Please return or renew this item by the last date shown. There may be a charge if you fail to do so. Items can be returned to any Westminster library.

Telephone: Enquiries 020 7641 1300
Renewals (24 hour service) 020 7641 1400
Online renewal service available.
Web site: www.westminster.gov.uk

11/11/13.

ꞀꞀᗡ

City of Westminster

By Frances Brody:

Dying in the Wool
A Medal for Murder
Murder in the Afternoon
A Woman Unknown
Murder on a Summer's Day

Murder on a Summer's Day

Frances BRODY

piatkus

PIATKUS

First published in Great Britain in 2013 by Piatkus

Copyright © Frances McNeil 2013

The moral right of the author has been asserted.

A CIP catalogue record for this book
is available from the British Library.

ISBN 978-0-3494-0058-7

Typeset in Perpetua by M Rules
Printed and bound by CPI Group (UK) Ltd, Croydon, CR0 4YY

Papers used by Piatkus are from well-managed forests
and other responsible sources.

MIX
Paper from
responsible sources
FSC® C104740

Piatkus
An imprint of
Little, Brown Book Group
100 Victoria Embankment
London EC4Y 0DY

An Hachette UK Company
www.hachette.co.uk

www.piatkus.co.uk

To a valued friend and insightful reader, Sylvia Gill.

Providence created the Maharajahs to offer mankind a spectacle.

Rudyard Kipling

One

Light found its way through the gap in the curtains. I sleep with the window open so usually the birds wake me before the clock does. Reaching out to stop the repeater alarm clock, I sent it flying from the bedside table onto the floor. It landed face up. Squinting at the luminous figures, I made out the time. Big hand at twelve, little hand at five, but I had not set the alarm. The ringing continued. Not the alarm, the telephone.

Somewhere in the garden, or the wood behind my house, a wood pigeon cooed itself silly. I stumbled out of bed, blinking away sleep. The ringing grew louder as I stepped onto the landing. Whoever was telephoning to me at this ungodly hour on an August Saturday morning did not intend to hang up and try again later.

As I hurried downstairs to the hall, my first thought was that something might be wrong with my mother or father. This anxiety led me to stub my toe on the foot of the hall stand. Cursing inwardly, I picked up the receiver.

At first, I did not recognise my cousin's voice, which irritated him.

1

'It's me, James.'

'What's the matter?'

James and I were close as children. His wife, Hope, died in March. For a fleeting moment, I wondered had he felt a sudden urge to pour out his heart.

'Kate, are you properly awake?'

'No.'

'You'll need pencil and paper.'

I sat down on the floor. Placing the telephone beside me, I reached for pad and pencil from the hall stand. 'Go on.'

'I'm telephoning to you from the office.'

'Why?'

Until recently, James was something in the War Office. After one of his rare civil service transfers, James now shuffled high-level documents in the India Office. He would not call me from there at this time without very good reason.

'Something important has come up. We have a sticky wicket your end of the pitch.'

As a very little boy, James spoke plain English. Then he went away to school. After that he became just as likely to speak cricket, rugger, or Latin.

'I'm listening, James.'

'This is sub rosa, Kate.'

Private. He knows that I have a party line with the professor across the road. 'My neighbours are on holiday. No one is listening in.'

'At my end, the line is secure.'

This was all a little mysterious so early in the morning. James clearly suspected that the telephone operator at my local exchange may be ear-wigging; a perquisite of an operator's job I supposed.

2

'I can give you no similar assurance. Send me a message via Wakefield.'

My father, superintendent of the West Riding force, has his office at Wakefield Police Headquarters.

'Time is of the essence.' He spoke in the form of an announcement. 'This is a government matter. If the telephone operator is still on the line, please disconnect now.'

His own pomposity slows James down but I refrained from saying so in case someone *was* ear-wigging.

Two seconds elapsed, three, four five. There was a click on the line. 'That's better. I can sense when someone is listening.'

'James, will you now tell me what this is about?'

'We need your expertise, Kate. An important person has gone missing in Yorkshire. I want you to find him.'

I hoped this was not to be so top secret that the identity of the missing person would remain anonymous and the location undisclosed. 'Who is he?'

'Maharajah Narayan Halkwaer of Gattiawan.'

'Spell the names, please.' My cousin behaves as though everyone is as well-versed in the people and places of Empire as he is himself.

'N-a-r-a-y-a-n, pronounced Na-rye-an. H-a-l-k-w-a-e-r. We say Halk-wear.'

My pencil needed sharpening, but the names were readable.

'We are keeping this quiet, so major discretion, Kate. People here know you're a good egg.'

I did not entirely like the sound of this. My idea of a good egg comes with a three-minute timer, bread soldiers and a pinch of salt. James's means something to do with play up and play the game.

3

'Where was he last seen?'

'Maharajah Narayan went riding on the Duke of Devonshire's estate yesterday. His horse returned without him.'

'How unfortunate.' It was more than unfortunate, and on two counts. First, southerners refuse to acknowledge the size of Yorkshire. At a guess, I would estimate the Duke of Devonshire's Bolton Abbey estate at fifty thousand acres. Second, the duke is Colonial Secretary. It would be tragic if a high-ranking Indian royal guest disappeared down a mine shaft on his land.

My cat, Sookie, appeared from nowhere, a speciality of hers; she head-butted my leg. 'Does he know the area?'

'Unfortunately, no. His father, Maharajah Shivram, and his younger brother, Prince Jaya, were guests at a shoot a couple of years ago but this is his first visit.'

'James, that estate is huge. You need to send out the troops.'

'A search is taking place. But Prince Narayan . . .'

'Prince? You just said he is a maharajah.'

'Yes but his father is senior maharajah. That is why I refer to our missing Indian as a prince. If I may continue?'

'I wish you would.'

'Thank you. Prince Narayan is a known practical joker. We are hoping there is some exaggeration going on, causing concern that may not be justified. We do not wish to intrude into his private life, overreact and turn this into some scandal.'

'What do you mean?'

'He is travelling with . . . I'll be polite and call her a companion.'

'And has she disappeared?'

'No. It is possible his absence is connected with some lovers' tiff.' He had my interest now. James lowered his voice to a whisper. 'Gattiawan is locked in a quarrel with a rival princely state. We must act swiftly to rule out any private action that may cause political difficulty.'

I groaned inwardly. This confidential civil-service-speak may mean a great deal to James and his colleagues. To listen to it first thing in the morning brought on a mild headache. I would have much rather heard more about a lovers' quarrel.

'The search is to be resumed at first light.' James's voice rose and took on an optimistic note, which for him is rare. 'He may be found as we speak. He was riding a high-spirited horse. Accidents happen.'

I had a nagging feeling that the India Office, teeming with old India hands and able to call on the army and Scotland Yard, should not be calling on Kate Shackleton.

'Why me? Surely this should be a police matter.'

'Kate, you are on the spot . . .'

'Not exactly.'

'. . . and you were recommended to my superiors not only by me but by a Scotland Yard commander. The chap you met at one of mother's suppers after a case of yours last year. Do you remember him?'

'Of course.'

'The commander has contacted the North Riding chief constable. The local man will be glad to have you on board.'

Commander Greathead had been most complimentary about my approach and methods. He was a valuable person to have on my side. It would be foolish to turn down the request. I quashed my misgivings.

'All right, James. I'll set off as soon as possible. What else do I need to know?'

Sookie sniffed at my stubbed big toe. Had she been a surgeon in a previous life?

'Gattiawan is an extremely wealthy state. The prince has a considerable amount of jewellery with him – from the state treasury and his own private collection.'

Curiouser and curiouser. 'Who is my contact? Am I reporting to his lordship?'

'The duke is in London. His steward expects you. Report to the estate office on your arrival. How soon can you be there?'

'Perhaps two hours.' I stood up. 'Will you be in your office to take my call, when I have something to report?'

'Yes.' He gave me his number. 'And, Kate, we have not spoken to the prince's family yet.'

'The family is in England?'

'They are in London. The senior maharajah and maharani and Prince Narayan's wife and young son are all staying at the Ritz.'

'Shouldn't you tell them?'

'No point in being alarmist without good reason. I want to rule out theft and foul play, hence the urgency, and confidentiality. Now you know as much as I do.'

I doubted that. He would brief me on a need to know basis. 'You mentioned a female companion.'

'Ah, yes.'

'Well?'

'You will learn about her when you arrive.'

'No, James. Tell me something now.'

He sighed. It was my guess that this female companion was the real reason that he had contacted me.

'Miss Metcalfe was a dancer at the Folies Bergère. Please ensure that she is not withholding information, or pocketing valuables.'

'Very well, James. I'll see what I can do.'

'Good luck, Kate. I know you'll do your best. You're one of the chaps when it comes to a caper like this.'

It was a little unnerving to hear James call me one of the chaps. I felt sure that being the Honourable James Rodpen's cousin, niece to Sir Albert and Lady Rodpen, put me in the pukka category with the India Office and the Colonial Office, but I do not feel the least bit pukka.

I was adopted as a baby. My mother, Lady Virginia, known as Ginny, excels at taking her ease and devouring novels. A duke's daughter, she shocked her family by marrying an up-and-coming police officer for love.

Last year, the view of myself as well-connected took a bit of a bashing. I met my birth sister; and my natural mother, who lives in a Wakefield slum. To her, it is home, and it is where I was born. After meeting them, and getting to know my niece and nephew, I looked up the definition of chameleon. The first part did not suit me, but the second part of the definition struck a chord. Chameleon, noun. an insectivorous lizard-like reptile, possessing the power of changing its colour.

What hue should I adopt to enter the portals of the Duke of Devonshire?

As I climbed the stairs, I wondered how to pack for the work of searching the countryside for a missing Indian prince. The Jowett is a sturdy motor, but I would not want to push her across the moors. Riding breeches and jacket would certainly be needed. Somewhere in the recesses of this house lurked rarely worn boots.

In a big house, there would be a boot room. Here there is a glory hole under the stairs. My house is on the small side, having been the lodge house, sold off by the owners of the mansion up the road, when their fortunes ebbed from middling to small riches.

I opened the wardrobe door. Since my dear cousin had no doubt sung my praises, I must look the part. I chose my smart costume for the journey. I pulled out a couple of summer frocks, a useful long cardigan and my summer hat and coat. I washed my face, brushed my teeth and combed my bobbed hair, damping it down at the back. I picked up my sponge bag. A glance in the long mirror, which need not be quite so long as I am five feet two inches, told me I would pass muster. As an afterthought, I included my pleated silk Delphos evening gown, which takes up no room at all and whose colours are gorgeous.

In the hall, I began to write a note for my housekeeper. Mrs Sugden has her quarters attached to the house, a situation that suits us both very well. As I wrote, the slap-slap of her slippers across the kitchen floor announced an impending interrogation.

Looking naked without her glasses, Mrs Sugden appeared in the hall. She wore her plaid woollen dressing gown, tied by its silk cord. Her long prematurely grey hair hung in a plait over her shoulder.

Surprise teetered on outrage. 'Where you off to at this time, without so much as a cup of tea?'

'On an urgent case. Cousin James telephoned to me.'

'I heard nowt.'

'I'm going to Bolton Abbey. An Indian prince has done a disappearing act and I'm to produce him, but this is all hush-hush.'

'I hope he's not dangerous.'

'You'll tell Mr Sykes won't you? And ask him to take over, until you hear from me.' My able former police officer assistant Jim Sykes would welcome the opportunity to step up and take charge.

She cast a beady eye over the valise and bag in the hall. 'Have you remembered your toilet bag?'

'Yes.'

'Have you packed a warm vest?'

'It's August.'

She sniffed. 'August! That means nowt out int' Dales.'

'Do you know where my boots are? Riding, walking.'

'Where they're supposed to be.' She opened the under-the-stairs cupboard door and disappeared, calling from the dark recess. 'Is the travel blanket in the motor?'

'Yes.'

It was then I had a brilliant idea, which would keep Mrs Sugden occupied so that I could escape.

'Mrs Sugden, I'm going to fetch the car. Would you glance at the Court Circulars in *The Times*? Tell me if you see mention of the Maharajah of Gattiawan.'

Mrs Sugden emerged triumphant with two pairs of boots, riding and walking. I took them from her.

She delved in her pocket for spectacles. 'The Maharajah of Gattiawan?'

'Yes.' I set the boots in the doorway with my luggage.

Mrs Sugden disappeared into the drawing room, where I pile far too many old newspapers on top of the piano. I called to her. 'Back in a while.'

I carried the bags and boots to the front gate. Buttoning my motoring coat, I walked up to my garage. It was a sweet

9

feeling to be out so early on a fine morning. Dew brought out the scent of late roses. Silvery cobwebs glittered on garden hedges.

My motor spends its nights in a converted stable at the top of the street. I opened the garage door and greeted my shining blue Jowett Short-Two. She still looks brand new and eager. I bought her less than a year ago with the proceeds from a particularly successful though sad case, one that attracted considerable notice. This was the case that brought me to the attention of the Scotland Yard commander and no doubt swayed the India Office and the Duke of Devonshire into trusting me.

My police superintendent father always drills home the need for preparation: proper preparation prevents poor performance. I would need a map.

'Shh,' I told the engine as I urged the motor from her slumbers, drove out and closed the creaking door behind me.

I drove to my front gate and began to load my valise, boots and trusty satchel. When not in use for a small passenger, the motor's dickey seat makes handy luggage space.

James's briefing had left me feeling less than well-armed for the task ahead. What was a maharajah of Gattiawan doing in Yorkshire? Why was he visiting Bolton Abbey before the start of the shooting season? Today was Saturday 2 August, so open season, but with ten days to go before grouse-shooting began, on the Glorious Twelfth.

James had not even told me when the maharajah and his companion arrived in Yorkshire.

I checked my watch. Ten minutes to six.

Mrs Sugden called from the doorway. 'I've found summat about maharajahs.'

'I'll be there in a tick.'

Fortunately, Mrs Sugden is a fast reader and *The Times* Court Circulars have the virtue of brevity. She placed the relevant pages on the piano stool, drawing it up to the chaise longue.

We sat side by side as she tapped the page with her ridged fingernail and read, 'The Maharajah of Kapurthala is the first Indian Prince to visit the British Empire Exhibition. He expressed his satisfaction with the Punjab Court exhibit. He has now returned to Paris, but will be back.'

'What about Gattiawan?'

Mrs Sugden is nothing if not thorough. 'Aga Khan . . . Maharajah of Rajpipla at the Savoy Hotel . . . Maharajah of Nawanger . . . They'll all know each other. Probably rivals, and one of them has done away with another, perhaps sent an assassin. It's like Shakespeare. Ah, here he is. The Maharajah of Gattiawan arrived at Marseilles yesterday in the SS *Malwa* on his way to London.'

I looked at the item, dated 26 April. It gave no indication whether the maharajah was travelling overland, or stopping on the way. 'Nothing else since then?'

She shook her head. 'Nowt else in Court Circulars, only an article about the good command of English among educated Indians, from the Special Correspondent in Bombay.'

There was nothing for it but to set off, feeling less than well-prepared.

I shrugged into my motoring coat.

Mrs Sugden followed me along the garden path. 'You don't have much luggage. Have you packed an evening dress?'

'The Delphos robe.' I opened the car door and got in quickly, before she had time for more questions.

She frowned at my choice of evening wear. 'I suppose that Delphos gown doesn't betray its age. But I can pack another bag for you.'

I started the motor. 'If I need anything else, I'll send you a telegram.' My mind already raced ahead. Prince Narayan of Gattiawan, where are you?

Mrs Sugden waved, folding her other arm around herself against the morning chill.

A sudden thought propelled her through the gate. She leaned into the motor. 'Be careful. They all carry daggers, and they're very good at strangling.'

'I'll try to stay in one piece, throat intact.'

As I drove away I heard her call something about the black hole of Calcutta, but my thoughts were already on the missing man, the lovers' tiff, and the mysterious Miss Metcalfe who had hooked herself an Indian prince.

James wanted to rule out theft and foul play. The Yorkshire Dales has its sprinkling of poachers. But jewel thieves, murderers? Surely not.

Two

The map lay on the passenger seat. I expected to consult it somewhere near Ilkley, and looked for a place to stop. Just as I was about to pull into the kerb, an arched bridge appeared on my right. Seeing it gave me a small jolt. My husband, Gerald, and I had visited Bolton Abbey one long ago, idyllic Sunday. We had driven across this very bridge.

I turned right, crossing the River Wharfe.

Bolton Abbey, in case you are wondering, is not an Abbey. It is the name of a village, loosely used to refer to the area that forms part of the Duke of Devonshire's estate. On that far off pre-war Sunday, Gerald and I visited the twelfth-century priory ruins, walked through woods, and listened to the fast-flowing river and the cascading waterfall. It must have been May, because I remember nodding bluebells. We had purchased sixpenny entry tickets for the pleasure of strolling round the grounds. Along with a horde of other visitors, we tripped across slippery stepping stones to the tune of nervous laughter and cries of 'Be careful!'

Glancing at my watch, I followed the narrow road. Almost eight o'clock, and the world had come to life.

Smoke rose from a distant chimney. A dog barked. A black grouse narrowly missed premature demise as it flew across my path. It occurred to me that I did not know the location of the estate office, nor the name of the steward.

Entering the village, I reached the smithy. I stopped the motor, believing that the blacksmith would direct me. The fire smouldered, but the place was deserted. Hesitating to knock on a cottage door, I drove on.

As I rounded the bend, I saw a creature that from a distance resembled a scarecrow. His trouser bottoms stopped halfway up his calves. He wore a striped, voluminous sleeved shirt, tucked in at the front but not at the back, its cuffs undone and hanging. He must have heard the motor but did not stop what he was doing. At first I thought he was scraping muck from the soles of his large boots. But then I saw that it was a childlike, almost ritualistic activity. He stood first on one foot, then the other, striking the sole of his boot against a large stone several times, with an urgent hit-and-scrape movement. As I came closer, I saw that on the last go he made a spark, presumably by the friction between the stone and the nails on the soles of his boots.

Only then, after the spark, did he turn and look at the car. As he did so, he raised his arms, giving himself the shape of a cross, and then began to wave like an injured pigeon attempting take off.

'Hello and stop!' His voice betrayed uncertainty. His breath came in short, nervous bursts as if he feared that by flagging me down he may have committed some grave error for which he would pay dearly.

I stopped.

His wild haystack of hair had been roughly chopped to

14

form the shape of a basin above his weather-beaten face. It was difficult to tell his age. Perhaps twenty. Too old to be playing a game with his boots and a stone.

'You be Mr Shackleton.'

Mister! Because I have bobbed hair? Not a good start, but a discussion of my sex seemed a bad idea. 'I'm expected?'

'Aye.' He waved an arm, indicating that I should follow him. He gave one last longing look at his stone and then walked close to the edge of the road, one foot on the grass verge, glancing back at me suspiciously as if half expecting to be mown down.

At snail's pace, I followed.

After a few moments, he stopped by a third-class railway carriage that stood on the verge, mounted on concrete fingers and stone chippings. A metal chimney protruded from the roof.

This seemed to me an ingenious use of an unwanted railway carriage. I remembered that the Cavendish Pavilion, where Gerald and I had taken afternoon tea on our visit here, was built along similar lines to a railway refreshment room. Gerald had commented on its architecture at the time, saying that the coming of the railway had transformed Bolton Abbey in more ways than one.

Had the errant Indian prince, practical joker, sent his horse back without him and secretly boarded a train, I wondered.

I climbed from the motor. 'Is this where I will find the duke's agent?'

He of the hob-nailed boots nodded.

Through the window of the carriage, I glimpsed a tall figure. He had his back to me.

The lad climbed an iron step, opened the door and

15

entered what must be the estate office. 'Here is that person you was expecting, sir.' He stepped aside to let me in, holding open the door with his bulky frame.

The interior smelled of tobacco, earth and sweat. A wood-burning stove in the centre of the carriage, its chimney piercing the roof, sported a battered black kettle.

A tall, sparely built man, clad in tweeds and gaiters, turned towards me. He had been studying a map that was pasted to one of the windows. His gaunt, unshaven face was as grey and tired as his worn jacket. From his slightly glassy-eyed stare, I guessed he had not slept. He blinked, as if believing me to be some apparition, and spoke with barely restrained annoyance. 'Can I help you, madam?'

Madam. This was an improvement. The skirt probably helped.

'I'm Mrs Shackleton. You are expecting me, I believe.'

He looked beyond me. 'Where is Mr Shackleton?'

The thatch-haired young man looked out of the door, as though there may be another person he had missed, running along behind the motor.

My poor sweet Gerald has not been seen, except in my dreams, since the last month of the Great War. 'It's me you are expecting.'

His mouth opened wide enough to nest half a dozen grouse chicks. He had expected a solid chap who would lift a little weight from his shoulders.

I spoke again, quickly, before he had time for words he may regret. 'Am I speaking to the duke's agent?'

'Yes, yes, that's me.' He recovered himself sufficiently to give me his name. 'Frederick Upton. I was led to understand that a Mister Shackleton would call.'

Clearly my fame had not travelled this far into the North Riding. One small part of me felt the need for apology, or explanation. All it would take to bring him to heel would be a flourish of my aristocratic connections, but I would not do that. Instead, I adopted a manner copied from my mother and aunt, of effortlessly putting men in their place by a show of social confidence. For my mother and aunt, that comes naturally. I have had to practise.

I handed him my card. 'Mr Upton, I was contacted by the Honourable James Rodpen this morning, on behalf of the India Office and His Grace the Duke. I am asked to investigate the maharajah's disappearance.'

His manner changed.

After a brief hesitation, Upton drew out a chair for me. 'I beg your pardon, madam. I must have misheard your title.' He took a seat himself, in the captain's chair, on the other side of a scratched and cigarette-scorched table.

'Please tell me everything I need to know, Mr Upton, including when Prince Narayan arrived in the area and when and where he was last seen.'

'His highness arrived by car on Tuesday last. He stayed one night with a Mr Presthope, in Halton East. On Wednesday, he came across from there. On Friday morning, he went riding, nice as ninepence, back mid-morning. In the afternoon, off he went again. He was on a fine Arab, and the horse came back without him, at eight o'clock last night.'

'Did it strike you as odd that he went riding twice in one day?'

He frowned. 'I hadn't thought about that, but no. He is a top polo player, the best in the world I'm told. He does not fish, so it is natural enough that he took his gun, to fit in a spot of deerstalking, and another ride.'

'Is deerstalking allowed, so near to grouse shooting?'

'The grouse are out on the moorland. He would know not to disturb them. The deer keep to the woods.'

'And did he ride alone?'

'Two grooms rode with him, Osbert Hannon, and Isaac Withers.'

'My dad,' piped up the lad in the doorway. Having drawn attention to himself, he now stared at his feet, and blushed.

'Joel, go make yourself useful. Keep your peepers peeled out there.' He waited until Joel had left, shutting the door quietly behind him. 'He can be a useful lad, but a little deficient in the brains department.' He folded his hands on the desk. 'To go back to what we were saying, the prince bagged a doe, a white roe.'

'Isn't it surprising that he shot a doe and not the male, with its trophy antlers?'

'It was the creature that came in his sights. A hunter sometimes takes the first shot he can. Very shortly after that, he rode off alone, possibly in the direction of Halton East.' He walked to the map on the window and jabbed a finger at it.

I moved to stand beside him. The place he pointed to was east and a little north of our present position. 'That's Halton East, where his highness stayed his first night in the area, with an old school friend.'

'How far is it from here?'

'Two miles.'

'And did he call on his old school friend?'

'He did not. Mr Presthope has joined the search, around

18

Embsay Moor.' Upton made a circle with his hand around the map. 'This is the area we've searched. Of course, he could have gone beyond. His highness is a young man, and a fine horseman, but accidents happen.'

'How many men are searching?'

'The local constable has a team of men and police dogs on the moors. Everyone from the estate who can be spared is out there. The head forester has a group combing woodlands. The water bailiff is searching every bend of the river. Gamekeepers are tramping the moors. The works manager and his men are inspecting every building. I felt sure we would discover him before nightfall. At eleven o'clock last night, I notified his lordship. We continued searching with lanterns, and began again at dawn. It's a mystery, Mrs Shackleton, a mystery.'

In spite of the seriousness, I almost smiled. I could hear James hymning my praises to the powers that be. My cousin, Kate Shackleton, has solved the most difficult of cases.

The stuffed shirts of government would be only too happy to pursue the matter quietly, to avoid turning a crisis into a news story and a political embarrassment. But the nagging doubt returned. Why me? India Office tentacles must stretch across the land; retired colonials who know India better than their own county, who are acquainted with the personalities and speak the languages.

'I'm told that the prince is a practical joker.' I turned away from the map. 'Is there a possibility he could have taken the train, or be paying another visit and enjoying himself at his lady companion's expense?'

Upton scratched his head. 'I doubt that. No one has left by rail. His Rolls-Royce is still here. There was one little oddity, but it amounted to nothing.'

'All the same, Mr Upton, do tell me. I want to have as full a picture as possible.'

Upton leaned against the edge of his desk, betraying his weariness. 'One of the men said that the coal merchant from Embsay, Deakin, saw an Indian on Bark Lane yesterday. When I asked Deakin about it, he said it was a mistake.'

I made a mental note to talk to this man. After all, James had mentioned a rival Indian state. Mrs Sugden may have been indulging in her usual flights of fancy when she suspected all Indians of carrying knives and being excellent stranglers, but an Indian wandering the lanes of the estate would hardly be mistaken for a local yokel.

'It's an odd thing for the coal merchant to have said.'

'He's an odd man. Some people will say anything to be stood a drink.'

I glanced at the map again. 'It's a huge area, Mr Upton.'

Upton's hands made fists. 'You'll be taking over I understand.' The words almost choked their way through his dry lips. 'I suggested we contact the barracks, but his lordship said to give it a few more hours.'

'Please telephone to his lordship, Mr Upton. Add my voice to yours regarding the need for troops to widen the search. You have done everything you can and you are the expert on the countryside.' He brightened a little at my praise. 'I want to find out a little more background by speaking to those in the royal party. He may have given some hint as to what was in his mind. Also, I want to see the men who accompanied him on his ride yesterday.'

He nodded. 'I'll have Osbert and Isaac sent to you. Will you work from here?' He glanced about the converted carriage in something like dismay.

'I'm sure you need this room yourself. I'll speak first to the prince's companion. Who else travelled with him?'

'His highness drove here with just his companion, Lydia Metcalfe.' As he spoke the woman's name, Upton's nostril twitched, betraying a powerful hint of disdain.

'How many servants?'

'Just one valet. The valet travelled by train, arriving before them with the bulk of the luggage.'

From what little I had heard of Indian royalty, it surprised me that the prince travelled with only a single servant. 'Isn't it a little unusual for someone of his rank to travel without an entourage?'

He sighed. 'It certainly is. Prince Narayan must be cut from a more modern cloth. When the prince's father and younger brother, Prince Jaya, were guests at his lordship's shooting parties the retinue would have populated a large village.'

'I take it that Miss Metcalfe and the valet are at Bolton Hall?'

A coughing fit stopped Upton from answering me. He picked up a stained pint pot and took a swig of cold tea.

I gave him time to recover.

'The prince is staying at the hotel, the Devonshire Arms.'

'Is Bolton Hall shut up?'

'In part. There is a skeleton staff. His lordship and her ladyship are expected on 9 August, with guests arriving on the tenth, in advance of the shooting.'

Neither of us voiced the thought that the duke may well need to change his plans, and soon.

There was something Upton was not saying. It puzzled me that Indian royalty was being accommodated at the hotel, not the Hall. I waited. Silence often prompts a fuller explanation than a demand.

'How can I put this delicately? Normally the prince would be a guest at the Hall, as his father and younger brother have been before him. But given that he is travelling with an unsuitable woman who cannot be received they occupy a floor at the Devonshire Arms.'

So, Miss Metcalfe was a person the establishment did not intend to acknowledge. Bring in the outsider. Bring in Kate Shackleton.

'I see. And does Miss Metcalfe have a maid?'

'No. Apparently she insists on looking after herself.' Having almost ventured into the territory of opinion, Upton's eyes lit with a sudden understanding. 'I expect they have asked a lady to come believing you might persuade Lydia Metcalfe to sling her hook.'

'She must stay put, Mr Upton. Everyone must stay put. You say the maharajah arrived by Rolls-Royce?'

'Yes. He drove himself.'

'Have the Rolls put under lock and key. Instruct the stationmaster not to issue Miss Metcalfe or the valet a railway ticket. This is not to suggest blame attaching to them, but any information they have could be vital.'

He nodded. 'I'll send word straight away.' He opened a drawer and took out writing paper. Then he turned to me. 'It ought to come from you. His grace said that you would be directing the investigation.'

He placed paper on the blotter and pushed the glass inkstand towards me, inviting me to use his pen. Ignoring his touch of resentment, I dipped the blunt nib. I wrote two brief notes, one to the hotel manager ordering the Rolls-

Royce to be impounded. The second, I addressed to the stationmaster, asking that no one be issued a ticket to leave Bolton Abbey station without my permission. This seemed to me a draconian but necessary order.

When I had finished writing, Upton opened the door and called to Joel. He gave the lad careful instructions about delivering the notes.

Joel repeated the instruction. Having a multiple errand brought a mist of confusion to his eyes. He bit his lower lip, and mumbled.

'Go to the station first. Hold that note in your hand. Give it to the stationmaster. Put the other in your pocket. Go to the hotel second. When you get there, take the note from your pocket and give it to Mr Sergeant.'

Joel released his lower lip from his teeth, leaving a livid mark on his pouting lip. Carefully, he slid one envelope into his pocket, and then he left.

'Tell me, Mr Upton, apart from this mysterious sighting of an Indian or not an Indian on the road, have any strangers arrived in the area recently?'

He opened a tobacco jar that stood on the table, and filled his pipe. 'I thought of that. We had the usual crop of day trippers last Sunday, but they all left by evening. There is just the normal round of deliveries.' He struck a match to light his pipe. 'I was hoping his disappearance would turn out to be a prank, because of the reputation he has as a practical joker. You never know when a creature like Miss Metcalfe is concerned. He may have it in his mind to teach her a lesson for something or other. Give her a fright.'

This seemed to me unlikely, but not impossible.

We talked for a few more moments. I studied the map on

the wall, trying to get my bearings. The River Wharfe snaked its way through the countryside. The places vaguely familiar to me were Strid Wood, and the Strid – the point at which a person with long legs and a brave but foolish heart might leap across the river. Down from the priory were the stepping stones, where Gerald and I had crossed.

Just then, the door flew open. Joel stood there, his mouth opening and closing as he struggled for words. He still gripped the letter to the stationmaster in his hand. 'He's got a stitch. He can't run any nearer.'

As if feeling the need to demonstrate, Joel grabbed his lower abdomen and leaned forward, groaning.

'Who's got a stitch? What's happened?'

Joel stared with wide, frightened eyes. 'Matty's took a stitch from running with his message. They've found him. Drowned.'

Three

Sitting on the iron step outside the estate office I pulled on my boots. I felt hollow inside. The man was drowned. I had come too late; failed before I had begun. Upton and Joel had hurried to fetch horses.

I heard them before I saw them; the clip-clop of hooves.

Upton was mounted on a brown mare, leading a white pony. Joel hurried along behind.

It is a long time since I have ridden. I mounted the pony clumsily, sensing Upton's impatience.

'We're going about a mile beyond Bolton Bridge, where the river bends before Paradise Lathe.' He turned and called to Joel. 'Stay here. If anyone comes, tell them where we are, and to wait.'

The gentle pony trotted quickly, needing little encouragement. I looked to my left, across the river. The ground rose steeply and became dark with trees. The slight breeze did not stir the leaves. Only the river rushed, as if determined to join our race as it noisily whooshed across boulders. The air smelled of grass and wild garlic.

Upton was a little way ahead. He called to me, his voice

scattering, so that I had to lean forward to catch his words.

'I don't understand. We searched the river yesterday.'

Wildflowers bowed under his horse's hooves; buttercups, daisies, wild pinks, poppies and meadowsweet.

I urged the pony to catch up.

A few moments later, Upton spoke again. 'The poor man must have been submerged, the Wharfe playing her tricks.'

A couple of ducks sailed sedately along the river, looking about them. A curlew dipped and called.

'How did it happen?' he asked, without expecting an answer from me. 'Maybe he stopped to let his horse drink, and scooped water for hisself. Being a stranger, he wouldn't know the river's treachery.'

'But he was young, and a fine horseman.'

Upton pulled ahead of me again, muttering. It sounded like, 'How could it come to this?'

Not far off, by a drystone wall, were two men. As we drew closer, I saw that they were standing a few feet from something on the ground. The something turned into someone, covered by a blanket. The searchers had come prepared.

Upton and I dismounted. I patted the pony. A creature alive in the face of death can be reassuring, and need reassurance.

I looked first at the men who had found the body. One was of medium height, with wiry sandy hair and a sun-freckled complexion. He looked shocked and bewildered, as if someone had hit him and taken the breath from his body. The second man was older, tight-lipped, with one of those grit-stone faces that is hard to read. His shoulders slumped. His arms hung heavy. As Upton drew near, this man bobbed onto his haunches and turned back the corner of the blanket that covered the head, and then turned it back a little more.

He revealed a deathly pale young man with luxuriant black hair that had begun to dry in curls. He was so slender that his ribs showed themselves one by one, a perfect cage, the river having stolen his shirt. In a painting, he would have been a shepherd boy. This was no Indian prince.

Upton dropped to his knees and stared.

After a long moment, he turned to me. 'It's Osbert Hannon, the groom I told you about. He went riding with the prince.'

'He's not much more than a child.'

'He's twenty-one, married these seven months, and his wife expecting. His two older brothers were lost in the war. He's his mother's only son.' Upton gulped and turned away. '*Was* her only son.'

I spoke to the older man, the one with a face of stone. 'He wasn't missing, was he? Osbert I mean.'

The man shook his head. 'He searched last night with the head gamekeeper. This morning him and Isaac was to ride about again, where they'd been with the Indian.'

'When did you last see Osbert?'

'About midnight, when some of us gave up the search, to start again at dawn this morning.'

Upton covered Osbert's face, and stood up.

The sandy-haired, bewildered man looked at me blankly when I spoke to him. 'I'm sorry to question you when you are so upset. I'm Mrs Shackleton, asked by the duke to represent the India Office. Did you see Osbert this morning?'

The bewildered man stared at me for a long moment, as

if my words had to enter his brain, be translated into another language, and spoken back to him. Then, he shook his head.

Upton picked up a stone and slung it into the river with great force. He wheeled round, turning on the two men. 'Why didn't you say who you'd found? I thought it was the Indian.'

The stone-faced man said quietly, 'Matty knew it were Osbert. He went running to find you, and then to get a stretcher.'

'God help Osbert's mam, sir,' added the other. 'And he's no sight for a lass in his wife's condition.' He ran his fingers through his wiry hair, making it stand on end.

Upton did not answer. He turned his back.

I stared at the horizon. White clouds scudded hastily across the blue sky; the world hurrying to mock the quick and the dead.

We spoke no more, until the fellow they called Matty came into view, carrying one end of a canvas stretcher with wooden rods.

Behind him came Joel, holding the other end.

They placed the stretcher on the ground. Upton picked up Osbert Hannon's body, as gently as if he were about to nurse a baby. As he did so, I noticed a nasty wound on the back of the young man's head. This could have been from the rocks on the riverbed, or it may have been inflicted before he entered the water. Upton laid Osbert on the canvas and covered him, as though tucking him in for the night.

'Matty, Joel, go on searching along the river.'

Matty nodded.

Joel looked blank. 'What for?'

'For an Indian, dead or alive. What do you think? I'm not

sending you on a bloody fishing expedition. Go as far as the weir. And keep your traps shut about Osbert till I say open 'em.'

The other two men had taken up positions at either end of the stretcher, waiting for instructions.

'Bring him to the estate office. Say nowt.' He turned to me as we walked towards the horse and pony. 'Thank God I didn't have the church bells rung to call off the search.'

The animals were grazing patiently. This time I mounted more easily. 'I must break the news to Osbert's wife and mother before I bring his body home to them,' Upton said as he swung into the saddle.

'Wait! The coroner will need to consider Osbert's death in relation to the maharajah's disappearance. There will be a post mortem, and an inquest. Have the body taken to Bolton Hall and notify the constable.'

The flat of Upton's palm went to his forehead. 'Of course. You're right.'

He called to the men and trotted up to them.

The wound on the back of Osbert's head may have been caused accidentally, when he fell into the water. But the river murmured murder. A man so young and lithe did not fall and drown. He was pushed. Why?

Four

I dismounted from the pony in the stable yard of the Devonshire Arms Hotel. This was where Upton told me I would find Isaac Withers, the man who, along with Osbert Hannon, had accompanied the prince on his ride yesterday.

Hearing the pony's hooves, an elderly man emerged from the furthest stall, squinting as he came into the light. He looked at the pony, and at me. Ledges of pocked flesh crossed his cheeks and either side of his mouth. Two warts gave him the appearance of a lumpy old tree.

So this was Joel's father, Isaac. Either Joel was older than he appeared, or he was the fruit of old loins. Whereas the son gave the appearance of a poorly clad scarecrow, the father appeared to wear every item of clothing that had come his way. In spite of the warmth of a summer morning, he wore gaiters on his trousers, two pairs of thick socks, grey and brown, a heavy overcoat, scarf and an old cap.

'Are you done with the pony so soon, madam?' The sheer amount of clothing slowed his movements. He hobbled closer, narrowing his eyes, waiting to hear where I had been, and why.

'Are you Mr Withers?'

'That I be.'

'Hello. I am Mrs Shackleton. I'm here to find out what has happened to his lordship's guest.'

Even his bushy eyebrows appeared extravagantly overdone. He raised them, giving a sparkle of surprise to rheumy old eyes that were exceedingly pink around the lids. 'Has summat happened to him?'

'Mr Withers, I need to ask you a few questions. When you have seen to the pony, please come and join me on that bench out there.'

'What do you want to know?'

'We'll speak when you are done. Five minutes?'

'I'm on me own, and I'm not as fleet as I were.'

'Then, when you are ready.'

I left the stable block and sat outside. On the bench, I stretched my legs, examining the toes of my well-worn boots. These boots have been my stand-by since the age of nineteen. Perhaps I shall still have them when I am ninety.

The tranquillity of this place was palpable. Yet it was not silent. Nearby, bees hummed in a patch of lavender. Birds sang. Above, small white clouds raced by; clouds with an appointment to keep.

After ten minutes, the sound of hobnail boots cut into the hum of bumblebees. I edged to the far end of the bench to give the man room. 'Please sit down, Mr Withers.'

'They call me Isaac.'

When he sat down, a smell settled between us – horse muck, animals, sweat, damp clothes dried out, stale tobacco.

He took out a clay pipe. 'Is it all right if I smoke?'

'Yes.'

31

I waited until he had filled and lit his pipe.

'Tell me about going out with the Indian prince yesterday, Isaac.'

'He's not found then?'

'Were you asked to go, or did you volunteer?'

'I'm better on a horse than on my feet these days, though I'll be joining the beaters when grouse-shooting starts. Mr Upton picked me and Osbert to go, on what whim I don't know. Me being the eldest and him the fleetest probably.'

'What time did you set off?'

He pressed his fingers on the centre of his forehead and rubbed his inner eye, perhaps to prompt his memory. 'Seven o'clock yesterday morning, that was the first time.'

'How did he seem to you?'

'He was right enough.'

'Was he friendly, aloof, did he ask any questions?'

'He wanted to know the lie of the land and asked about the grouse shooting. I pointed out Hazelwood Moor and Barden Moor. We took him through the Valley of Desolation, White Doe Path, all around. He were asking about Embsay Moor and the grouse butts. I gave him fair warning over the disused shafts up there, and peat pits.'

I made a mental note to ask Upton whether the shafts and pits had been searched, but given the man's thoroughness, I felt sure they had, if searching such places was possible. A thought struck me. Perhaps the prince would never be found.

'What was he like?'

Isaac sucked on his pipe. 'Not like any man I ever did see. Something special about him. You'd say he was royal even if you didn't know it.'

'Can you explain?'

He thought for a moment. 'I seen the king when he came here shooting twelve year ago. You know it's the king but that's because you know he's the king. This one, even the horse took to him. It's a horse with a wild streak, likes no one, tosses its mane, mount me if you dare. But when he came near, mild as a lamb it lowered its head and nuzzled his hand.'

'So were you surprised when the horse came back without him?'

'Surprised? I were fair flabbergasted.'

The curling tobacco smoke smelled sweet, too sweet.

'What else can you tell me?'

'His highness wanted to shoot. Said he'd shot his first tiger at ten, and shooting was what he were after.'

A sudden coughing made him thump his chest.

'When you went out with him the second time, in the afternoon, did you notice any change in his mood?'

'How do you mean?'

'Did he seem upset, or more caught up in his thoughts?'

Isaac shook his head. 'Not as I noticed. You'd have to ask Osbert. It's not up to the likes of me to take notice of a personage's frame of mind.'

'Tell me about the afternoon.'

'He left us by the stables and stalked up into the woods, after deer. Her ladyship made a deer farm on the park. There was five hundred head until four year ago, roe and sika. He said to wait and we'd hear a shot, or his whistle. We thought we could be there till doomsday. Them deer sense when someone's out walking with a gun. But sure enough we heard the shot. If I'd been there, I might have stopped him.'

'Why would you have stopped him?'

For the first time, he turned and looked at me full on, incredulity in his small, rheumy eyes. 'Why? Why? Didn't I say? He shot a white doe. The man shot a white doe, God help us. I went to the churchyard this morning to pray, but it's too late. My bones tell me it's too late. To shoot the white doe is sacrilege.'

What had upset the man so much? In my experience of country people there is nothing they like better than felling an animal, carrying home a carcass, large or small.

And then it dawned. This was the land of the white doe. I tried to remember the Wordsworth poem, *The White Doe of Rylstone*. Emily and her soft-paced doe trek across Barden Moor to visit the grave of her murdered brother at Bolton Priory. When Emily dies, the faithful doe continues the journey. I had seen an engraving of the doe, lying beside a grave, the embodiment of gentleness and fidelity.

In a world of long-held superstitions, where a four-hundred-year-old legend is alive and well, the prince had offended local sensibilities.

'He blundered out of ignorance then.'

Isaac grunted. 'Don't tell me he didn't know. You should hear him speak, like the duke himself. That Indian is more English than I am. Everyone knows the story and if you ask me . . . '

The clip-clop of hooves and clatter of cartwheels stopped his speech. We both looked up as the horse-drawn cart approached, on which the stretcher holding Osbert Hannon lay.

Isaac and I stood until it passed, he clutching his cap.

The grit-stone man who had helped pull Osbert Hannon from the river flicked a whip that missed the horse's flank.

When the cart moved out of sight, Isaac said, 'I knew it would end badly. God bless us. Where are they taking him?'

'To the Hall.'

'Where was he found?'

He would know soon enough. I answered him to watch his reaction. 'In the river.'

Isaac closed his eyes. 'Drowned?'

'Yes.'

His breath came in rapid bursts. We both sat down again. Isaac pulled and twisted his cap. His hands were shaking.

I waited until his breath returned to something like normal. 'Isaac, when did you part company with the prince?'

'After he shot the deer, he left it to me and Osbert to take it to the barn. We would have gone on with him, for the pleasure of watching him ride, in spite of the deer. But he insisted. He'd go on alone. I expect we held him back, not being such fine riders.'

I sensed there was something he was not saying.

'What time was that?'

'About four o'clock.'

'Did he ask for directions anywhere?'

'Not as I remember. Osbert said he went towards Halton East. I were too upset about the doe.'

'Did he give a hint of going somewhere?'

'No. The good lord had another plan for him. The river claimed the heathen. The earth takes its revenge. An eye for an eye, a tooth for a tooth, an Indian prince for the white doe.'

'Isaac, I have just one more question. When did you last see Osbert Hannon?'

'Osbert? He'd have no hand in such an impossible deed. Are you saying he drowned the Indian?'

'When did you see him?'

'It was last midnight, when some of us gave up, so we could come fresh to task in't morning.'

'You must have been bone weary.'

'That we were.'

'And did Osbert have far to go?'

'Not far, up by the Coney Warren.'

'And you?'

'Why, less still, at Strid Cottage.' The creases in his face deepened. He stared from frightened eyes. 'Tell me it's the heathen just gone by, not Osbert.'

Upton would by now have broken the news to Osbert's family. 'I'm sorry, Isaac. Osbert is the one who was taken from the river.'

Isaac shut his eyes. Colour drained from his gnarled face. The pipe clattered to the flagged ground. 'Then it's true.'

Terror rolled off him in waves.

'What is true? What are you afraid of?'

'It's the wrath of the maid, and the heavens that protect her, her and white doe. It's begun. Osbert dead. The heathen prince missing. It'll be me next.'

Five

Bolton Hall has the eccentric appearance of having been created by someone who would have preferred to build a castle. Originally the fortified entrance to the Priory, designed to keep out marauding Scots, it was extended by the Bachelor Duke, William Spencer Cavendish, 6th Duke of Devonshire. He allotted the task of extending the building to his protégé, the head gardener.

I had parked on the road and approached the front of the building along the path, with a broad smooth stretch of lawn to my right. Perhaps it had been the choice of this same head gardener to plant trees so close to the front door that they would surely block the light.

Some other caller had shown scant regard for the grass. A three-seater Crossley Bugatti was parked half on the path, half on the perfect lawn.

The door was opened by a young maid who had been crying. She sniffled as I gave my name and told her that I was here in connection with Osbert's death. She looked as if she may burst into tears again so I quickly asked 'Whose motor is that?' This was partly to divert her from distress, but also out of curiosity, for it occurred to me that a member of the Duke of Devonshire's family may have driven here at speed.

'It's the doctor's motor, madam. He is with poor Osbert now.' Osbert's name brought a fresh tear to her eye. Either he was closely related, or she had been in love with him.

'I'm here to see the doctor. Has anyone else arrived?'

She stepped aside to let me in. 'Mr Upton brought Osbert's mother and Jenny, and then he left.'

'Jenny must be Osbert's wife?'

She winced. That answered my question. The maid was in love with Osbert. There are times when stating the obvious seems the only thing to do. 'You've all had a terrible shock.'

She nodded. Slowly, she turned and looked in the direction of the two Mrs Hannons who were seated by the fireplace in the great hall. 'They are over there, waiting to see Osbert. The doctor is not ready for them yet.'

'Thank you. I shall wait with them.'

'Very good, madam.' As if suddenly aware that she had let out her secret to a stranger, she said, 'We was all of us at school together. We was all of us pals.' She hurried away.

As I had guessed, the hall was indeed dark, and also dingy. Small wonder the duke and duchess used this residence only during the shooting season. The place gave me the shudders.

The two bereaved women sat motionless on straight back chairs near the enormous empty grate. As I walked towards them, my footsteps echoed to the rafters.

On the opposite side of the hearth was another chair. I picked it up and brought it across, hoping they would not mind if I joined them.

I introduced myself to the women and expressed condolences. The older Mrs Hannon was thin, with work-worn hands. She glanced at me, puzzled.

I heard myself speaking too slowly, deliberately. 'I was asked here to search for the Indian prince.' The younger woman appeared not to have heard me. 'I am so sorry that your husband, your son, has died.'

'Did you see Osbert?' the older woman asked. 'Are they sure it's him?' She was still wearing her pinafore. A strand of grey hair had escaped from her pinned-up plaits and hung in a wave, touching her shoulder.

'Yes.'

'We have to wait. The doctor has to see him.' An absurd glint of hope came into her eyes, as if the doctor might perform some miracle. 'But he is drowned. Is that for certain?'

'Yes.'

She reached out and touched the wrist of the heavily pregnant young woman beside her, who did not react. She stared ahead, without seeing.

This was no time to be questioning them, and yet I had to.

'Have you been offered something? Tea? Brandy?'

The older woman nodded.

I could see no sign of refreshments so took the brandy flask that I carry in my satchel for emergencies and offered it to her.

She shook her head. 'My poor lad went too early to work this morning. They kept him out half the night searching and then he was up at dawn. But I don't understand. Do you think he saw that Indian in the water and went to help, or went to drag him out?'

'I don't know. The Indian has not been found.'

'That river. That damn river. I hate it. Why did it want my boy?'

'Did he seem very tired this morning?'

Jenny spoke at last. 'He wanted to search with the others. They were ordered to carry on searching for the foreigner. Why couldn't he have stayed in his own country?'

Good question. He came here because we went there. He came here because this is the heart of empire. 'Did it upset Osbert that the Indian prince shot the white doe?' Not wishing to hint at suicide, I added quickly, 'Perhaps it preyed on his mind so as to distract him?'

The older Mrs Hannon shook her head. 'Osbert thought all that stuff silly. Big rodents, that's what he calls deer, brown, white or any shade between. Pests.'

At a tapping sound, the younger woman raised her head and looked towards a door that opened on the far side of the hall. A man in his late thirties, leaning on a cane, gazed across at us.

The younger Mrs Hannon started to breathe more heavily. Glancing at her, I saw that she must be very near her time. Her hand went to her belly, as though she had to block the ears of her unborn child.

As he limped towards us, walking stick marking time, I realised this must be the doctor, owner of the Bugatti. He was dressed like a country doctor, in good tweeds. His fine fair hair was touched with grey. He pushed it back from his eyes. 'Mrs Hannon, and Mrs Hannon, you may come through and see Osbert now.'

In order to use the telephone and report to James, I had been led through dark corridors and rooms with closed curtains to a study where three walls were covered in book cases.

He spoke over a crackly line. 'Is there a connection between the groom's death and the prince's disappearance, Kate?'

'It's too early to tell.' A grandfather clock by the door chimed the half hour. Half past ten. 'The search is continuing.'

After a long pause, James said, 'Let me know the moment you have more news.'

'Of course. And James . . . '

'Yes?'

'Nothing. I'll speak to you later this afternoon, news or no news.'

I disconnected. I had wanted to ask whether they had yet alerted the Indian family. But that was up to them, to the India Office and the Duke of Devonshire.

Compared to the politics of the situation, my task seemed straightforward: find the missing prince.

I had rashly told the housekeeper who led me to this room that I would find my way back.

Shutting the study door behind me, I entered the gloomy corridor and turned left. In the next room, maids were busy at work, one on a stepladder by the window, the other leaned on a polishing mop, a sob in her voice as she spoke. It was the maid who had opened the door. 'Poor Osbert. I can't believe it's true.'

'Well it is.' The older woman teetered unsteadily on the ladder as she turned to deliver her advice. 'So snap out of it. His lordship and her ladyship will be here tomorrow. Tears won't polish a floor.'

After twists and turns in the corridor, I miraculously found my way back to the starting point, the great hall.

The doctor was sitting in the chair that had been occupied by Osbert's mother. He stood as I approached, holding the back of the chair with one hand and extending the other to me, introducing himself as Lucian Simonson.

'So you are Mrs Shackleton. Upton, the agent, told me you were called in by his lordship.'

'By the India Office.'

'Amounts to the same thing, I dare say.'

He glanced at my ring finger. 'And am I right in believing you are Gerald Shackleton's widow?'

'Yes.'

It still gives me a shock to hear a stranger speak Gerald's name. And that small, cruel word, widow, always seems as though an unspoken adjective waits to be attached: poor, rich, grieving, merry.

We sat down, side by side, turning our chairs one towards the other. 'Small world, Mrs Shackleton. I've heard a little about you. And your husband and I knew each other at Leeds Infirmary before the war; an excellent surgeon and a fine man.'

For a while, we reminisced, not about the war, where Dr Simonson had earned what he referred to as his gammy leg, but about the summer of 1913, which seemed like yesterday, but a yesterday in a different world.

I brought the conversation back to the here and now. 'Has the constable been notified of Osbert Hannon's death, doctor?'

'Upton sent one of his men to find him, and left word with the constable's wife to call headquarters at Skipton.'

'Did you know Osbert?'

'Only by sight. Healthy young chap. I never had cause to treat him.'

'I'm glad of the opportunity to speak to you, Dr Simonson, because I wonder whether there is any connection between the prince's disappearance and Osbert's death. I know you cannot answer that question directly, but you may be able to venture an opinion as to how he died.'

It seemed to me too much of a coincidence that one of the last men to see the maharajah had been found dead.

Dr Simonson pulled one of those faces that indicate the difficulty of venturing an opinion. 'The coroner will order a post mortem and we'll know more after that. The family live on the other side of the river. His way to work brought him along the path to the Strid, where he would leap across, something he has been doing without mishap since he was a child.' He took a silver cigarette case from his inside pocket, flicked it open and offered me a cigarette.

I accepted.

'What preliminary conclusions have you come to regarding Osbert Hannon's death, Dr Simonson?'

He lit our cigarettes. 'Good question. You want to know whether he was dead when he entered the water.'

'Yes.'

He sighed. 'When I was called here, I knew that the search was underway for a missing prince. My examination seemed therefore to call for particular thoroughness. I was an army doctor, Mrs Shackleton, not a surgeon like your husband, but we were called upon to venture into areas beyond our particular expertise. I have taken a good look at young Osbert.'

'Did he drown?'

'You noticed the abrasion to the back of his head?'

'Yes.'

'It could have been done when he hit a rock. If he toppled backwards, it would be harder for him to save himself.'

'Did his wife and mother see the abrasion?'

'No.'

I was not sorry to hear that, yet part of me feels it is better to know everything, even the worst. 'So was he alive when he fell, or when he jumped? Perhaps he saw someone struggling and tried to save them.'

'He could not swim. If he did try to save someone then he was brave or foolhardy.'

I looked the doctor in the eyes, blue-grey, honest eyes that met mine. Yet he seemed to be evading a direct answer. Eventually, he said, 'Determining whether a person drowned can be difficult. Sometimes it is a matter of excluding other possibilities. Water in the lungs is not necessarily an indication. We know that he left home at dawn. His wife was sleeping but his mother was awake and heard him go.'

I thought how upset the young wife must be that she had not seen her husband leave for the last time.

'Do you think that because he searched so late and rose so early, he was simply tired and lost his footing?'

'That is a possibility. It would not take him long to reach the Strid, where he may have slipped. That would give him several hours of submersion, long enough for water passively to enter the lungs.'

'I see. That is what you meant when you said drowning can be difficult to determine.'

He thought for a moment, and then decided to say more. 'I noticed no sign that he clutched at anything, no weeds or grit under his fingernails. That might indicate that he fell and was unable to help himself, overcome by the ferocity of the river. It could also mean that he twisted as he fell and hit his head on a rock. Most cases of this kind are accidental. Suicide seems unlikely in his case, a young fit man with everything to live for.'

'Could the wound on his head have been inflicted by someone?'

'That is not out of the question. I'm waiting for an ambulance to take the body to Skipton hospital.' He tapped the ash from his cigarette into the fire grate. 'He seems a well-liked young man, well loved even, if the reaction of the females hereabouts can be relied upon. Two of the maids in tears, a village lass knocking on the door to ask if it's true.'

There was nothing more to be said on the subject, not yet at any rate. I thanked the doctor and rose to go.

He walked with me to the door, his stick tap-tapping.

'Is there anything I can do for Osbert's mother or wife do you think?'

'That's kind of you, Mrs Shackleton, but I don't think so, not just yet. I will wait and see if they have any questions. After that I need to investigate something that's spreading among the village children, a spate of vomiting and diarrhoea. You'd be well advised to keep your distance from the little blighters.'

As I left, I wondered whether Osbert, the recently married Romeo with a pregnant wife, had ended his romantic escapades. If he were still breaking hearts, then a father or a sweetheart may have wanted to teach Osbert a lesson. A push, a shove, a little harder than intended. But that seemed unlikely. And it brought me no nearer understanding why or how the prince had gone missing.

Six

The reception area of the hotel was deserted. I tapped the counter bell. Moments later a stout, twinkly-eyed fellow, as broad as he was high and with a nose to make Mr Punch proud, emerged from an inner office wiping crumbs from his mouth with one hand, and with the other hand fastening a reluctant button on his braided navy jacket.

'Good morning, madam.'

'Good morning. I'd like a room please.'

He pursed his lips, allowed his eyes to pop, shook his head and let out a breeze expressive of doubt. 'I'm sorry. We are not accepting guests at present.'

'Do you have a room available?'

'Oh yes. But not for . . . '

'Not for what?'

'It's nothing to do with your being an unescorted lady.'

'What is it to do with?'

'We are in an unusual time, and not knowing who might come through the door I have instructions to be careful, and can say no more.'

I took out my business card and handed it to him. 'Please give this to the manager. Say I wish to speak to him.'

He held the card at a good distance and scrutinised it. 'Please wait. There is a seat over there.' He nodded towards the window.

I stayed put.

The manager was not long in coming, hurrying towards me. Of medium height, as wiry as his commissionaire was stout, he walked with ramrod-stiff gait, as though a cord of steel ran up his backbone.

He wore a dark suit, which somehow looked wrong. Here was a man I would expect to see in khaki. His small neat moustache said Military Man. 'Mrs Shackleton, I do beg your pardon for this slight. I was tipped by the India Office to expect you.'

Well thank heaven for that.

He made a small bow. 'I'm Sergeant. Clive Sergeant is my name and sergeant is the rank I rose to. I alerted staff to be wary of newspaper reporters. My apologies that Cummings applied this caution to you.'

Cummings, the commissionaire, ambled up, straightening his shoulders.

'You have luggage?' Sergeant asked.

'In my car, the blue Jowett.'

'Cummings, see to Mrs Shackleton's luggage. The garden room.'

'Yes, sir.' Cummings stopped short of saluting.

'Now if you'll come this way, Mrs Shackleton. I took the liberty of having my wife stand by to make you a breakfast. I believe you left home at an ungodly hour.'

'That's very good of you, Mr Sergeant, but I am here to interview the prince's valet and his companion.'

'They are not going anywhere, madam. I've seen to that. Following your instructions, the Rolls-Royce is under lock and key. No one, including the prince's companion, will have access to it. As to the valet, he is standing by, waiting for his master's return. So, this way if you please, to the dining room.'

Breakfast sounded suddenly tempting. What's more, this man would make a good ally.

A few moments later we sat at a window table in a pleasant, half-panelled room that looked out onto the garden. Someone must have been peeping through the circular glass in the door that communicated with the kitchen because almost straight away a waitress appeared, carrying a tray.

Mr Sergeant waited until she had gone and then risked a small smile. 'I will see that you are well looked after, Mrs Shackleton. I served under the general, your grandfather, Lord Rodpen, on the Northwest Frontier. We all admired and respected him greatly. It will be an honour to assist you in any way I can in this dreadful business. I am most distressed to have let us all down by losing so important a guest as the Gattiawan heir.'

Of course he was not to know that the venerable grandfather, General Rodpen, was mine only by virtue of adoption.

He stirred his tea. 'And now this terrible business with young Osbert Hannon.' Sergeant lowered his head. 'Poor boy. What a blow. As if we haven't suffered enough losses already. He was his mother's only remaining son.'

'So I understand, and leaves a young widow.'

'How could someone so fit and agile have such a mishap?'

'Mr Sergeant, did Osbert seem in any way perturbed after escorting the prince yesterday?'

Sergeant shook his head. 'Not a bit of it. I saw him in the afternoon. He told me that the prince bagged a doe, and that he and Isaac had taken it to Stanks's barn. He said that the prince had gone on alone, to explore the moors. Last night, Osbert joined the search party and was out until the early hours.' Sergeant stroked his moustache. 'Surely to God Osbert wasn't so wearied that he slipped crossing the Strid. Local lads are so confident they can leap it that sometimes they misjudge. Osbert would have been in a hurry to rejoin the search at dawn.'

A breakfast was placed in front of me by the waitress. I gazed at bacon and egg, black pudding, fried bread and mushrooms.

'Is that all right? My wife said you may prefer a kipper or a boiled egg, but I told her, I said that the general always liked a fried breakfast.' He scrutinised the plate, and tutted. 'She left off the kidney.'

'It's all right. I don't want kidney, thank you. This should see me through the day.'

'You're sure?'

'Positive. Perhaps while I eat you would be kind enough to tell me something about Gattiawan. Having served in India you must know a great deal about the place.'

'About India, yes. It is a land of extremes, Mrs Shackleton, riches beyond the dreams of avarice, alongside the most abject poverty and starvation.'

'What is Gattiawan like?'

'Most of my time was spent on the frontier. I have never

been to Gattiawan, or any of the princely states. I know that they are allowed to get on with their business as they please, as long as they pay taxes to the crown.'

I thought back to my schooldays, and the lessons on Peoples of the Empire. 'There are hundreds of princely states, I think.'

'Yes, five hundred and sixty or more, taking up about a third of the land. I do know that Gattiawan stood by us during the Great War. There are those in India who when push came to shove for the war effort said, "England's need is India's opportunity". Not to put too fine a point on it, they wanted us gone from India. But Maharajah Shivram and his son Prince Narayan fought alongside us. I would shift heaven and earth to find the prince.'

The breakfast was getting the better of me. I pushed the black pudding to the side of the plate. 'Mr Sergeant, *The Times* court circular item referred to the Maharajah of Gattiawan's arrival in Marseilles on the SS *Malwa*. I take it that was the senior Maharajah, Shivram, Prince Narayan's father.'

'Yes. The Indian princes have all manner of titles, nawab, nizam, rao, rawal, but in Gattiawan they use maharajah, which I believe is rather superior to a mere rajah.'

'But Prince Narayan is also a maharajah? So there are two maharajahs in the family.'

'Strictly speaking there are three, Maharajah Shivram, his missing son Narayan, and Narayan's young son. At the age of seven a prince who is in line to be ruler officially takes the title. It can be confusing, but it helps that we more commonly refer to them all as princes.'

A surfeit of princes did not entirely clear the confusion.

If I could find Narayan, I would at least put a face to the middle one.

'Did Prince Narayan and Miss Metcalfe travel on the SS *Malwa* with the family?'

'No. They were already in Paris and came to London to visit the British Empire Exhibition.'

'What brought him to Yorkshire in advance of the grouse shooting?'

'They came by way of Derbyshire – Chatsworth. Miss Metcalfe is from these parts. I believe the maharajah wanted to see where she grew up – her original habitat, I suppose you might say.'

'What kind of man is he?'

'He is handsome, extravagant, courteous, rides well, a superb sportsman, every inch a prince.'

Now I really did want to find him.

I placed my knife and fork on the plate. 'Please thank Mrs Sergeant for that excellent breakfast. Now I really must speak to the valet, and Miss Metcalfe.' I pushed back my chair.

'Who will you see first?'

'The valet.'

Sergeant rose from the table. 'Miss Metcalfe . . . ' For the first time, he hesitated. 'She is in her room now. If, as I hope, the prince returns, he will be angry if she has not been treated courteously. On the other hand, if the Indian royal family arrive and she is here, that could be highly embarrassing.' He sighed and spread his hands in a helpless gesture.

'Mr Sergeant, what would you do in the army?'

'I would have the day's orders, and contingency plans.'

We walked to the door. 'Our day's orders must be to find

the maharajah. As yet, we do not need a contingency plan. Miss Metcalfe could have useful information. Did anyone else travel with the prince?'

I had already asked this of Mr Upton, the duke's agent, but I am not above asking the same question twice, in case I elicit a different answer. This time I did not.

He paused by a well-tended aspidistra. 'Prince Narayan and Miss Metcalfe drove up together. The valet, Ijahar, came by train. That is the extent of the entourage.'

'Strange. My Meeks encyclopaedia had photographs of Indian princes, seated on elephants, surrounded by ranks of soldiers and countless servants.'

'Mrs Shackleton, it is unheard of for such a man to travel with a single valet. He should have aides-de-camp, secretaries, launderers, drivers, drummers and trumpeters and their servants, servants' servants, and a dozen minions. It is Miss Metcalfe's influence that they travel like "normal people", as she puts it. She cannot abide hangers-on. If it were up to her, he would leave his valet behind, but Ijahar is so loyal he would have run after the motor all the way up the Great North Road.'

His description of Miss Metcalfe almost tempted me to see her first, but my uncle always maintains that if one wants to find out about a man, there is no better source of information than his valet.

'Does he speak English, this valet?'

'Yes, in his fashion.'

We reached the bottom of the stairs. 'So, Mr Sergeant, please lead the way to Ijahar.'

As we climbed the stairs, Sergeant said, 'The man's pestered the life out of my staff. Every five minutes asking,

Have they found my master? He is in and out of the hotel like a jack-in-the-box, staring across the countryside, as if he'll divine where the prince has got to.'

Prince Narayan, Lydia Metcalfe and the valet occupied the entire first floor. From the landing window, I looked across at a spectacular, sunlit view. Only gently moving clouds cast a shadow across the scene.

Sergeant pointed to a closed door. 'Ijahar is in there. Will I come in with you?'

'No. Thank you, Mr Sergeant. I will introduce myself.'

Seven

I tapped at the door. It was flung open by a young, thin Indian who stared at me from anxious eyes. One eyebrow had been obliterated by a great scar. He wore a white turban, tunic, baggy trousers and dhoti. The man looked at me expectantly, a smile beginning to form. 'They have found his highness?'

'I'm afraid not. Are you Ijahar?'

It was a stupid question. He could hardly be the night porter, disturbed in an illicit nap.

'I am Ijahar.'

'My name is Mrs Shackleton. I am here at the request of the Duke of Devonshire, to investigate your master's whereabouts. May I come in?'

The poor man seemed taken aback, and alarmed at the prospect of being alone with me. I wondered whether it would have been better to let Mr Sergeant stay.

Ijahar opened the door wide, and propped it with a shoe, which did not do the trick. He then placed a smoothing iron there, to hold the door open.

I watched in disbelief. Was he afraid I might slam the door and ravish him?

The room was little more than a linen cupboard. Pipes ran along the back wall, against which lay a roll of bedding. The slatted shelves held neatly folded clothing. On the floor was a doubled blanket, covered with a slightly scorched sheet and next to that an impressive collection of clothes irons and smoothing irons, one perched precariously on an unlit Bunsen burner. A shelf held an array of clothes brushes.

'You take very good care of your master, Ijahar.'

He nodded enthusiastically. 'I am dressing him since he was a child.'

Talking in a cupboard, albeit a large cupboard, did not seem a good idea.

'I have a few questions. Let us go into your master's room, where we can speak more comfortably.'

The thin face clouded with doubt. The scar on the absent eyebrow seemed to stretch. 'He is not liking it if you go in his room, memsahib.'

'I will take responsibility, Ijahar. I need to see the room.' Still, he hesitated. 'It is better if you show me. I could ask the manager.'

He sighed, and nodded. 'You follow me please.'

We stepped along the landing to the next room. Ijahar withdrew a key that hung on a ribbon around his neck. 'Manager Sergeant says keep it locked. Let no one in.'

'But you are letting me in now.'

'I hear manager Sergeant talk to you outside my door and say my name.'

The room was opulent. I felt sure that the prince had brought his own furnishings. Rich silks in shades of plum and dark grape covered the chairs and bed. Scarlet silk pyjamas and a dressing gown monogrammed in gold thread lay on the bed.

'For his return. And I draw a bath.'

'So you expect he will return soon?'

'Yes, yes. He likes to trick, to joke, ever since young. In his palace, when guests come, to eat, he has a train go round and round the big table.' He smiled. 'Up he speeds it, so guests reach out, and what they reach for, food, cigar, drink, chocolate, is gone.'

This confirmation of the prince's reputation as a practical joker gave me a small glimmer of hope, though I felt little sympathy for a man who would crack such a bad joke as to have a whole estate, a whole village, down tools to search for him.

An Elizabethan table stood by the wall. On it was a writing case, and typewriter. In the corner of the room stood a heavy old safe.

'Did your master say anything to you before he went out yesterday afternoon?'

'Yes, memsahib.'

'What did he say?'

'He said Ijahar.'

'Just your name.'

'Yes. He was in good mood. Sometimes he say, You.'

'And then what?'

'I dress him. I put on his boots. Bring his gun.'

'Did the maharajah receive any messages or visitors before he went out yesterday?'

'Not yesterday. Day before. Mr Presthope only.'

I remembered that this was the old school friend under whose roof the prince and Miss Metcalfe had spent one night.

'Mr Presthope of Halton East?'

He nodded.

'Do you know what they talked about?'

Ijahar shrugged and shook his head.

'And are any of your fellow countrymen in the area?'

'Countrymen?'

'Yes, any Indian gentlemen, only it was thought someone may have been seen in the area on Friday.'

'No, memsahib, only my master and me.'

'I must look into the writing case. This is not to pry into your master's affairs. It is part of my investigation. Do you understand?'

He hesitated, as if expecting to hear his master's footsteps and to be caught in a moment of betrayal. All was silence.

'Very well, memsahib.'

'And I want you to be witness that I am taking nothing.'

'Very well, memsahib.'

I lifted the writing case a little nearer. I saw that under it was a telegram. I unfolded it. It was dated August 1, yesterday. What a strange message. It read simply, "Ides of August" and was signed "C".

We had read *Julius Caesar* aloud at school. Afterwards we ran about warning each to beware the ides of March, thinking this to be some villainous band of outlaws. It was disappointing to learn that the ides referred to the middle of the month. In some months, like March, the ides was the fifteenth. If I remembered correctly, in August the ides fell on the thirteenth. This cryptic message sounded like a warning. And who was "C"?

The sandalwood writing case had a key in the lock. I opened it. Placed on top of the envelopes was a typed note.

Received from Maharajah Narayan Halkwaer the sum of £10,000 (Ten Thousand Pounds) for disbursement by Thurston J Presthope, Esquire to Mr Tobias Metcalfe in accordance with said Maharajah's instructions.

T J Presthope   31st July, 1924.
Thurston J. Presthope,
Sandmoor Hall,
Halton East,
North Riding of Yorkshire

Presthope was the man the maharajah had stayed with on his first night in the area. Who was Tobias Metcalfe? Why, if the maharajah wanted to give him money, did he not do so himself? It seemed extraordinary that the maharajah had handed over such a large sum the day before he disappeared.

A further cursory glance through the writing case revealed what looked to be verse, exquisitely penned in an Indian script on blue bond paper, decorated with tiny hand-drawn flowers. Poetry. There were a couple of letters in what I took to be Urdu. There were also notes in English, but nothing that gave a hint of an invitation that would explain an absence.

'Has anyone, apart from you, been in this room since your master left?'

He shook his head. 'I have the key.'

'What is in the safe?' It struck me as careless that a receipt for ten thousand pounds was left in a writing case.

'My master's jewels and the dubte suraj ki chamak.'

'The dubte suraj ki chamak?'

'Gattiawan diamond, called glow as sun goes down.'

The newspapers had been generous with their information about the Koh-i-noor diamond, Mountain of Light, the empress of jewels that formed the centrepiece of the Great Exhibition at Crystal Palace in 1851. Now it was on display at the British Empire Exhibition. 'What is the dubte suraj ki chamak like?'

'It is like nothing else.' He lowered his voice to a reverent whisper. 'Dubte suraj ki chamak, a pale pink stone, weighs 186 carats.'

'That is bigger than the Koh-i-noor.'

He joined forefingers and thumbs to indicate its shape and size, about four inches. 'Diamond of the Mughal Emperors, mined in Golconda. In a time of war it was hidden in milk pudding.' He raised his fingers to a point. 'Around it, silver star diamonds and golden as moon diamonds. From top grow peacock feathers.'

'Feathers?'

He nodded eagerly. 'Emeralds, rubies, pearls, sapphires.'

Much as I wanted to see this extraordinary gem, I decided against asking Ijahar to open the safe. My anxiety for the maharajah increased to the weight of one hundred and eighty-six carats. The man must be mad to have driven here carrying such a jewel. The car could have crashed. He could have been robbed. He was either extremely foolish or very daring. Perhaps both.

'Why did he bring the diamond here?'

For a moment, it seemed that Ijahar might tell me something, but he clammed up, pursing his lips.

'Ijahar, you know something. You must tell me. I am here on behalf of His Majesty's Government.' And so I was.

59

Hearing myself say this aloud gave me a shiver of surprise at the gravity of such responsibility.

'I only hear them say.'

'Say what?'

'I do not listen.'

'Of course you don't. What was said?'

'The king comes here to shoot. My master will show him the diamond.'

'I see.'

I did not see. It was news to me that King George would be coming to Bolton Abbey for the grouse shooting. James must have known but had chosen not to tell me. I wondered what other pieces of information I would have to ferret out before I found the truth. I glanced once more at the note regarding disbursement of monies. It seemed careless to leave this lying about.

I had never met Thurston Presthope, but I did not like the sound of him. I added this old school friend to my list of people to interview. And then a thought occurred to me. Why not leave this here, or appear to leave it here? Set a trap.

'Ijahar, I want to use the typewriter to write a note. Will you wish to stay while I do this?'

He nodded. 'I stay, memsahib.'

'I shall use a piece of paper from your master's writing case.'

I took a sheet of writing paper from the case and rolled it into the typewriter. I copied the note exactly. Now here would come the hard part.

I took the paper from the typewriter. Ideally, I would have liked to trace and practise Thurston Presthope's signature.

Since my notebook was handy, in my pocket, I took it out, and tried my hand at the flourishing scrawl, twice.

I then forged Presthope's signature on the newly-typed note.

Ijahar had lost interest. He was smoothing the pyjamas on the bed. I put the original note in an envelope, and slid it into my satchel. My forgery, I returned to the writing case.

Ijahar turned his liquid brown eyes on me. The scar where his eyebrow should have been took on a livid cast as he stood in the rays of sunlight that poured through the window.

'Ijahar, I need to speak to Miss Metcalfe now.'

Tobias Metcalfe, the intended recipient of ten thousand pounds, must be some relation to the maharajah's paramour. Perhaps Lydia Metcalfe had put in a plea for financial assistance for her father, or a brother.

Eight

'Her room, memsahib.'

The words uttered by the valet held a hundredweight of loathing. He rapped on the door, and then hurried away.

A voice called 'Enter, truant!'

I stepped into the room. Lydia Metcalfe was seated at a walnut dressing table, applying lip rouge. Through the huge oval mirror, she glanced at me in undisguised disappointment. Straight away I realised that Ijahar had emulated the prince's knock, to upset the woman he disliked.

She swung round on the stool. Of course, she was beautiful. What else might I have expected? Nineteen or twenty years of age, I guessed, with high cheekbones, flawless pale skin and full bow lips. No fashionable bob here. Her mass of waving red hair had been tamed into luxuriant pleats and loops. I could see why the maharajah had fallen for this most modern work of art.

'Miss Metcalfe?'

'Who the hell are you?' Her London accent sat uneasily with such stunning looks.

'That's a yes?'

'Oh, witty, eh? Yes I'm Lydia Metcalfe. What of it?' She took a swig of something that looked like water. But a trained detective knows gin when she spots a bottle of Gordon's next to the perfume spray.

'I am Mrs Kate Shackleton, here at the request of the India Office to investigate the maharajah's disappearance. May I have a word with you?'

'What about?' She picked up the bottle and topped up her glass. 'I thought they were too busy searching for Narayan to bother me.'

'The search was resumed at dawn.'

'By the halt, the lame and the blind. They don't want to find him do they, your precious India Office, because they can't stop him.'

'Stop him?'

'They can't stop him marrying me.'

She rose gracefully to her feet, moving as if about to take her place on stage at the Folies Bergère. Tall, with long slim legs and a great deal of front, she wore a clinging silk dress the colour of young nettles. The row of emeralds at her throat was spectacular enough to form the solitary display in a high-class jeweller's window. It was matched by the bracelet dangling from her wrist and a solitaire emerald on her ring finger. She made sure I saw it.

Now was certainly not the moment to enquire after the prince's wife and child. I tried not to gawp. 'You are engaged?'

She shot me a look that said she missed nothing, including my surprise. 'Yes. In the Hindu religion a man is allowed to marry four wives. He has only the poetry-writing princess. She was foisted on him, betrothed when they were children. It's me he wants and he is in a hurry.' I would have liked to ask why but decided against it. She told me anyway. 'He saw the way the Aga Khan looked at me when we were dining at the Savoy.' She downed the contents of her glass, glaring at me from big summer-blue eyes. Her animosity was ebbing. She looked a little defensive, as if expecting criticism.

'You must be anxious about your fiancé.'

She softened a little when I referred to the prince as her fiancé. 'You'd better sit down.' She indicated a bucket chair, covered with a gold satin throw. I sat down somewhat gingerly, half expecting to slide off.

Jamming a Sobranie cocktail cigarette into a long holder, she sat on the bed. 'If you'd had the shock of your sweetheart taking this long about his business, and no word of explanation, you'd be knocking it back yourself.'

'When did you last speak to the prince?'

She threw the word back at me. 'Prince! He's a maharajah. One day he will be king of Gattiawan. But of course Britain doesn't like Indians to be called kings. They like to keep the monopoly of that to themselves. Are you here because they're pointing a finger at me? Are you instead of a detective?'

'I am a detective.'

'Well then, I expect you'd like a clue. Gretna Green.'

'Gretna Green?'

'I told him it would be very romantic if we could elope to Gretna Green.'

'Did he say that he was going there?'

'It wouldn't be an elopement if he went alone, would it? I think he's making some arrangements, checking that the marriage would be valid, arranging a Hindu marriage to follow. When he came back from his ride yesterday, he brought me a four-leaf clover and said, Be mine.'

'It's unusual in a man, to know the meaning of flowers.'

'I teased him about it. I said it would take more than a weed to make me stay with him forevermore. He said there would be an even better surprise for me when he returned. And I knew it was to do with our wedding.'

'So you believe he went to make some arrangements.'

'If we'd been in London he would have sent one of his minions but they can't be trusted. I'm teaching him to do things for himself.'

'Have you told the police what you have just told me?'

She laughed. 'Our village plod? It's none of his business. I got rid of him.'

'How?'

'Oh, he came sniffing round, looking down his nose at me. I turned on my smoulder, his legs melted and he ran away.'

'I wish you had told him because it sounds odd that the maharajah would go straight from deerstalking into making arrangements for a marriage.'

'Are you saying I'm stupid?'

'Of course not.'

'When you are wealthy beyond dreams, you can do anything. He could have had a car waiting.' She spoke with more hope than conviction.

I waited for her to listen to how weak and unconvincing her words sounded.

'All right, if you must know, I am worried. Narayan can barely stand to be away from me for more than an hour or two.'

'So you have been by his side, apart from the riding, since you left London?'

'I didn't say that.'

'Miss Metcalfe, I'm not asking questions to be intrusive. I want to try and piece together events. If you tell me anything that he said or did when he was with you, something that made you believe he might act out of character, or have a plan to go somewhere – apart from Gretna Green – I could extend my enquiries. The physical search of the estate here is the most useful approach, but we can also build a picture, do you see?'

'It's a picture you want? Well put this in your picture. I want my maharajah back. If someone has hurt him, I'll kill them.'

'Is there anything else you can tell me? You left London when?'

She leaned back against the pillows and kicked off her shoes. 'We drove a week ago Friday from London to Chatsworth. Narayan dined with the Duke and Duchess of Devonshire last Saturday. Of course, I wasn't invited.'

'Why was that?'

She laughed, showing perfect teeth. 'I'm not the right sort, not pukka. I suppose you must be or you wouldn't be here, but you seem all right.'

'Was there a particular reason for the visit to Chatsworth?'

'He didn't say so, but I know it was to do with the Gattiawan diamond. The Koh-i-Noor diamond is on display at the British Empire Exhibition. Narayan and I went together to see it. His father had mentioned that perhaps they might loan the Gattiawan diamond for display during the second part of the exhibition, when the Koh-i-Noor is returned to the king.'

'And after Chatsworth?'

'We stayed in Derbyshire for a few days. For once we gave that damn valet the slip. Narayan sent him here on the train. It's ridiculous, a grown man expecting someone to dress him. I can't abide the thought of some maid messing about with me. I do for myself, thank you.'

'Did you meet anyone, talk to anyone, who may have followed you here, from London, or from Chatsworth?'

'No. We didn't tell anyone where we were going. I didn't know myself. Narayan said it was a surprise. I expect he'd talked to Devonshire about it, about coming up here for some riding and shooting. And I believe he thought because we're far-flung here, I would able to stay at Bolton Hall. I knew I wouldn't, and I wouldn't want to.'

'Tell me about staying the night in Halton East.'

She pulled a face. 'Narayan was told Bolton Hall was still "shut up", but that if *he* wanted to stay there he could. They're not so subtle, these fancy aristocrats of ours. But of course, I'm meant to know my place, and they're not above trying a bit of nose-rubbing.'

'That must have upset you.'

'Not likely it didn't.' She shook her emerald bracelet at me. 'Do I look as if I care to mix with boring old farts? They won't put up with me and I won't put up with them. Narayan knows that, and he admires me for it. We spent one night with that so-called friend of his, Thurston Presthope. They were at school together. I saw through him straight away. He said his wife is away. It's obvious that she's left him. He doesn't pay his servants. He's a gambler, and a waster. There was a dead moth on the dining room table. I said to him, "What's that doing there? Do you have a wager on how long it will take to turn to dust?" Of course Presthope had to pretend to be amused.'

'What does he do, this Mr Presthope?'

'He's a so-called gentleman, which means he does nothing and hasn't two ha'pennies to rub together. He called here on Thursday. I expect he asked Narayan to lend him money.' Her startling eyes flickered with a sudden idea. 'Presthope's behind this.'

Before she had time to say more, there was a tap on the door. She made as if to leap up eagerly, then recovered her poise and leaned back, calling as she had to me, 'Enter!'

A fair-haired young chambermaid appeared in the doorway. 'Miss Metcalfe, I'm to ask if you need any help with your packing.'

'Packing? Why would I be packing?'

'The Indian gentleman, the maharajah's manservant, madam, he said you are leaving.'

Lydia picked up the ashtray and flung it at the chambermaid, missing her by a hair's breadth. 'Tell him that! Tell him I'm going nowhere till Narayan comes back.'

The chambermaid bolted from the room.

'I'll swing for that wretched creature, by God I will. I'll tell Narayan, sack him, or I leave you.'

Her emerald bracelet glinted as she raised her glass and took another drink of gin.

'Miss Metcalfe,' I tried my soothing voice. 'Is it possible that the valet expects the Indian royal family will be arriving, because of Narayan's disappearance?'

'What of it if they do? I have a right to be here.'

Bravado. Another moment and she would start to cry.

'Who is Mr Tobias Metcalfe?'

'My father. Why?'

'I believe I heard one of the estate workers mention him, and it occurred to me . . . No it's nothing.'

'What?'

'I wondered whether the maharajah's true purpose in coming here was to ask your father's permission to marry you.'

Her eyes widened. 'D'you know, I bet that was it. It would be just like him to play by the rules. When we arrived on Tuesday, the farm was our first call, at Narayan's insistence. He particularly wanted to see my father but he was out of luck.'

'Why was that?'

'My father wasn't there. He and my brothers stayed clear until we had gone. Narayan talked to my mother.'

'Did he mention marriage?'

'He might have said something to Mam, while I was looking round the farm. My mother always tries to give me a job, tries to draw me back in. I went to collect eggs. But Narayan would get short shrift from Dad if he asked permission to marry me. I know exactly what he'd say.'

'What?'

'The usual. Narayan's married already, his skin's the wrong colour, I'm old enough, I've been pleasing myself all my life. Shall I go on?'

'Not unless it helps to get it off your chest.'

She refilled her glass and took a long swig. Her face was now flushed, her eyes a little glassy and fierce.

'I don't understand why Narayan is taking so long. He's too used to his comforts, and that servile creature massaging his toes, or whatever he does.'

'We'll find him. Miss Metcalfe . . . '

'My name's Lydia. Stop calling me miss, stop rubbing it in.'

'Lydia, I've never yet looked for a missing person I haven't found.'

'Well then why are you talking to me and not out looking? Do you think I have something to do with his disappearance, that I've murdered him and shoved the body under the bed? That bloody valet tells lies about me. Narayan doesn't listen. He loves me. He would not do this to me, just disappear. Do you think someone is keeping him away from me against his will?'

'This is not bandit country, Lydia.'

It seemed unkind to remind her that she was the one who demanded her lover travel without an entourage.

I took my leave of Lydia Metcalfe, puzzling over the fact that the prince had used a go-between to bribe Lydia's father into approving a marriage he abhorred.

The sound of sobbing drew me to a room across the hall. The young chambermaid was huddled over the wash basin, splashing water on her face, and crying piteously.

'Oh dear. Did that ashtray hit you? Let me see.'

'N-o-o-o, it, it didn't hit me . . . '

'Then what's the matter?'

'Nothing.'

'Doesn't look like nothing.'

Through her sobs, she choked out an explanation. 'I had some bad news today.'

I am sorry to say that where a polite person would pretend not to notice distress, a detective must perforce stick her oar in. It is not an entirely hard-hearted practice. The poor girl looked in need of comfort.

'It's the last straw her flinging the ashtray at me. I was keeping up well. I only cried a bit. I would've cried later, on my own time, except he'd hear me and be glad.'

'Who on earth would be glad to hear you cry?'

'My dad.' She gave in to a fresh bout of tears and sought in vain for a handkerchief.

'Here, take mine.'

'Thank you.'

'Sit down. Give yourself time to recover.'

Whether this was the right approach, I had no idea. Perhaps the Bolton Hall servant had the better way, ordering her young workmate to snap out of it.

I sat beside the girl as she cried. 'What is your name?'

'Rachel Simpson.'

'Rachel, are your tears for Osbert Hannon?'

She snuffled. 'Aye, and for me an' all. He should've married me. She snatched him from under my nose. They'll see when she has the bairn. They'll all know how she caught him.'

And some of them may resent him enough to kill him. Love, hate, jealousy, they are all strong motives for murder.

I filled a glass with water. 'Take a sip, Rachel. You'll feel better if you tell me about it.'

I listened to the old, old story, at the same time following another train of thought.

An old memory nagged at me.

I had been at a dinner party at Aunt Berta's. We ladies had withdrawn, ostensibly to play cards but really for a good old gossip. Someone had told a tale about a maharajah who worshipped a sixteen-year-old Spanish dancer. When she refused his advances, he wrote to her father three times, finally offering a hundred thousand pounds if the girl would marry him. It worked.

Knowing of Mr Metcalfe's animosity, it made sense for Prince Narayan to use a local man as go-between to offer money to Lydia's father in exchange for his blessing on their marriage. The prince was used to having someone else take care of his business. Who better than his old school friend, Presthope?

But what if that old school friend found another use for the money?

Of course Presthope may have acted honourably and passed on the ten thousand pounds, or the offer of it, to Tobias Metcalfe.

That may have been the final insult to an independent-minded farmer whose daughter was no better than she ought to be.

Nine

A death and a disappearance. Was there a connection, I wondered, between the drowning of Osbert Hannon and the failure of the maharajah to return to the hotel? What if the crime, if crime there be, arose not because of a practical joke or foul play involving an Indian prince, but because the local Romeo had overstepped the mark, and somehow the maharajah had become entangled? Or because the offer of ten thousand pounds for the purchase of his daughter had enraged Mr Tobias Metcalfe?

As I walked towards the stable to find Isaac Withers, a bulky, uniformed figure emerged from the police house.

Even someone without my well-honed detection skills would have recognised the man as the local constable. Stupidly, I had not troubled to ask about him, or learn his name. He had a fleshy, not unpleasant face, with the drooping jowls and liquid black eyes of a boxer dog. His crooked buck teeth gave the unfortunate impression of an ominous smile.

'Constable?'

He turned towards me. It is always best to observe procedure, and I should have left a card with his wife.

I introduced myself and told him that I had been called by the India Office.

'Have you by gum?' He frowned. 'Well I was out on the moorland since dawn, and no message has come to me about you.'

So much for James's claim that he had smoothed my way.

I handed the officer my card. 'Please do check with . . .' I almost said 'your superiors', but did not want to start out on the wrong foot, 'the chief constable.'

He glanced at the card, holding it by the corner as though it may need to be fingerprinted later. He gave a sideways glance as if hoping to spot a receptacle for used tram tickets into which he could drop my card. Reluctantly, he thrust it in his pocket. 'Now I have important investigations and am now performing the task of coroner's officer in connection with a drowning, so ...'

'Just a moment, officer.'

'A moment is what I am short of.'

'Has anyone checked whether the maharajah may have left the area by car or train?'

His lips twitched. An eye did the same. 'Everything that needs to be done is being done. I wish you good day, madam.'

In other words, keep your snitch out of our business.

With that, he strode off towards Bolton Hall, leaving me to find Isaac Withers.

I delayed doing so for just long enough to return to the hotel, contact my housekeeper and ask her to pass a message to my assistant, Jim Sykes. Check the railways. Contact local companies that hire out cars and drivers. Find out if anyone has had dealings with an Indian gentleman. He may have enquired about travelling to Gretna Green.

Mrs Sugden repeated my words back to me, with a touch of astonishment on the 'Gretna Green.' I realised it did all sound preposterous. Besides, the maharajah had his Rolls-Royce. But he may have preferred to sit in the back of a car with his mistress.

When I emerged from my telephone call, the commissionaire was loitering at the desk, busily perusing a sporting paper. He folded it as I came near.

'Mr Cummings, I wonder if I could trust you to make an enquiry for me?' I slid half a crown across the desk in a casual manner, as if I had never wanted it in the first place.

'Of course, madam.'

'Would you find out for me whether the maharajah made or received any telephone calls, or sent a telegram or a letter?'

Afternoon sun filtered through branches, giving the green world a bright glow. I was walking with Isaac, along the woodland path that led to the Strid. He had told me the name of the local constable, Brocksup, though I feared I had shot my bolt when it came to establishing cordial relations in that quarter.

I now wanted to see the place where Isaac believed Osbert Hannon fell into the river. The old man picked his way carefully as the ground sloped. We had tethered the horses when the way became narrow and steep. I followed Isaac as he sure-footed his way across crevices to a large flat rock that took us perilously close to the deep drop.

Below, water raged over rocks, its roar drowning out all

other sounds. As a cloud passed overhead, we and the grey stone darkened. Waves of foam leapt and sparkled.

Isaac pushed his hands into his pockets. 'This is the Strid. We warn young uns not to jump across, but we all done it.' He pointed to the opposite bank. 'Osbert wends his way from the Coney Warren. He'd arrive on yon side, and leap across. The young uns scorn the bridge.' We stood in silence, listening, as though the river might murmur a confession.

His face had turned red and the veins in his neck bulged. The poor man was deeply upset. 'Even in winter he leaps it. Happen he was weary from searching into the night, or just that second misjudged.'

I stared at the torrent, until the noise and strife of the river seemed to come from inside myself. Aside from the turbulence of the water, this place had a most tranquil air, as if nothing bad would ever happen. It was possible to hold these two thoughts simultaneously: this spot holds threat, danger; what a peaceful place, such an air of serenity.

Isaac said softly, 'Osbert's not the first, nor will he be last to come a cropper here. An age ago, the boy of Egremond perished. He's sung of by the poet.' Half to himself, Isaac murmured some old lines. 'Where the rock is rent in two, and the river rushes through, 'Twas but a step, the gulph he passed; but that step – it was his last!'

I broke his mood. 'Isaac, you know the river. If Osbert did fall in here, would it be feasible in those hours between dawn and mid morning that his body would be swept to where the river bends, by Paradise Lathe where he was found?'

Isaac shook his head. 'Who knows what tricks this river will play? I know of a case where weeks later a body was found miles off, and another poor soul caught in the deeps who never did emerge to be buried as a Christian. One thing I do know.'

'What's that?'

'The river would never have swallowed him if he had not played a part in slaying the white doe. We have brought a curse on us-selves, him and me.'

'You weren't there. You told me yourself you were by the stables, waiting to hear a shot or a whistle.'

Isaac was not listening. I knew full well that nothing I said would shift his belief. The idea would fester in him. He would turn to the death of the doe for explanation of any and every misfortune that came his way between now and eternity.

'Isaac, I believe Osbert was popular with the local girls.'

'Aye. There's no denying it.'

'Might he have found himself on the wrong side of some father, brother, or a rival?'

'He were safely married.'

'That won't stop tears dampening a fair few pillows.'

'What are you driving at, madam?'

A young rabbit appeared, sniffed the air, and made a dash for cover.

'It's most likely that Osbert's death was a terrible accident and nothing whatsoever to do with the shooting of the doe. You spent a lot of time with him.'

'Everything he knew about horses, he took from me.'

'Did anyone threaten him, some jealous sweetheart, or an angry brother?'

Isaac turned back towards the path, making out he had not heard me.

We began to walk back towards the horses.

'Who's been saying summat?'

'I've kept my eyes and ears open, that's all. It could be nothing. Tittle tattle.'

'Aye, tittle tattle, but I've heard nowt.'

I made a guess, knowing only one name. 'Tittle tattle about Rachel's father?'

Isaac gave a mirthless laugh. 'You're on a dead end there. He wouldn't drown the lad. He'd thrash him fair and square. A stationmaster has a position to keep up.'

'Yes. I'm sure you're right. It was just a thought.'

The pony whinnied as she saw me. I had learned her name: Betsy. If my riding lessons had included a pony such as this beauty, I might more readily have taken to the saddle.

If horses could talk, the maharajah's Arab might save us a lot of time and trouble. It is most annoying to think that an animal might have a solution. Oh for a way to interview a horse.

Focus, Kate, I told myself. I must tuck away the information that the stationmaster may have had it in for Osbert, and now concentrate on trying to find the maharajah.

'Isaac, I want you to take me on the morning ride you did with the prince. Perhaps it will jog your memory. I want you to tell me if he paused anywhere, or said something that might have given a hint as to what was in his mind that day. Anything, however small, or if you saw anyone on the way.'

Isaac shook his head. 'He didn't say much, just wanting to know the lie of the land. He was after inspecting the butts beyond Hazelwood Moor, where he'd be shooting come the twelfth. We took him across by stepping stones and up through the Valley of Desolation.'

'Then take me there.'

If it were true that the maharajah expected to be shooting on the twelfth, then Lydia was wrong in her assumption that they would very shortly elope.

We rode on in silence, retracing our path alongside the Wharfe. The ruined abbey seemed to say that it had seen all this sort of endeavour before, and it was to no avail.

Gingerly, my pony trod alongside the stepping stones, following the bigger horse. Both Betsy and I were relieved to reach land on the other side. She gave a little shake, which made me smile, for the water, though fast flowing here, was not deep.

We climbed a little, and trotted through woods and a gate into meadowland. Either by instinct or familiarity, Betsy avoided marshy patches. Here was a horse who did not like wet hooves.

'It's beautiful, Isaac. What's this place called?'

'It's the Valley of Desolation.'

'But it's not a bit desolate.'

'It was once, when a storm came through and destroyed every tree, laid waste and flooded the land.'

'By the time you reached this place, had the prince said anything, made any comment?'

'We inspected the grouse. It's been a good year for the chicks. See, there's a couple there, feathers tucked in because they're warm. Fluff 'em out when it's cold.'

Enjoy yourselves while you can, little grouse. You'll have a rude awakening come the Glorious Twelfth, not so glorious for you.

We rode across the Moor, inspecting grouse butts until I felt saddle sore. When we came across a hut we dismounted to check that it was empty, although the area had already been searched.

Enough was enough. I told myself that I should be interviewing the mysterious Thurston Presthope, the friend who had been trusted by the maharajah as emissary to Lydia's father, or seeking a report from Upton as to the progress, or not, of the search parties.

But having come this far, I would persevere. We had exhausted the possibility of the prince's morning ride offering any clues as to his whereabouts.

'Isaac, what about the afternoon?'

'Ah,' said Isaac, as if suddenly interested, and as if this was what I should have asked him all along. 'He lost interest in grouse in the afternoon. That was when he shot the white doe.'

By now, I had a slightly sick feeling from being so long in the saddle. 'Show me where.'

'That's easy. He was in Westy Bank Wood when he shot doe.'

'Take me there.'

We rode in silence back towards the river, this time crossing a wooden bridge. I was becoming as superstitious as the old man. Somehow I thought that if I could ride the same ride, see the wood where the maharajah stalked the deer, something might occur to me, one of those sudden insights that come when least expected. Straight away I regretted this as it meant that we did not enter the wood at the nearest point, but rode on, towards the hotel, and then veered round.

Isaac rode up into the wood. 'This was his way. Of course he was on foot, stalking.'

We entered the shady wood that smelled of fern and wild

garlic. Pansies, honesty and campion nestled in the grass. At that moment, all I wanted to do was clamber off the pony, find my way to the stream that gurgled somewhere nearby, take a cooling drink and sit in a shady spot.

We rode on in silence, horse and pony patterned with shadows as we moved between the trees under branches lit by the sun.

The pony stopped suddenly. She had seen a cage on the path. In it was a live crow. At that moment, a single shot rang out. Betsy whinnied and reared. I patted her neck and spoke a few words to calm her.

A second shot followed rapidly on the first. This time it took all my strength to hold her still.

'What's going on?'

Isaac called back to me, waving an arm at the caged bird. 'That's a bait crow. Its own kind have come to find it. My lad is shooting them. They're destructive devils.'

The wood turned from idyllic to sinister.

The crow in the cage let out an unearthly sound.

And then a human sound followed; a shriek of terror.

The sound came from deep within the wood where trees grow too closely together for a horse to pass. I dismounted, as did Isaac. We hurried through trees, pushing aside branches and treading fern. There, in a clearing, were two dead crows. Beside them stood Joel. His gun lay on the ground.

'Nay lad.' Isaac stumbled towards him, his voice hoarse, his breath laboured. 'What ails thee?'

Joel was white and trembling, terror in his eyes, his striped shirt wet with perspiration. He opened and closed his mouth but no words came.

I made him sit down with his back to a tree and dip his head towards his knees. He made whimpering noises and pointed towards a holly bush.

Isaac made no attempt to move. 'That's the place the highness shot the white doe.'

I walked towards the holly bush. A dead crow had fallen there. I moved as Joel would have, towards the crow. *And then I saw him.*

There, behind the bush, lay a body, partly hidden under branches. Someone had made a hasty attempt to conceal the dead man. The least glimpse told me who this was. Staring at the figure on the ground, I almost lost my balance. This could not be real. He did not look real. My stomach churned. I tasted the fried breakfast in my throat. Keep a hold of yourself. You will not be sick, not now.

During my wartime nursing in the VAD I had seen death at close quarters but could not suppress the shock of its finality, that terrible knowledge that here was a life snuffed out too soon.

I turned, to see Isaac looking in my direction.

I walked back to them.

'Is it him?' Isaac asked.

'It is.'

Isaac held his hand to his head and closed his eyes. 'He's in the exact same spot where the doe was killed.'

'I didn't do it,' Joel whimpered. 'I shot the crows, that's all. I didn't see him.'

Isaac put a hand on his son's shoulder. 'Nay lad, you couldn't have killed him with them cartridges.'

'No one is blaming you, Joel.' I wanted them gone, so that I could gather my thoughts and examine the area. 'Isaac, fetch the constable. If you cannot find him, speak only to Mr Upton or Mr Sergeant. Tell them where to come.'

When father and son had gone, I went back to where the body lay. I carry with me an Ensignette pocket camera that produces three-by-two inch pictures. I could have done with a better one for this task, but it would have to suffice.

I photographed the branch-covered body. My first thought was that the initial search had been insufficiently thorough, and the body had been missed. But as I looked at the lifeless form through the tracery of branches, I saw that the prince's hair and clothing were dry. If he had lain here since yesterday, the body would have been wet with dew. No crow had pecked at his closed eyes, no animal had nibbled here. I looked around. The nearby fern lay deeply crushed where someone had trodden. There was a broken branch, but broken branches abounded. I saw no torn scrap of clothing to indicate that someone had carried, or dragged, the body here. The crush in the fern was deep enough to indicate that whoever moved through that area had carried something, or someone, heavy. Roundabout, the dry ground showed no footprints. I took another photograph. Even in death, Maharajah Narayan Halkwaer of Gattiawan cut a noble and handsome figure. A tracery pattern shaded the prince's cheek. As I clicked the shutter, images imprinted themselves onto my brain, like the pictures in a macabre fairy tale. A smooth, untroubled brow and sensuous mouth held my gaze. There was something regal and impressive in the way he lay, like a figure on a cathedral tomb. His well-cut forest-green jacket and trousers spoke quality. His soft boots were buffed to a high sheen. I had the strange feeling that any moment he would sit up and call for his valet to take off his boots.

As my eyes grew accustomed to the gloomy wood, I saw through the carelessly placed branches that blood had dried around his heart, where a bullet had penetrated. I reached through and touched the jacket. Dry as my own.

That was when I saw the rifle, lying at the side of the body. I have little knowledge of guns. But I know that after a person has fired, he would break the gun, take out the ammunition for safety, and ride with the gun open. This gun was not broken.

I looked again at the branches to see whether I could spot anything unusual such as a scrap of cloth.

Something about the way the body was laid struck me as odd. He had not simply fallen but had been 'arranged'. At first I could not put my finger on why I thought this. There was no crossing of the hands on the chest, though the eyes were closed. The face looked quite calm, no grimace here in the face of death. His arms lay by his side. I bent down to take a closer look at the right hand that I could see most clearly. The fingers were not curled but in a relaxed position. His nails were carefully manicured.

Nearby, a branch cracked. Someone was approaching.

Feeling like the ghoul of Bolton Abbey, I took one more photograph.

The duke's agent, Upton, hurried along the path on foot, followed by two men carrying a stretcher.

The men placed the stretcher by an elm tree and went quietly away.

'It's the maharajah?' Upton asked, following the direction of my gaze towards the body. 'We searched. How could we have missed him?'

I could have hazarded several guesses, but now was not the time.

We looked across towards the man who once had everything, who had entertained at a table so big that a miniature train chugged around it with drinks, cigars, chocolates; a man whose everyday jewellery could buy not just the estate of Bolton Abbey on which we stood, but the whole of Yorkshire, and have change to pay for Paris. Riches beyond measure had not saved Narayan's life. Had riches beyond measure hastened his death? A prince, a warrior, his life should not have ended ingloriously on strange soil.

'Constable Brocksup is on his way,' Upton said. 'He was telephoning to Skipton for the inspector. His wife is alerting the bell ringers to be on hand to ring out the news, but not until Mr Brocksup has seen for himself.'

'Is the doctor still at Bolton Hall?'

'Now that I think of it, I saw his Bugatti by the hotel. I should have alerted him.'

Minutes slowed to an eternity. A squirrel scuttled up a tree. Upton lit a cigarette. It was perhaps not much more than twenty minutes until the constable arrived, out of breath from hurrying.

Upton began to introduce us.

'We've met,' Brocksup said curtly. He walked towards the body, squatted on his heels and took a look. As he straightened up, he said, 'You may leave this to me now, Mr Upton, Mrs Shackleton. I will take charge until the inspector arrives.'

'What about the bell ringers?' Upton asked.

'Give them the nod.' He took a sketch pad from under his arm, and produced a pencil.

'I have taken photographs. But I expect the inspector will bring your own photographer.'

It was as if I had not spoken.

Ostentatiously, the constable began to sketch.

Upton and I were well and truly dismissed.

When we reached the path, Upton whispered, 'He's an odd cove. Don't take his abruptness amiss, that's just his way. And he's quite an artist. He'll sketch the maharajah in a most lifelike fashion, down to the curl of an eyelash.'

Something told me that Scotland Yard's techniques had not yet reached the North Riding.

I glanced at the constable, intent on his drawing. 'Mr Brocksup!' He raised his head.

'I shall inform the India Office of the maharajah's death.'

Whether he liked it or not, I also had a job to do.

Ten

At the road, I parted company with Upton. He walked towards the priory church. I urged the pony in the direction of the hotel.

Before we had gone many yards, the church bells began their ominous toll, announcing the death, calling off the search. The pony's hooves clip-clopped, giving me the eerie feeling that we were joining in the announcement to unseen multitudes: the prince is dead; the prince is dead.

How Lydia Metcalfe would take the death, I could not imagine. If she had gone on drinking gin at her earlier rate, she may well be comatose by now.

I trotted Betsy into the hotel stable yard. Joel was agitatedly grooming the horse that Isaac had ridden. The creature picked up on Joel's mental state. It stamped, whinnied and drew away from him.

When he heard Betsy trot into the yard Joel dropped the brush. Moving with a dreamlike sway, he clattered across the cobbles and took the pony's bridle while I dismounted, not looking at me.

I spoke gently, trying to bring him back from whatever

place his thoughts had taken him. 'Thank you for alerting Mr Upton to come to the wood, Joel. You did well.'

He stared blankly and then began to nod himself into speech as if moving his head turned a key. 'You said not to barge into the hotel. I didn't barge into the hotel. I made straight for Mr Upton's office.'

'Does Mr Sergeant know about the prince's death?'

He shook his head. 'I didn't barge into the hotel. You said not to barge into the hotel. I didn't barge into the hotel.'

'Where is your dad?'

'He didn't barge into the hotel.'

'Where is he?'

'In there.' Joel indicated the stable. 'All this has sent him right dizzy. He had to sit down. He's an old man and not up to this malarkey.'

I popped my head round the stable door. Isaac was seated on a bale of hay, trying to light his pipe. He dropped a match into the hay and made no attempt to stop it catching fire. I hurried up to him and killed the flame. 'Isaac, you don't look well.'

In a stall behind him, a black stallion pawed the ground. 'That Arab is useless. No one'll want to ride him no more. He'll be a horse of death now.'

'I'm sure he won't. It's not the horse's fault, any more than it is yours.'

'Nothing to say for hisself neither.'

'The horse?'

'Aye.'

'Where do you make tea here?'

'We don't.'

'Then come with me. You've had a bad shock.'

Without another word, I took the pair of them to the

kitchen door of the hotel, ushered them in and asked a surprised kitchen helper to provide strong sweet tea.

Moments later, I found Mr Sergeant in his office. As briefly as I could, I told him about finding the body. 'I did not mean Isaac and Joel to keep the news from you. It was to keep Miss Metcalfe and Ijahar from arriving and disturbing the scene before the police came.'

Sergeant gulped. 'I thought as much when I heard the church bells. There could be no mistake?'

'No. The constable is with him, waiting for his inspector to arrive. And I need to telephone the India Office.'

'This is terrible.'

'I know.'

'And in Westy Bank Wood, you say? The wood was searched yesterday evening.'

'Mr Sergeant, I saw the doctor's car outside. Has the constable sent for him?'

'I don't think so. The doctor was having a drink in the bar last time I saw him.'

'Then would you please tell him the news.' It did not surprise me that in his excitement at telephoning for his inspector, the constable had forgotten to call for the doctor.

'I'll tell him now. And will you come?'

'Not yet. I had better make that call. And I expect the India Office will want the valet to know, so that he can ensure that Hindu customs are observed. But let me see what they say.'

Sergeant sighed. 'This will devastate Ijahar. I've never seen a man so utterly devoted to his master. He will want to ensure the body is treated with respect.' He picked up his hat, and put it down again. 'I will leave you to your telephone call, Mrs Shackleton.'

The local operator answered quickly. I gave her the telephone number for James at the India Office, and then waited for her return call. After several moments, the telephone's loud ring startled me, and I realised how on edge I felt.

'Kate, you have news?' James spoke in a neutral voice, keeping hope, or dread, at bay.

'I'm sorry to tell you that Maharajah Narayan Halkwaer is dead.' I paused, to let him take in the information before adding, 'I found him in Westy Bank Wood. The local constable is with him, waiting for the inspector to arrive from Skipton. There is a doctor on hand.'

'How did he die?' James asked.

'A gunshot wound to the chest.'

'Gunshot?'

'What appears to be his own gun is beside the body, unbroken.'

James did not speak straight away. In my mind's eye, I saw him clutching his pen, writing down my words, his hand not entirely steady.

'When did you find him?'

'Almost an hour ago. It has taken this long for the constable to arrive and for me to get back here and be put through. And James, I don't believe that is where he died. The body was covered with branches, as if to disguise its presence. That area was searched yesterday.'

Silence.

I had the impression that he covered the mouthpiece with his hand and was speaking to someone else in the room. I waited.

'Where are you calling from?'

'The manager's office at the hotel.'

'Stay there. I will telephone back to you.'

'James, wait! You need to alert Scotland Yard. The area where he was found should be carefully searched. I don't believe the local police are up to that. He did not die there. This is not an accidental death.'

'Kate, everything will be taken care of from this end. You will hear from me shortly.'

He disconnected the line, without giving me any indication as to what 'shortly' might mean. It was frustrating to be confined to a room when there was so much more I might do. I wished I could be confident that the inspector from Skipton would properly examine the scene and establish what path had been taken by the person or persons who carried the prince's body to that spot and covered it with branches. And why that spot? It may be that the doe was shot there, as Isaac said. But it was just as likely Isaac would have said that of whatever place the body was found, because of his obsession with the creature.

There was something Isaac was not telling me, but what? That possibility of a link to Osbert's drowning still niggled. Had some irate father or sweetheart come close enough to take a shot at Osbert, missed and hit the prince? Villagers would close ranks in the face of an outsider, but Osbert would feel responsible, may have threatened to talk, and lost his life because of that.

For a good half hour I sat on the manager's chair, paced the room, sat down again, closed my eyes, tried to fathom how and why the prince had died. The means was clear enough – a gunshot wound. But who had pulled the trigger, when, where and why?

I answered the telephone the instant it rang, announcing

my name, disconcerting the operator who was clearly unused to such a speedy response.

A moment later, James came on the line.

'The Colonial Secretary is on his way to see Maharajah Shivram Halkwaer, to break the news of his son's death. He expects that the family will travel to Yorkshire tomorrow. I shall be making arrangements for a private train.' Perhaps it was my imagination, but I thought I detected a touch of reproach in his voice. I had done my job, but not well enough. My task had been to find the maharajah alive. James hesitated. 'Will you wait at Bolton Abbey until I arrive with the family tomorrow?'

'Of course.'

'His lordship will speak to the coroner and the chief constable.'

'Is there anything I can do, James?'

'Just one thing, regarding the Metcalfe woman; throw her off the pitch. I'm told her parents are tenant farmers somewhere nearby.'

'Consider it done.'

'Good. I don't want her in sight of the family when they arrive, or near the prince, nor any of his belongings. She is a menace.' He spoke with the kind of vitriol I would have reserved for the killer.

'All right, James. You make your point.'

'Does she know about the death?'

'No, or she would have had something to say by now.'

'Keep it from her for at least an hour. She mustn't be able to lord it over the family, saying she knew first.'

'What about the valet? I expect he should be told so that he can ensure the proprieties are observed.'

'You're right. Thanks, Kate. Oh and you are invited to stay at the Hall.'

The thought of staying at Bolton Hall gave me the shudders. 'It's all right. I have a room here at the hotel.'

I wondered what the Gattiawan royal family, used to the sumptuous life of a palace, would make of Bolton Hall. It might be good enough for the king but I doubted it would match Gattiawan standards.

'Very well. I shall see you tomorrow.'

'All right.'

'And Kate?'

'Yes?'

'Thank you.'

When I left the manager's office, I sought out Rachel, the chambermaid who had been the object of Lydia Metcalfe's ashtray-throwing wrath earlier. She looked drained, and should have been in bed with a hot-water bottle.

'Rachel, has Miss Metcalfe stirred from her room?'

'No. Mr Sergeant made me look in on her. She's in a dead stupor. I closed the curtains. Let sleeping dogs lie.'

'Thank you.' I would have liked to say more but feared too much sympathy might result in a fresh outburst of tears.

I walked up the stairs, to check that Lydia really was in a 'dead stupor', and not dead.

Close up, I watched the rise and fall of her ample chest. It would be time enough to tell her about Narayan's death when she woke. Give her a while longer of blissful ignorance. In the meanwhile, I would break the news to the valet, and hope that the poor man would not bring down the ceiling with his howls.

Eleven

Although it is only a short distance from the hotel to Bolton Hall, I decided to drive. Ijahar had been back and forth between Hall and hotel, silent as a ghost, carrying cloths and incense.

I had barely driven a few yards when Isaac emerged from the stable. He stepped in front of the motor as though desirous of dying under the wheels.

I braked.

He spoke rapidly, a little out of breath. 'I mun know. Does blame attach to me, or my lad, or to Osbert?'

'No. I'm sure not. Why should it?'

'Then let me come with you, tell the constable about the horse.'

He was not making sense, but I could hardly leave him in the middle of the road, and his son was nowhere to be seen.

I stepped out of the car to help him in. He moved slowly and clumsily. As I was about to set off, Mr Sergeant appeared from the direction of the Hall.

'I'm asked by the duke's housekeeper to spare her some

of my staff. She has every room in the place to be ready by tomorrow for the Indian party.'

I was not sure what to say to that. If he expected me to don a pinafore, he could think again. 'I don't suppose they'll set off at the crack of dawn. And perhaps they will travel with just a small entourage.'

He shook his head. 'You don't know Indian royals, Mrs Shackleton.'

Sergeant hurried on his way.

When I reached the Hall, there was just one motor parked at a careless angle – the Bugatti belonging to Dr Simonson.

Isaac made no move to leave the car.

'Do you want to stay here, or will you come inside?'

'Yes, I will stay here.' But he immediately climbed from the car. We walked to the entrance, then came to a halt.

'Sit on that bench, eh?'

He refused but then sat down, clutching his arms around himself as if to keep warm.

Perhaps he and Joel would be sent for to help at the Hall, and that would give him something else to think about.

'Did you hurt your arm?'

'No. It hurt me.'

'Just rest awhile.'

I entered the Hall without knocking as the door was slightly ajar. Dr Simonson was seated just where I expected – at the side of the great hearth, smoking a cigar.

On the balcony that surrounded this room, a maid hurried along, clutching a polishing mop.

Simonson stood as I approached and waited until I sat down beside him.

'Is the police inspector here, Dr Simonson?'

'He has left to consult with the chief constable. I said I would wait until the ambulance comes to take the prince's body to Skipton for a post mortem. It is to be done quickly, out of regard for the family.'

'Did you examine the body?'

'Yes. It is a long while since I examined two bodies in one day.'

'May I ask what was your conclusion?'

'It is too early for conclusions.'

'Were you able to establish the cause of death?'

'You have probably already done that for yourself, Mrs Shackleton.'

I had not put the question well. I wanted an interpretation, not facts. 'From what I saw when I looked at his body, he appeared to have been shot at close range. The entry wound was small.'

'Yes, a small round puncture hole, and the exit wound a slit.'

Before I had time to voice my suspicions that Narayan did not die where he was found, Dr Simonson said, 'Death would have been instantaneous. That may be a comfort to his relatives.'

'Could it have been an accident?'

He looked at me quizzically. 'That will be up to the coroner to decide.'

'How long has Prince Narayan been dead?'

'Difficult to say with certainty, rigor mortis has set in.'

'I don't believe he died in the spot where he was found. I think someone took his body there.'

The doctor threw the stub of his cigar into the empty

grate. 'You would have to voice that suspicion to the coroner, or his officer, Mr Brocksup.'

'Where is the prince?'

'He is in a room at the rear of the building.' Simonson snapped his fingers. 'How could I forget? That is the message I have for you. The valet asked to see you.'

'Really? Where is he?'

Simonson reached for his walking stick and stood up. 'He has been to the hotel and come back twice, bringing incense and I don't know what else. I told him that he must not touch the body. He simply wanted to sit, to keep watch. The housekeeper chose a room that is cold the whole year round.'

'Not difficult in a place this size.' I felt a chill as we walked through the hall. 'Is Osbert Hannon laid out here also?'

'No. His body has already been taken to the hospital.'

We entered a corridor, climbed a couple of steps, turned left, hit a blank wall, turned right, entered another corridor and walked into a room so dim that I just missed bumping into furniture that was covered with white sheets.

I sniffed the air. The scent of jasmine and roses mingled with mildew.

'We're coming closer,' Simonson said.

The door was open a fraction.

'Ijahar, you asked for Mrs Shackleton.' The doctor strode into the room. 'She is here.'

But I was looking beyond Ijahar to the face at the window. Isaac was outside, peering in. An oil lamp burned under the window. In its glow, Isaac's lumpy face turned into that of a devil. Isaac saw me. He moved away.

Ijahar hurried towards me, as if I were his long-lost friend.

On the floor behind him lay Prince Narayan, his body covered in a cloth of gold. A table should have been brought in.

The doctor read my thoughts. 'The valet insisted the stretcher be laid on the floor, their custom apparently.'

Ijahar bowed. 'I must have flowers for his body. They do not listen. I must have them now.'

'I see. Ijahar, what happened to your eye?' One eye was half-closed, and bruised.

He ignored my question. 'I cannot leave my master.'

'Look here, Ijahar.' Dr Simonson did not hide his irritation. 'If I'd known what you wanted I would have told you. It's not Mrs Shackleton's place to gather flowers. And you know that your master will be taken away shortly.'

'It's all right. I'll do it. What kind of flowers, Ijahar?'

'All flowers, roses, jasmine, the gold flowers, and the other, the one called . . . not a flower . . . '

'A herb?'

Under other circumstances, a walk in this garden on a sunny afternoon would have been sheer bliss. But here we were. The scent of wallflowers took me back to walks in the park. I picked some, along with marigolds. They grew in such profusion that they would not be missed. We had decided to keep to certain colours, so as not to make too gaudy a display. I concentrated on gold and yellows. Dr Simonson took out his penknife and cut white and yellow roses. He dropped them into the trug, sucking at his finger.

'Are you all right?'

'Just a thorn. I've got it now.'

'He wanted herbs, too. Better look in the kitchen garden and hope the cook doesn't wallop us.'

We walked round to the back of the house.

Simonson stopped by a pot of basil. 'What kind of herb do you think he wants?'

'I don't know. Mint? Lavender?'

I spotted the lavender. 'Let me have your penknife will you? The stalks on this lavender look quite tough.'

'I'll do it. Though given his royal blood, I should think laurel will be needed.'

When I heard the sound, I thought for a second that Dr Simonson had pricked his finger again, or his gammy leg had given way. But the groan, like that of a hurt animal, did not come from him. We both heard it at once and looked at each other.

'Over there!' Dr Simonson pointed to clumps of over-grown herbs close to the wall.

We hurried towards the sound.

I was closer, and saw him first. There, below a window, lay Isaac, half-hidden in the greenery, helpless, groaning, a vague expression on his face, his mouth drawn to one side, his lower lip on that side hanging down and dribbling spittle. The smell of mint grew stronger as I knelt beside him. Without looking through the window, I realised this was where Isaac had peered through at the prince's body. How long he had lain here, I did not know. 'It's all right, Isaac. The doctor is here.' I loosened the top buttons of his shirt.

Simonson had set down his walking stick. He limped towards me at a brisk pace. He crouched down beside Isaac. 'Now old chap, don't worry. We have you.' He rolled Isaac onto his side, at the same calling to me. 'My bag in the motor. Iodide potash.'

As I hurried away, he was saying, 'Can you speak to me? Tell me your name.'

I ran to the car and picked up the doctor's bag. Iodide potash. He would need to take it in water, or milk. One of the maids was spreading a wall hanging over a bush. I called to her to bring a glass of water to the kitchen garden, double quick, and to have someone bring a blanket.

By the time I got back, the maid was hurrying towards us, spilling water from the glass as she ran.

I took the container from the doctor's bag. 'How many grains?'

'A dozen.'

I dropped the grains into the water.

'Now hold steady.' He held Isaac by the shoulders. 'Try and sip what Mrs Shackleton is going to give you.'

I put the glass to Isaac's lips and tilted it. More went down the poor man's chin and jacket than into his mouth. His eyes stared into mine, as if his glance could tell me what his tongue could not.

'Isaac, don't try to speak. I'll tell Joel you are in good hands.'

But he did try to speak. It came out as gibberish.

'Stay with him, Mrs Shackleton. He knows who you are.'

Someone brought a blanket. I tucked it around Isaac as best I could, then sat beside him, keeping him steady, holding his hand as the two of us crushed mint.

After what seemed an age, Dr Simonson returned with two orderlies in navy blue ambulance uniforms. Slowly and carefully, they manoeuvred Isaac onto a stretcher.

'Where are you taking him?'

'These men came to take the prince to Skipton Hospital.

But they can come back for him. I'm sending the old chap to Beamsley Hospital, and hoping they'll take him in. They only have nine beds.'

We followed the men through the garden.

'What is the matter with Isaac?' I knew but wanted to hear him give me the proper words.

'He's had a stroke. That weakness you see is hemiplegia.'

'Paralysis of one side of the body.'

'Yes.'

'Will you be able to do anything for him?' I had seen the effect of trauma on the brain during my war service, and knew how difficult it could be to treat.

'It is possible there could be some improvement, over weeks and months. It depends on the amount of iodine that can be absorbed by the system.' He picked up the abandoned trug of flowers and handed it to me with a small smile. 'Look, I'm going to follow along behind and see him safely in.'

At the ambulance I tried to reassure Isaac. 'I'll tell Joel where you are. Try not to worry.'

I watched the ambulance set off. For a few yards, the doctor drove behind the slow-moving vehicle. I guessed that he would grow impatient, and overtake.

Ijahar, no doubt having grown tired of waiting for a floral delivery, was suddenly at my side, head bowed, thanking me, taking the basket of flowers from my hand, hurrying away. By the time I turned to look at him, he was disappearing back into the Hall. The poor fellow did not want me to take too good a look at his swollen eye. I might play the nurse and keep him from his master.

*

I found Joel swilling the stable yard, sweeping the wet cobbles with a stiff brush.

'Are you on your own, Joel?'

He leaned on the brush. 'Aye. Dad's at the Hall.'

'It's about your dad I've come. I'm sorry to say he was taken poorly in the grounds of the Hall.'

The blood drained from Joel's face.

'Dr Simonson is taking care of him.'

'Where is he?'

'He is on his way to Beamsley Hospital . . . '

Joel let go of the brush which fell to the ground. 'Hospital?'

'. . . to be kept an eye on for a day or two.'

'I mun go to him.'

'Not today. Let him settle. Perhaps tomorrow . . . '

In his haste to be off, he tripped over the brush as he ran, falling flat on the cobbles.'

'Joel, wait!'

He picked himself up and began to run, out of the yard, past the car, along the road.

Perhaps I should have run after him, called to him, or offered to take him to the hospital. But I could hear James's voice telling me to make sure Lydia Metcalfe was out of the way. Had she yet heard that her lover was dead?

Twelve

Mr Sergeant quick-marched across the hotel lobby.

'Seeing you enter those doors is like watching the cavalry ride over the hill. Come this way, Mrs Shackleton. I must speak with you privately.'

He drew me into a small office beyond the reception area and closed the door.

'Have you seen his highness's valet?'

'Yes. He is standing guard over the prince's body. He had me and the doctor picking flowers.'

'Yes, yes, he would. He will want to cover the body with blooms. The man is determined to do everything properly for his master. He has been back and forth running at the double.'

Sergeant showed every sign of continuing without taking a breath, so I squeezed in my words quickly. 'It is a good thing Dr Simonson and I were in the garden. We found Isaac there. He has suffered a stroke.'

'The poor man!'

'When I told Joel that his father has been taken to Beamsley Hospital, he just hared off. I hope he will be all right.'

'Oh he will. Joel will find his way to Beamsley. Poor Isaac. I am not surprised he has been taken ill, after everything that has happened.' Sergeant let out a sighing breath. 'I thought being a hotel manager would be a relief after all the battles and strife. I feel as if I'm back on the front line.'

'Has something else happened?'

'Did you notice Ijahar has a black eye?'

'Now that you mention it, I did notice his eye was blood-shot and half closed.'

'She smacked him in the eye.'

'Who?'

'Lydia Metcalfe.'

'So she has heard about Narayan's death? I told him to be quiet about it.'

'He came back from the Hall, looking for what he wanted in their trunks and in the prince's room. Miss Metcalfe heard the door banging. She came out just in time to hear Ijahar asking me if there were cedar trees on the estate for the cre-mation.'

'How awful. Is that how she found out?'

'Yes. She just slugged him.'

'But what a thing for him to ask. I can hardly believe he is talking about cremation. Does the man think he can light a fire and burn a body?'

'He wasn't thinking clearly. Next thing, Lydia Metcalfe is all over the hotel, telling anyone who will listen that the duke himself had her man done away with so that he could grab the Gattiawan treasure.'

'Where is she now?'

'In her room. She has quieted down but I can't have her staying here.'

'It is all right. I have already been asked to persuade her to go to her people.'

'Thank heaven for that.'

'I'm told they farm nearby.'

'Yes, near Halton East.'

'Then I'll see what I can do.'

'She was asking for you. And the Indian family will be distraught enough without having Lydia Metcalfe in the vicinity.' He shook his head sadly. 'The prince was such a vital and valiant man, Mrs Shackleton. Not many men who are ladies' men are also men's men, but he was.'

'Mr Sergeant, would you please have the Rolls brought to the front of the hotel?' A brilliant thought struck me. If Lydia could be driven to her relations in style, she may agree to go willingly.

'I will.' He grimaced. 'She is not an easy person to deal with. Do you want me to come up with you?'

'No. It will be better if I speak to her alone. Have a pot of tea and toasted teacakes sent up.'

I would like something, even if she did not.

'Huh! It will take more than currant teacakes to bring her to some semblance of civility.'

Lydia Metcalfe lay on the bed. One leg anchored her to the floor. I wondered whether the room might be spinning round her. The empty gin bottle lay on the bedside cabinet.

'Miss Metcalfe, are you awake?'

A groan.

'Lydia, it's Kate Shackleton. We spoke earlier.'

'Haven't lost my marbles since this morning. I know who you are.'

'And I know that you have heard the news about Narayan. I am so sorry that you heard in such an unfortunate way.'

She began to cry. 'That creeping miserable toad wants to burn him. He's already burned his clothes.'

'What do you mean?'

'I saw him through the landing window. He lit a fire and burned Narayan's clothes and his boots. Unclean, you see. Everything to do with a body is unclean in their eyes. I despise the toad, and I despise every pathetic person in this damned hotel.'

I hoped that she was wrong about the prince's clothes having been burned. But I had a horrible feeling she knew what she was talking about.

'How did he die? They didn't tell me how he died.' She sat up, swaying a little. 'Aren't you going to tell me either? Don't you know?'

'There has to be a post mortem, but I spoke to the doctor.'

'And?'

'The doctor says he would not have suffered.'

'How did he die?'

'From a single gunshot wound to his chest.'

'Who killed him?'

If she had not, earlier, been drunkenly announcing that her maharajah had been murdered, I would not have said what I did. 'It was an accident.'

She clenched her fists. 'What kind of accident?'

Sharing suspicions with a woman who had drunk far too much and already turned violent twice today – once throwing the ashtray at the chambermaid and the second time bashing the valet – it seemed a good idea to try and wind her down a little.

'A tragic accident. He was riding, holding his gun. That Arab had a bit of a reputation, but Narayan had wanted it, had chosen it specially.'

'He would.' Her voice was barely audible.

I was winning. 'Possibly the horse baulked, and the gun went off.'

'Oh my God, poor love.'

I hoped she would not ask me questions, such as where he was found, and why it had taken so long.

'Do you want to see him?'

If she did, I would try and have the valet whisked out of the way on some pretext. Because once the family arrived, her opportunity to say goodbye would be gone.

'No. I don't want to see him lying dead.'

She rubbed her hands over her face that was streaked with tears. Annoyingly, she still looked beautiful. She always would.

I went to the wash basin, wet a face cloth and handed it to her.

She took it. 'Do I look a sight?'

'You could look worse.'

'He chose me. Indira was foisted on him when he didn't know any better.'

She had told me that already.

'He must have thought a great deal of you.'

'He built me a palace. He filled it with the finest of everything. You should see my palace in Gattiawan. He would have married me. They can, you know. They can marry four times, but I would have been the last and the only one. And he would have married me soon. Someone has stopped him.'

I filled a glass with water and handed it to her.

She sniffed. 'It's water.'

'Tea is on its way.'

'Why have you come?'

This was a bit rich, given that Sergeant said she had been asking for me. 'I wanted to tell you myself, about the maharajah. I'm sorry I was too late.'

The arrival of tea saved my having to tell her I had come to escort her off the premises.

Rachel called out but would not step into the room.

I took the tray from her and carried it to the dressing table. Pushing aside a pile of jewellery, I set the tray down.

'Have something to steady you. This is best, believe me. I've lost someone, and I know. Don't let people you despise see you like this.'

Given that Lydia seemed to despise most people, and for the present had excluded me from the list, my words did the trick.

It surprises me that after a death, items so taken for granted, such as a fluted white china teapot and cups edged with gilt, turn into objects of delicate beauty, as if seen for the first time.

'There's another reason why I'm here.' I poured two cups of tea. 'Lydia, don't jump down my throat.'

'What reason?'

'Narayan's family are on their way from London. Once they arrive, they will sweep in and be the only ones who matter.' The jewellery caught my eye. 'Don't be here. Take what is yours in case there is any dispute. Go to your people. It's not so far is it?'

'So that's why you're here.' Her hand shook as she took the cup from me. 'That bloody wife of his, Indira, when I was in my palace, she sent servants to poison me. Is she coming?'

'Yes.' I assumed she would be, though I did not know. 'I have asked for the Rolls-Royce to be brought to the front of the hotel, in the hope that you'll agree to stay at your family's farm for now.'

She perked up at the mention of the Rolls. 'They're giving me my car back?'

'Yes.' We were not returning the car to her, but now was no time for details. 'I'll ride with you.'

'Why?'

Think quickly, Kate. 'Because I want to interview Thurston Presthope. He lives at Halton East, I believe. You can point me in the right direction.'

'That rat. I saw through him. Out for what he could get. He borrowed money from Narayan, didn't he?'

'Something like that. I want to make sure what has happened does not release him from his debt.'

'He should pay me. Narayan would want that.'

'I don't want to hurry you, Lydia, but it might be a good idea to pack your jewellery.'

'I will.' She came to life, revived by tea, or thoughts of saving her booty from the Halkwaer family. 'What about my clothes, my furs?'

'I will have them packed and sent on.' I took out my notebook. 'I'll list what you're taking, and what's to follow.'

The sooner she was gone, the better.

And now that I had decided to interview Thurston Presthope, I wanted to lose no more time.

Thirteen

There is a first time for everything. This was my day for driving a Rolls-Royce. I had to sit forward in the seat to reach the controls.

'It's my car,' Lydia said peevishly. 'Let me drive.'

'Get in. I'm driving.' My patience ebbed. 'It doesn't run on gin.'

'Oh yes it does.'

'Oh no it doesn't.'

She started to laugh, in a drunken slightly hysterical way, but climbed into the passenger seat.

We set off. I prefer drinkers who drop off to sleep. But I needed Lydia to stay awake, being unsure where along this twisting lane her parents' farm was. The consolation was that I could not go far wrong, following the winding road between Bolton Abbey and Halton East. I noticed farm buildings to our left. 'Is that it?'

'No. That's New Laithe. Stop the car. Let me drive.'

I guessed she wanted to turn up at her family's farm appearing to be in charge. 'You might not stop. I don't want to be taken to London.'

'Don't put ideas in my head.'

'It's better that I drive. Your family will think you have a chauffeuse.'

This remark seemed to please her. 'You're right. Stop the car. I need to sit in the back.'

I stopped the car. She climbed out, stepped in a puddle, cursed, opened the rear door and poured herself in.

I set off.

'There's a cattle grid. You'll see the turn after that.'

In under a mile, the motor grumbled across the cattle grid. Lydia waved in the direction of a muddy, cow-trampled lane. 'Up there.'

Being a farm, the entrance had a gate. We sat, seeing who would give in first and open it. Neither of us wanted muddy feet.

In the end, I capitulated, probably because I wanted to decant her more than she wanted to be decanted. Stepping gingerly, I lifted the rope from the gatepost and pushed the gate. When I turned, I saw that Lydia had changed her mind and clambered into the driving seat.

I gave in gracefully, stepping aside as she drove through the gate, but not far enough aside to avoid being splashed with mud.

'Hop in,' she smiled. 'My brother might drive you back on his motorbike.'

I climbed in beside her, ready to grab the wheel if we looked like hitting a barn.

Unfortunately for her, no one from the house was watching our grand arrival.

She pipped the horn. A woman's face appeared at the window.

Satisfied, she climbed out, clutching her valise of jewellery.

I passed Lydia her overnight bag before sliding across into the driving seat.

Now was not the moment to intrude on Mrs Metcalfe.

As Lydia was ushered into the house, I turned the motor around. She called after me, something about her car.

Beyond the gate, I had to pull in by the side of the road when a herd of cows meandered towards me. They were followed by a man of about fifty years old, corduroy trousers tucked into boots, an old army shirt and a tweed jacket that had seen better days. I took a chance.

'Mr Metcalfe?'

'Who's asking?' When he touched his cap, pushing it back slightly revealing a balding head, the gesture was one of country courtesy, not deference. Here was a man singularly unimpressed by a Rolls-Royce.

'Mrs Shackleton. I've just given your daughter, Lydia, a lift home.'

He gulped slightly at the mention of Lydia's name. His open face betrayed such mixed emotions that I half expected him to say I could take her back where she came from.

Family loyalty prevailed.

'Oh aye?'

'She had some bad news. Her companion was found dead a few hours ago.' I watched him carefully for any sign that he may have had something to do with the prince's death.

'I heard church bells.' He glanced at the herd of cows. They were smart enough to have given me a wide berth and were carrying on without him, udders swinging. 'Where did they find him?'

'In the woods.' That information would already be spreading so I was giving nothing away. 'Mr Metcalfe, I was brought in to investigate the prince's disappearance. This may seem like an impertinence, and irrelevant under the circumstances, but did he ask for Lydia's hand in marriage?'

He hesitated. 'How can he, when he's already wed?'

'Did he?'

'He left a letter for me with the wife.'

'When was that?'

'Tuesday.'

'Do you mind telling me what was in the letter? It could be important.'

'It was of no importance to me. I chucked it on fireback.'

A cow made a lowing sound. Mr Metcalfe adjusted his cap.

'Did he send anyone to intercede for him?'

'I reckon he knew better than that.' Mr Metcalfe nodded a goodbye.

As he moved away, I looked back and saw the cows waiting patiently by the gate.

If Mr Metcalfe were telling the truth, then the maharajah's old school chum, who was meant to 'disburse' money to Mr Metcalfe, was better off by ten thousand pounds. No mean sum.

Mr Sergeant had given me the address of Thurston Presthope's house at Halton East, but it was Lydia's description of its neglect that drew me to it. It was the type of house that might once have housed a local squire. Constructed of stone, it stood no-nonsense square, with more than its fair share of sash windows, although two of them had been bricked up, possibly to avoid a long-ago window tax. In the evening sunlight, the windows looked dirty, one with a drooping curtain.

A drainpipe had come away from the wall. There were slates missing from the roof.

I stepped out of the Rolls.

It was a long time since the gate or the house had enjoyed a lick of paint. The gate took a bit of pushing as it was missing a hinge. Weeds grew through cracks in the path that led through an overgrown front garden to the porch. I raised and dropped the brass knocker.

After a long wait, during which I considered knocking again, someone called through the letter box to me about mislaying the key and saying I would have to wait. Eventually, after much shuffling about, the door opened. An elderly housekeeper looked from mud-spattered me to the mud-spattered white Rolls-Royce.

'I don't know if the master's in.'

I produced my card.

She squinted at it. 'I'll ask.'

She left me waiting in the porch, with the door open, while she climbed the stairs slowly, leaning heavily on the banister.

The grandfather clock ticked fitfully and failed to chime on the hour of six. It was slow.

'Who the devil is she and what does she want?'

'She's one of them rich eccentrics,' I heard the house-keeper say, 'covered top to toe in mud but driving a big car.'

An interested sound issued from the man's throat.

A moment later, Presthope appeared on the staircase.

From the corner of his mouth, he hissed, 'Why didn't you show her into the parlour?'

He then composed himself for what I took to be his version of a grand entrance, pulling in his belly, throwing back his shoulders, and probably – although I could not see – tucking in his buttocks and spreading his toes. He wore a silk smoking jacket, shabby dark trousers, and – from the stench – last week's hair lotion. Cast in a melodrama as a younger man, he would have been the romantic lead. Now he was seedy and down at heel.

'Come in, dear lady. Excuse my housekeeper's rudeness.'

I smiled. 'She was not at all rude, Mr Presthope. I am the intruder. Mrs Shackleton.'

'I have heard all about you from Upton. You found my good friend's body.' His voice oozed charm, confidence and deep regret. No doubt the money the maharajah had entrusted to him would see him right in the spruce up and style department.

He hesitated in the hall before leading me into a dining room. 'I'm sorry we haven't lit fires. It's so warm.'

We stood by the dining room table. I noticed that a side table held a photograph of a school cricket team. A young Prince Narayan and Presthope stood side by side.

He pulled out a chair for me. 'I've asked for tea to be brought, unless you would like something stronger, after such a shock.'

'Tea will be grand.'

'I apologise for the scratchiness of my situation here, but my wife is in town, staying with her mother.'

From the look of the room, his wife had been staying with her mother for a very long time.

He sat in the carver at the head of the table. 'I can't believe that Narayan is dead. We were such good chums at school. Of course, as a sportsman, he excelled – cricket, polo, rugby. Such a loss, such a great loss. I am so glad to have seen him just once more.'

'That is what I want to ask you about, Mr Presthope. You see, the Indian royal family will be arriving shortly, along with the duke and duchess. I want to be able to give his lordship a clear account of events so that he will be able to answer Maharajah Shivram Halkwaer's questions.'

'Of course. And if Maharajah Shivram wishes to speak to me, I should be glad to attend his highness.'

I bet you would. Here was a man with an eye for any opportunity.

'When did you last see your friend?'

'He stayed here four days ago, for one night. We had arranged the visit by letter. He was motoring from Derbyshire and unsure of his precise day of arrival, but he wired me the day before.'

'You must have had a lot to talk about.'

'Oh we did. He was in excellent spirits. We reminisced about schooldays, horses, motor cars. My wife being away it was not so awkward with Miss Metcalfe. She has turned into a fine looking woman.'

I played the simpleton. 'I would have thought if your wife were here, it would be less not more awkward to entertain Miss Metcalfe.'

'You jest, Mrs Shackleton. If my wife were here there would have been an extreme difficulty in receiving Lydia Metcalfe. Her family farm nearby and she is . . . well, being a gentleman, I shall be kind. She never did fit in, from being small. Country life did not suit her. She was sent to live with an aunt in London.'

'Is that why your guests spent only one night here, because of the possible scandal?'

'No! I would have accepted her, for his sake. But she objected to the lack of comfort. We plan some changes here, you see. The bathroom was not to her liking. And I dare say his highness is used to a great deal better.'

That surely must qualify for the understatement of all time, yet he did not blink an eye. I waited.

'The Metcalfe farm was their first port of call, and then they came here. Respectable folk, the Metcalfes. It tells one something that Lydia did not get on with her own parents.'

'So you did not approve of their engagement?'

He hesitated just a little too long before shaking his head in what he must hope would appear a wise and telling manner. 'He would not have married her.'

'Oh? I thought perhaps a wedding was planned and you were to be best man.'

He gave me an oily smile. I could see a compliment forming as he looked at me.

'My dear lady, if you were to be maid of honour, I would be best man at any wedding. But I can assure you there was no such plan.'

I ignored his clumsy attempt to flirt. 'She wore an engagement ring.'

'A bull wears a ring through its nose but expects no nuptials, pardon my bluntness. He met her at the Folies Bergère. His other lady friends were immediately banished to the outer darkness, suitably recompensed, of course.'

If they had been suitably recompensed, I guessed that no

117

previous mistress of the prince would trouble herself to risk a noose by shooting him. But a liar and a rogue who stood to gain a great deal of hard cash, and probably thought it his due, would have no such scruples.

'Where were you on Friday afternoon and evening?'

He stared at me. 'What? You don't imagine . . . '

There was a kick at the door.

Presthope pushed back his chair. 'You can't get the staff these days.'

He walked to the door and flung it open. Keeping his voice low, he said, 'I've told you. Put the tray down, and then open the door. Don't just boot it.'

'What? Pardon?' The housekeeper did not lower her voice. 'You want me to bend down and spin meself dizzy? Well I can't do it, and I can't hold a tray and turn a knob, not with my rheumatics.'

So spoke a woman who had not been paid her wages, and remained loyal to her absent mistress.

The door closed.

Presthope came to the table with the tray that had been thrust at him.

'Excuse my housekeeper. I keep her on out of pity.' He pushed the tray in my direction. 'I was here on Friday afternoon, with my accountant.'

I hate those moments when it is left to me to pour tea, especially tea so weak it is not worth the trouble. But I did it, not wishing to interrupt my line of questioning by a debate about who should play mother.

'You say you saw the prince just that one night?'

'Yes. The constable asked me did Narayan ride across here to see me on Friday. Unfortunately he did not.'

'What about Thursday?' This was the date of the note when the prince had handed money to Presthope.

He shook his head as he took a careful sip of tea and only just refrained from pulling a face. It was stewed, and cold.

'You were at the hotel on Thursday I believe, connected with an exchange of money?'

'I did call at the hotel, but on another matter, to meet an associate in the bar, not to see Narayan. I did bump into him though. Has Miss Metcalfe been making accusations against me?'

'Why should she?'

'Because I know her. In Narayan's imagination she was some sort of goddess but I know her to be a jumped up money-grubbing farm girl. Her father and brothers cannot make light of her way of life as I do, being a man of the world. As long as she confined her activities to London and foreign parts, they were not compelled to reckon with her immorality. But for her to wave her doings under their noses must have been hard for them to stomach.'

'Are you suggesting they are capable of murder?'

'I am suggesting nothing, and casting no aspersions. It simply occurs to me that if you are making enquiries into Narayan's death – which I sincerely hope will turn out to be a tragic accident – then you should be apprised of the local situation.'

'Thank you.' The man was not above throwing mud in every direction to divert attention from himself. 'You say you bumped into the prince at the hotel.'

When he saw I would not let go, he relented. His eyes narrowed. 'I don't wish what I am going to say to be widely known, Mrs Shackleton.'

'I am sure if it has no bearing on the prince's death, then I would have no reason to divulge whatever you have to say to me. But I am trying to establish as full a picture as possible.'

He nodded. 'Very well. I shall be candid.'

That would be the day.

'I have had some financial difficulties lately, death duties and so on. Last Thursday, Narayan pressed two hundred pounds on me, and insisted I regard it as a gift.'

'I see.'

What a liar, and yet so persuasively spoken. If I had not seen the receipt for ten thousand pounds with my own eyes I may have believed him.

If he were right about the men of the Metcalfe family, hatred of Narayan would give them a motive for murder. But ten thousand pounds was no paltry sum. And an old school friend could come close enough to press a trigger.

How could he lie so confidently after having signed that he had taken possession of the money?

Fourteen

The hotel room that until yesterday had been occupied by Prince Narayan now looked very different. The silk throws and cushions had gone. Clothing that had been set out for him to change into after his ride no longer lay on the bed. Yet there remained a heady whiff of something like jasmine, and a sharp scent of sandalwood from the writing case on the Elizabethan table by the window.

The hotel manager, Mr Sergeant, came to join me. At my request, he opened the writing case. 'What am I looking for?'

'A receipt recording a monetary transaction between the prince and a third party.'

He picked up the stationery and the blue bond paper bearing the poem in a strange language, decorated with tiny flowers. I was glad we could not read the script. I guessed it to be from Narayan's wife.

'Nothing like that here.'

He closed the case and locked it.

I went to the fireplace. A small fire had been laid, but not lit. Scraps of charred paper lay between the logs.

Small wonder Presthope was so confident and had lied to me in such a bare-faced way, saying only that his friend had 'given' him two hundred pounds. Somehow, when Ijahar was in and out, back and forth from Bolton Hall, taking incense and cloths of gold, Presthope – or some emissary – had, they thought, destroyed the note. He was not to know that I had kept the original. My forgery had fooled him. I felt a frisson of pride at having copied his signature so well.

'Anything else?' Sergeant said.

'Was Mr Presthope in the hotel today?'

'If he was, I did not see him. I can ask the staff.'

'Has anyone been in this room apart from the valet and the chambermaid?'

'It is possible. Ijahar came back for the prince's laying out clothes, and then for every bit of silk, velvet, muslin that was on the chairs, the bed, and in the trunks, and for some ointment and incense. Given the state of the man, he may have failed to lock the door.'

'Yes, I suppose that is possible.'

'Shall I question the staff?'

'That would be a good idea. I know you'll be discreet.'

'Very well, and now my wife asks will you come to the dining room. She will cook you a chop.'

'Thank you but there is something else I need to do. Does anyone in the area have a dark room and photographic facilities that I can use? I have a film to be developed and printed.'

'Sorry, no one in the hotel. There is a photographer in Skipton but he does not live on the premises and his shop will be closed now.'

'That's a pity. But never mind, I'll drive home, and come back early tomorrow.'

'Wait a minute. We do have one keen photographer nearby. Dr Simonson at Embsay. Shall I telephone to him?'

'There's no one in the village? Nearer to hand?'

'Not that I know of.'

It would be a lot nearer to drive to Embsay than to Leeds and back. That decided me. 'Then yes please. It's a bit of an imposition on a Saturday evening.'

Not only did the doctor let me use his dark room, he shared the shepherds pie left for him by his housekeeper. We tucked in while my prints were drying.

'Do you take the *British Journal of Photography*, Mrs Shackleton?'

'Yes I do.'

'I have quite a collection, passed to me by my father. Did you know that Sir Arthur Conan Doyle, when he was a young medical student, wrote accounts of his photographic adventures, to supplement his income?'

'No. That's news to me.'

I do know Sir Arthur slightly. He is a friend of my aunt and uncle. But I decided against mentioning this to Dr Simonson.

When we had finished the shepherds pie, he pushed the plates to the edge of the table and crossed to a bookshelf in the corner of the room, returning with a pile of old, well-thumbed magazines. He opened one and turned the pages.

'Hark at this, eh? He writes of himself in the third person and never by name. He refers to himself as The Doctor, and he is travelling with The Commodore. So witty. Listen to this: "The Commodore is not a conversationalist. Though more lively than the proverbial tombstone, he is taciturn when compared to an eight day clock. Clearly, a third companion was necessary . . . The Genius." They sail the coast line from Eddystone.' He ran his finger down the page. '"None of our results did justice", he says. Don't you know the feeling?'

'I do indeed.'

He set the magazine down on the table. 'It was reading Arthur Conan Doyle that lured me into photography. I thought the adventure part sounded like a great lark, not that I travel far now.'

'Did you take your camera with you during the war?'

'Heavens no. I thought I'd have plenty of time for taking photographs when I got back, if I got back.'

I almost told him that my husband, Gerald, had carried a camera with him to the end, but I am trying to wean myself away from mentioning him in these sorts of situations. I busied myself looking at the illustrations in the journal.

He opened another copy and scanned it. 'Here, read this.'

'You read it to me.'

'Conan Doyle is talking about not being able to capture colour. He says, "Are we never to have the yellow of the sand and the green of the grass and the blue of the ocean transferred to our plates? It seems to me that a standing fund should be put by as a reward, to attract the researches of chemists and physicists in that direction." He had a point, eh?'

'Perhaps we would be even more disappointed in our efforts if we had colour.'

'Oh I don't think so. What brought you into photography?'

'My aunt and uncle bought me a Brownie for my twentieth birthday.' The old journals were dusty. I pulled a hanky from my pocket as a sneeze began. 'I enjoyed taking pictures but it was not until I visited Frank Meadow Sutcliffe's studio in Whitby that I began to take it seriously.'

'Oh? I've never visited Whitby, or Sutcliffe's studio.'

'You should.'

I turned the conversation quickly, before he took my comments as an invitation. I liked the man but after all, I had known him just a few hours. 'I think my prints will be dry. Would you like to see them?'

'Not before pudding, thank you.'

'Of course, tactless of me.'

He laughed. 'Not at all.' He rose from the table, gathering up the plates, turning his back to me. 'I had better not see them, Mrs Shackleton. I was drafted in to do the autopsy and prefer not to have the complication of having seen your photographs of the body in the wood, however professionally expert.'

It was a kind of rebuke and a closing down of the conversation.

On the way back to the hotel, I noticed a light still on in the police house. My knock was answered by Mrs Brocksup, a tall, angular woman with grey hair done up in a bun above her head. I introduced myself.

'Here are some photographs for Mr Brocksup to pass to the coroner.'

She took them from me. 'I'll hand them to him.'

I thanked her, and wished her goodnight, once again with the feeling that my photographs were not wanted. I would be glad to see the back of this day, and hoped that James's arrival tomorrow might mark a change of some kind.

It was eleven o'clock when, back at the hotel, I asked Mr Sergeant to lock my photographic negatives in the safe.

Like Dr Simonson, Sergeant showed no curiosity.

At the time, I had accepted Simonson's explanation of why he did not want to see the photographs. Now, I thought again. Neither man wanted to see because he did not need to know, and therefore did not want to know. There was something very military in that attitude.

Sergeant turned the key. 'All done.' He slipped the safe key into his waistcoat pocket.

It occurred to me that a retired army man, like Sergeant, falls into a position of trust, such as hotel manager, for services rendered, and because he is known to be reliable. Not exactly 'one of the chaps', the wrong social background, the wrong school for that, but utterly reliable all the same.

Fifteen

In Westy Bank Wood, a spindly-limbed young white doe paused by a felled tree. Head raised, it sniffed the air and looked about nervously from big round eyes. Suddenly confident of being unseen, it lowered its snout and nudged a branch aside, and another, until it revealed a man's face. The maharajah rose like a spirit. Wordlessly, he called for his horse. Betsy, the white pony, galloped towards him from one direction and the Arab stallion from the other. As the horses hurtled towards him, about to collide, about to trample the maharajah and the doe, a suffocating sense of panic flooded over me.

The doe fled.

A disembodied voice said, 'He is too young.'

I woke, unable to see or think because of the power of the dream. Outside, a dawn chorus chirped, mocking my fears. Slowly, I remembered it was Sunday morning. I took in the unfamiliar bed and the strange room.

What did the dream mean? It could be something or nothing. After the events of yesterday, it was hardly surprising that my mind struggled to take in everything that had happened.

Unwilling to return to haunting dreams, I swung out of bed, still feeling a little shaky. It was not yet 6 a.m. I would go for a walk before the world came to life.

At the small basin in my room, I brushed my teeth and washed.

Looking through the clothes that I had brought, I now saw everything was wrong. How dowdy that old tweed costume I had grabbed in such a hurry. It would have to be the walking boots; not exactly a good pairing with my summer coat.

As I dressed, the sentence from the dream rang in my ears. 'He is too young.' Who was too young?

The maharajah, I supposed. He was too young to die.

I drew back the curtains. Of course being the country it was not too early for people to be out and about. Beyond the hotel grounds, I saw a familiar figure walking along the path towards the hotel. It was Upton, the duke's agent. He walked like a man who had been hollowed out. Every step seemed an effort. I turned away, feeling like a spy.

My room was at the wrong side of the hotel for me to see the wood, but not seeing it made it that much more real, a dark and mysterious place that called out the word murder. I could not shake off the dream. Perhaps it was trying to tell me something. Are we cleverer than our dreams, or do they outsmart us?

The best way to dispel the dream would be to stroll to the wood. The hotel was eerily quiet as I walked from my room to the entrance. I wondered would the doors be locked from the night before. Fortunately, someone had been up and about. I closed the door quietly behind me and turned to walk through the village.

It was a relief to stroll along the road in such silence. Even the birds had disappeared into the woods or some other haunts. After the manic activity of the day before, the very air, with its slight breeze, urged me to slow down.

As soon as I noticed a path leading to the trees, I took it. Of course that was a mistake. The path meandered and led me higher than I intended. I somehow missed the way to the place where the prince had lain.

Trying to picture the map in the estate office, I realised from the slope of the hill and the farm not far off, that I was near Stanks's farm. If I went by it, I should be able to turn and find my way back to that fateful spot in the wood. Had it been cordoned off by the police, I wondered. James would want to look at it. So, too, may Narayan's father.

Smoke curled from Stanks's farm chimney.

I realised I was on their land and that the working day had already started. Hens pecked across the yard. I strolled towards the gate, intending to leave quickly. That was when I saw the barn. It must be the one where the doe had been taken. What if it was exactly like the doe in my dream?

Quietly, treading like a thief, I pushed open the barn door, just enough to allow me to squeeze in.

It was dim inside after the brightness of the morning. I blinked and glanced about. There hung the white doe. In my mind, it was a small, delicate creature, like the one in Inchbold's painting. In reality, it loomed much larger than I imagined, smooth and magnificent, in spite of being inelegantly trussed by its limbs to the rafters. There was something ancient, almost sacramental about viewing this upside-down creature. I suddenly understood how animals can be imbued with qualities and powers beyond knowledge.

I sat down on a bale of hay and contemplated the beast — so calm and regal, in spite of this undignified ending.

My semi-worshipful staring at the deer would bring me no nearer to finding who murdered the prince.

I averted my eyes from the doe and took out my notebook and pencil. Jot something down, I told myself. James will be here today and will want to know everything. But all that came to my mind were questions. If, as Lydia claimed, her maharajah was so keen to marry her, why had they not married in Paris? She must have told Narayan what her father's attitude would be and that his blessing was unlikely.

Why come to Yorkshire?

They were free agents. No reason why they should not come here. Perhaps the maharajah really did want to see Lydia's birthplace, if he were so besotted with her. He clearly thought he would be able to persuade Mr Metcalfe to give way.

Of course the prince was also here for the sport. Being here would give him the run of the Duke of Devonshire's estate before the hordes arrived for the glorious twelfth.

Since Lydia was unwelcome at Chatsworth, Narayan may have wanted to test how it would be here. He had never been on a shooting party at Bolton Abbey. Perhaps he thought being near her parents' farm would give her somewhere to visit and something to do. He would feel easy knowing she had family nearby.

He had another reason to come here, renewing the acquaintance of his old school friend, Thurston Presthope.

Perhaps there was some assignation that he had revealed to no one. If there had been an Indian in the area, was this someone the maharajah had arranged to meet?

What enemies did he have, and who would benefit by his death? Thurston Presthope had much to gain, if he believed he could pocket the ten thousand pounds that was to have persuaded Mr Metcalfe to give his blessing to his daughter's marriage.

There was still the question of whether the coal merchant did or did not see an Indian on Bark Lane. By the time James arrived, I would try and have an answer to that question at least.

Sometimes, when investigating, I feel that a small fact has escaped me, or there is some person I have overlooked. This time, there were just the tiniest facts and only two suspects in sight. There was the respectable stationmaster, suspected because of his anger at his daughter's love for the man who had jilted her, Osbert Hannon. I must meet the stationmaster, and soon. But my earlier theory that the stationmaster fired at Osbert and hit the maharajah now struck me as unlikely.

Both Presthope and the stationmaster knew the area well. I was convinced that the maharajah's body had been moved. Whoever moved the body must be familiar with the area, and confident enough to choose a time and place when he would be unobserved.

I put away my notebook without writing a single word.

A bluebottle appeared and buzzed about the unblinking eye of the dead doe. Hating to witness the creature so pestered, I stood to leave the barn.

As I stood, so did someone else.

The figure rising from a kind of trough at the far end of the barn almost made me jump out of my skin. Straw clung to his hair and to his striped shirt.

I froze; so did he.

'Joel?'

He climbed from the trough, picked up a cap and twisted it in his hands.

Act normally. Behave as if you see people climbing out of troughs every day.

'I've done nowt wrong!' He stayed glued to the spot.

'I'm sure you haven't. Did I disturb you?'

He shook his head.

'You probably have permission to be here. I don't.'

'Did you come to see her?' His voice sounded strange and unreal in the echoing barn.

It took me a few seconds to realise that he was asking me about the doe.

'Yes. She is a beautiful creature.'

He moved closer, staring lovingly at the doe, waving the flies away with the cap that I recognised as belonging to Isaac.

Joel glanced at the door, as though I might prevent his reaching it.

'I ought to be going. Will you walk out with me, Joel, or are you working here today?'

He shook his head. 'I don't want to go home.'

'It must be lonely there, without your dad.'

'Aye.'

'Did you see him yesterday?'

He nodded.

'How is he?'

He gazed at the doe, as though she was the one who had enquired after his father's health.

'Dad's right badly.' He looked towards the barn door.

I did not want him to bolt, as he had yesterday. He may have helpful information. Besides, I felt pity for him. He seemed so puzzled, and alone.

'I'm glad they let you see your dad.'

'He tries to speak but it comes out wrong. His feet are cold.'

'He will be taken good care of there.'

Joel moved closer to the doe.

'She is beautiful, Joel, a fine animal, she would not have suffered. The prince was a good shot.'

He stepped back quickly. 'I saw his ghost. I smelled his ghost. There's two ghosts now, him and Osbert.'

'Perhaps it was a dream.'

'I smelled him. I smelled the Indian.'

'What kind of smell?'

'Sweet, like flowers.'

'When was this?'

'In the night and just now.'

'There was no one here but me. There are no ghosts.' I must keep him talking, keep him by me. What was he afraid of, and what did he know? 'The dead won't hurt you.' He was unconvinced. 'Probably we should go. They are out and about at the farm. Do they know you are here?'

'No.'

'Then we are both trespassers. Shall we walk a little way together?'

He pulled on the cap.

'You haven't eaten. Let me see if I can get something for breakfast and I will walk back with you. It may not be so bad to go home if someone is with you.' The mention of food seemed to cheer him. 'You stay here. I'll see what I can get.'

'I'll stop by the gate.'

'All right. Be sure you wait for me.'

Knocking on the farmhouse door would be good cover for my trespassing. And perhaps I might speak to someone who would have helpful information – though I hardly knew what questions to ask.

I walked to the farmhouse. The girl who answered the door was about twelve years old. She looked surprised to be asked for milk, bread and eggs, but left me waiting and came back moments later with half a loaf, eggs, not very well wrapped in a bit of old sacking, and a jug of milk. 'Have you fetched a jug, missis?'

'No.'

'Then you mun fetch this one back soon as you've done.'

'Right. I will.'

I paid her, though neither of us was sure what the amount should be. She asked too little, I probably gave too much.

I pictured walking back to Joel's cottage, making tea and frying eggs.

Joel put paid to my thoughts of a rustic breakfast. He cracked two eggs into the jug and offered it to me. When I refused, he drank it down in three or four gulps.

He put the rest of the eggs, and the bread, in his pockets.

'Wait here, Joel. I'll still walk you back to your cottage.'

I returned the jug.

It was gratifying that he had waited. As we walked down the incline towards the road, I put my question to him; or one of my questions.

'I heard that there was an Indian on Bark Lane on Friday. Did you happen to see him, or did you hear that story?'

'No.'

That was simple enough.

'Have you seen any Indian, apart from the prince?'

'Yes.'

Hope leapt.

'When, and where?'

'On Friday. The one who wears white. He carried the prince's gun from the hotel. He is a small man with a scar on his eyebrow.'

'I see.'

'I told the constable. He asked me all about it and about shooting crows. He said I mun tell, because I saw prince dead. But I am mixed up. They will blame me.'

'No one will blame you for what happened to the prince.'

'My brain is not good. Everyone knows it.'

'No one will ask you a hard question. Let me ask you another question, Joel. Is that all right?'

'My brain is not strong because my head is big and a breeze cools my brain.'

'A cool breeze can be good.'

'Not for the brain.'

'This is my question. Do you have any idea how, when everyone searched the wood for the Indian prince's body on Friday, it was not there?'

'I have to go now.'

I caught his sleeve as he set off to run. 'Wait! It's all right. I won't ask any more questions.'

'No one mun seek me. Tell them not to seek me.'

I had handled our encounter badly. I wondered who or what he was afraid of.

The day looked set fair. Having upset him, it seemed only

135

kind to walk him home. He said the road would be a better way, but I wanted to look again at the Strid.

He hesitated. 'Do you want your eggs back?'

'No. You keep them. But I want to walk through the wood.'

He recognised a bargaining position, and gave way.

I asked no more questions. He volunteered no information. We kept pace, in what I hoped was companionable silence. A squirrel dashed across the path a little way ahead and scaled an elm. We walked into a patch of sunlight. The river murmured gently. The peace of the wood might drive away his bad dreams, though the poor lad might have nightmares for the rest of his life after what he had seen. My own early morning dream came back to me. The image of the dead man rising was vivid enough, but more dramatic still were the words spoken aloud by an unseen presence: 'He is too young.'

Who was too young? My first thought had been of Prince Narayan, a still young and handsome man. Osbert Hannon was too young to drown in the Wharfe at age twenty-one. My husband, Gerald, missing in action in the last year of the Great War, was too young to leave this world. Was it one of them, all of them, or someone else? Isaac Withers was not too young to have suffered a stroke, but here was his son Joel, forever a child in his muddled mind.

The Wharfe grew noisier as we neared the Strid. Joel became agitated. 'It's laughing. The river is laughing.'

The roar of rushing water filled my ears. I turned to look and moved a little closer, mesmerised by its power. Huge perpendicular masses of grey rock hemmed in the torrent that then forced itself through a gap with a great whooshing force. At the point where a young man might leap, the ledges of rock reached out, as if wanting to be joined once again after their ice-age sundering.

He hung back.

My eyes were drawn to a small, plodding figure on the other side of the river. A young woman eased herself onto a rock, holding tightly to her apron. When seated, she stared into the water. If she noticed me, she did not acknowledge.

Joel called to me again.

I walked back to him. 'Who is that?'

He would not look.

After several minutes, the young woman slid from the rock and took a few unsteady steps towards to the fast-flowing water, still holding her apron. I recognised her. It was young Mrs Hannon, Osbert's widow. My God, was she about to throw herself into the river? I opened my mouth, ready to call to her, but my voice came out too softly and was drowned by the rushing current.

Joel came nearer. 'It's Jenny. Osbert's Jenny.'

As she drew closer to the edge, she put her hand in the bunched up apron and drew out flowers, throwing them into the water, repeating the action until the river was strewn with buttercups, daisies, rosemary and meadowsweet. She stood and stared into the water. Finally, she turned and stepped away. With the burden of her apron of flowers gone, she walked steadily back up from the rocks to the path. Slowly, she disappeared from view.

After that, we walked on in silence, under a sky now filled with clouds.

Eventually, Joel turned as one path led from another. 'It's round here.'

Moments later we arrived at a stone cottage with a lop-sided door and neglected thatched roof.

He hesitated. 'I'll be all on my own.'

'Be brave.'

Sixteen

Having changed from my boots, I drove to the railway station. What would the stationmaster be like, I wondered. He was a man with a respected position. Osbert had promised to marry his daughter, had married another, and yet still dallied with Rachel. Protection of a daughter's honour was a powerful motive for murder.

More mundanely, I would learn the arrival time of the London train. I could also enquire about any strangers who may have been seen in the area during the week, or whether there had been any unusual activity.

A curious dog barked as I passed a neat cottage garden. A curtain twitched. This was not a place where a stranger would go unnoticed. I rounded the bend and there was the station. As I climbed from the car, the powerful stench of paint hit my nostrils. Obviously the station had to look its best for important visitors. A porter, brush in hand, called out to me to be careful of wet paint. I walked through the gate sideways, not having brought sufficient changes of clothing to risk paint smudges.

The railway lines gleamed in the sunshine, as if they knew

an important train was expected. Planters filled with begonias, geraniums and lobelias were arranged with military precision along the wall. Stillness reigned, the silence broken only by distant birdsong.

Through the clear circle in the opaque glass of the stationmaster's office door, I watched as a rotund, florid-faced man stared into a small looking glass as he clipped his short grey moustache with nail scissors.

I stepped to one side, to be out of his view, and waited several moments, long enough for him to finish attending to his facial hair.

When I looked again, he was examining a roll of red carpet that stood in the corner of the room. I knocked.

He put on his cap and opened the door.

I introduced myself.

'I heard you were here, madam, looking into things. And you're the lady got poor old Isaac into the hospital.'

'I would like to take credit, but that was the doctor's doing.'

'You were there, madam. A gentleman always does the right thing in the presence of a lady.'

I felt sure he was wrong about that, but now was not the time to argue about the doctor's integrity.

'Mr Simpson, would you be so good as to tell me the timetable for today.'

He puffed up a little at my use of his name. If he asked me how I knew it that would give me an opportunity to mention his daughter. He did not. I would have to find some other way of introducing that topic and testing out his feelings about Osbert Hannon.

'A special train is on its way from Kings Cross, to Leeds,

to Skipton scheduled to arrive here at 7 p.m.' He consulted a sheet of paper. 'There will be three first-class carriages and five third-class carriages for staff. The duchess will travel in the first compartment with the two maharanis, wife of Maharajah Shivram Halkwaer, and Maharani Indira, who is the unfortunate widow. Her young son, Prince Rajendra is with them. They will be accompanied by a maid or maids. Prince Jaya will join the royal train at Leeds. In the next carriage will be the Right Honourable James Rodpen and aides-de-camp. A fleet of Bentleys will be here to meet the train and take the party to Bolton Hall.'

'What about the Duke of Devonshire and the senior maharajah?'

'They will be arriving by aeroplane.'

'Goodness, I would never have expected that.'

'Nor me neither, madam. But that looks like the future. God help the birds is what I say.'

'Are you expecting many other visitors today?'

'Oh no. Today's sightseers are being turned back at Skipton. They're being told that Bolton Abbey is closed to visitors today.'

'Tell me, have there been any other Indians arriving by train this week?'

'Only the servant. He came with a little placard, giving details of his destination, and in charge of a tremendous amount of luggage.'

It would have been too good to be true that another Indian had arrived. But there were other stations. 'Mr Simpson, has there been very much activity at the stations along your line this week?'

He shook his head. 'No more than usual. The mail arrives,

141

the mail is despatched. People take their goods to Skipton market to sell and others go to Skipton market to buy.'

'Have any strangers arrived here, or at your neighbouring station?'

'No. Not here, and not at Holywell.'

His curiosity was aroused. 'You're thinking of that story madam, started by Deakin.'

Was there no news that did not travel faster than I? 'It was just a general enquiry, Mr Simpson. I am trying to establish a pattern for what life is normally like in this very peaceful spot, so that we may reassure the Indian family.'

It was as if I had not spoken. He saw straight through my words.

'I understand, madam. That Deakin, he sees all sorts when he's in his cups, which is most of the time, and he'll tell any tale to ease a pint out of a body. Mind, I'm not criticising him, due to the war he had. It takes some people down a certain path if you follow my meaning. My wife counts every bag of cobs and nutty slack that man delivers.'

So Deakin was regarded as a drunkard, and a cheat who gave short measure in his coal deliveries, and was generally disliked. But was he lying when he said he saw an Indian, or when he said he did not?

Mr Simpson stroked his moustache thoughtfully. 'I wonder if I might ask you a question, madam?'

'Of course.' Was this the moment when we could discuss Rachel and her love for Osbert?

He pointed to a couple of trunks labelled Miss Lydia Metcalfe, Dorchester Hotel, London.

'The trunks?'

'No. The red carpet next to them. I am debating with myself whether it is appropriate, under the circumstances, to roll out the red carpet. We don't run to black you see, and given the tragic accident, red may seem a little tasteless.'

'It's a dark red, and it will be most suitable I'm sure. I notice that the maharajah's valet has laid out his master's body without regard to our usual mourning rules. They do things differently I believe.'

'That is a relief. Then we shall lay the red carpet. The senior maharajah and his lady have been here with Prince Jaya, for the grouse-shooting, and so it will be just the same as always, in spite of the tragic accident to the maharajah.'

Tragic accident. I wondered whether those were his own words, or what he had been told by someone.

'Mr Simpson, about the other death, the one that is closer to home.'

He grimaced. 'Has my Rachel been blubbing at her work?'

'She has been very brave.' I sighed, hoping to convey a great deal of sympathy rather than nosiness. 'I have the impression that Osbert broke more than one girl's heart.'

He saw through me. 'I've heard that you are a detective.'

'Yes.'

'Well, madam, there is nothing to detect in relation to Osbert's death. A good hiding was on the cards for him, but not a murder. He was the only support for his mam, and for the foolish lass who wed him. I would have sooner sent my Jenny out of harm's way to live with her gran than have her take up with a young philanderer so light in his ways. But we should not speak ill of the dead. Perhaps he would have made a good father and husband had the lord spared him.'

He stopped, and gulped. 'I hope nobody says I've done away with him?'

'Is anyone likely to think that?'

'Nobody would be so foolish. But there's a lot of loose talk in a village. If they're slandering me, they're leaving Metcalfe alone.'

'The farmer?'

'Aye, and I can vouch for both of us, myself and Tobias Metcalfe, there's no truth in it.'

'What are they saying?'

He bit his lip. 'You hadn't heard. I should've kept my gob shut.'

'Tell me.'

'No father would want his lass to take up with a foreigner, but he wouldn't have shot the man for it.'

'Then who is saying he did, and where are they saying it?'

'Oh you know what men are like when they've had a drink. The Indian hadn't been missing five minutes. It was in the Elm Tree. But I know Tobias Metcalfe and he's no such fool. Folk don't want to believe there could be two tragic accidents falling out of a clear blue sky. But it has to be that, because otherwise the finger points at one of us.'

Those words again; tragic accident.

Back at the hotel, I availed myself of the telephone in Mr Sergeant's office and put in a call to my housekeeper. It was clear from my conversation with the stationmaster that what little gossip swam to the surface here came from men in public houses. If anyone was likely to catch a good bite, it would be my able former policeman assistant, Jim Sykes.

As I waited for the connection, I glanced at this week's *Craven Herald*, open at a page giving an account of the maharajah's visit to Yorkshire.

Moments later, Mrs Sugden's familiar voice assailed my ears. 'You didn't pack enough clothes and you're regretting that shabby costume.'

'Well all right, yes I am, but that is not why I am telephoning.'

'What's up then?'

'Please take a message to Mr Sykes. Tell him he would very much enjoy a fishing break at the Devonshire Arms, Bolton Abbey, and today would be an excellent time to begin.'

'I'll go round there now. And I'll ask him to fetch another suitcase for you.'

'Thank you, Mrs Sugden.'

'Oh and your mother telephoned yesterday. She has heard that your cousin is coming to Yorkshire.'

Panic rose. Whenever my mother hears I am investigating in a picturesque place, she feels the urgent need to make an immediate excursion to that particular spot.

'If she calls again, tell her I know all about James's visit and it is to do with work. I have to go now.'

I straightened the *Craven Herald*. There on the front page was an advertisement, announcing that Mr Deakin, Coal Merchant of Embsay, would supply cobs and nutty slack by the hundredweight.

It was high time for me to discover whether Mr Deakin really had seen an Indian on Bark Lane last week.

As I drove away from the hotel, Cummings appeared in the doorway, his jacket undone. That man must spend an inordinate amount of time undoing and doing up his buttons. He waved to me. Perhaps he was hoping for another half a crown, even though he had not earned the first one.

Seventeen

Reaching Embsay, I parked the motor by the church and walked in what I hoped was an inconspicuous fashion along the main street, looking about until I spotted the coal merchant's house.

A small plump woman in patterned pinafore, her hair almost covered by a turban, answered the door on my first knock.

'Mrs Deakin?'

'Yes.'

'I'm Mrs Shackleton. I'm sorry to disturb you on a Sunday morning but I wonder if I might speak with your husband.'

She hesitated, before answering me in hushed tones. 'Well, you know, he's still sleeping.'

'I could walk about and come back in half an hour or so.'

'If it's coal, I can take your details.'

'No. I do need to speak to him. It won't take long.'

'He's not in any trouble is he? If it's about that delivery to the farrier's house, he's adamant he left the eight bags.'

'It's just a question I have, concerning the Indian prince, and a sighting Mr Deakin made on the road.'

'He was mistaken. He's said he was mistaken. It was just something that came up over a pint in the Elm Tree.'

'All the same, I do need to speak to him.'

'You better come inside.'

The door opened straight onto a tidy room, cheerfully furnished with, as might be expected in a coal merchant's house, a goodly fire burning. The room felt almost unbearably warm.

'Sit yourself down. I'll see if he's stirring.'

Mrs Deakin climbed the stairs to the room above. Sound travelled well in the small cottage, but she spoke so softly I could not make out her words.

Mr Deakin's answer came clearly enough. 'Can't a man have his bit of peace and quiet, woman? Who is she?'

More murmuring.

'What does a posh woman want with me?'

Murmur, murmur.

'Tell her she can wait.'

Mrs Deakin reappeared. 'He says he won't be long. Will you have a cup of tea? I'm just about to make a pot.'

'Thank you.'

From upstairs came a cacophony of coughing, wheezing and spitting, followed by loud pissing in a pot.

Shortly after that, Mr Deakin appeared, dressed in trousers as black as his coal and a worn khaki shirt, braces dangling. He was a stout man, bearing a belly designed to hold a great deal of beer. 'How do.'

'How do you do, Mr Deakin. I'm Mrs Shackleton,

looking into the recent events at Bolton Abbey, on behalf of his lordship.'

'What's to look into?'

'I want to try and account for the hours when the prince went missing, so that the coroner will have a full picture.'

Mrs Deakin poured tea into two dainty china cups and a cream pint pot decorated with a cottage scene. She pushed a teacup and saucer towards me with a small smile. 'There you are, madam.'

'Thank you.'

Deakin clutched his pint pot with both hands.

'It was something you said, Mr Deakin, regarding seeing an Indian on the road on Friday.'

He took a mouthful of tea, pulled a face, turned and spat it into the fire. 'No sugar in this, woman.'

She took the mug back from him, and began to spoon in sugar.

'That were summat and nowt. It turns out gipsies had come to camp, somewhere over by Skipton Moor. Well some of 'em are brown as nuts, and that's who it was. A gipsy.'

'What time was that?'

'Don't ask me. I've that much on I couldn't say.'

'But it was Friday afternoon.'

'Or Thursday. It could've been Thursday. He were on a bike.'

Mrs Deakin stirred several grains of sugar into her own tea. She looked surprised. I wondered if the bike was a recent addition to the story.

'It were Friday, love. I know because you came in and told me, and I'd been baking for the church fair.'

He took a big sup of tea. 'Well then Thursday, Friday, I don't know.'

'I've never seen a gipsy ride a bike.'

'Are you calling me a liar, missis?'

'Of course not. So this gipsy, he had cycled across from Skipton Moor. Is that a way off from here, Mr Deakin?'

'They get about don't they?'

'What did he look like?'

'Dark-skinned.'

'Tall, short, well-built, slim?'

'It's hard to tell when a person's on a bike. On the slight side.'

'Old, young?'

'You can't tell can you? Gipsies don't age like we do. I only caught a glimpse of him.'

'What was he wearing?'

'Nothing out of the ordinary, I don't remember.'

'Which way was he going?'

'Why, towards Halton East.'

Flames shot up the fireback as coal crackled and split. I had kept my coat on and began to feel a little faint.

'They come round, you know,' Mrs Deakin chipped in. 'Do you want any odd jobs? Will you buy a piece of lucky heather? That kind of thing.'

Deakin snorted. 'Aye, and you're soft enough to say yes.'

The conversation was going nowhere. I could sit here until the middle of next week and be no wiser.

'Well thank you, Mr Deakin. Sorry to have disturbed you so early. If you think of anything else, you can contact me at the hotel.'

I handed him my card. How much longer I would be at

the hotel, I did not know. Once James arrived, I guessed my usefulness, such as it was, would be at an end.

Mrs Deakin walked me to the door.

I thanked her for the tea and took a few steps, waiting for her to close the door.

When she had done so, I walked back, and listened to hear any aftermath.

Sure enough, Mr Deakin berated her for waking him, and for not sending the busy-body packing. He reminded her that if they wanted a quiet life, the less said, the better.

As I returned to my motor, church bells began to chime.

A coal merchant might sleep late on a Sunday. A farmer would not. It was time to pay a visit to the Metcalfes' farm. How much resentment did Lydia's father and brothers harbour towards the maharajah for making Lydia his mistress? Enough to kill him?

Eighteen

Once more I drove to the farm gate and stopped the car. Climbing out without stepping into a deep puddle and a muddy track proved impossible. Squelching back into the driving seat, I headed for the farmhouse.

The woman who answered the door had the same high cheekbones as Lydia, the same summer-blue eyes, only her eyes lacked Lydia's youthful sparkle.

I introduced myself. 'I'm Kate Shackleton, the person who drove Lydia over here yesterday.'

'Oh, it was you. She's asking for her car.' Mrs Metcalfe looked beyond me to the Jowett. 'That's not it.'

'No. That's my motor. The Rolls is back at the hotel.'

'Come in if you like.' Mrs Metcalfe held the door open. 'She's still in bed.'

I wiped my feet on the mat and offered to remove my shoes.

'Don't bother. Step on the matting, and sit yourself down.' I stepped into a large square kitchen, filled with the aroma of slow-roasting lamb. 'She'll have heard you drive up, and she'll hear us talking. I'm not calling her again.' Mrs

Metcalfe pulled out a chair for me at the kitchen table. 'Are you a friend of hers?'

'No. We only met yesterday. I was asked by the India Office to investigate the disappearance of Maharajah Narayan Halkwaer.'

She sat down opposite me, reaching for a large cabbage. 'I'll have to get on with this. I've men to feed. Sunday or no Sunday, they've work to do.' She tore at the cabbage. 'So that was his full moniker, Maharajah Narayan Halkwaer? It suited the poor man.' Mrs Metcalfe tore a leaf from the cabbage, shredding it, dropping the strips into a basin of salted water.

'What did you think of him, Mrs Metcalfe?'

'I could see the attraction right enough. He was good-looking and a real gentleman. And he was that interested in our family. He even wanted to know the hour of Lydia's birth.'

'And were you able to tell him?'

'I was indeed. It was twenty to ten in the evening – October twentieth.'

'Why did he want to know?'

'To have her horoscope cast.' She paused in her cabbage shredding. 'I had all on keeping a straight face.'

'He must have cared for Lydia very much.'

'He wanted her father's permission to marry her. Well what was I supposed to say to that? It's not our way is it, for a man to have two wives. He wanted to be sure of her you see. He struck me as the jealous type. Good thing his wife didn't feel as jealous.'

Perhaps she did. Lydia had said that the maharani tried to have her poisoned. Of course, that could be Lydia's sense of the dramatic coming into play.

153

'Lydia's dad didn't put in an appearance, so the maharajah left a letter with me.'

This fitted with what Mr Metcalfe had told me when I saw him bringing in the cows.

I wanted to ask where Mr Metcalfe and his sons were on Friday, when Narayan was shot. One way would be to sit here chatting, pretending that I was waiting for Lydia to grace the room with her presence, or I could jump straight in. I chose to jump. 'Mrs Metcalfe, there'll be an inquest into the prince's death. Because I was charged with finding him, I have decided to gather as much information as I can, to be passed to the coroner. You'll know that he died of a gunshot wound?'

She stopped shredding cabbage. 'Lydia told me. She says you reckon it was an accident.'

'I said that, yes.'

'But you don't believe it?'

'That will be up to the coroner to decide.'

'Do you think Lydia killed him?'

'No. Do you?'

'She has a temper on her.' She ripped off more cabbage leaves, shredding rapidly, her long fingers tearing at the leaves. Dead insects floated to the top of the water, above the cabbage. She fished them out and put them on a newspaper where a caterpillar wriggled. 'Lydia wouldn't kill the goose that lays the golden eggs. And she is cut up. It's real enough.'

'It never occurred to me for a moment that Lydia killed Narayan, Mrs Metcalfe. Shooting would not be her style.'

'Whose style then?'

154

This woman did not believing in circling round a topic, so I met her on her own ground. 'I believe your husband was upset that Lydia took up with an Indian.'

She crossed to the big stone sink, tipped the cabbage into a colander, and turned on the tap.

'We're past being upset at what Lydia does. But when she brought the man here, announcing to everyone for miles around that she's no better than she ought to be, her father was none too pleased.'

For a Yorkshire woman to own up that her man was none too pleased was the equivalent of any other person admitting rage verging on insanity.

'Was he displeased enough to go after him with a gun, Mrs Metcalfe?'

'Oh and I'd tell you if he was?'

'You'd tell me if he wasn't.'

'Then I'll tell you.' She chopped the hard stalks of the cabbage and dropped them in the colander with the leaves. 'My man was here all day Friday, all day Saturday, and so were my sons. I'll vouch for them, though that'd count for nowt, but so would Tom, our labourer, and so would the feed man who called, and so would the coal merchant, and a flock of lambs if they could speak.'

'Someone who is out and about as much the feed man and the coal merchant must see what's going on, and whether there are any strangers in the area. Did either of them mention anything to you?'

'I've nothing to do with Deakin, except watching him tip the bags, and letting him know I count them. My husband deals with the feed man. You'd have to ask him.'

She went to the range and opened an oven door. I

watched as she basted the meat. 'Are you after stopping for your dinner? I can set another place.'

'Why would you have me for dinner when I've all but accused your husband of murdering the Indian?'

She set the tray of meat on the hearth and spooned potatoes around it, basting them, too. 'Because you'd be a fool if you didn't think of that, and Lydia told me you are on the clever side. What do you think crossed my mind soon as I heard the man was dead? But my man and my lads didn't do it. I can promise you that. I made my own enquiries.' She put the meat and potatoes in the oven.

When she came back to the table, her face was pink from the heat of the fire.

I smiled. 'I can see where Lydia's independent streak comes from.'

'Well if that's so, it's all she did take from me.' She came back to the table, lifted a cover from a bowl of Yorkshire pudding mix and began to whisk it. 'I've six kids and Lydia is the one that was born different, like some fairy child. She couldn't be doing with this place. Hated it here. Would she help in't house? No. Would she help on't farm? No. And she hated school. Beat her, bribe her, nothing worked. In the end I sent her for one summer holiday to my sister Emily. Emily married one of the fellers from the circus that came to Skipton. He'd been a tightrope walker and lodged with our family. When they married, they settled down to keeping a public house in London, the Earl of Ellesmere in Bethnal Green. Lydia got it into her head when she was seven years old that she must go to London and visit her aunt. We packed her off with a label on her coat, for the summer, for peace and quiet. Our Emily only had lads. She wrote to me could she keep Lydia till Christmas. Come Christmas, Lydia had a part in a pantomime, so could she stay till Easter. Emily sung Lydia's praises to high heaven. How good she was in her lessons, and singing and dancing, and French. They'd a concert room in the pub and she was on that stage from the minute she got there.'

'And she never came back?'

'No. That was it.' She placed a teacloth over the bowl of Yorkshire pudding mix.

'You must have missed her.'

'I've three good sons, and two daughters who do fit in to the life here. Lydia never belonged to me. It's a funny thing for a mother to say, but it's true. I only had her for that short time, till she could walk and talk, and make her wishes known.'

'Have you ever seen her perform?'

'No, and not likely to. She was in a chorus at one of them London theatres. Next thing Emily knew, the whole lot of them tripped off to Paris. Well, Lydia wasn't old enough. Our Emily went after her but she wouldn't come back. There's no stopping Lydia once she sets her mind to summat.'

'I believe Paris is where she met the maharajah.'

She crossed to the sink to fetch the cabbage. 'Well you know more than me then. Emily wrote to tell me Lydia had taken up with an Indian prince. You could have knocked me down with a lamb's tail when the two of 'em turned up here last Tuesday, Lydia shaking her jewels at me.' She tipped the cabbage into a pan.

'And have you or your husband seen the prince's friend recently, Mr Presthope who put them up on Tuesday night?'

'No. We have no cause to go to Halton East, and a man like him wouldn't have the time of day for us.'

I believed her. That meant Thurston Presthope still had the ten thousand pounds that he was meant to offer to Mr Metcalfe.

'How did Mr Metcalfe and your sons take to seeing Lydia again?'

'Still on that line are we? The lads were pleased enough to see her. Course her dad's not speaking to her. He doesn't like that Lydia took up with a darkie, no matter how high-placed the man is. The races shouldn't mix, according to him. And of course he knew the man was married. He said he'd stick our Lydia in a harem and she'd never get out again, and that would be her comeuppance.'

'Did your husband meet the prince?'

'No. He kept out of the way.' She began to scrape carrots. 'Said he didn't want to clap eyes on him or he wouldn't be answerable for his actions.' For the first time, she stopped what she was doing and rested her arms on the table, looking at me steadily. 'That's why my first thought was the same as yours. But I was wrong, and so are you.'

'But he was murdered.' The voice came from the door on the far side of the room. Lydia glided in, wearing a peach négligée and matching satin robe and slippers.

'You didn't stop up there long enough. There's still onions to chop and gravy to make.'

Lydia came and sat at the table. 'I was listening to you and just thought it was time to come down and add my tuppence worth.' She looked at me. 'It was murder. That's why I let you bring me here. It might have been me next.'

158

'I am not saying it was murder, Lydia. I am just trying to gather information.'

She examined her nails. 'Narayan would not have accidentally shot himself. He has been handling guns, and horses, since he was a child.'

'Accidents happen. It will be for the coroner to decide.'

She took a nail file from her pocket and began to move it carefully around her thumb nail. 'That's why the coroner doesn't want me there. I'd speak up.'

'Who said the coroner didn't want you?'

'Oh you don't know everything then? Our good and true constable called. Full of himself because he is coroner's officer for two deaths, when all he's ever done is clip lads round the ear and tell farmers to keep their sheep under control. "You won't be needed, Miss Metcalfe." Translated into English, that means sling your fancy hook.'

'You're right. I didn't know.'

'They wouldn't want me to take the stand, tell the truth and shame the devil.'

Mrs Metcalfe began to chop an onion with ferocious speed.

'Tell me, Lydia, do you know whether there were any of Narayan's fellow countrymen in the area, any other Indians?'

'Not that I know about. Why do you ask?'

'A story I heard. And I'm trying to explore every possibility, whether there was rivalry with another state.'

'There is always rivalry between Indian princely states. The British government sees to that. One state has a seventeen gun salute and wants an eighteen gun salute like their neighbours; another has a nineteen gun salute and wants a twenty-one. It's all nonsense. Doesn't amount to a row of beans. I know who would have it in for him – the British government.'

'Why?'

'Because they can. He embarrasses them. He puts them all to shame. He is a better man than any of them, a better sportsman, cleverer, knows how to enjoy life – to live, not just exist. And I'll tell you who would have worked with them, for a price, Thurston Presthope. That's why he fleeced Narayan while he was still alive.' She fumbled up her sleeve for a hanky. 'I want my car back. I want to get away from here.'

'When will you go?'

'As soon as they give me my car back.'

I rose to leave.

'Not stopping for your dinner then?' Mrs Metcalfe asked.

'Thank you, but I have to go. It was nice to meet you.'

'And you. Not every day someone steps across the threshold and accuses my family of murder.'

Lydia walked me into the yard.

She stayed on the mat by the front step. 'What did my mother mean by that?'

'She wanted me to know that your father did not shoot Narayan.'

Lydia snorted. 'She would say that.'

'Do you think he did?'

'He doesn't have the nerve. Hitting a small girl who wouldn't play the part of mother's little helper was more his line. He would not have got within a foot of Narayan.' She looked at my Jowett. 'What a dinky motor.'

'It suits me very well. Mile for mile I'd trust it more than your Rolls.'

'Take you up on that. When I get my Rolls back, I'll give you a run for your money.'

Nineteen

Mr Sergeant strode from his office as I was about to enter the hotel lounge.

'Mrs Shackleton, enjoyed your drive, I hope?'

'Yes thank you.'

'You missed breakfast.'

'Guilty. But I'll be more than ready for Yorkshire pudding and whatever joint of meat you are roasting.'

'Glad to hear it.' He gave me a conspiratorial glance and continued his stroll to the desk, indicating that I should follow. He did not speak until we were well away from the lounge. 'Another guest has arrived this morning.'

This was not news to me. I had seen the familiar car parked outside. It had belonged to me for a very long time, until I bequeathed it to my assistant, Mr Sykes. He insisted on having it painted black, which was just as well or our motors would have passed for close cousins.

I had no intention of revealing to Mr Sergeant that I had sent for reinforcements. 'This must be a busy time of year for the hotel.'

'I was unsure whether to turn him away. But he seems

genuine. He is here to fish and has all the right tackle for brown trout. I don't believe that a newspaper reporter would go to such trouble, and he shows no curiosity about recent events.'

'Mr Sergeant, you have a business to run. Welcoming guests is what you do.'

He relaxed a little, but his worried frown did not entirely disappear. 'You are probably right. He shows no sign of having heard about the tragic accident, but then, reporters are crafty.'

There were those words again: tragic accident. I could understand that Mr Sergeant would wish to avoid scandal in the press concerning the late prince and Lydia Metcalfe – but their affair was common knowledge. If he were so sure that Narayan had died in a tragic accident, what was there to hide?

'Would it be so terrible if he is a reporter? The story is bound to come out.'

'You are right. I just hope I have not let a viper into his lordship's nest, though I believe there will be one reporter allowed in to tomorrow's inquest.'

So he also had information about the inquest. I was beginning to feel like Mrs Shut Out.

'Is there more news of the inquest?'

'His lordship has given permission for it to be held at the Hall, eleven o'clock, tomorrow.'

'If your angler guest tries to wangle his way in, that might be the moment to suspect him.'

'This is a terrible imposition, Mrs Shackleton, but would you mind, if the opportunity presents itself, speaking to the gentleman and telling me if you think he is a newspaper reporter? If so, is he the one that is in the picture?'

What picture, I wondered.

'Not at all, Mr Sergeant, our being fellow Jowett owners gives me the perfect opportunity. I will speak to him before lunch.'

He thanked me profusely.

Of course, it would not do to appear too eager to chat to a strange man, even if that strange man were well known to me.

I made my way to my room for a spit and lick.

As I turned from the wash basin, I noticed a familiar suitcase by the wardrobe – my own suitcase. How had Sykes found my room number and unlocked the door? Not for the first time, I was glad to have him batting for my team, as cousin James might say.

I placed the suitcase on the bed and snapped it open. Mrs Sugden had cleverly packed my violet afternoon dress and jacket, a suitable colour for mourning. The silk pink patterned dress with cap sleeves also looked good. Ever practical, my housekeeper had also included bath salts as well as writing and carbon paper.

I would ask Mr Sergeant to loan me a typewriter.

Having decided on the violet, with black Cuban heel shoes, I made my way to the lounge, feeling a little guilty at having dragged Sykes away from Rosie and the family on a fine Sunday.

He looked happy enough, seated by the French windows, reading the *Sunday Pictorial*. We exchanged a polite greeting.

I took a seat nearby and picked up a magazine.

After a few moments, he offered me his newspaper, and I accepted, allowing myself to be drawn into conversation.

The positioning of our chintz-covered chairs afforded

a pleasant view of the garden, and also gave Sykes a view of the door. Although no one was in earshot, as far as I could tell, we uttered a few pleasantries before I said, 'You went into my room with the suitcase. That was taking a chance.'

'Everyone was otherwise occupied and I was very quick.'

Sykes would make an excellent burglar. He has tried to pass on his lock-picking skills, but my abilities are a pale shadow of his.

'Tell me something about your plans to fish, so that I can assure the hotel manager of your bona fides.'

'He's still suspicious of me, after my grand performance? That's an army man for you.'

'He believes you may be a newspaper reporter, here to dig the dirt on the late prince and his paramour. I'm also beginning to think myself half mad because apart from Lydia and her mother I am the only one who suspects foul play. Everyone else is at pains to proclaim the "tragic accident", well, accidents, to be precise.'

'Plural?'

'One of the grooms who rode with the prince has drowned. That may or may not have been accidental. I am inclined to think not.'

'Because . . . ?'

'Too much of a coincidence. He was young and fit. I find it hard to believe that he slipped while leaping the river.'

'And the prince?'

'He died of a gunshot wound to the heart. Now there is the faintest of possibilities that his horse baulked and it *was* an accident. But in that case, he would have lain where he fell and would have been found on Friday. His clothing was dry. He had been covered in branches. It was not even a very proficient job.'

'So whom do you suspect?'

'Either someone local, or connected with a rival Indian state, or he may have become inconvenient to the British government.'

Sykes let out a whistle. 'Now I wish I really were here for the brown trout. What are the police up to?'

'With a piece of charcoal in his hand, the local constable is the Leonardo of the North Riding, sketching the scene and ignoring my photographs. Unfortunately, he is acting as coroner's officer and intent on brushing me aside.'

'Ignoring you? Doesn't the man know that's a hanging offence?' He glanced beyond me towards the door and then evinced a sudden interest in a newspaper.

I took the hint and asked about how he planned to spend his time at Bolton Abbey.

Sykes captivated me for six long minutes on the topic of rods, lines, nets and bait, until Mr Sergeant had given up his eavesdropping.

'All right then, boss. Tell me what you want me to do.'

'Blend in. Have a drink at the Elm Tree in Embsay. There's a coal merchant called Deakin who saw an Indian on Bark Lane on Friday afternoon and now claims he did not see an Indian, but a gipsy on a bike.'

'A gipsy on a bike? No.'

'That's what I thought. Whether it was something or nothing, I would like to know. Also, an old school chum of the prince's, Thurston Presthope, is now trying to defraud the royal heirs of ten thousand pounds. He believes he will get away with it because the prince asked him to buy the goodwill of his mistress's father, Tobias Metcalfe. Presthope thinks no one else knows about it.'

Briefly, I told Sykes about Lydia Metcalfe, and my visit to the farm.

'It's the men round here who are the best gossips, Mr Sykes. So you won't be sorry to hear that I want you to frequent the local public houses.'

'No sacrifice is too great, Mrs Shackleton.'

'I shall type a report for my cousin. He is the one who gave me this assignment and will be arriving this evening. What room are you in?'

'Seventeen.'

'Expect a copy under your door sometime this afternoon. The chartered train is due at seven.'

Sykes folded the Sunday paper. 'I considered taking the precaution of signing in under a false name – "Mr Fish" – a scrupulously neat gentleman angler of impeccable habits.'

'And did you?'

'I decided against.'

'That's a pity. I should like to see scrupulous neatness and impeccable habits.'

'Shall we have lunch?'

'Don't push your luck. You're just a passing angler. I have my reputation to think of.'

'I'm a passing angler who will attend evensong at the church. There are bound to be homilies about the dead. It's the kind of topic that could interest a murderer.'

'And then?'

'I shall just have to force myself to try the local ale and be generally agreeable to the populace.'

Through the open window came a distant hum. Two waitresses appeared on the lawn, looking up at the sky.

We went out through the French windows and gazed up to the heavens. Sykes sidled across to the waitresses.

Mr Sergeant came to join me, shading his eyes as he looked up. 'That'll be his lordship and the senior maharajah. They've flown from Croydon.' He blinked and screwed up his eyes as the plane came closer. 'It's a de Havilland 50.'

'You can tell that from here?'

'It's an interest of mine.'

The hum of the aeroplane grew louder. It dipped a little.

'Where will it land?'

'I don't know. I expect the pilot has his eye on some long stretch of ground over there.' Sergeant glanced towards Sykes who was chatting to the two waitresses. 'What did you find out about our new guest, Mr Sykes? He's a bit over-curious for my liking.'

Twenty

After lunch, Mr Sergeant had his office typewriter brought to my room, along with paper and a fresh sheet of carbon paper. No self-respecting private detective would use someone else's carbon paper, to be perused by any nosey parker capable of reading inside out.

I used two sheets of carbon paper, top copy for James, second copy for the coroner, third copy for me and Sykes. After making a few preliminary notes, I began to type.

As my fingers hit the keys, I realised how furious I was with the whole business of feeling pushed to one side by the coroner's officer. I must not take out my annoyance on the typewriter, or every p and every o would have a hole in it.

> To: The Hon James Rodpen
> From: Mrs Catherine Shackleton
> cc: Coroner
> 3rd August, 1924.
>
> <u>Report into the circumstances surrounding the disappearance and discovery of Maharajah Narayayn Halkwaer at Bolton Abbey</u>

Following your telephone call on Saturday 2 August, I drove to Bolton Abbey where I met Mr Upton, the Duke of Devonshire's land agent at his office. He and the hotel manager briefed me as follows:

Prince Narayan booked into the hotel on Wednesday 30 July, with his companion Miss Lydia Metcalfe. They had arrived the previous day and stayed with T J Presthope, Esquire, of Halton East. His highness went riding on the morning of Friday 1 August, accompanied by grooms Isaac Withers and Osbert Hannon. In the afternoon, he went deerstalking in Westy Bank Wood and shot a doe. According to the escorts who carried off the doe, he then rode on alone. No other sightings have been reported

Further enquires reveal the Prince to have been in good spirits. He rode an Arab known to be a powerful horse but a breed to which he was accustomed. When the horse returned without its rider, a search was immediately undertaken, continued into the night, and resumed at dawn on Saturday.

I rode with Isaac Withers, following the route of the morning ride. We then entered the wood. At 3 p.m., in Westy Bank Wood, we came upon Withers's son, Joel, who was about his business of shooting crows. He cried out in alarm at having seen the Prince's body, concealed by branches. (Photographs passed to coroner's officer, Constable Brocksup.)

Mr Withers notified the duke's agent who duly arrived and we stayed by the body until Constable Brocksup took control of the scene. The maharajah was taken to Bolton Hall where formal identification took place by the valet, Ijahar. From there, the deceased was taken to Skipton hospital for post mortem examination.

I stopped typing. It is strange that in a language as rich in synonyms as ours there is no word that carries the same weight as tragic. I was loath to use the word, given that it tasted wrong in my mouth, having been used to describe what happened to Narayan as an accident. Yet to leave such an incident without an adjective seemed heartless. Distressing would not do, not in an objective report. Shocking? Shocking it must be.

This shocking event has touched the lives of those who came into contact with the Prince. Osbert Hannon, the twenty-one-year-old groom who accompanied the maharajah, was found drowned in the Wharfe on Saturday morning, having left home at dawn to join the search.

Attending Bolton Abbey, to offer his services if required, Isaac Withers suffered a stroke and is now in hospital, robbed of speech.

Miss Lydia Metcalfe is staying with her family at their farm. She expresses a desire to leave for London.

Mr Thurston Presthope of Halton East provided hospitality to Prince Narayan and Miss Metcalfe on Tuesday 29 July. While, in the presence of Ijahar, searching the maharajah's writing desk for sight of any invitation he may have received that took him out of the area, I came across a note signed by Mr Presthope acknowledging the receipt of ten thousand pounds to be paid by Mr Presthope to Mr Tobias Metcalfe, Lydia Metcalfe's father. I placed this item in the hotel safe. I have reason to believe Mr Presthope, or someone close to him, gained entry to the room and destroyed a similar sheet of paper that I left in place of the receipt and that Mr Metcalfe received no such amount.

One other item in the maharajah's room is a telegram received on Friday morning with the text Ides of August, signed C.

It is never hard to know what to put in a report. The hard part is what to leave out.

In conclusion, the puzzle remains as to why, when the wood was thoroughly searched, the body could have lain there for twenty hours. From my cursory examination, it appeared that this was not the case. The Prince's clothing was dry. The state and placing of the body indicated to me that he had died elsewhere. No doubt the post mortem examination will cast light on this possibility.

In a small community, the tragic death of Osbert Hannon was deeply distressing. For this to be followed by the discovery of the Prince's body in the woods has shocked inhabitants, here and in the outlying districts. The events may have precipitated Isaac Withers's stroke. Under such circumstances, rumours and hearsay abound. Further enquiries may reveal more information about the circumstances surrounding events at Bolton Abbey.

There ended my report. They would see from the photographs that the gun was unbroken.

I signed and folded the sheets and put them in envelopes.

When I looked up, I saw that Sykes hovered outside.

I opened the window.

'I heard you stop typing.'

I thrust an envelope at him. 'Go away. You will be mistaken for a peeping Tom.'

I shut the window.

Suddenly, tiredness hit me. I had been up at dawn two mornings running, and had eaten a tremendous Sunday dinner. When James and the Indian family arrived, I would need my wits about me. I shut the curtains and thought about entering the land of nod.

There was a knock on the door.

I opened it to find Mr Cummings, every brass button done up, looking shifty, glancing right and left.

He handed me a piece of paper. 'The prince sent a telegram from the post office on Wednesday morning, addressed to Mr Mohinder Singh Chana at the Ritz Hotel in London.'

I glanced at the paper. The message read simply

TWENTY-ONE FORTY

It was signed NH.

'This was it?'

'Yes. Please destroy it. My cousin would be in serious trouble if this comes out.'

'Do you know whether there was a reply?'

'I don't know if it was a reply but his highness received a telegram on Friday. I've written it on the back.'

I turned the paper over. This was the same telegram that the prince had tucked under his writing case:

Ides of August
C

'I never would have done this as a rule, but you are working for his lordship. All the same, if this prying comes out my cousin's livelihood is at risk.'

'Here.' I reached for my purse, and gave him another half crown. 'What time did he receive the telegram on Friday?'

'I gave it to him myself when he came back from his morning ride, about twelve o'clock.'

'Did he say anything?'

'He opened it then and there, and he looked pleased.'

'Anything else?'

Cummings slipped the half crown in his pocket. 'He said he'd do a bit of deerstalking that afternoon.'

'You look as if this surprised you.'

'I thought he'd want to be with his companion. They were inseparable all day Thursday. Later, when I went up to tell him that Isaac and Osbert were here, I heard Miss Metcalfe complaining about him going out again. He said this would be his only opportunity to go shooting, because he had a surprise for her later.'

There was a noise in the corridor. Cummings looked about him, and then scuttled off.

My tiredness fled. From what Cummings said, this cryptic telegram signalled the prince's imminent departure from the hotel, otherwise he would have had plenty of time to go deerstalking before the grouse shooting began on the twelfth.

Ides of August.

What was significant about this date in August?

Slipping the cryptic notes in my pocket, I decided not to rack my brains. Answers have a habit of emerging in their own good time.

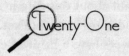

Twenty-One

Waiting is the hardest part. At 6.30 p.m., I sat on the edge of the ornate memorial fountain, a little way up the road from Bolton Hall. Usually, I like fountains, and enjoy watching them cascade, catch the light, and create the feeling of being freer than air. But this creation, dominated by an enclosing heavy stone structure, did not tempt me to trail a hand in the water.

In half an hour the train would arrive, bringing the Indian family, grieving mother, widow, fatherless child. James would alight from the train and into a waiting Bentley. I would hand over my report, to him and to the coroner.

What would happen then? James would thank me oh so politely on behalf of the India Office and the British government. He would tell me that my services were no longer required.

Or he might say, 'You are quite right, Kate. This was no tragic accident, this was murder. It must be properly investigated.'

'He was murdered.'

The voice startled me. I looked up to see who had

176

spoken. It was Mr Upton. He, like me, was waiting for what might happen next – the arrival of the Indians. Yesterday morning, he had looked tired and a little put out by my arrival on the scene. Between then and now there had been a subtle change in his manner, as though something had been taken from him. But what? And was he speaking about Osbert, or about Narayan?

'Who was murdered?'

He pointed to the inscription on the fountain. 'Lord Frederick, second son of the 7th Duke of Devonshire. This fountain was built in his memory. He was Gladstone's private parliamentary secretary. When Gladstone tried for conciliation in Ireland, Lord Frederick took on the job. He travelled to Dublin with Earl Spencer, bearing a message of peace. They did for him in Phoenix Park.'

'Won't you sit down?' Was Upton trying to say that he, like me, believed there had been foul play here at Bolton Abbey?

He shook his head. 'Jobs to do. There's all the extra work at the Hall, and we've lost three men.'

'Three?'

'Osbert drowned, poor Isaac beyond help in the hospital, and now Joel.'

'What has happened to Joel? I saw him this morning.'

'No one knows. He has run off. Who can blame the lad?'

'Shouldn't someone be looking for him?'

'He knows his way about. Daft as he is, he has a notion of self-protection. No one wants to be called at the inquest.'

'Why not?'

'He doesn't want to be called, I should have said. He is afraid to speak in public, and lost without his dad.'

He touched his cap and strode off in the direction of the Hall.

No one wanted to be called, he had said. Did he include himself in that? I would like to be called.

After a few moments I followed, wishing I had detained him, questioned him, to discover whether he knew something I did not.

I walked to the priory and wandered among the gravestones until I heard motor car engines on the road. Curiosity drew me to look as the fleet of Bentleys came into sight. To observe people climbing out of the cars, I had to walk away from the priory, round to the side of the house, where a tree screened me from view.

The Duke of Devonshire and a stately Indian, who must be Narayan's father, Maharajah Shivram Halkwaer, flanked by lines of staff, waited to greet the arrivals. The maharajah wore Indian dress in a dull red. I have seen the duke on only a couple of occasions and he was at a distance from me, but unmistakeable. He is a solid-looking man with a ruddy complexion. I have heard him likened to a walrus, but with a strong jaw.

The first car, with curtained rear windows, drew up at the front of Bolton Hall.

Footmen stepped forward to open the doors of the car. The Duchess of Devonshire stepped out first. In a caring gesture, she held out a hand to an older woman, dressed in a white sari, her bowed head covered. That must be Narayan's mother. Next a younger woman stepped out. She also wore white. Taller than her mother-in-law, and the duchess, she held herself erect, creating a sense of a space around her. That space was invaded straight away, by a little boy aged seven or eight who scampered from the car. A young woman servant came after him, but he shook her off and went to his mother, immediately assuming a more dignified stance.

From the second car came an elegant man in his early twenties, dressed in a beautifully cut long dark jacket in the Indian style. Slim and handsome, he looked neither right nor left but walked straight to the senior maharajah. Although they did not touch, and the younger man bowed, some powerful emotion passed between them, almost electrifying the air. It was so private that I turned away, even though I could not be seen from my spot by the tree.

Or so I thought, until a man in a dark grey suit and black turban spotted me, making me feel caught out. From the way he glanced about him, I thought he must be a bodyguard. What a pity Narayan had not travelled with this observant man. James walked on the man's other side, and did not notice me.

I set off to walk back to the hotel, hoping that James would come to find me before very much longer.

And then I saw a sight I shall never forget. A long line of Indian servants, dressed in white, walked along the road carrying vast amounts of luggage, in their hands and on their heads. I stood aside to let them pass.

Behind them came carts, full of luggage, pushed by more servants. They gave the appearance of being here to stay for a very long time.

I was sitting in the hotel garden when James appeared, taking long strides across the lawn. James stands six feet tall in his stocking feet. He stood six feet tall in his stocking feet at age fifteen, but willed himself to grow no taller. As he came closer, I noticed how much thinner he looked than when I saw him earlier in the year, at Hope's funeral. Never less than immaculately turned out, he is a good-looking man, with a small, fair moustache and neatly parted light brown hair, turned a shade darker by pomade.

He smiled and shook my hand, sitting down beside me on the bench. 'Glad of the opportunity to stretch my legs, Kate. That was a long journey, Leeds, Skipton, and then here. It felt never-ending.'

'I saw all the Bentleys.'

'Assembling the family and their entourage is like deploying three regiments to the same part of the front line.'

'Who has come?'

'Uncle Tom Cobley and all. Fortunately, they have brilliant aides-de-camp.'

'And I saw the aeroplane this morning.'

'They flew from Croydon. The duke travelled with the maharajah, his doctor and two aides-de-camp.'

'Doctor? Is the maharajah a sick man?'

'No. But that's probably because he always travels with a doctor.'

'They must have taken it very hard.'

'They certainly did. They're all utterly devastated. Narayan was the heir, and a fine man.'

'That little boy I saw, is he Narayan's son?'

'Yes, and next in line. The little Prince Rajendra. He has sisters, two girls at home in India who have yet to find out that their father is dead. I don't believe the little boy fully grasps what has happened.'

Neither does anyone else, I thought, but now was not the time to say that.

'I take it that the women in the car with the Duchess of Devonshire are the prince's wife and mother.'

'Yes. They are all shell-shocked.'

'And the other young chap, in the second car with you?'

'The maharajah's younger brother, Prince Jaya. He'd been in Edinburgh with a school friend so came via York. It was awful in that train, Kate. I'm not over-sensitive to atmosphere, but that train! I swear it wasn't powered by steam but by grief.' He stood up. 'Let's take a turn around the grounds. My legs have died on me.'

'And who was the Indian in the dark grey suit and black turban, travelling with you and Prince Jaya?'

'Oh, Mohinder Singh Chana. Bright chap. Aide-de-camp.'

The man to whom the maharajah had sent the mysterious telegram. Twenty-one forty. The man who had sent the cryptic reply: Ides of August.

James looked at the view across the river. 'It's so beautiful here.'

'Yes. Pity that it's taken a crisis of Empire to bring you to Yorkshire.'

'I know. It was kind of you to invite me after Hope died. But I've been busy at work. I had to keep doing something to fill my brain, and stop me thinking.'

'I suppose that keeps you out of a house full of memories.' I took his arm and steered him towards the road. He must see the wood for himself, the spot where Narayan had lain. But he did not know that was in my mind and continued his train of thought.

'It's not so simple. We got in each other's way, Kate, Hope and I. I was thinking about her on the train journey. If I was going down the stairs, she was coming up. If I wound the

181

gramophone, she was just about to read her book. And now I feel so bad about this. When she went on a visit, I felt relieved. And I know she was always glad when I went to work.'

'That's how people rub along most of the time, James.'

'But I didn't want her to be gone.'

'If you were Thomas Hardy, you'd write some very moving poems about feeling guilty. But would she want you to feel guilty?'

'No. And at least we had the chance to say goodbye.' He touched my arm lightly and I knew he was thinking of how I lost Gerald. 'Sorry. I shouldn't be deviating from the task in hand. Blame the train and the sense of loss that wound round the steam and smoke.'

I thought about the darkness of Bolton Hall. After Indian palaces and the best London hotels had to offer, it seemed hardly the best place to house a grieving family.

'James, I have a report for you, and have copied it to the coroner.'

Perhaps my report would carry more weight if it came via James.

'Oh? Can you tell me what's in this report?'

'I would rather you read it, and then I can tell you what is not included.'

I pulled the report from my satchel and handed it to him. We paused in our walk while he read it.

'I wish everyone I worked with was as succinct as you. Thank you.' He put the report in his pocket. 'But that's a bit of a bombshell you're dropping, saying that the maharajah did not die at that spot. Are you accusing someone of murder?'

'I can't accuse someone when I don't know what happened. But you need to see the place where he was found.'

'The coroner is at Bolton Hall now, speaking to his lordship, arranging for an inquest to be held at the Hall tomorrow. I'll hand this to him personally.'

'Well then, do you want to do that first?'

'He won't be leaving yet, and he does already have your photographs.'

'Good.'

We had almost reached the place behind Bolton Hall, where the ground slopes up to Stanks's farm, and one can enter the wood.

'It's this way – up the hill.'

'Lead on then,' James said.

James listened without speaking as we crossed the narrow lane and began to climb towards the wood. Fortunately, my Cuban heels were just about adequate for the gentle slope. Leaving out only the information about the prince's mysterious telegram, which could cause serious trouble for Cummings and his cousin, I told him everything that I had found out, and, more importantly, what I had not found out – such as where Narayan had died. 'It's important that we find the place, because there may be some trace or clue as to what really happened. The more I've thought about this, the more convinced I am that Narayan was murdered on Friday, his body hidden somewhere, and then produced, ready to be found on Saturday. It is too much of a coincidence that on Saturday morning one of the grooms who was with him was found drowned. He knew something. Perhaps he saw who killed the prince.'

'Your photographs, Kate, do you have extra copies?'

'No. But I do have the negatives in the hotel safe so can make more if needed.'

'I'll let you know.' His stomach rumbled. 'Excuse me. It was impossible to eat on the train. It would have looked so heartless.'

I looked at the ground, to avoid being tripped by tree roots, or stubbing my shoe on small rocks. An extraordinary tree caught my eye. It appeared to have two legs, the centre of its trunk having been worn away, and yet it stood as sturdily as the rest.

'There's something else you should know. This may be important because of what you said about the rivalry between Gattiawan and a neighbouring state. The local coal merchant told fellow drinkers in the Elm Tree that he saw an Indian on Bark Lane on Friday afternoon. Later, he changed his mind, and said it was a gipsy.'

'Have the police talked to him about it?'

'Who knows? Nobody tells me anything unless I ask, and I can't exactly start interviewing the police when I don't know how far you want my remit to extend.'

I was on the point of saying that my trusty assistant would make his own enquiries but something in James's manner made me hold back.

'So, this is the fateful wood.'

'Yes.'

James glanced down at his shoes, but followed me without another word.

The evening had grown chilly, and chillier still as we entered the shady wood. We walked in silence along the path. James stopped dead, and stared. 'What's that crow doing there?'

The crow in the cage was silent, no doubt weakened by its prolonged captivity.

'It's a bait crow.'

'I know it's a bait crow, but what's it doing here?' He strode to the cage and looked closely. 'I don't see how this catch opens.'

'Be careful.'

He took off his jacket and held it in front of his face, putting one hand into a sleeve and reaching down. 'I've got it.' A moment later, he stepped back.

The crow flew from the cage, its wings flapping, darting at James as if it would gladly peck out his eyes. He waved his jacket at it and for a few seconds it was not clear whether crow or man would win.

Then suddenly, the crow flew away, darting through the trees and disappearing out of sight.

'That was very kind of you, James, to release the bird.'

'Kind my foot. If Maharajah Shivram or Prince Jaya want to visit the spot where Narayan was found, I don't want them tripping over a crow.'

We stood very still. A light breeze rustled through the trees. Far off, a blackbird called.

'James, there is something I should tell you. Over there, that is where the body was found. This area should have been cordoned off pending a police search.'

'I expect they have found everything they need.'

His complacency annoyed me.

I took his hand. 'Come on, I'll show you exactly where he was found.'

He stepped gingerly, fearful of pulling threads in his trousers. Near the holly bush, I pointed to where the body had lain and gave him an account of coming along this way with Isaac, and seeing Joel.

'You are not suggesting this Joel Withers shot the maharajah?'

'No. He is a timid young man, and a little odd, but he was afraid when he saw the body.'

'That's natural enough.'

'There is something wrong, something I can't put my finger on.'

He turned and strode back to the path. 'It will be up to the coroner to review all the evidence in the case.'

'Well I hope he does.'

James picked up the empty crow cage, and looked about. On the other side of the path, tall nettles grew against a felled tree. He flung the cage beyond the nettles. 'Come on. This place makes my flesh creep. Woods are all right for boy scouts and for exercising dogs. Let us get back into the sunshine.' We walked back along the path. 'When you spoke to Lydia Metcalfe about the death, what did you say to her?'

'She was in a bit of a state. I hinted to her — well, more than hinted, that his horse had baulked and his rifle had gone off. But that was only to keep her quiet.'

He nodded approvingly.

'She didn't believe me.'

'But you said it. That's the main thing. It is exactly the explanation that we thought most likely.'

'We?'

'In the India Office. May I explain something to you?'

'I wish you would.'

We were on the downward slope, making our way back to the road.

'Gattiawan is politically important to British interests. There has been unrest in a neighbouring province, some hot-headed nationalists stirring up trouble. We are in negotiations with Maharajah Shivram regarding his taking a controlling interest in that province, and increasing the Gattiawan gun salute from nineteen to twenty-one. It would be most inexpedient for this tragic death to impinge on delicate negotiations.'

He spoke in an irritatingly soothing tone. 'The family need to be able to grieve, to take back Narayan's ashes to a sacred river, to have a narrative that they can pass on to his young son, and to his daughters.'

'What about the truth? What if an Indian from a rival state was sent to kill the prince?'

'Kate, we rule in India because we know how to do things properly . . .'

'What do you mean by properly?'

'As far as I can gather, no one but you believes there was foul play.'

'The family will want the truth.'

'And they shall have the truth. But we will do it properly.'

'Properly means examining the facts, sifting stories, corroborating statements.'

'We have our way of doing things. Maharajah Shivram trusts us.' He spoke slowly, as if explaining multiplication tables to a six-year-old. 'We have given India a language, a system of law, a trusted civil service of the highest quality, railways, and an army. They look up to us because we know how to go about things in the right way.'

'That was why Lydia Metcalfe spoiled the picture. You

only ever like Indians to see the cream of the British crop, and their wives, sisters and daughters.'

'Precisely.'

He offered me his hand as we reached the stile.

'Is that it then? Are my services dispensed with?'

'Of course not. I am authorised to give you payment in recognition of your success in finding the prince.'

We had reached the lane. The rumbling sound of a cart caught my attention. A handcart with very large wheels came into view, loaded with timber and an old chest. It was being pushed by the stony-faced man who had pulled Osbert Hannon from the river.

James did not meet my glance when I looked at him. He simply said, 'It's for the cremation.'

'Cremation?'

'The coroner will issue a certificate tomorrow, granting permission. I've forgotten the name of the place.' He stopped the man who was pushing the cart. 'Where is it you are taking the timber?'

'To the Valley of Desolation, sir. And his lordship ordered this chest be given up, to help make the right sort of fire. It is an old cedar wood, and the kind that is preferred for Indian cremation.'

He walked on.

The stark reality of watching the timber being trundled along gave me the shivers. 'Why such a hurry?'

'It is Hindu custom not to delay. If they were at home and the body lying in state, things may have been done differently.' James held out his hand. 'I had better get back to the Hall. Thank you for everything you have done.'

I took his hand. 'What happens now?'

'I will call for you tomorrow morning, at least an hour before the inquest. I expect the coroner will issue a certificate authorising cremation.'

Sykes appeared from the direction of the river.

I was continuing my walk back to the hotel. Although there was no one about, he maintained his guise and hailed me as one might greet a fellow hotel resident.

There was no point in telling him of my conversation with James. My former policeman assistant would rightly be outraged at the thought of a suspicious death not being fully investigated. My approach was different to his. I would investigate anyway, leaving aside the outrage.

'Do you want to hear about the church service?'

'Yes.'

'Only you seem preoccupied.'

'No, it's all right. Tell me.' I slowed my step and looked towards the river. It was a fine evening. The sun glowed red. 'Let's walk by the water. We can come back up to the hotel separately. Don't want to start tongues wagging.'

We left the road and walked the grassy slope towards the Wharfe. Finally, he said, 'It was so very sad, that service. There's a beautiful west window and the evening sun shone through. It lit up a very pregnant young woman, the widow of an estate worker who drowned. The older woman with her was in shadow. It seemed most odd.' That was a rather poetic observation for him. 'The duke was in his pew. I suspect he had instructed the parson to keep his homilies short and to the point. There were prayers for the souls of Prince Narayan and for Osbert Hannon. And he had a warning, too.'

'What sort of warning?'

'He said that no one in this congregation, indeed in this village or on this estate, should believe the superstition that the death of a white doe brought ill fortune. These were tragic events and no one could fathom the ways of the Lord. And they must not forget to pray for Isaac Withers who was sorely afflicted and being cared for in the hospital. That was the signal for the organ to shatter the silence, and for the choir to strike up. Afterwards, I saw the duke talking to the young widow and Osbert's mother, which I thought was very kind.'

'Yes. It's so shocking, a terrible blow for them.'

'People congregated outside after the service. There was speculation about whether there would be grouse-shooting this year, and a rumour that King George would have taken part but won't now be coming.'

'Nine days to go. I can't see any shooting happening on the twelfth.' A flock of slipstreaming birds passed overhead. 'That coal merchant, Deakin, the one I told you about – I don't suppose he was at the service?'

'No. But Mrs Deakin was. Someone did ask her about her husband having seen an Indian in the area. She claimed not to know anything about it.'

'She does know!'

'I'm sure. But I don't believe we should set too much store by what that man said. I gained the impression that he would not be a reliable witness.' My assistant never fails to amaze me. I am quite good at drawing people out individually, but he has the ability to work a crowd. 'Oh and I chatted to the verger. He said it was typical of Mrs Hannon and her daughter-in-law even at a time of such grief to be concerned about a young man who has gone missing from his cottage, and from his work.'

'Joel Withers?'

'Yes.'

'He is a simple soul, scared of his own shadow. I came across him this morning, sleeping rough in the barn, where the doe is hung. He was reluctant to go home alone. Poor fellow woke from a nightmare.'

'What kind of nightmare?'

'He thought the prince's ghost was in the barn with him. The poor chap saw a spectre rising from the hay, he smelled him, he probably even heard him. If you can find where Joel is hiding, I should like to speak to him again. I would hate for him to come to harm.'

'I wonder if it's too late for me to take a look at that barn, or see if I can find Joel's hiding place.' He looked at his watch and spoke the time aloud.

As he did so, something clicked for me. Twenty-one forty. Twenty minutes to ten. Prince Narayan had telegraphed the time of Lydia Metcalfe's birth to Mr Chana in order to have her horoscope cast. Mr Chana had done as he was asked. He had sent an answer that not everyone would understand. A favoured day for the marriage of Lydia Metcalfe to Prince Narayan Halkwaer was the Ides of August. Presumably Chana was sure that the prince would understand this, or perhaps Chana had been deliberately ambiguous. And did the wording contain a threat?

191

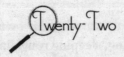

Twenty-Two

On Monday morning, at breakfast, I exchanged polite good mornings with the other guests in the hotel dining room, two elderly couples and a gentleman with the reassuring appearance of a retired city bank manager.

Sitting not far from the door to the kitchen, within hearing distance of clattering pans and a chattering Mrs Sergeant and her waitress, I ate a leisurely breakfast of bacon, egg, mushrooms and fried bread. If James was as good as his word, he would not be long in calling for me and giving me more information about the inquest to be held at Bolton Hall. I assumed that it would be an affair of a few moments, to be opened and adjourned until a later date. Until that was done, investigations stood still for me. It was too soon to expect an acknowledgement of my report. James might hope for a verdict of accidental death, but a coroner, with all the independence and traditions of his office, would not be satisfied with such an interpretation.

Sykes was not at breakfast. I guessed that he must already be up and about his business. If a brown trout had information, he would fillet it out.

No sooner had this thought occurred to me than I saw him, seated outside in the garden.

When the waitress brought my coffee, I asked her to bring it outside. 'It's such a lovely morning.'

She carried the coffee out for me. My fellow guest waved his newspaper. 'Good morning, won't you join me, Mrs Shackleton?' The waitress gave me a questioning glance.

'I will join Mr Sykes.'

I sat down beside him.

He tapped the newspaper. 'Interesting titbit of information here.' Until the waitress was well out of hearing, he regaled me with a story of an extension to the sewage works at Esholt, and the daring plan of the Jowett brothers to have four cars drive civic dignitaries through the tunnels on the day of the opening ceremony. 'You have to hand it to them. When it comes to promoting their motors, they're not backward in coming forward.'

'Is that true? Cars driving underground?'

He handed me the newspaper. 'Here it is in black and white. It must be true.'

I glanced at the paper.

As I did so, he leaned in and said quietly, 'No sign of your missing Joel Withers, but I did take a look at the barn where the doe is hung.'

'Poor Joel seemed quite cut up about it. What with that and his father's stroke, I'm not surprised if he has crawled off to lick his wounds. I only hope nothing bad has happened to him.'

'I wonder if there is more to it.'

'Such as?'

'He told you he saw the prince's ghost, and that there was a smell.'

'Scent rather than smell. What of it?'

'You believe the prince did not die in the wood so I thought it worth checking the barn.'

'Did you find anything?'

'Not a bullet, though I did look for a bullet. Not traces of blood, though it would take more light and more time than I had. But there was a smell.'

'Joel said it was a sweet smell.'

'And so it was, in the straw, something like perfume among the other more usual whiffs to be found on a farm, faint but definite.'

'Perhaps some courting couple had been there.'

'This was not cheap scent that a country girl might dab behind her ears, something more exotic than that. Of course it won't last, and would not stand up in court, but that barn warrants closer examination.'

Before we had time to say more, I saw Mr Sergeant approaching from the direction of the Hall. I thought he looked in our direction, and that he would wave. As he drew closer, I realised he was not seeing me, not seeing anyone. The man who usually walked so decisively, so ramrod straight, now slouched and dragged his feet. Something had happened. My first thought was of Joel, the nagging feeling that he may have come to harm.

Sykes noticed the change in Sergeant, too, but we did not comment. Time would tell what had brought about this transformation in the once-confident hotel manager.

'What next for me, Mrs Shackleton?'

'Go on looking for Joel. I'll persuade James to ensure there's a thorough search of the barn.'

James arrived on the dot of nine, striding across the garden, waving.

Some people yawn when they are tired. Others yawn when the world is not going their way. James falls into the latter category.

'What's up?'

'Nothing.' He spoke without any great conviction. 'I didn't sleep well, that's all. Always takes me a while to become used to the quiet of the country after London.'

He reached out a hand, as if I needed to be hauled from the garden bench. 'Come on then, old girl. I know you'll want to see this through to the last wicket.'

I held out two hands and let him pull me from the bench. 'Lead on.'

As we walked back across the grass to the road, I told him about the possibility that Narayan had died in the barn. 'It should be examined carefully.'

He made one of those agreeing yet non-committal sounds perhaps best represented by the letters huhuum.

'I realise it could be awkward to mention it at this time, but given that the inquest will be opened and adjourned . . .'

James stopped in his tracks. 'Who said that, that it would be opened and adjourned?'

'I just assumed it would.'

'Well, no. There has been some fairly solid evidence gathering. I believe it is hoped there will be a verdict.'

'I don't see how.'

'Unless I am very much mistaken, it will be game, set and match this morning.'

James must be totally naïve to believe that within these few short hours there could be a satisfactory outcome. Suddenly I understood why Mr Sergeant had dragged himself back along the road. He must have been to see the coroner's officer. But what had taken place to bring about such a change in the upright Mr Sergeant?

'So a full inquest is to be held at Bolton Hall. Isn't it unusual to hold an inquest in a private house?'

'Not at all, apparently. I'm told there are a number of precedents for doing so, dating back to the Middle Ages.' Before I had time for another question, he said quickly, 'And tomorrow there will be an inquest into Osbert Hannon's death, at Skipton.'

As we came in sight of the Hall, I noticed that Dr Simonson's car was parked crookedly on the side of the road, behind a black Austin.

The front door of Bolton Hall stood ajar.

I paused by the entrance. 'Just a minute, James. Before you usher me in, tell me something. Mr Chana, could he have been here on Friday?'

'Good heavens, no. He was at the Ritz. I saw him there myself.'

That made sense. The telegram advising Prince Narayan of a propitious date for his marriage must have been sent on Friday morning. Only my increasing suspicions of almost everyone made me wonder whether Chana was here, and someone else had sent it on his behalf.

A smartly dressed young footman threw back his shoulders as we approached, greeted James politely, and ignored me.

'This is Mrs Shackleton. Here to see the coroner's officer.'

'Come this way, madam.'

James squeezed my arm. 'Thank you, Kate. You're a brick.'

If I had held a brick at that moment I know what I would have done with it. This full inquest must have been on the cards since he arrived. He had simply kept quiet about it.

The young footman led me up to the gallery and from there into a room with creaking floorboards. A worn oriental rug covered the centre of the floor. Constable Brocksup sat behind a highly polished mahogany table. He did not stand to greet me.

'Good morning, Mrs Shackleton. Please be seated.'

I scraped back the chair. A more uncomfortable seat has never been glued together in the history of joinery.

'As you know, I am the coroner's officer.'

'Yes, Mr Brocksup.' When threatened with being bullied into submission, take the initiative. 'And you will have received my report, and photographs.'

He frowned, adding indentations to his tramline brow. 'Indeed. Thank you. I will be obliged if you do not mention the photographs to anyone. We are dealing with Hindus, Mrs Shackleton. The family would be most distressed to know that photographs were taken of the deceased.'

'Oh?'

'It would offend their beliefs to know that such photographs existed.'

'I am sure I have seen photographs of a royal Indian lying in state prior to a funeral.' I was not in the least sure of this, but did not wish to accept his claim that photographic evidence would offend sensibilities.

197

'That is as may be, but the circumstances of your photographs render them distasteful and inadmissible.'

Why was I allowing this man to wrong-foot me? I seethed but refused to be ruffled. 'The relevance of my photographs is that they show a body that has been placed, rather than one thrown from a horse, a body that someone has made a crude attempt to hide. This indicates that his highness died elsewhere.'

'That is your interpretation.' He slid my report from a folder. 'Your report will satisfy your obligation to the India Office. Unfortunately, it contains speculation and hearsay and so is inadmissible. The family will be obliged to you for giving information about the receipt for ten thousand pounds signed by Mr Thurston Presthope. But you will appreciate that the coroner must rely on medical evidence and the testimony of eye witnesses.'

'If the maharajah's riding clothes had been examined, they may have given an indication of where the body was between his disappearance on Friday and his being found on Saturday afternoon.'

Brocksup moved his fleshy lips, causing his jowls to dance. 'The valet burned the clothing. That is the usual Hindu practice after a death.'

'Did you bring me here to advise me that my photographs and my report will be ignored?'

The jowls spread as he attempted to make a pleasant face, to appease the little woman. 'Of course not, Mrs Shackleton. The coroner will consider every item put before him.'

'Am I to give evidence?'

He pushed back his chair. 'This is not a court of law. If there is some point of clarification that is required, or the coroner deems you have something of use to contribute, then you will be called.'

He stood, indicating that the interview was over. 'Thank you, Mrs Shackleton.'

When I did not budge, he walked to the door. With rudeness disguised as courtesy, he held it open for me.

'Don't you care to find out what happened? You are a sworn police officer.'

'I know my duty, madam.'

On the gallery, he walked one way and disappeared through another door; I descended the stairs.

So his interviews were complete. I was the very last person to be dealt with, to be silenced.

The grand entrance hall was already being transformed. Two rows of chairs had been set out in a horseshoe shape. A table had been brought in. One chair was placed at its centre, and another at the end, presumably for the coroner and his officer.

I watched as three servants brought in seven more chairs, the minimum required for an inquest jury.

The young footman who had led me to the coroner's officer stood by the grandfather clock. He opened the door and began to wind a cloth around the pendulum to mute its chime.

Even the clock must be silenced.

The encounter with the coroner's officer had left me feeling a little sick. I went out for fresh air.

James was talking to Mr Chana, he of the black turban who had exchanged telegrams with the prince.

I wandered away from the Hall, towards the ruined abbey. There on the grass, clover grew. Narayan had found a four-leaf clover for Lydia. James and I once searched for a four-leaf clover when we were children. Now I could not remember whether we found one, or simply ate the sweet-tasting clover flowers.

Usually in life, the prospect of a dreaded event is worse than the event itself, nothing being good or bad but thinking makes it so. But this was something new. The words foregone conclusion came to mind. Everything would depend on the coroner. He could declare foul play. It was within his power to commit a suspect to be detained and charged.

But without a proper investigation, suspicion fell widely and settled nowhere. It would be up to me to change that.

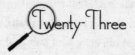

Twenty-Three

The butler stood sentry outside the main door of Bolton Hall. He gave a small bow and opened the door for me. It was 10.20 a.m. by the grandfather clock.

I took a seat on the second row of the horseshoe arrangement.

Mr Sergeant and Mr Upton arrived together. Both acknowledged me, but went to stand by the great hearth where the fireplace was large enough to roast an ox. Only a couple of logs burned there, more for cheer than warmth, giving off the smell of wood-smoke. I was able to watch the two men without seeming to do so. The hotel manager no longer looked as subdued as when I caught sight of him earlier, but then he was not aware of being observed. Even now, he held himself not quite so straight and tall; a man who had lost a nugget of inner certainty. The duke's agent lit Sergeant's cigarette. If Upton was in any way perturbed, he did not show it.

The outer door opened again. Thurston Presthope burst in with his look-at-me stride. He tried to catch my eye. I looked ahead, hoping he would keep his distance. He did not. In a moment, he was standing over me, belching Turkish cigarette smoke.

'Mrs Shackleton, how pleasant to see you here.' He gave me a patronising smile that said, You thought me a little down-at-heel, well look at me now! He was certainly well turned out in what must have been his very best suit and a sharply starched shirt with high collar. He had polished his shoes and buffed his nails. 'I believe a relation of yours is with the royal party.'

'You are well-informed, Mr Presthope.'

He sat down on the chair next to me, pulling at the creases in his well-pressed trousers. 'Have you mentioned that the prince gave me a small gift?'

'No.'

This was quite true. I had not passed on Presthope's misinformation about receiving two hundred pounds from his friend.

'So wise, my dear Mrs Shackleton. You see, I know the Indian. Indian royals are very touchy about that sort of thing. They would consider it deeply vulgar to have such a trifle mentioned. I shall naturally, given my friend's untimely demise, give that money to a charity. Do you have a favourite charity? I know many ladies do.'

I was supposed to simper the name of some good cause. 'Do you have the cash with you? Give it to me and I'll pass it to Osbert Hannon's widow.'

'What an excellent idea, but no. I don't carry cash. Later perhaps.'

He hurriedly excused himself and went to join Sergeant and Upton by the fire.

At twenty-seven minutes past ten, Constable Brocksup came through a heavy oak door at the far end of the hall.

Behind him came Dr Simonson, his cane tapping a rhythm on the tiled floor. Brocksup indicated that the doctor should take a seat on the front row of the horseshoe. He then turned his black eyes on the three men by the hearth. As if drawn by magnets, Sergeant, Upton and Presthope took their seats at the far end of my row.

One moment later, the butler led in seven men who, apart from a parson in his dog collar, at first glance looked so like each other, with their dark suits and high collars, that it took a few moments to distinguish their features. The banks, insurance and solicitors' offices of Skipton must be missing their key officials this morning.

Finally, the Duke of Devonshire, distinguished, gravely preoccupied with guiding his guest, escorted Maharajah Shivram Halkwaer to the front row. The maharajah wore an immaculately tailored Savile Row suit and silk shirt. Prince Jaya, similarly attired, led the widowed maharani, his sister-in-law, to a chair. All eyes were on them, and one could not help but feel great sympathy, and respect for their dignity. The prince was most solicitous, waiting until the maharani was seated, ensuring she was comfortable. Watching them enter, I had a better look at her today than yesterday. She was elegant, with high cheekbones and fine features. Perhaps because I was the only other woman in the room, I had the impression that she noticed me. Her pale sari gleamed in sunbeams of light from a high window. It was not to do with posture, but the family radiated an air of bereavement and pain.

James came next, alongside Mr Chana in his charcoal suit and a black turban.

Finally, the soft-soled coroner glided soundlessly into the room.

Chairs scraped the floor as we rose until he took his place behind the highly polished table. With his white hair and open, pleasant face, he had the appearance of a benevolent uncle.

He broke the ensuing silence in a cultured, kindly voice that sounded oddly intimate and out of place in this vast hall.

'Your highness, your lordship, ladies and gentlemen, let me begin by expressing deepest condolences to Maharajah Shivram Halkwaer and his maharani, who is too distressed to attend this inquest, to Maharajah Narayan's widow, Maharani Indira, and his brother, Prince Jaya on the loss of a dearly loved son, husband, brother, and of course father, to Rajendra, Menaka and Priya, and to family, friends and associates who respected and honoured the late Maharajah Narayan Halkwaer and who will miss him dearly.'

A fall of soot made a gentle patter in the hearth. Wood smoke wafted into the room.

The coroner spoke again. 'May I remind your highnesses, your lordship, ladies and gentlemen, this is not a civil or a criminal court. We are here to establish the circumstances surrounding the tragic death of Maharajah Narayan Halkwaer. Our concern today is to establish when, where and how he died. To that end, I shall be calling witnesses. I shall do this in the form of a narrative, beginning with his highness's arrival in the area.

'We know he motored from Chatsworth, arriving in the area on Wednesday. He passed one night at the home of Mr Thurston Presthope, of Halton East. Mr Presthope.'

The coroner's officer called Mr Presthope.

Presthope stood, drew back his shoulders, threw out his chest and strode to the side of the coroner's table.

After being sworn in by Brocksup, and swearing to tell the truth, the whole truth and nothing but the truth, Presthope painted a picture of a happy reunion with an old school pal, a convivial supper, a hearty breakfast and a friendly parting when the maharajah set off for Bolton Abbey. Only when prompted by the query as to whether that was the last time he saw his friend did Presthope hesitate, glance at me, and offered the additional information that he paid a courtesy visit to the hotel on Thursday, to ensure that the maharajah was comfortably ensconced. This was at variance with what he had told me. Such a practised liar should know better than to improve a previous lie.

Presthope returned to his seat, well pleased with himself.

The coroner said, 'Mr Sergeant, would you please step forward?'

Sergeant wiped his palms on a white handkerchief which fell to the floor as he stood. I moved a little to allow him to pass me. He trod on my toe without noticing. Yet when he took his place by the coroner's table, his stand to attention and taking of the oath steadied his nerves.

In answer to the coroner's question, Sergeant confirmed that he was the hotel manager and had done all possible to ensure Maharajah Narayan Halkwaer's comfort and enjoyment.

'His highness chose a horse, a spirited Arab. He had already ridden on Friday morning. He rode later in the day, having no complaint about the horse. At 8 p.m. in the evening, the horse returned without him, and the search began.'

'You say the prince had no complaints about the horse, Mr Sergeant. Have there been previous complaints?'

'Yes, sir. Some less experienced riders have found that horse difficult to handle.'

'Did you not feel some concern when the maharajah had not returned by 8 p.m?'

'No, sir. I knew he had a friend in the area and that he wanted to explore the countryside. Of course as soon as I was alerted to the horse coming back riderless, we began to search.'

'Thank you, Mr Sergeant. You may step down.'

Sergeant hesitated, and then with something like relief returned to his place.

It was then Upton's turn.

Once sworn, he explained that as the duke's agent he had taken charge of the search, which included Westy Bank Wood.

'Mr Upton, did you yourself search Westy Bank Wood?'

'No, sir. It was searched by the head forester and his men.'

'Can you explain why the maharajah was not found on Friday evening?'

Maharani Indira, Narayan's widow, gave the slightest movement, a straightening of her shoulders as if some blow might follow soon.

Now I saw why Upton had appeared so hollowed out and so changed when I had seen him in an unguarded moment early yesterday morning. He felt obliged to either cover up the forester's incompetence, or to lie, or both. He explained how thoroughly the wood had been searched, and yet was forced to admit that some part may have been missed.

'Is it possible that the body lay undiscovered that night?' the coroner asked.

Upton's answer came out in a mumble.

'Please repeat your answer, Mr Upton.'

'It cannot be ruled out that we missed his highness's body, sir.'

'Thank you. You may step down.'

Although the room held no more seats than needed, Upton looked about him as if he had forgotten where he belonged. And then he returned to his seat, holding each chair for support as he moved along the row.

Would I be called? I wanted to speak up and say what I felt to be true. Yet the thought of having to say words no one would want to hear put every nerve on edge and made me feel physically weak. It was as if a jelly filled with thorns encased me.

Besides, by the time Constable Brocksup had given his evidence, it seemed to me that the verdict was inevitable.

Brocksup consulted his notebook. 'We treated the deceased with extreme respect.' He lowered his head, as if to indicate how extreme a level of respect. 'Having due regard to the scene and to the removal of the deceased, having seen a bullet wound in the area of the heart, I searched and found a bullet lodged in the trunk of a tree, which I removed with a hunting knife and took for examination.'

Next came Dr Simonson's account, which the coroner asked him to present to the court in layman's terms.

The doctor stood. For a moment he hesitated, his walking stick having fallen to the floor. I thought he was considering whether he should take the few short steps without it. He picked it up and tapped his way forward, notebook in hand. He confirmed his name, and said, 'I found a lacerated wound on the chest which extended upwards to the back. This proved to be the track of a bullet.'

'What would be the effect of that injury?' the coroner asked.

'It would cause instantaneous death.'

'Thank you, doctor. Is it possible to estimate the time of death?'

'It is not possible to be precise, but I would say death occurred something under twenty-four hours prior to the body being discovered.'

'You say the track of the bullet extended upwards.'

'Yes, sir.'

'If the horse, which we have heard described as a spirited creature, was startled and bolted or baulked, and the prince was holding his gun, with an eye for a shot, could that account for the positioning of the bullet?'

There was the slightest hesitation, as when someone is offered a single choice and would prefer another. 'Yes, sir, it would.'

Thanking and dismissing the doctor, the coroner shuffled out a page from his notes. 'I have here a report from Mr Daniel Robson, gunsmith of Skipton. Is that gentleman present?'

He was, having slipped in late and unnoticed. A long-faced man, shoes polished to high gleam, he gave a slight bow in the direction of the Duke of Devonshire and the maharajah as he stepped forward.

Like the other witnesses, the gunsmith took the bible in his hand.

'Mr Robson, will you tell this court what you have told me?'

The gunsmith explained how he had matched the bullet to the weapon carried by the maharajah.

When the man resumed his place, the coroner turned to the jury. 'Gentlemen of the jury, do you have any questions?'

Small huddles and whispers followed as the jurors talked amongst themselves.

The jury foreman, a clergyman, spoke as if from the pulpit. 'Is Joel Withers here, to give his account of finding the maharajah?'

'Sadly, no. His father, who had accompanied the maharajah on Friday, suffered a stroke. Joel Withers is by his father's side.'

In the lull that followed, I raised my hand, like some schoolgirl asking to leave the room. The coroner looked past me.

I scraped my chair as I stood.

'Mrs Shackleton.' The coroner spoke my name like a teacher taking the class register, but at least he knew it.

'Yes.'

By way of explanation, he announced to the room, 'Mrs Shackleton, niece of Lady Rodpen, daughter of the Lady Virginia, is staying at the hotel.' He was delaying the moment when I would speak. 'You wish to say something?'

'When Joel Withers made his hue and cry in Westy Bank Wood, I was there, riding with Isaac Withers, Joel's father, around the paths taken by the maharajah the day before. I sent the Withers father and son to alert the constable.'

Why were these words coming from my mouth? I wanted to cry murder. I wanted to say that evidence had been ignored, destroyed, fabricated.

The coroner studied me over spectacles now perched just above his nostrils. 'Is there anything you would like to add?'

Because I was not speaking from the front of the room,

the people on the row in front turned to look at me: the duke, the maharajah, his son, the widow, and James. Only Mr Chana did not turn his head.

I noticed that Indira had a permanent wave in her hair. I saw the sadness in her eyes, and I could not speak.

The coroner said, 'Mrs Shackleton.'

I heard myself say, 'He looked very peaceful.'

Then I sat down, despising myself.

At first, I could barely hear what the coroner said as he brought this part of the inquest to a close. A choice of verdicts . . . horse baulked . . . gun went off . . . accidental . . . or open verdict . . . if you harbour doubts.

Surely they must harbour doubts.

I could have made sure they did, but I had failed.

Twenty-Four

Another moment and I would have hotfooted it back to the hotel and said goodbye to Bolton Abbey for good. Sometimes a person just has to acknowledge that she has been well and truly defeated.

I was halfway across the lawn when Mr Chana caught up with me.

'Mrs Shackleton.' He spoke in a deep, cultured voice. 'Her highness the Maharani Indira invites you to view her husband's body.'

I stared at him.

Anyone else might have spoken again, added a word of explanation. He did not.

My image of Prince Narayan was of him lying near a holly bush, covered in branches, dead crows nearby. Would I like to see him once more, to have a different picture? It would never blot out my first sight of him. But this was an invitation. To refuse would be churlish.

'I accept.'

He gave a small bow. 'Please come with me. I am Mohinder Singh Chana.'

The main hall had cleared of people. We walked beyond the chairs, to a ground floor corridor. I wondered whether the 6th Duke of Devonshire had ever regretted handing the task of extending this house to his head gardener. The corridors were a veritable rabbit warren, taking us around a corner, through a passage, up a step, around another corner, and another onto a landing dark enough to grow mushrooms.

'May I ask you a question, Mrs Shackleton?'

'Yes.'

'You mentioned in your report a receipt for ten thousand pounds, signed by a certain gentleman.'

'I did.'

'Is that receipt secure?'

'Yes, but the gentleman in question does not know that. He may think it turned to ashes in the grate.'

'Thank you.'

I caught the sound of retreating footsteps and glimpsed a man in traditional Indian dress disappearing around a corner.

At a closed door a robed Indian stood sentry.

'The men have left the room free. Excuse me if you know this, but you must not touch the body.' He nodded to the sentry who opened the door.

We stepped inside.

The shutters were closed, the room dim. The air was filled with the scent of jasmine, carnations and roses. Oil burned in lamps around the huge fireplace. An oddly shaped alcove gave the room the appearance of too many walls. But what drew my eye was the figure of Narayan. He lay on the floor, richly embroidered purple and pomegranate silks spread under him. All but his face was completely covered in flowers, roses, marigolds, pinks and carnations. In the subdued room the blooms provided a splash of life and colour that belied the scene of death. His arms were by his sides, also covered in blossoms. The body was angled so that the head lay in the direction of the alcove.

There were many colourful cushions on the floor, studded with jewels and tiny mirrors. The widowed maharani sat on the floor, a small boy beside her.

Close up, Indira was more beautiful than I had thought when I first saw her. Her husband must have been mad to take up with Lydia.

Unsure of what to do, I gave something that approached a curtsey and expressed my condolences.

She waved at a cushion near to her.

I sat down.

'Women do not usually come to see the body. It is thought too emotional, you see. My mother-in-law keeps to her room.' She spoke to her son. 'See, Rajendra, how peaceful your father looks.'

Now that my eyes were accustomed to the gloom, I saw that Narayan lay on a stretcher, eyes closed, arms straight by his sides. Both man and stretcher were so covered with flowers that I had thought he had been laid on the floor.

She motioned to Mr Chana who stood in the doorway. He came across, took the child by the hand and left the room.

'At the inquest, you said my husband looked peaceful when you saw him in the wood.'

'Yes.'

'Yes you agree you said that, or yes, he did?'

'He did.' I searched for the word. 'He looked regal.'

'Not like someone who had been thrown from a horse.'

'I can't say.'

'No. I suppose not.'

'It is a lovely custom, to cover the body with flowers.'

'You will notice that his feet point to the south. This is the direction his soul will travel, the direction of the dead.'

'Yes I see.' Something I could not quite grasp niggled at me. Had this been part of a dream? I had a feeling I should know something, but what?

'Did she look on his body?'

I knew very well whom she meant but did not answer straight away. Did Indira know about Lydia? Of course she must. Narayan had built a palace for Lydia near his own. Lydia had claimed that Indira tried to have her poisoned.

'I'm sorry, I'm not sure what . . .'

'Not sure whether his whore saw him, or not sure you should tell me?'

'She did not see him.'

'Good.' We sat in silence for a moment. 'I am his only wife. We were betrothed when I was seven years old. I gave him a son and two daughters.'

Sometimes the choice is between saying nothing and saying something stupid and banal. 'It will be hard.'

Hard? Yes. Not as hard as for the poor young widow left carrying Osbert Hannon's baby. Or perhaps a different kind of hard.

She said it again. 'I am his only wife.'

Perhaps, although she looked so calm, grief had unbalanced her. I did not answer her.

'Tell me that statement is true.' The urgency in her voice made me turn and look at her directly. She saw my confusion. 'He was planning to marry her. He asked our astrologer to cast her horoscope and forecast a propitious day. Has he married her, his whore, disregarding the day, without telling me, in some private ceremony?'

'No.'

'I like to think he would not have done it, not married a prostitute.'

We sat a while longer.

'Is there anything I can do, your highness?'

'Thank you, no. You may go.'

As I left the room, Prince Jaya, who had escorted Indira into the inquest was waiting outside. He gave a sad smile. 'Thank you for your words at the inquest. I am the man who has lost the best of brothers.'

He went into the room, and I felt glad for Indira that she had her family to lean on.

But what test had she put me through, I wondered, as Mr Chana escorted me back through winding corridors. And did I pass?

'Are you staying for the verdict?' It was Presthope, standing nonchalantly on the lawn in front of the house, smoking. 'Foregone conclusion, I'd say.'

I did not answer him but walked away, towards the Priory Church. I would sit there and have a few moments of peace and quiet.

He followed me. As he came closer, I realised he had been drinking. He thought it was all over.

'Pretty little speech you gave there, Mrs Shackleton, even though you were not called. Perhaps the coroner did not realise your importance, the importance of a private detective.' The idea amused him greatly.

215

'Mr Presthope, you told me that you borrowed two hundred pounds from the maharajah.'

'No, Mrs Shackleton. I told you that he gave me that amount as a gift.'

'He entrusted you with a great deal more.'

I was giving him an opportunity to be truthful, to return the money. Even a disreputable rogue deserves a chance to be honest.

Presthope smiled with reptilian charm. 'I noticed your dissatisfaction at the inquest, but please do not take out your failure on me. I can guess how you came up with your story, that I have somehow taken advantage of my friend. It must have come from the farmer's daughter, our charming Miss Metcalfe. I thought better of you than that you would believe such lies.'

He lurched towards me, wagging his finger, and then drew back as he saw Mr Chana emerge from behind an enormous rhododendron bush and saunter by.

'Lies? Well that is all right then. I thought perhaps you had murdered the prince for his money.'

His arms dropped by his side. 'What? You think I killed Narayan?'

'Did you?'

'Why would I? He was my friend.'

'But you were not his friend.'

'Women don't know the meaning of friendship. Friendship sometimes means holding back the truth. My alibi is watertight, which if you were anything of a detective you would have verified. You don't know, do you? You haven't heard what they're saying in the village.'

'I have a feeling you're going to tell me.'

'Since you suspect me, then yes, I will. The word is that halfwit son of Isaac's killed him.'

'Joel, but why would he?

'Everyone knows he doted on the white doe. It was his pet. He's fed and nursed the creature since it was a kid. Joel killed Narayan because he shot the damn doe. Why do you think Isaac had a stroke? Because he knew, he knew that his son is a murderer. It wouldn't look good, would it? Not for his lordship, not for me, not for the village, not for any of us.' His mouth tightened as he stood an inch away from me, intimidating, breathing fumes on my head as if he would like to set my hair alight. 'It's Joel Withers who will be strung up if you cry murder. How humiliating would that be? A royal prince murdered at the heart of Empire by a village fool. If you make accusations against me, I shall tell what everyone knows.'

I did not let him see the effect his words had on me. What he said made a terrible kind of sense. It explained Joel's fear and dread, his nightmares. It explained his father's distress. It explained why everyone insisted on the explanation 'tragic accident'. No doubt poor Joel would be dealt with quietly. He would be locked away in some asylum and forgotten.

I took a step back, but only so that I could look Presthope in the eyes. He would not know how deeply shaken I felt. 'Then do that, Mr Presthope. Accuse a poor young man whose father was so distressed by the death of a prince that he will never recover. Do that, Mr Presthope. Heap more coals on your own head.'

I continued to the church and went to sit inside, trying to regain some composure.

I do not know how long I sat there, but when the church bells rang I nearly jumped out of my skin. Then I realised that the chimes were to call us back to the inquest. A verdict had been reached.

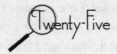

Twenty-Five

We took our places in the hall.

The jury filed in.

This time, James sat beside me. Perhaps he feared I might once more intervene.

The widowed Maharani Indira was not in her seat. It was occupied by the Duchess of Devonshire. I could imagine the duchess saying kindly that Indira should be with her mother-in-law. Her ladyship would attend for her, and report the verdict to the women.

The coroner turned to the mild-mannered clergyman.

'Gentlemen, have you reached a verdict?'

'We have, sir,' the clergyman replied softly.

'What is your verdict?'

'Accidental death.'

I glanced at Narayan's father. Maharajah Shivram Halkwaer closed his eyes and lowered his head. Prince Jaya turned to his father as if to protest.

The maharajah paid him no heed.

The coroner asked the clergyman jury foreman, 'Is your verdict unanimous?'

'It is. We extend our deepest sympathies to the family.'

For the first time, the coroner fidgeted, twisting his pen. He thanked the jury for their verdict and spoke words of regret and condolence for a life cut short. He put down his pen. 'I am issuing a special certificate to permit cremation of the body of Maharajah Narayan Halkwaer in accordance with Hindu funeral rites. Because the laws of this country do not allow for cremation out of doors, His Grace the Duke of Devonshire has given permission for a temporary structure to be erected at an appropriate location on the estate.'

We stood until the coroner had left, followed by the Duke and Duchess, the maharajah and Prince Jaya.

Presthope stood to leave. Mr Chana walked up to him, as did Constable Brocksup who touched his arm and put his lips close to Presthope's ear. The three men climbed the stairs to the gallery. Presthope turned and gave me a look of poisonous hatred.

'You tried to warn him,' James said.

'I thought he should have the opportunity to tell the truth.'

'That was kind of you, but probably ill-advised.'

James and I watched as the three men went through a door on the right.

When the hall had emptied of all but me and James, we sat side by side and lit cigarettes.

'It was a whitewash, James.'

'I knew you would think that.'

'The nicely constructed story about the horse that baulked, about the body being undiscovered, it's tosh. Narayan did not die in that spot. He was taken there.'

'So you keep saying. There is no evidence to point in that direction.'

'Not if no one wants to find the evidence.'

'It is better this way.'

'Yes. I see that. Better for all concerned that there be no suspicion of foul play.'

'Thinking like that will do no good. The family have accepted the verdict.'

'No, the brother has not accepted it. Did you look at him when the verdict was announced? And Indira . . .'

He gave me a sharp look. 'What about her?'

I decided against confiding in him. 'Well, she wasn't here, was she? Because any fool would know this verdict was decided in advance.'

'The maharajah has accepted it. That is what matters. Prince Jaya will follow his father's lead.'

'And what happens now?'

He scratched at his neck under the stiff collar. 'The maharajahs of Kapurthala, Rajpipla, Nawanger and Kalathal, and the family from Baroda, are all either in London or on their way to London and have expressed an intention to come and pay their respects.'

'So they will be coming for the funeral?'

'We are discouraging them, but cannot easily forbid it outright. On the other hand, not having them here may make it appear that we are arranging a hole-in-the-corner funeral, not showing due respect and regard for the late prince's position. Given how long it takes for their entourages to move, having the cremation tomorrow may make it difficult for them.'

'There is some other reason, something else you are not telling me.'

James went to fetch an ashtray from a side table. He set it on a chair between us.

'What is it? Why are you being secretive?'

'All right, but it's unlikely to mean anything to you. Kalathal is in dispute with Gattiawan about mineral rights. It would be politically inexpedient to give various people an opportunity to congregate.' He tapped ash from his cigarette. 'But if they are to congregate, what better place than here, under the nose of his lordship, Colonial Secretary?'

Why did I keep coming back to that sighting of the Indian seen, or not seen, on Bark Lane by the coal merchant?

A sudden commotion by the door distracted us. The young footman was trying to stop a man from rushing into the hall.

I recognised the stationmaster. He ran up to James. 'I have a message for his lordship. That dolt tried to keep me waiting.'

'What is it?'

'I tried to telephone, sir. No one answers.'

'Spit it out, man.'

'I have taken a call from Kings Cross. Five maharajahs have between them chartered three trains. They are on their way now, coming for the funeral.'

James is hardly ever perturbed. He blinked. He opened his mouth. He closed it. He blinked again.

'Are you sure? This could be some foul practical joke.'

'I am sure, sir. Telegrams are due any moment.'

James dismissed him with a gesture. 'Then make ready.' When the stationmaster had gone, James said, more to himself than to me. 'Where on earth will we put five maharajahs and their entourages, and how will we keep them apart?'

'If they have combined to charter trains, they are already acting as one.'

Some power struggle from the distant sub-continent was snaking its way towards the heart of Yorkshire.

Twenty-Six

I walked up the hill towards Westy Bank Wood. The afternoon was still, with barely a breeze. Clouds, sometimes so busy racing across the sky, now looked as though they had been painted on a blue backdrop for a school play.

Smoke rose from the chimney at Stanks's farm, curling into the air.

I entered the wood and walked the path towards the spot where the bait crow had waited for death or release. Some of the trampled ferns had bounced back. Others lay broken and flat. The trees nearest to Prince Narayan's resting place were birch, oak and ash. I looked carefully at each tree. It was on the ash that I found the bullet hole. So that part of the inquest findings was true. A bullet, supposedly matching the one from the prince's gun, had been removed from where it ricocheted into the tree. Being no firearms expert, I had no way of knowing whether this bullet came from the prince's gun and, if so, whether it first entered his heart.

Through the trees, the sun shone fitfully, but well enough for me to use my watch as a rough compass. I removed my wrist watch, held it with 12 o'clock at the left and moved my arm so the hour hand – it was 2 p.m. – pointed at the sun. By my watch turned compass, I calculated how Narayan had lain. His head was north, his feet pointed south.

His eyes had been closed and his arms had lain by his side. For someone who took a tumble from a horse, he landed surprisingly neatly, and in accordance with tradition for the Hindu dead.

I re-fastened my watch.

'What are you thinking, Mrs Shackleton?'

The voice startled me. I turned to see the maharajah's younger brother, Jaya, followed by two young servants dressed in white. The prince had changed from his dark suit and now wore Indian dress, black trousers with a satin sheen, a rich dark plum jacket and a small hat. He was handsome, and knew it. I thought of Mrs Metcalfe's comments about the maharajah. Here was another man who would break hearts without trying.

'Good afternoon, your highness.'

'Good afternoon. This is where my brother was found, I believe.'

'Yes.'

'Where was he, exactly?'

I showed him.

He bowed his head and murmured a few phrases in a language soft and flowing.

'How did he really die?'

I stopped myself from saying that I did not know.

'A tragic accident.'

'I am not sure I believe that. Do you?'

'I can think of no other explanation.'

'One wonders why a man who had successfully stalked a

225

deer and had it carried off chose to ride on, still carrying his gun, as if about to shoot again, although any deer would have run a mile at the sound of hooves.'

Why had I not thought of that? Others must have. I said nothing.

'Is the coroner's verdict final?'

'The coroner is impartial. I have not heard of challenges.'

I felt uneasy, but how could I side with this total stranger who, for all I knew, was merely testing me?

He shrugged. 'My father accepts the verdict. He is more apt to believe that the British play by the rules of cricket. He is so full of grief that he has no energy to make a fuss, as he would put it.'

'Do you wish to make a fuss, sir?'

'That is not my place. But I want justice for my brother, if justice is called for.' He turned away and spoke again in his own gentle tongue.

The smallest barefoot servant stepped forward, carrying flowers. Jaya took the flowers from him and spread them on the ground.

The second servant stepped forward, bearing two dishes, which Jaya took from him and placed at the foot of a tree. Yet a third servant appeared and produced jugs.

Jaya poured, saying, 'Milk and water. So my brother's soul does not go hungry. The priest will do this tomorrow but perhaps Narayan's soul will be in a hurry. For justice, he must wait a little longer.'

He dismissed the servants with the slightest of gestures. 'Tell me what you know, Mrs Shackleton. It will go no further.'

I recognised that line. It is one I use myself. 'I know nothing, your highness.'

'It will be worth your while. Chana tells me you have saved my family from being fleeced by my step-brother's so-called friend.'

'I am glad to have been of help. And I am sorry for your loss. There is nothing more I can say.'

'You can't say, or you won't say?'

Here was a young man confident in his own authority, used to having answers on demand. It was not up to me to tell half tales to a stranger.

'Excuse my intrusion into the ceremony for your brother.'

He gave the slightest acknowledgement.

I turned and walked away.

So Jaya, too, suspected foul play. And the Halkwaers' fellow maharajahs were on their way; to pay last respects, or to seek political advantage, or both.

I changed my mind about leaving Bolton Abbey that very afternoon. This story was not yet over. I felt sick with myself for watching the inquest twisted to suit an anodyne verdict. But perhaps I had got the wrong end of the story. Maybe it was true, and I was mistaken. What if the body had lain undiscovered? It is ridiculous to expect everyone to search as meticulously as they ought, or to behave rationally in the face of death. Joel was not the kind of person to do something logical. If he had seen a body, and it frightened him, perhaps he had tried to cover it with branches. He might have feared the crows would pluck out the prince's eyes.

It was not rational that Joel should abandon his house and sleep in a barn near a dead doe, unless what Presthope said of him was true.

On leaving the wood, I walked along the track to Stanks's

farm. I would take one more look at the barn, and at the doe. Perhaps Joel had gone back there.

When I saw that the doe was no longer hanging from the rafters, a mad picture came into my mind of Joel lowering the animal and taking it for burial in a special place. A more likely explanation was that it had been carried to Bolton Hall, to be served as venison pie.

In the dimly lit barn, I breathed in the scent of hay and damp. Walking towards where Joel had lain sleeping, I looked around. A hoe, a scythe and a bicycle wheel had been left by the wall. There was a battered milk churn and some old machinery.

Perhaps it was because the light was so dim but the smells struck me as more vivid than before. Sykes had been right. Where Joel had lain, on the straw, there was another scent – unless my nose deceived me. It was faint, yet heady, like jasmine.

This was where Narayan was shot. He had come to look at the doe, and so had Joel. Joel had picked up the gun and shot the man who slaughtered his pet. He hid the body in the straw, where no one would think to look. They would be searching for a rider who had been thrown from his mount. When attention was diverted elsewhere, Joel carried Narayan's body the few short yards back to the wood, where he had been told to shoot crows. He covered it with branches, and then heard the horses as Isaac and I rode along the track. Small wonder he had been startled and cried out.

Isaac knew. He knew what his son had done, and it was too much for the old man to bear.

I removed my gloves, picked up some straw and sniffed. Now it smelled only of straw. In the gloom it would be easy to miss some scrap of fabric, a dark hair. Would there be any point in trying to drag the constable here? Not unless I was prepared to accuse Joel. The sooner I found him myself, the better it would be. At least I might know what to do.

A footstep made me turn. I expected to be accused of trespass and quickly tried to think of some explanation for my being here.

He loomed large, dressed in black. For a brief moment I did not place him, but just knew that here was no farmhand. The voice, oily, insinuating, threatening, struck me like a blow. Thurston Presthope.

In the confined space, he appeared huge as he bore down on me. 'I haven't thanked you. I haven't thanked you for ruining my life.' He drew closer, slowly, taking his time, blocking my way. 'What was it to you that I saw a way out of my money troubles? You went running to the aide-de-camp. Because he's good-looking? Now the Halkwaers intend to call in the debt. His lordship insists on it. I told them you would deny the story. And you will.'

'No. It's too late for that.'

'Mustn't let the side down. All to be done so nice and quietly, the shredding of my reputation.' He came closer. 'Tell them you are mistaken about that piece of paper. Give it to me.'

'Get out of here.'

'Leave the scene of the crime? Where our village fool revenged his white doe? I saw you on the hill, Mrs Busybody. There's a price for poking your nose into what doesn't concern you.'

'They'll come after you. I saw you being led upstairs.'

'They do not have that precious scrap of paper.'

He grabbed the satchel from my shoulder, tipped its contents into the trough of hay. It was my moment to get out but I was not quick enough. He grabbed me by the arm, then the shoulder and flung me backwards. I struggled, trying to get up but he kicked me, then bent and picked up my brandy flask. 'Like a tipple, eh?'

He twisted my arm, forcing me to my knees as he rifled through the papers, flinging my hairbrush aside, a penknife, a flashlight. 'Proper little detective. Where is it?'

'They have it already.'

'Liar.' He had my wrists in one hand. With the other, he unscrewed the top of my brandy flask. 'It's your word against mine without that paper. I told them you made a play for me, that you're a tart, a woman scorned.'

My breath was coming so fast I thought I would choke. He forced the brandy flask into my mouth. Brandy trickled down my chin. Just for a second, I could not breathe at all and felt myself go limp. That was when he pushed me backwards and stuck his hand up my skirt. He had let go of my wrists. As he flung himself on me, I thrust two fingers into his eyes, and in the second when he shifted his weight, from somewhere came the strength to struggle free of him. I ran towards the door. He was after me in an instant. I picked up the scythe and brought it round the back of his knees in a sweeping movement. He fell, giving me time to pick up the milk churn and wallop him in the guts.

Then I ran.

Once out in the open I would be all right. Keep saying that. Keep running. There was no one to call, no one nearby to help me.

Halfway down the hill, I knew Presthope was catching up

with me. I had to get to the road, and then where would I run? Too late I knew that I should have raced to Stanks's farmhouse for help.

Presthope was close behind. I turned and saw him bearing down on me. Then by some miracle, he tripped.

Later, I had no idea what made me jump into his car, or how I managed to start it.

Only when I screeched to a halt outside the hotel, did I slowly become aware that I could not stop shaking, and that I had lost a shoe.

Never have I been so glad to see Jim Sykes. He was sitting outside the hotel, nursing a pint.

'What on earth has happened?'

No words would come.

He opened the hotel door. 'Come on, come inside.'

'I don't want anyone to see me.'

'It's all right. I'll walk you in. There is no one about. You can do it.'

It took hot sweet tea, several hours, a bath and the ministrations of Rachel before I could trust myself to speak, before I could begin to think straight. No, not straight, just think.

Rachel agreed to believe that I had taken "a funny turn", but I think she knew something bad had happened and that I wasn't letting on.

I wanted to go home, crawl into my own bed, and never come out again. I wanted my mother. But if I gave in, then Presthope would have beaten me, and I would not let him do that.

When I forced myself to think, it was as if I had to split

myself in two, with the stronger part of me telling the use-less me what to do.

'Rachel, tell Mr Sergeant to open the safe for me, and ask Mr Sykes to meet me at the front entrance.'

She hesitated. 'Yes madam, if that's what you want.'

When she had gone, I thought I would give her five min-utes. I looked not at my watch but at the clock because for some odd reason I did not want to see my own hand, or wrist. I felt such a coward, and so stupid.

After five minutes, I made myself leave the room. Mr Sergeant, of course, knew of my "funny turn".

'Are you feeling any better, Mrs Shackleton?'

'Yes, thank you. That envelope I gave you, Mr Sergeant, I'll take it now.'

He took the envelope from the safe.

At the door, I gave it to Sykes. 'This is a receipt for ten thousand pounds that the maharajah entrusted to Thurston Presthope. Hand it to Mr Chana, no one else.'

'Is that who did this to you? Presthope.'

'Yes.'

He clenched his fists. 'Anything else I can do?'

'My satchel is in Stanks's barn, and there's a shoe . . . '

He looked away. 'Did he . . . ?'

'No.'

'I'll . . . '

'Don't. Just do as I ask. And I need you to find where Joel Withers is hiding.'

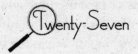

Twenty-Seven

The knock on my room door startled me. I had been lying on the bed, staring at my eyelids.

'Who is it?'

'I say, Kate, are you all right?'

'Why shouldn't I be all right?' I opened the door.

James looked peeved. 'No need to snap my head off. You do look a bit peaky.'

'Have you come to see me off the premises?'

'Why on earth do you think I would want to do that? I've been looking for you. Well done on your masterly intervention. You added just the right touch to the inquest.'

I sat in the chair. 'Not the touch I wanted.'

He perched on the corner of my bed. 'We need your help.'

'To do what? Help whitewash another inquest? There will be one tomorrow, in Skipton, on poor Osbert Hannon.'

'I know this has been hard for you, and we greatly appreciate it, really. I want to show you something, in the prince's room.'

If I refused, it would be out of character. He would know something was wrong. 'All right.'

The trouble is, curiosity will be my downfall. I daresay if some evil-eyed monster promised me an interesting revelation in the corner of a dark alley, I would be fool enough to follow, even after my nightmare in the barn.

We walked up to the first floor.

The door to Narayan's room stood open. I heard voices in a foreign tongue, one threatening and angry, the other pleading and whining.

When we entered, I saw Mr Chana, the aide-de-camp. He stood by the open safe. A pile of fabulous jewels gleamed on the dressing table. I moved closer, to look at the magnificent pieces. There was a seven-strand string of the most perfect pearls I have ever seen, diamond cufflinks and tie pins, emeralds, Cartier watches, and brooches – a ruby surrounded by diamonds, and a diamond surrounded by rubies.

'These belong to the maharajah? The brooches and pearls?'

Chana spoke coldly, without looking at me. 'Some are ceremonial.'

Next to the jewels were the boxes and bags they had come from, boxes of carved cedar wood, delicate ivory, cherry wood embossed with gold leaf, a light wood embossed with brass, a circular container decorated with silver. The bags were of dark velvet, scarlet, plum, mulberry and black.

Ijahar was staring at the jewels. He trembled and shook his head, speaking in a plaintive voice. 'I do not know. She must have taken it.'

James looked at the gems. He touched my arm. 'The

thing is, the Gattiawan diamond is missing. It is needed for the cremation.'

I stared at James, not fully taking his meaning, not connecting a diamond with a cremation.

'His highness must be carried to the cremation ground covered in jewels, and the most important jewel is the . . . '

'Dubte suraj ki chamak.' When I spoke the words, the three men all looked at me.

'You know where it is?'

'No. But I did take an inventory of the jewellery Miss Metcalfe took with her. The diamond was not one of the pieces. Perhaps it is in the hotel safe.'

In an instant Mr Chana bounded towards the door, issuing an order to Ijahar who began to return the jewels to their containers and place them in a Gladstone bag.

James and I followed Chana downstairs. Sergeant was in the office, a mug of tea on the desk beside him. He looked up as Chana tapped on the door.

'The safe if you please, Mr Sergeant. An item that Maharajah Narayan gave into your keeping.'

'Certainly.' Sergeant took a key from his pocket and crossed to the safe in the corner. We watched as he turned the key and opened the heavy door. He reached in and took out a velvet bag with the shape of a box inside. This he passed to Chana.

Sergeant moved to turn the key and lock the safe.

'Mr Sergeant, would you also please give me my negatives?'

'Negatives?'

'Yes. I left them with you on Saturday.'

'Ah, those negatives.'

'Yes, those negatives.'

'I'm sorry, Mrs Shackleton. I thought you knew.'

'Knew what?'

'The constable came asking for them, on behalf of the coroner.'

'How did he know where they were?'

Sergeant did not look me in the eye. There was little point in remonstrating, and saying that those were my negatives. He had done as he was told, which was why he had this job, a man who knew the proper order of things.

I turned and left.

Curiosity drew me upstairs again. I wanted to see whether the box in the black velvet bag really did contain the Gattiawan diamond.

I entered the hotel room. Straight away, from Ijahar's expression, I knew that the prized diamond had gone

The jewellery box taken from the bag stood open. It held an exquisite emerald four-leaf clover pendant, earrings and brooch set in white gold.

I knew in an instant for whom this gift had been intended. 'I believe this was the surprise the prince promised Miss Metcalfe.'

Ijahar came to life. He spoke excitedly, first in his language, and then to me saying, 'She, she, Miss Metcalfe. She has the dubte suraj ki chamak.'

'Ijahar, when did you last see the diamond?'

'Sometimes in a pouch that his highness is wearing.' He brought his hands from throat to chest, to indicate that the maharajah wore the diamond around his neck.

'Was he wearing it when you dressed him to go out riding on Friday?'

He shook his head.

'Did you ask him where it was?'

'No, memsahib. I do not ask.'

If it were known that the maharajah sometimes carried his diamond with him, that knowledge would give motive enough for foul play.

'She, Miss Metcalfe. She looks at the jewels.'

That made sense. Why else would Narayan have had her surprise present locked in the hotel safe?

'She is at her family's farm. I drove her there. Her trunks have been sent to London by rail, to the Dorchester.'

'Then they must be sent back. And Kate, she must not be allowed to leave the area.' I stared at James, sending him the message to do his own dirty work. He left the room saying, 'I'll get on to the Dorchester now.'

Chana looked at the emeralds. His mouth tightened. 'My prince was the most generous of men.'

If he had said aloud, 'For generous, substitute gullible', it could not have been more plain.

'Mr Chana, why did the maharajah take the risk of travelling with so precious a diamond?'

'When from childhood a person is surrounded by protectors and devoted servants, he feels inviolate.'

'And trusting.'

He gave a small bow. 'Thank you for sending your emissary with the note. My prince liked to do things properly. He wanted to marry on a propitious day and to have the blessing of that woman's father. Now I must return to Bolton Hall and report.'

He left, followed by Ijahar carrying the Gladstone bag of jewels.

237

I stood looking out of the window, watching as Mr Chana and Ijahar were driven back to the Hall.

James was in the doorway again, looking crestfallen. 'Please Kate, give me your support. My mother said I wasn't cut out for the India Office, and I am beginning to think she was right. So, unfortunately, are my superiors.'

He looked sad and helpless, just as he did when he was a little boy wanting to join big boys' games.

'What do you want me to do, James?'

'I know you won't feel inclined to help, and I do not blame you one bit. But we have less than twenty-four hours to find the dubte suraj ki chamak. It must be part of the funeral ceremony. Do you think it is possible that the Metcalfe woman has it?'

'I don't know.'

'Will you at least probe her about it? Perhaps appeal to her better nature.'

'Why don't you? She may be susceptible to your charming smile.'

'She won't trust me not to take the matter further if she has the diamond. But we will not, I promise. If she has it and hands it over, there will be no repercussions. You might remind her that her family's tenancy on the farm is due for renewal.'

'If she has that diamond and feels generous towards her family, they won't need a tenancy.'

'It is known worldwide. Even she would not dare risk trying to sell it. Please, Kate.'

I did not want to go, but neither did I want to stay in my room, jumping out of my skin at every little sound.

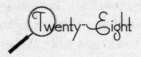

Twenty-Eight

James no doubt congratulated himself that he had so easily persuaded me to tackle Lydia about the diamond. He was not to know that I had a reason of my own. Somewhere at the back of my mind was the thought that if I found the diamond, I would find the murderer. One success may lead to another. Joel Withers could, conceivably, be the killer. If not, such a priceless jewel would provide a motive for murder.

I slowed the motor and came to a halt as a herd of sheep slowly crossed the lane encouraged by a border collie. A shepherd urged them on, raising his cap to me as the last animal entered a gate on the opposite side.

A little way on, I turned the motor onto the track that led to the farm. The wheels squelched through mud. Once more I climbed from the car, opened the gate, drove through, and closed it. I could see the British aristocrats' and Indian royals' attraction to being surrounded by servants willing to leap about and do the dirty work.

Lydia must have heard the car. She opened the farmhouse door.

'I heard the church bells. What is the verdict?'

We went into the kitchen. I looked about, but there was no one else there.

'I know you got friendly with my mother. She is always friendly to outsiders, constantly imagining that any female she comes across would be a better daughter than I.'

We sat down at the kitchen table. 'Where is she?'

'In the dairy.' She took out her cigarette case. 'Well, what was the verdict?'

'Accidental death.'

She snorted. 'They killed him.'

'Who?'

'If I knew I would tell you. Perhaps his lady wife, the poet, sent someone to take a pot shot. I suppose her spies would have told her he intended to marry me. What did they say at the inquest?'

'The horse baulked. The gun went off.'

She lit her cigarette. 'Huh! Exactly what you told me. You should be pleased then. I thought about it afterwards, and I knew it was nonsense. Narayan has been shooting tigers since he was ten. He is the world's top polo player which means he rides a horse better than anyone in the universe.'

'I came to tell you the verdict, Lydia, but also to ask whether you know where the Gattiawan diamond might be found. According to tradition, Narayan's body should be decked with jewels when it is carried for cremation.'

She balanced the cigarette on one of those tin ashtrays made by boys in a school metalwork class. 'Are they taking him back to India?'

'No. That would not be practical, not in August.'

'What then?'

'The duke has given permission for cremation in the Valley of Desolation. It will be tomorrow.'

She blew her nose. 'I can't believe it. I can't believe I'll never see him again. He was the most glorious man I ever knew. Of course I treated him badly . . . how else could I have kept him for so long?'

'Lydia, do you know where the Gattiawan diamond is?'

'How should I know? I suppose that miserable Ijahar says I have it. If he does, he's a liar.'

'When did you last see it?'

She thought for a moment. 'He wore it to dinner with the Duke of Devonshire at Chatsworth last Saturday night. He put on his ceremonial garb.' Her mouth turned down. 'I mocked him, of course.'

'And that was the last time you saw it?'

'Yes. Because I wasn't invited to Chatsworth, and I was asleep when he came back.' She jutted her chin. 'So ask the Duke of Devonshire. For all I know, he got his honoured guest drunk and took it. Isn't that how their sort always gather loot? Grab, grab, grab. King George has the Koh-i-noor diamond. Why shouldn't one of his dukes snatch the dubte suraj ki chamak? I know our top dogs want it for England. Narayan let that much slip. There's some shenanigans going on about it in high places. I'm not supposed to know that. Don't tell them I know.'

'What kind of shenanigans?'

'Some tit for tat. But I don't know. And they mustn't think I do.' She looked suddenly afraid. 'They all hate me.'

I stood to go.

She walked with me to the door. 'Can I have my Rolls-Royce back now?'

'I don't think so. Not until they find the diamond.'

She snapped her fingers. 'Got it! Thurston Presthope. I wouldn't put it past him to have taken the diamond. He borrowed money from Narayan. Tell that to the powers that be.'

The powers that be. That is exactly what they were. Not for the first time, I wondered why I had been chosen for this task. Perhaps it was because if someone had to fail, it had better be me, and not a charmed member of the inner circle, or the forces of law and order.

'Tell me now, Lydia, if you know where the diamond is. Your father's lease on this farm is due to expire. They will hold that over him. They will turn the place upside down.'

'Then damn their eyes. And damn them for locking up my Rolls-Royce.'

Twenty-Nine

A persistent tapping on the casement woke me from a dreaming sleep. I had closed the curtains tightly against last night's moonlight and now could not see whether it was day or night. Someone hissed at me through the slightly open window.

I went to see who it could be. The figure stepped back. He was dressed in white and gave a small bow.

I opened the window wider. 'Ijahar, what are you doing here?'

'Memsahib, the maharani will see you.'

'Now?'

He nodded.

Never let it be said that I declined a royal summons. 'Give me a few moments. Wait by my motor.'

'Your motor?'

'It's blue.'

I dressed quickly and left the room.

Unfortunately, not another soul stirred, and the outer doors were still locked.

I went back to my room, and climbed out of the window, feeling like a character in a girls' adventure story.

Ijahar stood by the car. When I asked him to get in, he shook his head and took two steps back indicating that he would ride on the step. Fearful of his falling off and my having to explain one more body, we compromised. He took his place in the dickey seat.

We entered Bolton Hall by a side door, a servants' entrance. A scullery maid turned away as we approached, averting her eyes as we passed, though I knew she had made sure of a good sly glance.

'This way, memsahib.'

I followed Ijahar up a steep, dingy staircase, a servants' staircase that led to an uncarpeted landing. A discreet door allowed servants to enter and leave their betters' rooms with a minimum of disturbance. The communicating door led to a carpeted landing. I followed Ijahar. He tapped on a door. No one answered. He opened it, and waved me inside.

The shutters of the room were half open, allowing a pale yellow light to illuminate the opulent woven rug on which silk, brocade and velvet cushions were placed. The rich colours of the rug and of the patterned cushions, mulberry, scarlet, wine and royal blue transformed the room into something out of the Arabian Nights.

Sitting on the floor is not something I do a lot. I gathered my skirt and chose a plum-coloured velvet cushion with moons and stars embroidered in gold thread.

On the rug were unrolled parchments and ruled foolscap of the kind on which musicians write their pieces. The parchments were held down at the corners by ornate gold paperweights. There were pens and different coloured inks. The papers were dotted with symbols and inscriptions.

Further off, to the side of the rug, were rolled parchments, tied with silk ribbons. Someone had been busy.

One of the parchments was decorated with signs of the zodiac. With a shiver, I wondered whether Prince Narayan's death had been foretold.

Gliding like a ghost, Indira stepped into the dimly lit room. Her slippers were woven of gold thread.

I stood to greet her.

She apologised for summoning me so early, and then sat down on a red-gold cushion embroidered with a pattern of pomegranates, motioning me to sit.

I waited for her to speak first.

'Thank you for coming, Mrs Shackleton. I could not sleep, you see.' For someone who had not slept, she looked perfect, with barely a shadow under her eyes. 'You are a widow?'

'Yes.'

'I thought so. We Hindus are taught from an early age to accept our lot on earth without complaint. Some are born into suffering and sorrow because in a previous life they were not pure in heart, and so did not find the way to God. But it is hard when you are not born into suffering and sorrow and it finds you regardless.' She glanced at one of the scrolls. 'You have noticed the charts.'

'Yes.'

'The astrologer must find an auspicious day for us to make our journey home with my husband's ashes.'

'And has he found such a day?'

'Not yet. You see, a day that suited my father-in-law was wrong for my son and his grandmother. A day that is right for them and me may prove unsuitable for Prince Jaya. But I expect you dismiss astrology.'

'I don't know enough about it to be dismissive.'

'Many Europeans regard it as mumbo jumbo but I have found that it accords with what will come to pass. My husband and I were married on a propitious day, and each day I gave birth was marked in my horoscope as propitious.'

If that was her belief, she must regret not having every day of Narayan's life cast. On Friday, he should have taken greater care.

'You have other children, your highness?'

'Yes, two daughters. They are in Simla with their ayahs – their nursemaids. My father-in-law thinks the journey by ship is too much for them. The youngest is only seven years old, the age I was when the Tika Raja and I were betrothed.'

'You were very young.'

'We married when I was sixteen and he was eighteen. If you had seen the two of us together on our wedding day, you would have thought we were a prince and princess from the Arabian Nights.'

I smiled. 'I can imagine, just by looking at what you have here, and how you dress.'

'He was educated in England. I was educated in Switzerland. At our wedding celebration, we realised we had both forgotten how to eat with our fingers. Later, we laughed about it.'

'What a happy memory.'

'I told you about our education so that you may understand. I feel not fully Indian, and not European either. I should not be here speaking to you, but holding a long silence, day upon day of silence. And I should ensure that my husband is treated in death as in life, with the respect and ceremony due to him. I wish you could retrieve the Gattiawan diamond in time for his funeral today.'

'So do I wish that, but it seems most unlikely.'

She sighed. 'Perhaps, perhaps not. You have something I recognise, persistence, a way of looking at the world with clear eyes. We have in common that we are widows, and we have something else in common.'

'Oh?'

'There are some matters that cannot be spoken aloud.' She fidgeted with the hem of her sari. 'These are the matters we most wish to know.'

'If we cannot speak of something, then how can it be brought into the open?'

'It is important to know. Because . . . Tell me your opinion of the inquest verdict. What did you think?'

'It is a plausible verdict.'

'It might be plausible, except that my husband was an exceptional horseman and an experienced huntsman.' She was echoing what Lydia Metcalfe had said. I made no answer. 'Servants talk, Mrs Shackleton, and some of that talk finds its way to me. There is a fine minaret by a lake, near Lahore. It was built by Emperor Jahangir as a monument to Mansraj, one of his pet deer.'

'Oh?'

She looked at me closely. She could not have said more plainly that she had heard about Joel Withers, the pet doe Narayan had shot, and the talk of Joel as having taken revenge.

'I hadn't heard that story, your highness. It must be unique, a monument to a deer.'

There was a tap on the door. She tensed.

The door opened. Ijahar bowed, 'Highness, the maharani is from her bed.'

She dismissed him with a nod. 'I must go. You will think about what I have said?'

She stood, and so did I. 'With respect, your highness, you have said nothing. I cannot read your mind.'

And I should have added that I could do nothing. If my suspicions were correct and Joel had shot the crown prince of Gattiawan because he killed a pet doe, then that information would be far worse to live with than a verdict of accidental death.

She hesitated. 'You are right. I heard that you are a private investigator. We understood each other at the inquest. I wrongly expected you to read my thoughts.'

'What are your thoughts?'

'I want to know who killed my husband. Your government will find out. They will need to know for their own information, but they will not tell me, or the Maharajah Shivram. Will you tell me, if you learn the truth?'

I hesitated.

She waited only for a few seconds for a reply I did not give. 'Perhaps you will, or perhaps not. After this visit, I will never set foot in this country again.'

'I am sorry that this place will have such bad memories for you.'

She waved her hand, dismissing my words. 'There is something else. I want to take the Gattiawan diamond home with me. It belongs to us. Its history links it to the Rajputs. My husband and father-in-law would have traded it for favours, but not now. It must be returned, so that it will adorn my son, Rajendra, when he becomes Maharajah of Gattiawan. Today my husband will go to the funeral pyre. It will be the first time in seven generations that a Gattiawan maharajah will be carried to the cremation grounds unadorned by the diamond. I believe that woman has it, that she grasped her moment to take it when Narayan did not return from his ride.'

Ijahar made a slight movement. A floorboard creaked under his foot.

'You will help me? You will try to recover the diamond?'

I hesitated, but found it impossible to refuse. 'I will try. Usually I look for missing persons. They can be difficult enough to find, but a precious gem . . . ' I almost added that it could be cut and sold, but that seemed too cruel.

'Thank you. The diamond must be returned. You will be well rewarded, Mrs Shackleton.' At the door she turned, 'Can you find your way out?'

'Yes.'

She was gone. Ijahar followed her, closing the door gently behind him.

After a moment or so, I left the room. Ijahar had led me through a concealed door, a servants' door. I found a stair-case, but not the right one. This was wider. Either the original architect, or the gardener who made the additions, had a sense of humour. I found myself on a landing with no way down. Once more, a servant pretended not to see me. I retraced my steps and followed the direction Indira had taken. This brought me to the minstrels' gallery.

Hearing a familiar voice through an open door, I glanced in.

James was speaking reassuringly to Prince Jaya, Narayan's younger brother.

Jaya waited until James had finished.

'Where is your British justice? I hear of it, but I don't see it. The man Osbert should not have been allowed to drown himself. He should have hanged for murdering my brother. And where is the Gattiawan diamond?'

They both saw me.

Conversation stopped.

'Excuse me. James, I was looking for you, but it can wait.'

Jaya gave a polite acknowledgement and took a small step back.

'What is it, Kate?'

'I'm going to Skipton, to the inquest. Just thought I'd mention it.'

'What inquest?' Jaya said sharply.

As if he had not traduced Osbert Hannon, I said, 'The inquest into the death of a young man, Osbert Hannon. He accompanied Maharajah Narayan on his ride. The next morning, when he was on his way to search for him, he drowned.'

Jaya's nose twitched with distaste. 'A royal prince deserved a better escort.'

I did not wait to hear more, but as I left them I caught James's placatory words. 'I realise that for your highness it is very hard to accept that your brother's death . . . '

Fill in the blanks, Kate. A tragic accident. The words were beginning to deserve capital letters.

Thirty

Osbert Hannon's inquest was to be held at Skipton Magistrates Court at 11 a.m. Having spoken to Dr Simonson after he examined Osbert's body, I did not know what else might emerge, but perhaps some small detail would shed light not just on Osbert's death, but the maharajah's.

I had driven a couple of miles along the road when I saw her. She walked slowly, with the plodding gait of someone who has a long way to go before nightfall. Where had I seen that walk recently? I slowed the motor. A few yards beyond her, I pulled in and stopped.

I turned to look at her. She was young, and pregnant. The dark cloak she wore was meant to disguise her condition but it flapped in the breeze. As she drew nearer, I recognised the soft round face of young Jenny Hannon who had come to Bolton Hall when Osbert's body was taken there. I had seen her walk by the river bank, throwing flowers into the torrent. Straight away, I knew where she must be going, and that she would never arrive in time.

As she drew near, I smiled. 'Are you going far, Jenny?'

'To Skipton.'

'So am I. Would you like a lift?'

Her whole body flooded with relief. 'That's what I want, a ride to Skipton. The coal merchant took me a mile on his cart but was turning off.'

'Come on then.'

She spoke more to herself than to me, saying, 'Thank you, Osbert.'

I got out to help her. She shuffled across to the passenger seat. When she was settled, I reached in the back for the motoring blanket. Though the morning was warm, the breeze would soon chill her. 'Here, wrap yourself in this.'

'Thank you.' She drew the plaid blanket around herself.

I had been riding with the canvas down, but now raised it and clicked the sides and roof in place. 'You must be going to the inquest.'

She took a hanky from a pocket and pressed it to her nose. 'I have to do it, though they said I shouldn't. My mother-in-law took a ride into Skipton with Mr Upton. She said I should stop at home, not be out showing meself to the world in my condition. After she had gone, I thought, no, I must go meself. What if Osbert is looking down on the inquest and says, There's my mother, but where's my wife? Or what if they try to say that Osbert did away with himself and I am not there to speak up for him?'

'Surely they won't.'

'A body doesn't know what they will say. And now that you have stopped for me, I know I am right to come. Osbert is looking down and taking care of me.'

She did not look taken care of, but nervous and edgy, as if dreading the ordeal of the inquest. I wish I could have radiated calm, but every nerve still jangled after yesterday's experience. And the image of Osbert lying on the river bank kept coming back into my mind.

As the motor roared into life, we fell silent. She stared ahead along the narrow lanes. We sped past fields and meadows, with always the fells high on the horizon.

Jenny could not make herself comfortable. She shifted in her seat and gave small gasps when a bump in the road caused a jolt.

Ahead of us, a sheep that had been grazing on the grass verge stepped into the road. It began to run ahead, as if herded by the vehicle. Stupid sheep. I slowed down and drove around it.

It must have been my morning for animals because a mile further on, we saw a running dog, a white terrier. It, too, ran ahead of the car as if pursued by devils.

'It thinks you're chasing it. Poor thing.'

The dog darted across the road. I swerved to avoid it. My passenger lurched forward and gave a small cry. I stretched out my arm to catch her. 'Sorry. Are you all right?'

She was turning round, looking back at the dog.

I felt sorry then, and thought I should have stopped for the dog. But today seemed difficult enough without animals throwing themselves in front of me. My mind raced towards the inquest. I felt churned up inside, the way one does when nothing goes right and each new calamity treads on the heels of the one before. After her initial outpouring, Jenny sat tensely silent.

Our journey was uneventful until we passed the church and came into the busy main street in Skipton where a brewer's dray and cart delayed progress.

'Do you know which way we go from here?'

She did not.

I stopped, and asked for directions to the courthouse.

Taking a left turn and a right, I spotted Dr Simonson's Bugatti, parked neatly this time. I pulled in behind it.

'I'll come in with you.'

Although the sun now shone hotly, she pulled her cloak around her. 'Will there be steps?'

As she struggled from the motor she gave a sharp cry.

Straight away, I knew what was coming. No wonder her mother-in-law had told her to stay at home.

She folded her arms tightly around herself, as though this may stop the force of nature.

'Take my arm.'

She opened her mouth to speak, but thought better of it and shook her head.

'Jenny, the baby is coming.'

She clamped her lips tight shut and did not budge from the pavement edge. Biting her lip, she started to nod.

I put my arm around her and had to make an instant choice. Get back in the car and find my way to a hospital, or take her into the building. Another small cry decided me.

'Don't worry. Take steady breaths.'

A man in clerical garb stepped smartly from the pavement into the road, to avoid us. I called to him. 'There will be a doctor in the coroner's court. Please ask him to come to the entrance.'

Perhaps the man was deaf. He hurried on.

We took a few faltering steps. She stopped, screwing up her face, rooting herself to the spot.

I called to a small man in a striped shirt who pushed a

huge racketing wheel barrow along the cobbles, repeating my request.

He let go of his barrow, calling, 'Watch me stuff,' and disappeared inside the building.

I manoeuvred Jenny closer to the entrance.

The wheelbarrow man reappeared. 'I've telled the porter.' He glanced about, checking on the security of his barrow, and then took Jenny's other arm. In this way, we managed to step indoors.

The man was gone in a moment, waving away my thanks.

In the entrance, the porter's cubicle on the right was separated by a window and a ledge with a bell.

The porter was in the hall, barring our way. A tall well-made man, he folded his arms as if to say entry forbidden, eviction no difficulty.

'You've come to the wrong place.'

'This is an emergency.'

He looked from me to Jenny whose cloak had now swung wide.

'You can't come in here for that.'

'It's your office or the hallway.'

He leaned towards Jenny, either ready to catch her if she fell or to spin her around and lead her out. 'There's the hospital on . . .'

Aunt Berta's voice required. 'No time! Fetch Dr Simonson from the coroner's office. This morning's inquest is into the death of this lady's husband.'

Aunt Berta would have added, My good man.

'You should have said.' Recognising defeat, he helped us into his little room.

Gingerly, Jenny began to lower herself onto his chair.

'Oh my God.' The porter turned and ran as her waters broke.

'I'm scared. His mam'll murder me for coming here.'

'She won't murder you before you've had the baby.'

'It int funny.'

I held her hand. 'I know. But isn't it a bit wonderful that you're a country girl and your baby's about to be born in a market town?'

She let out a wail.

'Is it a boy or a girl?'

'Supposed to be a boy.'

'He'll be able to say "My life began in Skipton". What a good start for him. And it's Monday. You couldn't have picked a better day. Monday's child is fair of face, a bonny boy to be born in a bonny place.'

We missed the inquest. Jenny Hannon held a tiny red creature, a boy. He had come into the world quickly, without fuss, as if he knew there was enough trouble already.

The porter provided tea. The older Mrs Hannon squeezed into the tiny office to inspect her grandson. Mr Upton, who had driven Mrs Hannon to Skipton, wisely took his leave. Dr Simonson and I had delivered the baby. He, being versatile, had then attended the delayed inquest. I had done very little, the porter having taken charge of the kettle and provided towels. All the same, I felt exhausted.

Now that it was all over, the porter could not do enough for mother and baby. He had made a couch of two chairs and assumed a proprietary air over the infant. 'If you're short of a name, mine is Arthur.'

Jenny did not look up. 'His name is Osbert.'

'Worth a try. It's not every day I allow my premises to be turned into a lying-in room.'

The doctor and I moved into the hall, carrying our drinks with us.

'What's the verdict?'

'Mother and baby are doing well.' He took a sip of tea and nursed his cup.

'You know very well what I'm asking.'

'Accidental death. Osbert Hannon was tired. He leapt the Strid as he always did, but this time missed his footing.'

'Was anything said that connected his death to that of Prince Narayan?'

'Not directly. Mr Upton said Osbert had searched into the night. Mrs Hannon said how early her son left home to join the search the following morning.'

'The bruise, the abrasion to the back of Osbert's head, you told me you would take a closer look during the post mortem, and discuss it with your colleague.'

'We could not say for sure, but the most likely cause was that the body bumped across the rocks as it was swept from the Strid to the bend in the river where it was found.' He put down his cup. 'Now what are we going to do about that mother and baby?'

'Good question. Shall we see what the grandmother says? Jenny will need bed rest.'

The porter had placed a board over his window. He now sat, somewhat disconsolately, at the edge of the room. He perked up when he saw us, and came to the doorway. 'Talk about cheek. The grandmother's complaining there's nowhere proper for the lass to lie down.'

'I don't want to lie down.' Jenny looked up at me. 'You

take me back, Mrs Shackleton. Osbert sent you to give me a lift and he wanted me to come back with you.'

That was a novel way for me to have my arm twisted.

'Doctor?'

'I might be able to find a hospital bed.'

Mrs Hannon scowled. 'Who'll pay for that? We've no money for hospitals. I would have delivered the baby meself if this lady hadn't brought Jenny into Skipton.' She looked at me accusingly, as if the baby's birth under inauspicious circumstances was entirely my fault. Perhaps she was right.

The question of how Jenny, the baby and the grandmother would travel home, now that Upton had already returned to Bolton Abbey, and the doctor had patients to see, was resolved by Dr Simonson.

He folded blankets from his car for Jenny to sit in my passenger seat, with the baby wrapped in blankets. The older Mrs Hannon, being too stout for the dickey seat, he promised to take to the railway station for the next train to Bolton Abbey.

Every cobble sent a jolt through the motor. As we drove out of Skipton, I noticed the hotel, and then saw a sign to the hospital. 'If you want to rest for a few days, don't think about the money.'

'Take us home. Little Osbert's dad is waiting to see him. His soul won't be free until he has seen his son safely home.'

There was no arguing with that. Driving as steadily as I could, I took us back along the roads we had travelled.

We were a mile on the road out of Skipton when she let out a cry.

'What's the matter?'

'It's that poor little running dog. Stop!'

'I can't see it.'

'Stop!' The baby began to wail. 'Back there by the wall. It's laid itself down to die.' She started to cry. So did the baby.

I stopped the car, climbed out and walked back. There it lay, the little terrier, once white, now caked with mud. Dead already, by the look of it. I drew closer. It opened an eye. It wriggled and gave a piteous whine as I picked it up gently and carried it back to the car.

'It's all right, Jenny. The poor little thing's not dead.'

'Give it to me.'

'No. It's probably running wild with fleas and ticks.'

'Don't let him run off, poor fellow.'

'I'll put him in the dickey seat.'

I wrapped him in my motoring coat, wondering how long it would take his fleas to lay their eggs in the seams, and set the dog down. He gazed at me with a look of almost human gratitude, and then closed his eyes.

When we reached the Hannons' cottage, I lit a fire, boiled a kettle and fried an egg for Jenny.

'I'm not hungry. Give it to dog.'

'No.'

'Halves then.'

'All right.'

Everything for the cradle was ready, along with swaddling clothes that I would leave for the grandma to apply.

Jenny lay back in her bed, the baby at her breast.

'His grandma will be here soon. I'll wait with you till she comes.'

She fell asleep. The dog fell asleep in front of the fire.

It now seemed years since early this morning when Indira had asked me to find the Gattiawan diamond. Such a request now seemed absurd.

I went outside to smoke, and to think. The dog came outside for a piddle, and went back in.

Eventually, Jenny opened her eyes. She looked a little better than earlier.

'Jenny, I have a question for you.'

'I'm too tired.'

'Was it Mr Deakin gave you a lift on his cart this morning?'

'Yes.'

'Did he say anything?'

'That I shouldn't be out. That I should have stopped at home.'

'Did he say anything about the business of the last few days, the things that have happened?'

'He said he saw an Indian on Friday afternoon on Bark Lane, but he was blowed if he would lose a day's work to speak about it in public.'

So Deakin *had* seen an Indian, a stranger. Now that the inquest was over, he felt safe in retelling his story. There was more going on than had yet been uncovered. After everything that had passed, I was determined to get to the heart of the matter, and learn the identity of this mysterious stranger.

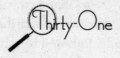

Thirty-One

The afternoon held calm and fine as I drove back towards the hotel from the Hannons' cottage, with blue sky, puffy white clouds and an obliging sun. Yet above the noise of the car's engine, strange sounds penetrated. I slowed down. Where were the noises coming from? Cymbals clashed. Drums rolled. And then I saw that a little further on, the road was lined with villagers. I drew onto the verge, and got out of the car. As I began to walk to where the villagers stood, a gunshot rang out, and another, and another, until I had counted nineteen. I found a spot by the memorial fountain among the spectators. It was their gasp I heard before I saw the start of the procession.

The tread of feet heralded an approaching army.

In a whirlwind of pomp, sound and colour, the procession came into view, led by two richly caparisoned elephants whose keeper twirled a golden rod. Bearers carried a stretcher that bore the late maharajah, covered in jewels that glinted and sparkled in the afternoon sun.

Dressed in ceremonial robes came Maharajah Shivram Halkwaer and Prince Jaya, and the little boy, Rajendra, with a red mark on his forehead. The Duke of Devonshire walked with them. I had never heard a bad word about him, and thought what a terrible thing that this had happened on his estate. A Sikh military escort marched behind, looking neither right nor left. A slew of maharajahs, old and young, bore themselves proudly, followed by more Indian soldiers carrying lighted torches, and by the men I took to be aides-de-camp, now dressed in white garments and scarlet sashes.

James pretended not to see me as he led a group including Sergeant, Upton and men from the estate. They were followed by the band of the North Riding police.

Behind them strode various musicians, beating drums, clashing cymbals.

When they had passed, we spectators lingered, marvelling at the scene that had just passed, the like of which we would never see again.

I walked back to the hotel with Rachel. She wanted news of Osbert's inquest. She took it calmly enough when I told her about Jenny's baby.

'I hated her, but now I pity her.'

As we passed the stable, I asked whether anyone had seen Joel, but she told me that no one had. 'They say things come in threes. I hope he isn't shot or drowned.'

On reaching the hotel, I made for my familiar bench at the rear of the hotel and sat down, mesmerised by the sky; waiting, trying not to imagine what would soon be enacted in the Valley of Desolation.

Down by the river, the flash of a fishing line flying through the air told me that Sykes was not far off. I would take a walk.

I strolled to the river, not making a beeline for my fisherman friend in case someone was watching from the hotel, though our secrecy hardly seemed to matter any more.

He waved as he saw me approach.

'I've kept a Wensleydale cheese sandwich for you. Made by Mrs Sergeant's fair hand. Thought you'd never get here. Did the inquest last this long?'

'No. Something else came up.' Briefly, I told him about Jenny and the baby, and the inquest verdict.

'You'll be hungry then. The sandwich is in the basket . . . oh, wait a minute, you won't want to see the bait, it'll put you off your cheese.' He reeled in his line.

From the basket, he produced a sandwich wrapped in a white tea cloth, a bottle of ginger beer and a glass.

It looked inviting and I realised I was hungry after all.

When he took a penknife from his pocket and released the bottle opener attachment, I saw that his knuckles were grazed.

'How did you do that?'

'Oh, a fish jumped out of my hand.'

'A fish called Thurston Presthope?'

'Looked more like a brown trout to me. But he won't be bothering you again.'

'I wish you wouldn't.'

'Well, when you don't get a bite, you have to do something.' He poured the ginger beer.

'I don't care about Presthope, but it would do my business no good to have you charged with assault.'

'No fear of that.'

I bit into the sandwich. Cheese and pickle. Can't beat it.

'Deakin, the coal merchant, he told Osbert's widow that he saw an Indian on Bark Lane.'

'I'm not surprised. He probably did. The man wants a quiet life, not to be questioned by the boys in blue and called to give evidence at an inquest, losing a day's work because of it.'

A couple of ducks came paddling up, waddling from the water to investigate my sandwich. 'Go away. The sixpenny visitors ruin you. You've had more to eat than I have today.'

"Do you want to know where Joel is?'

'You've heard something?'

'Seen, more like. I was up before daybreak and saw smoke rising on the horizon. An hour later, the sky in that spot was clear, so I knew it hadn't come from a cottage or a farm-house chimney. I did a little exploring. He's living rough in the woods. Made himself a bender, as they call it, shaping branches like gipsies do. He has a blanket, and a tucked away little pot.'

'Did he see you?'

'No. Maybe he was off shooting a hare. I kept out of sight until he came back, with summat in a bag slung over his shoulder. I didn't let on.'

'I wonder why none of the estate workers found him and persuaded him to come back to work.'

'They'll know where he is right enough. They're turn-ing a blind eye until it's all over. They suspect he may have shot the prince.' He looked at me steadily. 'Did he, do you think?'

'I don't know. But perhaps it's time to find out. Where is this bender? Joel must be lonely, and in need of a visitor.'

'Be careful, Mrs Shackleton. You wouldn't weigh his brain

against a calf's, but if he had a hand in the prince's death he could be dangerous.'

'I helped his dad. That will count for something with him.'

Sykes began to pack up his fishing gear. 'Let's go together. I can show you.'

'No. I don't want to scare him.'

'If that's what you want.'

'It is. Where will I find him?'

'Drive beyond the remains of an old tower, Barden Tower. The wood is a little way on from there. On the map it's called Nelly Park Wood. Walk through the wood, across a bridge, and by a waterfall. You'll come to a ford, he's camped out a little ahead of that off to the left, away from the path. It's about four miles from here. If you walk, you get to the ruined tower beyond the Strid.'

It was not the four miles to the wood that decided me to drive, but the four miles back. Checking that I had walking boots in the motor, I set off along the road that took me by Bolton Hall and up into the country. The only difficulty about coming this way was that in summer landmarks can hide behind branches, and one wood looks very much like another. People who know the names of their woods do not feel the need to erect signposts or nameplates for the convenience of strangers. Eventually, I spotted the tower. I stopped, consulted the map, and then continued to what I took to be the edge of Nelly Park Wood. There, I changed into my boots and slipped on a long cardigan.

Waterfalls and rushing water may never again hold the same appeal for me. How to do this, I wondered. Pretend to

265

be on a country walk. Stumble across Joel. Say, Excuse me young man, have you shot anyone lately?

Brambles and ferns had grown over a path. Sykes must have been a secret boy scout to have located this spot. Just as I began to think I had taken a wrong turn, there was the bender. A blanket lay over the bent branches, as if to be aired.

I drew closer. 'Joel!'

No answer.

Perhaps he was asleep.

I peered inside. He had spread bracken on the ground, giving the hollowed out space the appearance of a child's den. A cooking pot stood just inside the bender, along with spoon and fork. He certainly showed signs of being able to take care of himself.

Now I regretted bringing the motor. If he was out and about, he might see it on the road and avoid coming back here.

Undecided whether to find my way back to the bridge and wait, or to sit here, I leaned against an oak tree.

From the corner of my eye, I caught a rapid movement. Expecting to see a bird or squirrel, I turned to look. It was the toe of a swinging boot. A boot, a trouser leg, a Joel, sitting on a branch high in the next tree. This was how the Cheshire cat materialised for Alice.

'Joel, what are you doing up there?'

'I been sitting here. Heard someone coming. Didn't know who it was.'

So much for pretending that I happened to be walking through the woods.

'People are worried about you.'

'Who?'

'I am. I wondered where you'd got to when you didn't come to work.'

'It was my fault. They know it was my fault.'

'What was your fault?'

'What happened was my fault.'

I wanted to hold up my hand and say, Stop! Would this be a confession of murder? I would be obliged to report it. No wonder his neighbours and workmates had let him disappear quietly.

He kicked his heels against the tree trunk. 'She was my pet, my little doe.'

He wanted to talk. I must let him speak.

Silence.

Now that he had begun, he must continue. I prompted. 'You were sad about the white doe, your pet.'

'Yes.'

Silence.

I glanced up at him. 'You saw the Indian prince in the barn, and you were angry.'

He was holding on to the branch with both hands. 'No. Didn't see him there, except in my dream. Didn't see no one. Just my doe.'

'But you were in the barn. I saw you. Yesterday.'

'I saw his ghost but not him. I only seed him in the wood, dead. Didn't see no prince till in the wood. Told you. You was there, with my dad.'

'Then why are you hiding? You haven't done anything wrong.'

The branch creaked a little under his weight. 'My dad is badly. I made my dad poorly.'

'Is that it? Is that why are you hiding? Because if so, you are wrong. What happened to your dad comes from inside, not from anything outside that another person does.'

'Because I told him. I made him poorly. I upset him inside.'

'How did you upset him?'

'He didn't tell me. No one told me. Only Osbert told me.'

'What did Osbert tell you?'

'When he jumped the Strid on Saturday morning, he said it couldn't be helped. He said he couldn't have stopped the Indian shooting her. I didn't know because my dad didn't tell me. Nobody did, 'cept Osbert. He telled me.'

'What happened when he told you?'

Joel rocked back and forth on the branch. It shook and groaned. 'I wouldn't let Osbert pass. He said I must let him pass. I wouldn't let him pass. He pushed me. I pushed him back. He fell. I tried to get him out the water. He floated away, bumping along, under and over, under and over.'

I sat down on the ground. It looked dry but a damp coldness seeped through my skirt and stockings. Above me, Joel's feet swung back and forth, back and forth, like the feet of a corpse hanging from the scaffold.

Joel Withers had killed Osbert Hannon.

Still his feet swung back and forth.

'My doe is gone. Osbert is drowned. My dad is poorly. I should have taken better care of my doe.'

Joel Withers killed Osbert Hannon out of love for a doe.

'Come down out of the tree.'

'Why should I?'

'Looking up at you is making my neck hurt.'

'I like to be up tree. I can climb higher, and you can come up here.'

'No thank you.'

I lifted his blanket from the bender, folded it and sat with my back to the tree trunk. If he came down clumsily, he would land on my head. That might be a relief. I would have a very good excuse for retiring from the case.

I have to go home now due to a headache – or a crushed skull – caused by a gormless lad who inadvertently drowned his friend because of a wild animal's death, and then fell on my head.

After a long time, Joel said, 'I don't know who to tell.'

'You have told me.'

'It is my fault. People with great fault go to hell.'

The wood was quite silent. Not a leaf stirred, not a bird called.

'Did you mean to push him in the river?'

'No. He can't swim. I can't swim.'

'If you didn't mean to do it, it was an accident.'

Manslaughter, a court might say.

'I went to tell her, to tell Jenny and Mrs Hannon. I dare not knock on the door.'

'Do you think you must tell them?'

'My dad said no. He said tell no one. But it mun come out of me.'

Was it too late for him to tell the Hannons, or too soon? 'Jenny is very tired today. She had a baby boy. She and the baby may be sleeping.'

'I'll tell 'em while they sleep. And I'll tell 'em when they wake. This morning there was no one there, not Jenny, not Mrs Hannon.'

'They were in Skipton. They are back now.'

He slid from the tree.

I stood.

He picked up his blanket and his pot.

'Wait, Joel. Let me come with you. We'll go together.'

When Mrs Hannon saw Joel, she was glad that he had come. She gave us both tea, and him bread, and asked him to chop wood and draw water from the well.

He did.

I sat beside Jenny and the sleeping baby.

When Joel brought the pail of water, Jenny waved him over. 'Come and look at the baby.'

He stared at the infant, and reached down to touch its tiny hand.

'You are a good lad, Joel,' Mrs Hannon said. 'The doctor says they will find a place for you near the hospital. You can make yourself useful to them there, and to the old folk in the almshouses, and you will be near your dad.'

Jenny handed the baby to Joel. 'Set him in the cradle you made. It's all ready for him. He'll like it.'

The rescued dog, scratching its ear and looking a little brighter, viewed proceedings from its spot on the rag rug.

When he had placed the baby in the cradle, Joel poured water from the pail to the jug.

'It was my fault Osbert fell in the water. I shouted at him for letting the Indian kill my doe. I pushed him.'

Jenny looked up. Her mouth fell open.

'Nay lad, you allus think summat is your fault. Jenny, pay him no heed.' Mrs Hannon turned to me. 'His mam died and

270

he thought it was his fault, isn't that right, Joel? These things are no one's fault. We mun go on as best we can.'

'What am I to do?' Joel asked.

'Get yerself off to yon hospital while they'll have you. And tek that little terrier with you if you must have a pet. We've enough mouths to feed here without a dog.'

Joel bobbed down on his haunches. Making a beak of his fingers, he caught a flea from the dog's neck. 'I'll have my work cut out taking care of this little fellow.' He squashed a flea's egg between his thumbnails.

I hoped that no one would take a shotgun to Joel's new pet. Heaven help them if they did.

'Come on, Joel. We'll let Jenny rest. I'll give you a lift to the hospital and we'll see how your dad is getting on.'

As we drove back along the road, I saw that a marquee and a dozen tents of various shapes and sizes had mushroomed on the hill at the rear of Bolton Hall. White-clad figures darted in and out, or perched on their haunches, looking about them, chatting to each other. I stopped the car as I drew level with Mr Cummings who stood by a wheelbarrow loaded with old army blankets.

He looked at us in surprise. 'You found him then? I could do with a hand here. Will you shift yourself, Joel?'

Joel stared at Cummings. I guessed that in his mind, Joel had already left this place and was at the hospital with his father.

'What's going on, and what do you want us to do?'

'Oh, not you madam. But you see, it's the maharajahs. They all arrived for the funeral. Each one brought a train-load of servants and hangers-on. There isn't room for them all inside.'

'And you don't look well. Are you all right?'

He shook his head. 'There's sickness going round the village. I hope you don't get it, madam, or you'll be feeling none too clever.'

I climbed from the car. 'Here, let me help you. Give me and Joel some of those blankets.' He made as if to refuse. 'Come on, I was in the VAD during the war. I'm used to lending a hand.'

When Joel got out of the car, the little dog jumped into the driver's seat and sat there, looking important. Perhaps he thought his new life would always include a flea picker and a chauffeur.

We walked among the tents, listening to the chatter of strange tongues, watched by hundreds of eyes.

A cross-legged man played a flute. From a basket in front of him rose a graceful snake, peering about with a curling movement of elegant indifference.

Suddenly a shot rang out. All the men in the makeshift camp jumped to their feet and stood statue still, heads bowed.

Another shot, and another. It was the gun salute. Prince Narayan Halkwaer had been surrendered to the flames.

Thirty-Two

Smoke still rose from the distant funeral pyre.

Reaching the hotel, I decided against looking about to see whether Sykes was loitering in the grounds, waiting to hear about my encounter with Joel. Having squeezed in so many tête-à-têtes, we would be in danger of raising eyebrows.

I was not in a hurry to see him. Once a policeman, always a policeman; he had been out of the force for several years, but never quite shook off his desire to put a hand on a person's shoulder and say, 'Come along with me, chummy.' I believe his biggest regret in moving into private detection was the lack of a pair of handcuffs. I did not want to hear the word manslaughter in relation to a young lad who would live forever with the nightmare of having caused his friend's death. If Joel insisted on repeating his story and someone went to the police, then so be it. I would do my best to see that he was well-defended.

Cummings was standing in the hotel doorway, staring across at the smoke. He touched his cap, held the door for me, and then followed me into the foyer.

At the desk he handed me my key. 'And there's a message for you, madam. Came earlier today.'

I took the envelope from him, recognising James's handwriting.

No doubt he was still at the funeral. I wondered how long it might last.

I would be glad when this day was over. The only bright spots were seeing a baby come into the world, and finding that the mangy dog on the road was still alive.

A bath and a change of clothing would be the best next step. I took the note back to my room, kicked off my shoes and slit open the envelope. James wrote,

Dear Kate,

Regarding the missing diamond, the constable has searched Presthope's house but there is no sign of the jewel. Presthope vehemently denies having seen it, much less stolen it. All the likely banks have been approached, in the hope that the maharajah saw fit to take a deposit box, but to no avail.

Fortunately, Mr Chana has recovered a goodly sum of the money Presthope acquired, but that is small consolation.

The main suspect in regard to the diamond remains Lydia Metcalfe. I attempted to have her trunks at the Dorchester examined. The manager refuses, insisting that she be present and a court order obtained. This is being processed. Since she is here and her trunks are there, the manager's intransigence will ensure no one gains access to her luggage in the meantime.

Please remain vigilant.

If you do not see me, it is because I am kept busy here with the new arrivals from Kapurthala, Rajpipla, Nawanger,

*Kalathal and Baroda. His Grace and my superiors were keen
that Maharajah Narayan be given a suitable send off but this
has caused much disruption. Arrangements are proceeding
smoothly. The astonishing Constable Brocksup managed to
commandeer two obliging elephants from a passing circus. The
difficulty lies in accommodating the Indian royal families.
Each family has brought its own team of cooks, each team
expecting sole occupancy of a kitchen. Since there is only one
kitchen at Bolton Hall, under the command of a very
determined woman who flourishes a wooden spoon in a most
aggressive manner, catering arrangements are posing an
insurmountable difficulty.*

   Your affectionate cousin,

   James

Unaccountably, his letter cheered me. Perhaps it was
because I knew I would shortly have supper, served from a
kitchen supervised by the excellent Mrs Sergeant.

Also, I had wondered who conjured the elephants. Arch
enemy Brocksup's initiative matched his cunning and his
contempt for me.

Reluctantly, I decided that James was on the right track
in suspecting Lydia Metcalfe of stealing the diamond. She
knew the combination of the safe in the prince's room; otherwise, he would not have had the surprise gift of emerald
clover earrings, necklace and bracelet locked in the hotel
safe.

I gathered up towel and sponge bag to head for the bathroom. Just as I was about to open the door, there was a tap
on the window.

It was Sykes.

Having a ground-floor room brings certain disadvantages.

I put down towel and sponge bag and opened the window.

He made as if he had just paused in that particular spot to smoke a cigarette. Keeping his back to me, he said, 'I was sitting round the back on our bench. I thought you would come to find me. What happened in the woods?'

'I saw Joel. He did not kill the maharajah.'

Sykes said. 'Didn't think he had, poor blighter. What ails him?'

'I'll tell you about it later.'

'Anything else?'

'We'll find a moment to speak after supper. I'll walk in the grounds.'

Sykes moved away from the window.

Once more I picked up my sponge bag and the bath salts that Mrs Sugden had thoughtfully packed. As I walked along the corridor to the bathroom, I wondered whether James and the India Office were cleverer than I had given them credit for.

Could the rivalry between Gattiawan and Kalathal have provided a motive for the maharajah's murder? Narayan was young, energetic, emotional, and probably ambitious. The Maharajah of Kalathal may have calculated that with Narayan gone Kalathal would prevail. There could be nothing more designed to knock the stuffing from a man than to take his son and heir from him.

By inviting the maharajahs to the funeral, perhaps the Secretary of State for India hoped to bring matters to a head and discover the culprit.

I ran the water, watching it swirl onto my bath salts.

Where was the Gattiawan diamond? It would be so easy to hide, so difficult to find.

An early night was called for. Supper over, no new inspiration as to the murder or the theft of the diamond came to mind. I dealt myself a hand of solitaire, determined not to cheat.

As I pondered about moving a seven of diamonds, there was a knock on the door.

What fresh hell is this, I wondered.

The answer to my 'Who is it?' was a murmur; a female voice. I turned the key.

It took a few seconds to realise that it was Mrs Metcalfe, and not Lydia. They are about the same height, and with a family resemblance in the way they hold themselves. It was the quality of the clothing that first told me this could not possibly be Lydia. Mrs Metcalfe was muffled up in a brown coat with turned up collar, a navy check scarf tied under her chin.

As I opened the door wider, the light fell on her troubled face and anxious pale blue eyes above a web of fine lines that I had not noticed before.

'Mrs Metcalfe, is something wrong?'

She nodded. 'I came across in the pony and trap.'

'You had better come in.'

'I didn't know who to tell.'

'Tell what?'

'I hope you don't mind my coming straight to your room.'

'How did you know which room I'm in?'

'One of the chambermaids was at school with my youngest daughter, but I don't want to get her into trouble.'

It was probably the same across the whole area. Everyone would have some friendship or kinship with everyone else. Small wonder that Thurston Presthope had been able to attempt fraud by destroying what he thought to be incriminating evidence, and that everyone knew that Joel made a pet of the white doe and had killed the prince, even though he had not.

'What is the matter?'

'Our Lydia has gone.'

'Gone where?'

'I don't know. That's why I've come to you. She went to bed last night, well, early hours of this morning I should say. She plays cards by herself and keeps the fire going till all hours. She'd been marching about, making a racket. She doesn't live by the same clocks as we do. This morning she was up at ten o'clock and had breakfast. She left the house at about eleven, and said she was going out for a drive.'

'What in?'

'That's what I said. I thought she must be coming to see you, since you have a motor. I said would she be in for dinner. No she wouldn't. Would she be in for tea? She might, she might not. Don't wait for her. Well she wasn't back at teatime; she didn't come in for supper. And I'd a lot on my plate today. She'll come back when she's ready, I thought. Only she didn't. I went to her room, and I see all her jewellery is gone and that little bag she had, and her case. Well they weren't in her hands when she went out so she must have stashed them somewhere. How could she go off like that, without a word?'

Very easily, I guessed, probably chuckling to herself at her cleverness. 'The Rolls-Royce is under lock and key.'

278

'I went to the railway station, made out I was passing like. Asked when the trains would be back to normal as I have a relative wanting to visit. Well they would have told me if Lydia had caught a train, mentioned it at least.'

So the bird had flown.

Mrs Metcalfe bit her lip.

And then it dawned on me. Lydia was not one to let a locked door block her route to freedom. 'Come on. We will take a look.'

Sykes had retrieved my satchel from the barn. I picked up my flashlight and put it in my pocket.

We walked along the hall. Mrs Metcalfe led the way to the hotel's side door. 'I don't want to cause a kafuffle.'

A moon was barely visible behind the clouds. In one of the stables, a horse whinnied.

The Rolls had been garaged in an unused stable, but which one? We walked from stable to stable. I shone the torch. A door swung ajar. Inside, a crowbar leaned against the inner wall.

Mrs Metcalfe picked it up. 'That's our crowbar. How did she walk the lane without drawing attention? She must have crossed the fields.'

'Thanks for coming to tell me. At least now you know.'

Mrs Metcalfe held the crowbar, as if weighing it. 'Not so much as a goodbye.'

We walked together to her pony and trap.

'Try not to worry.'

'I'm past worrying about Lydia. It's how her dad's going to rant and rave about her just up and offing.'

'Do you have any idea where she may have gone?'

'Where else but London?' She sighed and placed the

crowbar on the seat. 'Well I'll know what to do if I'm set upon by highwaymen on the way home.'

I watched her turn around the trap. The pony trotted steadily out of the stable yard and along the road.

At times like these, I am glad that my father is chief superintendent of the West Riding Constabulary. I preferred to have more definite information before putting James in the picture.

Back in the hotel, I noticed that Mr Sergeant's office door was ajar. He had been avoiding me since the embarrassing moment when he admitted having passed my photographic negatives to the constable.

I tapped on his door. Acting as though there was no rancour between us, I asked for the use of his telephone.

Of course, he could not do enough for me. 'Please feel free, Mrs Shackleton.'

He tactfully exited the office, but before he had time to disappear, I took advantage of his contrite attitude. 'I would much appreciate it, Mr Sergeant, if you could send a message to Mr James Rodpen at the Hall and ask if he will find time to call on me as soon as convenient.'

He agreed and straight away summoned Cummings.

I closed the office door, and placed my call.

After a waiting time that seemed like an eternity, the call came through.

Mother answered. 'Kate! Mrs Sugden tells me you are still at Bolton Abbey. How lovely! Will you be staying long?'

I knew that tone. It was a prelude to her saying that she might just consider joining me.

'Not much longer. In fact I may be going to London.'

'Then you must visit Aunt Berta. I had a letter today. She tells me James is in Yorkshire.'

'Actually James and I are collaborating on something to do with his work, and I'd like to speak to Dad about it if he is there.'

The penny dropped. 'I see, yes. Well I am glad to hear James is with you.' She tried to hide her disappointment and almost managed it. 'Your father is at my shoulder. Goodbye, dear.'

'Bye.' Now I felt bad. I would have to arrange some pleasurable mother and daughter outing soon.

My father listened to my request. 'That should not be too difficult, Kate. A red-haired woman driving a white Rolls-Royce along the Great North Road is bound to have attracted attention. And you have the number plate?'

I did, and gave it to him.

'Stay by the telephone. I will see what I can do.'

For thirty-five minutes, I sat by the office telephone. Finally, it rang.

'Do you have a pencil?' He wastes no time in coming to the point.

'Yes.'

James burst in. 'What is it? I came straight away . . . '

He saw that I was on the telephone, and stood over me, trying to listen. I pushed him away as I jotted down details.

'I have sightings in Doncaster, where she stopped for petrol at 1700 hours, and at Retford, where she was cautioned for driving too fast. She has now stopped for the night in Grantham, registered at the hotel as Miss Lydia Metcalfe.'

'So she is using her own name. And what hotel?'

'I'm coming to that. It's the Angel and Royal. Apparently,

it is where Richard III signed the Duke of Buckingham's death warrant.'

James peered over my shoulder as I wrote.

'Is there anything else I can do, Kate?'

James heard the comment. 'Have her arrested!'

'Shut up, James. Thanks, Dad. I'll call you back if we need any more help. Oh, just one thing. If she makes any telephones calls, it would be useful to know whom she contacts.'

'I'll do what I can.'

I put down the telephone. James was practically hopping from one foot to the other. 'We must stop her.'

'We have no grounds for her arrest. We know where she is going . . .'

'Where?'

'London of course. You could have someone from Scotland Yard waiting at the hotel, with a court order. There may be time for one of the maharajah's representatives to catch a night train, and to search her luggage.'

James is never happy until he has had a good grumble. 'How could they be so careless as to not keep a proper eye on the stables? I gave strict instructions.'

'Osbert Hannon and Isaac Withers were the mainstay of the stables. Don't forget how many men have been commandeered to deal with everything that is going on at the Hall. No one expected Lydia Metcalfe to turn up with a crowbar . . .'

'A crowbar?'

'And break in.'

James lit a cigarette. 'Why did no one see her here, or on the road? All this in broad daylight.'

'Everyone was caught up with Osbert Hannon's inquest, or the cremation. And you have seen what people are like round here. They play their cards close to their chest.'

'Once she gets to London, she will be able to lose herself and pass on the diamond.'

'Assuming she has the diamond.'

'Why else would she disappear without a word?' James drummed his fingers on the manager's desk. 'With her protector gone, she took one last gamble by stealing the diamond.' He snapped his fingers in an unfamiliar gesture of decisiveness. 'We will do this together, you, me, Chana and Scotland Yard. How fast do you reckon Lydia Metcalfe will drive?'

'About twenty-five miles an hour?'

'There must be an overnight train.'

A sudden thought struck me. Earlier in the day I had passed the aeroplane, looking lonely and out of place in a nearby field. 'How long did it take the duke and maharajah to fly from Croydon?'

'No time at all. That beast eats up the miles, well over a hundred an hour.'

'There's the answer. Pull some strings, James. You, Mr Chana and I will take to the air.'

Thirty-Three

The pounding on the door was accompanied by Mr Sergeant's voice. 'Mrs Shackleton! An urgent telephone call.'

'Thank you. I'll be there in a jiffy.'

Hurriedly, I finished dressing and made my way to his office.

Sergeant ushered me in. 'It's a police superintendent.'

As if needing to be sure he had discharged his duty, he handed me the receiver. For a few seconds, he hovered, perhaps hoping to catch a few words. So I simply said, 'Hello,' and not 'Hello, Dad.'

'I have a message from the manager of the Angel and Royal. Miss Metcalfe asked him to telephone the Dorchester to say that she would arrive at about two o'clock.'

Mr Sergeant closed the door behind him.

'And has she left yet?'

'Yes, and without paying her bill. You'll have your work cut out with that one. Be careful!'

'We will. Everything is under control. We're a crack team, and we'll be travelling by aeroplane.'

'Then I'd better not tell your mother. She'd love to take to the skies.'

We were in a rather nice Bentley, driven by the duke's chauffeur. Mr Chana sat in front.

James and I sat in the back. I could tell he was excited at the prospect of a flight. 'We're lucky to have the aeroplane this morning. She'll shortly be on her way to Copenhagen, to take part in the reliability trials between Copenhagen and Gothenburg.'

'Will we all fit?' Most of the pictures I had seen of flying machines showed single-seat affairs, or space for a single passenger.

'It has cabin space for four passengers. We'll be fully enclosed, Kate, so don't fret about your hair. The pilot sits behind us in an open cockpit. And don't worry, because he is very experienced.'

'Don't keep telling me not to worry. You will make yourself nervous.'

The motor came to a halt by a field gate.

The aeroplane sat in a field of stubble, its engine running.

The chauffeur opened my door and I stepped out, and through the gate.

An engineer dressed in navy overalls, goggles on his head, came to meet us.

James bounded forward to chat to him.

Mr Chana fell into step with me. He had taken my valise from the chauffeur and carried that in one hand and his own Gladstone bag in the other.

'Have you flown before, Mr Chana?'

'I took lessons at the same time as Maharajah Narayan. He

285

had planned to undertake a long distance flight, and we would have a machine with dual controls.'

'You were the aide-de-camp closest to him?'

'Yes. It will be a source of eternal regret that I allowed that woman to persuade him to travel alone with her and just the fool of a valet.'

Something nagged at me. Now was not the moment to ask, against the background of a noisy engine and a spinning propeller. But in expressing regret, Chana had let down his guard and it would be foolish to miss the moment.

'Mr Chana, who else besides you and the astrologer knew that Maharajah Narayan intended to marry Miss Metcalfe in about ten days' time?'

There was a brief hesitation, and then it was as if a steel shutter came down. 'The maharajah and I took several flying lessons. He had a talent for it.'

He had heard me, but that was his answer.

No comment.

I had been clumsy, and my question was badly timed.

The stink of oil filled the air. Empty Castrol tins lay on the ground.

It was obvious from the way my cousin and the engineer parted as we approached that James had asked him to reassure me.

The man was a typical airman type, tall, good-looking and with the obligatory moustache.

'Anyone not flown before?' he bellowed to be heard above the noise.

I put up my hand.

'Some ladies fear giddiness, as when going up in a lift or looking down at the ground from a great height. This won't

286

be the sensation you'll have today. It is the connection with the ground that causes dizziness. Remove the ground, remove the sensation. Be prepared for a thrilling experience, dear lady.'

'I don't easily become giddy.'

'Glad to hear it. By the time we touch down in Croydon, I guarantee that you will be a convert to aviation.'

He took the bags from Mr Chana and shimmied up the ladder into the cabin, and back down.

We moved closer to the noisy plane.

'Any questions?' the engineer shouted.

'Will we fly By Bradshaw?' James asked.

'We will, and cruising at 95 miles per hour.'

James clambered up first, waiting in the cabin doorway to give me a hand. 'Flying By Bradshaw means we follow the railway lines. I have some flying lessons booked so have been reading up.'

I took my seat, next to the luggage.

James and Chana sat on the row in front.

Behind me, the pilot tapped to gain my attention, gave me a big wink and a thumbs up.

Within moments, we were revving across the field of stubble. With inches to spare before the drystone wall would have brought us to a crashing halt, the plane began to rise.

I looked down at the receding, flattening ground.

We crossed the countryside. The pattern of fields mesmerised me, with so many shades of green, tiny doll houses, and villages whose inhabitants paused in their work to look up at the sky.

Thirty-Four

Our journey in the aeroplane and from Croydon aerodrome in an official motor car created a sense of camaraderie between James, Mr Chana and me. Like the three musketeers, we entered the Dorchester Hotel

In all my visits to London, I had never before set foot in the splendid Dorchester with its high ceilings, sweeping staircase, tiled floor and golden walls adorned with gigantic, ornate looking glasses. Small wonder that Lydia wanted to return if she had become accustomed to such opulence.

A minor royal glided by in her finery, totally self-absorbed, seeing no one.

We three walked towards the desk. James paused, and with the merest gesture attempted to dismiss me and Mr Chana in the direction of two gilt chairs. 'Take the weight off your feet. I'll ask for the manager and ascertain state of play.'

By this, I took it that he meant to find out whether an officer from Scotland Yard had arrived with a court order, demanding that Lydia's trunks be inspected, and whether Lydia had registered.

Chana was quicker off the mark than I. 'Since I am named

in the court order as representative of the Maharajah of Gattiawan, I must come with you.'

James threw me a crumb. 'Keep your eyes peeled, in case she flits through. It is almost two o'clock.'

They left me to sit on a gilt chair by the wall. Naturally, James thought himself on home ground. As his country bumpkin cousin, I might offer a flat vowel, or call the looking glass a mirror.

Two well-clad Arab women, only their darting eyes visible, glided through the foyer, followed at a respectful distance by a heavyweight male retainer. An Indian woman and her daughter, their richly coloured saris gleaming, descended the stairs in stately fashion. Who was that actress, I wondered, her pearls glinting against the dark red silk dress?

After a few moments, James and Mr Chana returned. James did not look pleased. 'She is not here, and they still insist that the trunks cannot be opened except in her presence.'

Chana glanced towards the door as someone came in. 'His late highness's suite is booked for the whole of August and the first two weeks of September. I expect she will take advantage of that.'

James looked at his watch. 'Where is she?'

We did not look like three relaxed individuals enjoying the pleasures of the hotel. A passing gentleman gave us an odd glance.

Chana marched to the door and brushed past the commissionaire, presumably to look out for the Rolls-Royce.

'James, if Lydia sees you and Chana before you see her, she will hightail it for the Ritz.'

'I suppose you are right.'

'Go order afternoon tea. Draw Mr Chana off from the door. I'll see what I can do about checking her whereabouts.'

'How do you propose to do that? If you tell me, I'll see to it.'

'Leave it to me, James. I still have a little influence at Scotland Yard.'

'I thought that friend of yours went to America to help the FBI.'

'He is not the only apple in the barrel.'

'If it's the assistant commissioner or the . . . '

'Trust me for as long as it takes you to order tea.'

I watched from the telephone booth while I waited to be connected to Scotland Yard.

James gathered up Chana. They walked across the foyer and entered a sitting room.

Now that my friend Marcus Charles had gone to America, I had lost that particular contact. But at a supper given by Aunt Berta, Marcus's boss, a commander, was most flattering in regard to my solving a particularly unpleasant crime. The commander's late wife had been a supporter of women's suffrage. After she died, he felt sorry about having roundly mocked her and took the revolutionary turn of becoming a lukewarm supporter of females, when he could be discreet about it. Fortunately men of such rank are almost always at their desk, and he was.

I gave the commander Lydia Metcalfe's description, the details of the Rolls-Royce, and the name of the public house where she was brought up by her aunt and uncle. I even included the fact that before taking on the public house, the uncle had been a tightrope walker with a circus and had attracted his first customers by walking the tightrope from his pub to the opposite side of the street.

'Yes I have heard all about this person, Miss Metcalfe. She sounds like a female who shops a great deal.'

'I don't believe she would go shopping before coming here. If she is at a West End store, she will almost certainly have an account in the name of Maharajah Narayan Halkwaer.'

'Stay by the telephone, dear lady. You are right to speak to me. I wish more of our men made use of this instrument but they seem absurdly shy of it.'

It was a good half hour before he returned my call to tell me the white Rolls-Royce was parked outside the Earl of Ellesmere public house in Bethnal Green.

I could have popped in to tell James and Chana, but it seemed a pity to disturb their tea. It would be quicker to find a taxi and go there myself. Taking out my notebook, I scribbled a message for the page boy to take to James. "Gone to fetch LM from her aunt and uncle's pub. Wait here, eyes peeled, in case I miss her."

That would teach him not to leave me sitting on a gilt chair.

One forgets what a large place London is, a series of villages each with its distinctive character.

The elderly cab driver had already shown barely suppressed surprise at my choice of destination. Now, as he pulled up outside the Earl of Ellesmere, the taxi driver whistled his admiration at the sight of the Rolls-Royce. 'Not often you see a motor like that in a street like this.'

'No indeed. Do you know this pub?'

'Sorry, missis, I don't. My fares is mostly up west. I'll have an empty cab driving back there, see if I don't.'

This was meant to prompt a decent tip, so I duly obliged.

'Do you want me to wait for you?'

'No thank you. I'll be coming back in the Rolls.'

'Good for you, missis. Enjoy it while you're young.'

I was not quite sure what he meant by that, but never mind.

As the cab drove off, a young constable swaggered towards me. He was a tall, well-built fellow who would pack a punch and not be slow to draw his truncheon.

'Afternoon, Mrs Shackleton.' He could not resist throwing out his chest.

'Good afternoon, constable.'

'I've orders to stay nearby, should you need me.'

'Thank you. I hope that won't be necessary. Perhaps you wouldn't mind keeping out of sight.'

He nodded, and tapped his nose in music hall fashion. 'Rely on me.'

He walked on a little way.

I glanced up at the name above the door, Landlord Joseph Mudge.

Pushing open the heavy, brass-handled door, I hoped no one inside had seen the bobby speaking to me.

Entering a pub alone is something I have to brace myself for. There is an odd sensation when a room of normal size becomes enormous and traversing it feels like crossing a continent. Heads turned to look as I stepped directly into a lounge bar with the usual wall seats, round tables and stools, and the usual smell of beer and old cigarette smoke. A large door to my right was emblazoned with the words *Concert*

Room. So this was where Lydia spent her childhood, tap-dancing her heart out, practising her smile, picking up the knack of conquering hearts.

Look as if you belong, I told myself as I approached the bar where a stout woman was polishing a glass. Beyond her was another bar, which I guessed must be the tap room.

'Hello. I'm meeting Lydia here.'

She looked surprised, as well she might. 'Lydia's in the back.'

I tried to look as if I knew my way to the back, but did not succeed.

She pointed. 'Door next to the concert room.'

I knocked.

Lydia's cheerful voice yelled, 'Come in, Freddie.'

I came in. Lydia sat at a round table covered in a check cloth. Opposite her was an older woman, her red hair wound around metal curlers partially concealed by a green cotton turban. Her head resembled a rock covered by cockle shells.

'Hello, Lydia.' In spite of not being Freddie, I marched up to the table.

Lydia glared at me. 'Where did you spring from?'

A quick lie was called for. 'Your mother said I'd find you here. I know how much you value your jewellery so I thought I'd pop in and let you know that one of your emerald earrings rolled under the bed at the Cavendish Arms.'

'Where is it then?'

'Waiting for you at the Dorchester.'

Lydia scowled.

The older woman pursed her lips and widened her eyes in an exaggerated fashion, 'Oooh, hark at that, eh? You don't even miss an emerald now, Liddy.'

In for a penny, in for a pound. I smiled at the woman. 'You must be Lydia's aunt Emily. Your sister says hello.'

'Does she now? Well you better sit down, Mrs . . . '

'Shackleton.'

'. . . and name your poison.'

'I'll have what you're having, Mrs Mudge.' There was a cheap tin tray on the table, etched with an image of the Taj Mahal. 'That's nice.'

Just keep on lying, I told myself.

The aunt picked up the tray. 'Isn't it? My present from India. Best out of harm's way.' She carried it to an over-crowded sideboard and slid it to stand at the back, behind flowers under a glass dome, candlesticks, a fruit bowl and a china dog.

'India. Doesn't it make you melt when Liddy talks about it?' She turned to her niece. 'Does your friend know about your palace, Liddy?'

Lydia smoothed her hair. 'I might have mentioned it.'

'Tell her. Tell her about the marble halls, the satin cush-ions embroidered with gold, the silk bedding, the parrot, the sunken bath. Tell her about the journey to the hills in the hot weather. Tell her about the elephants. She loves it there, don't you? It's become her spiritual home, and we're all going to visit one fine day.'

'It's true. India gets under your skin. I shall go back. That palace and everything in it is mine.'

'Tell her about how the maharajah gave you the pick of the treasure and . . . '

'Not now, Auntie. What about that drink?'

The aunt walked to the door that led to the bar. 'You never know, I might meet a prince myself, when your uncle isn't looking.' She hoisted her skirt above her knees. 'But I'll need them stockings you promised me.'

'You'll have to wait until I go to Paris, Auntie.'

The door to the bar swung closed behind her aunt.

Lydia whipped round to face me. 'All right, what d'you want?'

'You. At the Dorchester.'

'Why?'

'You left the farm without telling anyone.'

'And is that a crime?'

'You were asked not to leave the area pending investigations into the missing diamond.'

'I have diamonds of my own. Why would I take that?'

'You tell me.'

'You'd like that wouldn't you?'

'Lydia, what are your plans?'

'To go out on the town with Freddie. You want to know a lot don't you?'

'If I don't ask you, someone else will. Scotland Yard is involved, and the India Office.'

She snorted, 'The India Office. The Indians might kowtow. I won't.'

'So is Freddie someone you can safely pass a diamond to?'

'He's a dancer, and a good pal. We were in the chorus together at the Little Theatre, my first job. And don't look at me like that. People swallow their grief in different ways. I take mine neat. And I haven't got their bloody diamond.'

'Is it true that you're going back to India?'

'Why shouldn't I? I have my palace there.'

'Without your maharajah to protect you, the establishment will have you turned back at the port.'

'Let them try.'

'The Indian Civil Service, the police, they will find some way of keeping you out.'

'I have as much right to be in India as anyone else. An Indian maharajah loved me. Can the British government say that? I don't think so.'

Her aunt returned with a tray holding a glass and bottles of Beefeater gin and dry vermouth. 'No sign of Freddie.'

'He's always late.'

The aunt placed the glass in front of me.

I took a sip. 'Don't know why you need curlers. This is strong enough to give you a permanent wave.'

She laughed. 'Oh, your friend's a card. You know how to pick 'em, Liddy.' When she had stopped laughing, she said, 'There's a copper outside, trying to play the invisible man. If Freddie sees him, he'll get the wind up. He hasn't been the same since that business blew up over his brush with big Albert in the back passage. All a shameful misunderstanding if you ask me.'

Lydia glanced at me. 'Is the copper with you?'

'Absolutely not. I've never had a police escort in my life. Not important enough.'

Mrs Mudge laughed. 'She's a card, your friend.'

'Nice gin. What are the cocktails like in the bar at the Dorchester? I've never had the pleasure.'

Lydia stood, 'Well then, since you were so kind as to find my lost earring, I'll stand you a treat there. Auntie, tell Freddie I'll see him another day.'

The woman's face became a picture of disappointment. 'Poor Freddie.'

'He shouldn't be late then, should he?'

A stout porter opened the door of a room on the second floor of the Dorchester. Lydia stepped inside the sumptuous room, and for a moment stood still and drank in the luxury while James, Chana and I looked on from the doorway.

We followed her in, to make way for a second porter who brought a trunk.

Lydia delved in her handbag and produced a key ring. 'Well, here we are, quite a party. Never thought you'd find yourself in my hotel room, did you, Mr Chana?'

Chana looked at James. 'May we proceed?'

James handed Lydia a piece of paper. 'Miss Metcalfe, this is an order taken out by Maharajah Shivram Halkwaer, requiring you to open your trunks in the presence of the maharajah's representative, Mr Chana.'

As she studied the paper with great care, James looked a little embarrassed. 'Perhaps you are tired after your journey and would like to have tea, or take a rest before we begin?'

Chana let out something like a muffled groan.

Lydia studied the paper. 'This says the hotel manager must be present.'

James and Chana exchanged a look.

'Well?' Lydia demanded.

There was a tap on the door. Another porter struggled in with a second trunk.

James turned to him. 'Please ask the manager to attend urgently.'

The porter stared, as if he could not believe his ears.

'Urgently,' James repeated.

When the man had gone, Lydia handed the paper back to James. 'It does not say how many trunks you wish me to open.'

'You sent two trunks from Bolton Abbey.'

'Ah yes, but I have another forty-eight trunks stored in the basement. What if I have colluded with a member of staff and a jewel of inestimable worth is folded in a nightgown and tucked in one of those forty-eight trunks?'

Mr Chana attempted to look through her. 'We will see all forty-eight trunks.'

'Fifty,' Lydia corrected. 'Must try harder in arithmetic, Mr Chana.'

Three hours later, Lydia opened the fiftieth trunk.

She took out writing paper and envelopes, holding up each envelope separately, to prove it contained nothing. She shook out a hand towel, embroidered with the Ritz Hotel initials; a hand towel embroidered with the Dorchester's initials. She held out a used tablet of soap for inspection. Picking up a packet of tea, she announced it to be Darjeeling, opened it and carefully emptied the contents into a large glass ashtray, allowing it to overflow onto the walnut dressing table. Over each theatre programme and each signed photograph of an actor, singer or dancer, she lingered. There were trinkets she must have had since childhood, cheap glass beads, a copper bracelet, an imitation pearl pendant. She waved a menu from the SS *Malwa*. Finally, she picked up a packet of sanitary towels, ripped it open and, with a flourish, placed pad after pad on the bed. She shook out a pair of stockings, which brought a flicker of interest.

She examined the toe of one, and discarded the pair in the waste basket.

'I need new stockings.' She smiled bewitchingly. 'Sorry to disappoint you all, but as you see, I am unable to produce the Gattiawan diamond, or any diamond. If you intend to dismantle the trunks for false bottoms, please reassemble and repack.'

Mr Chana gave a curt nod to James and to me, and marched from the room.

The manager gazed at the mess of Lydia's life that was strewn on the bed, chairs, dresser and across the floor. 'Regarding the storage fee for the trunks, Miss Metcalfe . . .'

Lydia ignored him. She wiped her brow in melodramatic fashion, pushed a couple of shoeboxes from a small velvet covered chair and sat down.

James asserted his authority. 'Not now. Miss Metcalfe is fatigued. She may like tea?'

'Oddly enough, I would. Thank you, Mr Rodpen. You are a gent.'

The manager hesitated for a moment before leaving in what I suppose might be called high dudgeon, but being a man used to controlling his feelings the dudgeon was not as high as it might have been.

'Miss Metcalfe. I am very sorry to say that after you have had your tea, I must invite you come to Scotland Yard to answer some questions.'

'Did you slip out and join the Metropolitan Police while my back was turned?' Lydia smiled sweetly.

James reddened.

'Thought not. Then go take a running jump, but before

you do, send a chambermaid to pack this lot. If you are all very lucky, I won't press charges.'

James has a terribly pompous manner when he wishes to adopt it, and I wish he would not.

'Very well. But I have orders. I shall reluctantly fetch a policeman.'

'Good. Fetch two.'

James turned to me, to see if I would follow.

I did not.

'Watch me.' She caught him by the sleeve.

She strode back and forth across the room, swaying provocatively. 'Well?'

James stared at her. He blinked a couple of times, and blinked again. 'Well what?'

'Could I walk like that if the diamond is where you think it is?'

James left, quickly.

I surveyed the wreck of the room.

A chambermaid knocked. 'You sent for me, madam?'

'Bugger off. I can pack my own trunks.' The chambermaid left. 'They're all light-fingered.' She began to scoop up her belongings, throwing them any old how into the nearest trunk.

James opened the door again. 'Mrs Shackleton, please remain with Miss Metcalfe until I return with the police officer who is waiting downstairs.'

He closed the door gently behind him.

'Lydia, if you know anything about the diamond, tell me now.'

She picked up a silk kimono. 'You bugger off as well. They have a little power and it goes to their heads, and every other bit of their body. Well let them do their worst. If they get on my wrong side, they'll never see their precious diamond again, not this side of paradise.'

'For heaven's sake, put a stop to this. If you know where the diamond is, say so. If not, stop pretending you do know. It won't do you any good.'

There was a tap on the door.

I opened it to a burly man in a crumpled suit, accompanied by a plain, slender woman in tweeds. He brought out his card. 'I'm Inspector Barker, CID, and this is Sergeant Wyles.' He looked beyond me to Lydia. 'Miss Metcalfe, I would like you to come along with us.'

'Will you give Miss Metcalfe a moment or two to repack her trunks, Inspector?'

A moment or two? We could be here for hours.

The inspector stared at the jumble of clothing, shoes, hotel and theatre memorabilia, lip rouge, powder, ships' menus and dance cards. 'Sergeant Wyles, please supervise this . . . activity. I shall wait on the landing.'

Wyles stood back for a moment, then gave a small sigh.

She and I began to pick up the debris of Lydia Metcalfe's life and place it in trunks with much greater care than did Lydia herself.

Was I envious when I saw the bag from the shop in Paris where Lydia bought her stockings? Perhaps, just a little.

When Lydia had left with the sergeant, I picked up a few odds and ends that had not found their way into the trunks; a receipt, a menu from the Paris Ritz, a ticket for the Folies Bergère, a kid glove stained by rain. There was something touching about the amount of useless stuff Lydia had held onto, taking up unpaid for space in the basement of the

Dorchester. I guessed there might be hotels in Paris, Rome, Amsterdam and Delhi where she had done the same. Perhaps there would be trunks in the attics of the Earl of Ellesmere in Bethnal Green.

And one of them might, just might, contain the Gattiawan diamond.

Thirty-Five

James and I watched from the hotel entrance as Lydia Metcalfe was discreetly escorted from the Dorchester by burly Inspector Barker and the slender Sergeant Wyles. Lydia turned to look at us before climbing into the waiting motor. Her make-up had worn off. She looked younger than her years. Her attempt at defiance frayed at the edges.

James and I exchanged a look. He sighed. 'One thinks of the sledgehammer and the nut, eh old girl?'

'I do believe you have a soft spot for her.'

'You have to give credit where it's due. She played a blinder. The lady has style.'

Slowly, James and I made our way out of the hotel.

'Where is Mr Chana?'

'Gone to the Ritz to pick up something for the maharani. He'll take a train back this evening.'

We waited at the entrance while the doorman hailed a taxicab.

Usually when I come to London, I stay with Aunt Berta, James's mother, so when we entered the taxi, James gave me one of his quizzical looks.

'It isn't over yet. We had better stay together for now.'

He nodded. 'Connaught Square, driver.'

We travelled in silence, unable to speak about what must now be happening to Lydia Metcalfe, and not in the mood for small talk.

'Far side of the square, driver.'

He paid the fare.

We walked up the familiar steps.

James's elderly butler, once my uncle's footman, greeted us. He had put on a little weight since I last saw him and his grey hair was thinner on top. In his own reserved fashion, Cooper liked me. His way of making a fuss was to say, 'Well, madam, here you are at last. Cook will be pleased.'

We had an early meal of comfort food, meat and potato pie and rice pudding.

Later, in the drawing room, James poured sherry. We sat on either side of the fireplace. I kicked off my shoes. There was something about this house that I never liked. The place echoed silence. On my occasional visits to James and Hope, I had watched them glide about like a pair of ghosts.

Now that Hope had gone to exchange pleasantries with her maker, the house, more than ever, had the atmosphere of a hollow tomb, awaiting the arrival of its first cadaver. It was the kind of dwelling that needed children, eccentric relations, hangers-on, cats, dogs, and canaries to expel the dreariness. I used to imagine something very bad must have happened here once.

James was oblivious to my feelings and I was careful not to say how gloomy the place made me feel.

He ambled across to a contraption in the corner. 'Did I

tell you I have a wireless? It works on a thermionic valve. I can see if there's a transmission if you like.'

'Not just now.' He looked so crestfallen that I claimed a headache.

'Funny that. Hope always caught a headache in this room.'

I was still trying to understand why the police thought that the humiliation of a strip search of Lydia Metcalfe at Scotland Yard would bring them any closer to finding the Gattiawan diamond. They were so clumsy, these men who thought they knew everything, that was what annoyed me. Willing to whitewash the foul play of Prince Narayan's murder, but prepared to commit an outrage on a 'wicked woman'. In purely practical terms, searching Lydia was ridiculous. I had to face up to the fact that we had arrived too late. There had been plenty of time for her to glad-hand the diamond to some friend or relation in the Earl of Ellesmere.

The police would no doubt be causing ructions there, with so many places in a pub where a diamond could be concealed. I had a sudden vision of a barrel of bitter being emptied into jugs and sieved for the precious gem.

Did she have the diamond or not? Sometimes I thought yes. But if she had it, then why did she hint that she had it, instead of issuing grand denials? 'James, do you think Lydia has the diamond?'

'I'm sure I don't know.'

'Do you think they think she has it, the India Office and Scotland Yard?'

'Possibly.'

'And possibly not. Perhaps they simply want to teach her a lesson. She rose above her station – an upstart East End girl who hooked an exotic and wealthy mate.'

'Many attractive girls do. My chum's maternal aunt . . . '

I never heard the story about the chum's maternal aunt because at that moment, the doorbell rang, loudly, persistently.

'It'll be a message from mother. She must have heard you are in London. Mark my word, one of her friends saw you at the Dorchester. She'll want to know why you aren't with her. She'll arrange a supper. If you wonder why she hasn't been trying to match-make for you of late, it's because she's busy arranging introductions for me.'

I know my Aunt Berta better than to imagine she would send a messenger. 'She would have telephoned. It's your stuffed-shirt friends who treat the telephone as though it is the invention of the devil.'

The butler brought in a card on a tray, but before James had time to take it, a tall, lean man with a lined face and grey hair appeared in the doorway. He was well into his sixties, trim and meticulously turned out.

By the way James sprang to his feet, and said, 'Sir?' I knew the man must be one of the high-ranking civil servants James so admires and tries to emulate.

The man was indeed a Sir. James introduced Sir Richard Hartington, Private Secretary to the Secretary of State for India.

'My cousin, Mrs Shackleton, the lady who has helped us so much in regard to Miss Metcalfe and the sorry business.'

I did not feel I had helped in any way at all. 'Shall I leave you gentlemen to talk?'

Sir Richard sat down opposite me. 'Please stay, Mrs Shackleton. I wanted to inform you that we have released Miss Metcalfe from custody, without achieving any information from her with regard to the dubte suraj ki chamak.

306

We are in a most embarrassing situation.' He looked directly at me, his grey eyes betraying no emotion. 'Do you believe she knows where the diamond is?'

'I believe she would like us to think that.'

He nodded. 'My thought also. But is she playing us along by pretending to know more than she does, or does she want us to think that she is pretending?'

Now that someone of his own sex and a higher rank had come onto the scene, James's sherry glass did a disappearing trick. He poured two glasses of whisky and handed one to his guest. 'Could she have passed the diamond to someone, sir?'

'The North Riding Constabulary have overseen a search of her family farm and of the house belonging to a Mr Presthope, with no results. Thanks to a telephone call from the superintendent of the West Riding Constabulary – your father I believe, Mrs Shackleton?'

'Yes.'

'We had a man posted at the Dorchester and at the Earl of Ellesmere even before you contacted the commander at Scotland Yard. If she has managed to conceal the diamond in either of those places then she ought to be signed up for the secret service. We are still conducting searches.'

James topped up my sherry. 'My cousin doubts that Miss Metcalfe has the diamond. She has another theory.'

'Oh?' Sir Richard took a sip.

'You won't want to hear it, Sir Richard.' I did not particularly want to repeat the highly speculative thoughts I had aired over the meat and potato pie.

'Try me.'

'Very well. I believe Miss Metcalfe had the opportunity to

take the diamond. The late maharajah bought a surprise present that he would have given her on Friday evening, jewellery in the design of four-leaf clovers, emeralds and diamonds.'

Sir Richard raised an eyebrow. 'Generous man.'

'But there is something else.' I recounted the story of the Indian on Bark Lane, Mr Deakin's retraction of his story, and that I did not believe the retraction. 'Ijahar, the valet, said that sometimes the prince wore the diamond in a pouch about his neck, perhaps as a charm, or just because he did not entirely trust it to the safe in his room. If there were a hostile presence in the area from a rival state . . . '

'In the shape of an Indian on the road last Friday.' Sir Richard finished his whisky.

'Yes.'

'Did you have any particular princely state in mind?' He raised a monocle to his left eye and peered at me through it.

I tried not to laugh at his antique gesture. 'I thought of Kalathal.'

'The Maharajah of Kalathal is at Bolton Abbey now.'

'So I understand.'

Sometimes James should keep quiet. 'That could signify a reconciliation, a putting aside of differences in the face of tragedy.'

Sir Richard ignored James. 'Did you know that the diamond has been in the Halkwaer family for seven generations?'

I did, but only because Indira had told me, so I pretended ignorance.

He continued. 'And do you know what state originally owned the diamond and was prevailed upon to make it part of a dowry in exchange for promises that were never kept?'

I did not know, but could guess.

James provided the answer. 'Kalathal?'

'Yes.'

'A motive for murder, Sir Richard?' I took a sip of sherry.

'No one has been murdered, Mrs Shackleton. The coroner's jury made that entirely clear. Maharajah Narayan Halkwaer died as a result of a tragic accident. Accidents happen.'

James, somewhat ineptly, tried to offer me support. 'My cousin, being an investigator, is inclined to suspect foul play.'

Sir Richard waved his empty glass at James. 'Shooting accidents are sadly more common than most ladies suppose.'

'Well that makes it very simple.'

'My dear Mrs Shackleton, you were asked for your expertise in finding the prince, and find him you did.' Sir Richard straightened his bow tie. 'Your suggestion gives us food for thought. We shall shortly enter discussions with the Maharajah of Kalathal. However, if you would care to assist us in another way . . .'

He waited.

So did I.

After a good half minute, he continued. 'When Miss Metcalfe has had time to sleep on the matter, I believe she will see sense. She appears to have taken a liking to you, and given how uncooperative she was this evening perhaps another approach may be more productive. I should like to be able to rule her out as a suspect in relation to the diamond. You might gain her confidence. We also need an assurance from her that she will not return to India.'

'Sorry, Sir Richard. Reluctant as I am to turn down an assignment from His Majesty's government, my heart would not be in it.'

He nodded graciously, acknowledging defeat, and then turned to James. 'Did you also strike up a rapport with the lady in question?'

James blanched. 'Not a bit of it.'

'Odd. She spoke flatteringly of you while she was in custody. Said that you were a gentleman.'

'I hardly had anything to do with the woman, offered her a cup of tea that is all, allowed her to take her time, no more than the normal civilities.'

'Still, we may ask you to keep an eye on her.'

Terror struck James. 'Isn't that a police matter?'

'Oh she can smell police a mile off, so she tells them, and I have no reason to doubt her.'

It was the first time I had spent a night under James's roof. The wallpaper in the bedroom was William Morris. On the windowsill sat an arts and crafts vase which held silk violets. I remembered Hope talking about it, and how pleased she was with her choice. She had sworn me to secrecy about the silk flowers as my aunt holds imitation flowers to be the height of vulgarity, and poor Hope lived to please.

After a surprisingly good night's sleep, I felt quite cheerful. This was because I had made a decision. Last night, I had telephoned Aunt Berta and arranged to meet her, for shopping and lunch. Later, I would take the train back to Bolton Abbey, and seek an audience with the maharani. I would apologise to Indira for not finding the diamond. Whether I would voice suspicions against the Maharajah of Kalathal was another matter. That was not my concern. After having lost possession of the gem for seven generations, perhaps it was Kalathal's turn to have the diamond back.

At 8 a.m., the maid brought my morning tea. She drew back the curtains on a bright sky. My tranquillity lasted less than ten minutes.

James knocked and opened the door without waiting for a reply. He stood in the doorway, looking dismayed, as when bigger boys went on an adventure without him.

'She's gone.'

'She? Lydia Metcalfe?'

He nodded.

'Well what did you expect? She's hounded, bullied, taken into custody, humiliated, threatened, and followed. What would you have done?'

'That's ridiculous. I would never be in that sort of position to begin with.'

'No, I don't suppose you would.'

He plonked himself on the bottom of my bed. 'But where has she gone?'

'When did they find out that she is missing?'

'Ten minutes ago. She slept in her room at the Dorchester. There was a constable posted on the landing. They had to force the door when she didn't answer the chambermaid's knock. She'd left the key in the lock.'

'She climbed out of the window?'

'How did you guess?'

'Not exactly a locked room mystery then.'

'But it was the second floor.'

'She's a dancer, James. That means she's agile. She was brought up in a pub by her aunt and her uncle the tightrope walker. If she'd been on the tenth floor, she would have left via the roof.'

'There isn't a tenth floor at the Dorchester.'

'James, go away. Let me dress.'

'Sir Richard has ordered me to find her. He said you might help me. He thinks that being female, and from the north, you may have an insight into how her mind works.'

'How does my being from the north come into the equation?'

'I don't know what he means, I'm sure.' James looked more miserable than usual.

'Lydia left Yorkshire when she was seven years old. An East End pearly king and queen would be closer to her than I.'

'You can ignore Sir Richard, Kate. I can't. Be a sport. You went to the Earl of Ellesmere. Do you think I should go there?'

I reached out to the bedside cabinet and handed him the items Lydia had dropped in the hotel room, the receipt for stockings from a Paris shop, the ticket stub from the Folies Bergère, the menu from the Ritz Hotel.

He stared at them. 'Are you saying she has gone to Paris?'

'My guess is that she did not spend five minutes in her room at the Dorchester. If I were her, I would have taken the boat train from Euston and be halfway across the Channel by now, out of the clutches of Scotland Yard and the India Office.'

James paled. 'You heard what Sir Richard said last night. He will order me to follow her. I don't like abroad, I never have.'

'Oh you'll like Paris.'

'Will you come with me?'

'No. If you meet the right people you will get on famously. I can give you two excellent introductions to people who know everyone. They'll find Lydia for you in no time.'

'What if she hasn't gone to Paris?'

'I think if our friends at Scotland Yard make a few enquiries, they will discover that she was on the boat train.'

'Did you know?'

'Of course not. But trust me, and cheer up. Make the most of this.'

He left, closing the door gently behind him.

Thirty-Six

'It makes me feel so modern to eat here.' Aunt Berta cut into her steak and kidney pudding. 'When I was your age, I wouldn't have dreamed that a place like this would have come into being. Something good came out of that war after all.'

Shopping spree completed, we were lunching at our favourite place, not glamorous but with its own charm – the VAD Ladies' Club on Cavendish Square. My feet ached, the mutton chop was overcooked and I felt heartily fed up with myself in spite of some successful purchases.

Aunt Berta does not miss much. 'Cheer up, Kate. You'll thank me for spotting that little hat. And you mustn't let James's moroseness rub off on you. He has that effect on people.'

'It is not to do with James, Aunt. The whole Bolton Abbey business is a disaster.'

This was my first big failure as a private investigator. And now I had encouraged James to go haring off to Paris in pursuit of Lydia Metcalfe. She had indeed boarded the boat train last night and would now be in Cherbourg. Whatever made me suggest that James follow her? My feelings of responsibility were heightened by Aunt Berta's delight that I had sent her son packing.

'My dear, it was a stroke of genius. James needs to be taken out of himself.'

'He didn't want to go.'

'Well of course he didn't but it will do him good. That boy doesn't know how to enjoy himself, and he's pushed from pillar to post in the India Office. He is not cut out for it.'

'Why did he move to the India Office?'

'They lighted on him because my father served on the Northwest Frontier.'

'Yes. The hotel manager at the Cavendish Arms served under him. He inspired great loyalty.'

'Well, you see, my father was cut out for the adventurous life. He was in India at the time of the mutiny, but his troops stayed loyal.'

'James believes our days in India are numbered.'

She waved her knife dismissively. 'Well of course he does. We shall be in India for another hundred years, at least. My father said so, and he should know. But, you see, my poor James would take the "our days are numbered" point of view. If he had been born into a different walk of life, he would be marching along Oxford Street with a placard telling us "the end is nigh". How can he expect to progress if he foresees an end to everything. Really! That is why he was far better off in the War Office, especially since there won't be any more wars.'

'Why did he agree to leave War?'

'The sad truth is he wasn't really cut out for that either.

War is a very convivial department. After all, they are doing what boys like best, planning for fisticuffs and destruction. Having James at their little soirees would be like going to the Folies Bergère with a parson.'

Over the pudding, we talked about Malcolm and Penelope, James's younger brother and his wife. Aunt seemed terribly pleased that they are producing children at an alarming rate.

Not until our dishes had been taken away did Sir Richard materialise, hovering in the doorway, glancing about the room full of females until his monocled eye alighted on us.

'Aunt Berta, there's James's boss.'

She looked up. 'Well if it isn't Richard. He took quite a shine to me once upon a time.' She waved him over.

He strode across the room. 'Ladies.'

Aunt Berta raised a gracious hand. 'Please, Richard, do join us for tea. Or would you prefer coffee?'

'Tea would be lovely, Lady Pocklington, though you may not feel so kindly towards me when you hear that I have despatched your son to Paris.'

'Really?' Aunt Berta feigned perfect surprise. 'He didn't mention it.'

'It was all a little last minute. Someone we want to keep an eye on. We value you your son most highly.' He allowed a silence.

Aunt Berta is good at codes. She excused herself, and headed in the direction of the ladies' room.

When she had gone, Sir Richard said, 'Your cousin has excelled himself, Mrs Shackleton. He discovered that Lydia Metcalfe left London on the boat train at midnight, and will have crossed the Channel by now. He has shown

considerable initiative in pursuing her to Paris. But I suppose you knew that.'

'He did mention it.'

The waitress brought tea.

He waited until she moved out of earshot. 'Shortly after
you left, there was an outbreak of bilious attacks among the
Indians at Bolton Abbey.'

'How unfortunate. I had heard there was sickness in the
village.'

'It is more than unfortunate.' His tone was so severe and
his look so charged with meaning that for a moment I
thought he was pinning the bilious attacks on me.

'I'm sorry to hear it.'

But I was not surprised, given the outdoor situation in
which the Indian servants had been billeted, and the lack of
hygiene available to them.

'Prince Jaya has been brought low, and his case is more
severe than first thought.'

'In what way?'

'He was brave about it, but their doctor was so concerned
that he called in a second opinion. The prince is nauseous,
has severe irritation, a rash, slowed pulse, his blood pressure
is low.'

'How awful.'

'Mrs Shackleton, it is more than awful . . . '

'I know.' I lowered my voice. 'A rash and a slow pulse indicate poison.'

Sir Richard looked round the room quickly, to see if ears
pricked at my words. If pricking occurred it was too discreet
to be noticed.

'When I first heard, I naturally thought that being

debilitated by the shock of bereavement, the prince had succumbed in a more severe way, but it very quickly became apparent that this was different in nature.'

'Has an emetic been administered? Is he responding to treatment?'

'Everything is being done that can be done, but it is too early to say. He may be fighting for his life.'

'Do you know how this poisoning occurred?'

'We are calling it severe food poisoning. The duke and duchess are devastated that this should have happened under their roof. They are trying to get to the bottom of it.'

'The practicalities of multiple cooks and shared kitchens will make it difficult.'

He groaned. 'Not to mention the entourages of bakers, cooks, tailors, washer-men and women, servants' servants, hairdressers, under-valets and sorcerers.'

'Do you suspect it was deliberate?'

'Frankly, and between us, yes. There is a great deal of cunning in the Indian. The death of Prince Narayan provided the perfect opportunity for a throng of princes to congregate at Bolton Abbey, ostensibly to pay their respects. Among the genuine mourners, we may have called down a nest of vipers. They should have left after the funeral but now linger, waiting for Jaya to die. You suspected foul play all along. I did not want to agree. For heaven's sake, we rule in India because we know how to do it and they do not. But princes dying at the heart of Empire, where will it end?'

It sounded to me as though it might end in erosion of confidence in the Empire, but this did not seem the most tactful response. 'Do you see a link between this poisoning and Prince Narayan's death?'

'It is possible. Naturally, our attentions are on safeguarding Maharajah Shivram and his grandson.'

'Why are you coming to me, Sir Richard? Surely you must have your own high-level investigators, and India Office experts.'

'Quite.' He took out his fob watch. 'I will be travelling North on the 4 p.m. train.'

'Then you must have a great deal to do. Have you time for a second cup of tea?'

'Mrs Shackleton, this is a terrible imposition.' He brought the full force of his old-world charm into a single smile and a deprecating tilt of the head. 'Will you return with me to Yorkshire? I have a car outside. Much as I hate to disturb your visit to your aunt, we need you.'

'Why?'

'The Maharani Indira asks for you. She is utterly distraught and will speak to no one else. Her mother-in-law is inconsolable. I think she has not stopped weeping, but at least she welcomes her ladyship's presence.'

'Short of supplying handkerchiefs, what on earth do you expect me to do? No one took the least bit of notice when I cried foul over the maharajah's death.'

'That was unfortunate, and it will not happen again. In answer to your question, I want you to speak to the women, to the senior maharani, and to Maharani Indira. They always know more than they are willing to disclose to men.'

I saw Aunt Berta in the doorway, hovering hopefully, and waved to her.

Before my aunt resumed her seat, Sir Richard said softly, 'My dear Mrs Shackleton, if you will agree to accompany me to Bolton Abbey, to pacify the maharanis, I shall take you into my confidence.'

I doubted that very much.

'All right, Sir Richard, I will come with you.' I poured tea for my aunt and Sir Richard, and then excused myself. Leaving them to talk about old times, I made my way to the ladies' room.

There, I wrote a note, which I would entrust to the club manageress to telegraph to Mr J Sykes at the Devonshire Arms Hotel.

Returning. Suggest Mrs Sugden will enjoy stay at hotel.

I signed, CS, for Catherine Shackleton, which I hoped might put staff at the local post office off the scent.

I wrote a second note, alerting Mrs Sugden to prepare for a visit to Bolton Abbey.

A little voice told me I would need reinforcements; people I could trust.

Sir Richard left Aunt Berta and me alone to say our good-byes.

'Aunt, what department was Sir Richard attached to before the India Office?'

'He was somewhere we don't mention, my dear. An office that does not officially exist, you know, somewhat of a secret.'

By taking me with him, to comfort and grill females, Sir Richard was giving a soft edge to his activities. But I had no doubt he would be ruthless.

Thirty-Seven

We boarded the 4 p.m. train at Kings Cross, having a reserved First Class compartment. Lazonby, Sir Richard's assistant, a slight, cheerful young man of about twenty-three, lifted my overnight bag onto the luggage rack.

'Can I get you anything from the restaurant car, Mrs Shackleton?'

'No thank you.'

'Take yourself off for some refreshment, Lazonby.' Sir Richard settled himself opposite me. 'Book a table for me and Mrs Shackleton, at about six, if that is not too early?'

It suited me very well. We would not arrive in Leeds until 8.05 p.m. and then there would be the journey on to Bolton Abbey.

When Lazonby closed the door behind him, I relaxed into my plush seat. The upholstery almost sighed and so did I. After the morning's shopping, my legs ached. I would have loved to kick off my shoes and might have overcome politeness, except that the tightness on my right toe spoke of a hole in my stocking.

Sir Richard, of course, was immaculate. Someone had

polished his shoes to a high gleam. He dashed a barely visible speck from his elegant pinstriped suit. Remembering what my aunt had said about his soft spot for her, it amused me to imagine that he might have been my uncle.

'What do you know about the princely states, Mrs Shackleton?'

'Next to nothing. That is why I wonder what made you pick me to go to Bolton Abbey.'

He leaned forward as though the surprise of my question demanded motion from the most still of men. 'You were highly recommended.' Some flattery followed which I decline to repeat. 'There was the additional complication of the prince's companion, and we were anxious not to escalate the situation before we knew more.'

I wriggled my toes, and prompted him to enlighten me about the princely states, hoping this would not elicit a marathon lecture.

'Four hours won't do this topic justice.' He gave a soft laugh when he caught my look of dismay. 'I'll try to leave out a few chapters and all verse. Your Aunt Berta always accused me of giving her too much information.'

Now he had made me feel bad. I volunteered that at least I knew there were over five hundred principalities.

'That's right, administered from Bombay or the Punjab, or by local commissioners. Some are large and powerful, others not much bigger than a field. Our treaties provide defence for the princes.'

'James told me how some of the states were our allies during the war.'

'Indeed. As well as providing financial and military support, they were our partners in curbing dissent and quietening the demands of the nationalists. Changed the relationship somewhat.'

From listening to the talk at Aunt Berta's dinner parties, I know that men in high positions speak in a kind of code and one must be alert to discover what lies behind their words. It is such an ingrained habit that they are probably unaware that we mere mortals speak differently.

'There was a change in the way we governed, dating back to the last century, but it goes back much further than that. The Rajputs supported the East India Company. The Marathas did not and suffered because of that. They have never forgiven the Rajputs.'

'And is Gattiawan Rajput or Maratha?'

'Neither. But they have connections with both through kinship. Traditionally, the Rajputs claim descent from the sun and the moon. The Marathas are farmers who rose from the soil by their own efforts. Vendettas still simmer, disputes pop up regularly, sometimes over claims to territory or minerals, other times over matters of status, precedence or *izzat*, meaning honour.'

He let this hang in the air and not for the first time it occurred to me that Indira's honour had been besmirched by her husband's affair with Lydia. If her family knew he planned to marry his cockney dancer, they may well have decided to put a bloody stop to that. Was the Indian seen on Bark Lane some emissary of revenge sent by Indira's family? Before I had time to ask about Indira's origins, he began again.

'After the Mutiny, Queen Victoria declared an end to the rule of the East India Company and the beginning of Crown Rule. The princes became responsible to the Crown, in return for protection. That relationship stayed the same until just five years ago when we established a council by royal warrant.'

I was trying my best to keep up. This, I guessed, was one of the changes that had followed the Great War. 'What difference did this council make?'

'I'm coming to that, my dear. The Chamber of Princes held its inaugural meeting at the Red Fort. Quite a spectacle, of course, the palace turned into a veritable fairyland with cloths of gold, huge thrones for King George's representatives who brought promises and guarantees from His Majesty.'

'What kind of guarantees?'

'Guarantees that princely privileges, rights and dignities would be maintained.'

Sir Richard remained still all the while he talked, without that need some people have for a hand movement, a sideways glance, a shift in position. He was waiting for some response from me. I had the feeling that perhaps he was coming to some point, hinting at a dispute within the Chamber of Princes that had led to a terrible vendetta against the rulers of Gattiawan.

'And has the Chamber of Princes flourished?'

'High hopes sometimes prove mistaken.'

He was beginning to exasperate me. I wanted something definite. A lecture in imperial history did not bring me any nearer to understanding who murdered the maharajah, and who may have attempted to poison his brother.

I tried to hide my impatience. 'Why doesn't it work?'

'All sorts of reasons: resistance to change; fears that private matters may become public; feelings of inferiority;

assumptions that the princes with more status will rule the roost. The chamber was designed to put an end to discontent but it has given the princes an even more inflated view of themselves. Now instead of consulting their own British state commissioner, they go over his head to the Political Department in Delhi. We now have less confidence that the loyalty of some states can be taken for granted.'

The terrible thought occurred to me that one of the states whose loyalty could no longer be taken for granted was Gattiawan, and the challenge to imperial authority had brought deadly consequences upon the Halkwaer family. If I were an imperial government, ridding myself of a turbulent prince, I would not ask Scotland Yard to investigate. I would bring in some female private detective who could be brushed aside when no longer required.

A cold chill ran through me.

'You are cold?' Ever the gentleman, Sir Richard instantly rose and closed the carriage window.

I wanted to ask a question, but dreaded the answer.

Like some facile lecturer steeped in his subject, Sir Richard talked on about India until I felt half dizzy and imagined a cornered tiger, a majestic elephant, a beggar and a prince shared our carriage, and that the carriage itself was draped in cloths of gold.

When the train slowed and halted at Grantham, no tea wallah came to the window tapping and offering cha, but a railway policeman knocked and opened our carriage door.

The policeman handed Sir Richard a note, waited for a moment, in case of reply, and gave a small salute as he left.

'I've asked for reports on Prince Jaya to be telephoned through to every station.' He sighed. 'No change.'

'Let us hope that is a good sign.'

I watched him carefully to see whether he betrayed himself in any small way by a look, or a shift in his movement. He did not.

When Lazonby returned to the carriage, Sir Richard informed him that there was no change in the condition of the maharajah's son.

We then made our way to the dining car.

As we waited for our meal to be served, I decided that the only way to satisfy my need for information was to ask direct questions. This, I knew, went against the grain of the civil service.

'You mentioned the rivalries between princes. Do you believe a fellow maharajah may have murdered Prince Narayan?'

'I don't like the word murder, Mrs Shackleton.'

'Then let me put it another way. Do you think that a fellow member of the Chamber of Princes, or someone outside the charmed circle, may have wished Prince Narayan harm?'

With great care, a waiter placed dishes of oxtail soup on the table.

'It is unlikely that such persons would go to extreme lengths.'

'I believe there is ill-feeling and rivalry between Gattiawan and Kalathal.'

'That is true, but usually more unites the princely families than divides them. They share blood and family ties, enjoy the same pastimes and ceremonies. Underneath the disagreements there is a sense of brotherhood between the princes. They may snub each other, partake in petty insults, allow feuds to fester down the generations, but they have grown soft under our rule and do not usually go out of their way to slaughter each other.'

There it was again, a little qualification, 'not usually'. My next question.

'And when the British Raj sees fit to intervene against some transgressing prince, what then?'

There was the slightest physical response from Sir Richard, a flicker in the eyes, a hesitation with the soup spoon.

'Oh it does happen, occasionally, although by and large we have no great complaints.'

'But when you do?'

'There have been cases when some ruler is discovered to be quite insane, or bankrupt, or has turned to criminal activities such as kidnap or murder. At such times, we deal with the matter appropriately, by insisting upon abdication and banishment.'

Now was my moment. He looked steadily at me across the table, clever enough to guess my thoughts, waiting for me to voice them.

'The transgressor will never see India again because of banishment, or something else?'

'Banishment, Mrs Shackleton,' he said firmly. 'We do not engage in assassination. That would give the princes far too high a view of themselves.'

I wanted to believe him. 'You spoke of nationalism.'

'Did I?'

'Not directly, but it is there in everything I hear about India – that during the war, England's need was India's opportunity.'

'Some princes did subscribe to that line of thought.'

'You tell me that under our treaties, we extend protection to the princely states. Could murder and attempted murder be a way for a dissident prince to announce that Great Britain cannot protect the princes, even on our own soil?'

The waiter took our soup plates and brought my plaice and Sir Richard's chop. 'Do continue, Mrs Shackleton.'

'All I meant was that the motive then would not be princely rivalry but nationalist ambition.'

He raised an eyebrow. 'You look at every wild possibility, Mrs Shackleton. I wish some of my colleagues had your imagination. If they had, we may have anticipated that the Chamber of Princes would be less than a roaring success.'

'There is time yet. It is five years old. How old are our upper and lower chambers? I think at age five, it is too early to speak of disappointment.'

I was no nearer bottoming Sir Richard's thinking when we reached Doncaster. Lazonby brought a message into the restaurant car from the railway police. Sir Richard slid it across the table to me.

Prince Jaya showing small signs of recovery.

'Well that is good news.' I pushed the note back to him.

He lit a cigarette and put the match to the slip of paper, holding it over the ashtray with finger and thumb.

When we reached Leeds, there would be other people about and my opportunity to ask the hard questions would evaporate.

'Ijahar, the valet, he is now at Bolton Hall.'

'Yes, or in one of those marquees that have been erected in the grounds.'

'He appeared devoted to his master and distraught at his

death. But if anyone wanted to do the maharajah harm, Ijahar would have been able to help them.'

'Now that really is wild. If you understood India, you would realise that is inconceivable. The depth of deference and respect of Indian servants for their masters is boundless. An inferior reveres his master to such a degree that if the prince threw a knife at him, he would stand and let it enter his heart rather than move. Put that out of your mind, Mrs Shackleton. Not the servant.'

One by one my possible list of suspects was being demolished by Sir Richard: not some kinsman with a grudge, not the British government, not a fellow prince, not a servant in league with a nationalist.

'A penny for them,' he said.

But I was not prepared to divulge the suspicion that remained. Perhaps he guessed. After all, I had been assigned to this task partly because there was a woman in the picture — Lydia Metcalfe. Now I was re-assigned because of another woman — Indira, the maharani, had asked for me. More than asked for me; she would see no one else. Did that indicate she thought herself under suspicion?

Avoiding this dangerous territory, we began to speak of other matters. Over the apple pie, Sir Richard reminisced about his youth. He recalled the year Aunt Berta was presented at court, and the balls that followed. He remembered a turquoise gown. When he and she danced it was like floating on air. She always had a full dance card, and she always saved a dance for him.

We returned to our carriage and chatted with Lazonby. I was conscious that bringing up Indira's name would not go unnoticed by the wise Sir Richard and the clever Lazonby.

There was something I needed to know, but what that something was remained a mystery to me.

We were drawing into Leeds station. Soon, the moment to ask would be gone. 'I liked the Maharani Indira. She struck me as so courageous at the inquest. What family is she from?'

Sir Richard was making those small movements that precede departing a train, straightening his shoulders, flexing his legs, moving his arms and hands ever so slightly. 'She is from a small state in the west, Gundel, an eleven-gun state, yet very emancipated.'

Lazonby rose to his feet and lifted down my bag. 'Isn't that a state that supports the education of women? Well, certain women I suppose?'

Sir Richard looked out of the window, as though needing to check the name of the station. 'Yes.'

It was such a small word, uttered without emphasis, yet markedly so, as if he wanted the word to drop into a pool of suspicion and send out the slightest ripple.

Just as casually, Lazonby said, 'There is a state that prefers a female ruler, Baroda. Perhaps Gundel will follow suit one day.'

I glanced at Sir Richard, but he made no response to Lazonby's remark.

I picked up my satchel. 'And if Baroda and Gundel, then perhaps Gattiawan might be next.'

Sir Richard gave the smallest of smiles in acknowledgement.

That was it then, I thought. I am here not because Indira asked for me, which I believe she did. I am here because Sir Richard suspects that Indira, that educated woman from an emancipated state, has taken matters into her own hands. Her husband betrayed her. She is not content to be under the thumb of her father and brother-in-law. Prince Narayan's death, Prince Jaya's poisoning, this represented Indira's grasp for power.

'Who will succeed as ruler when Maharajah Shivram dies?' I asked.

'Succession is in Shivram's gift. He could decide on Jaya, who is the son of his second wife, or he could appoint Jaya or Indira to act as regent for Narayan's son, Rajendra.'

'Rajendra may be of age by the time Shivram dies.'

'Unlikely. Shivram's father died at sixty. Shivram is fifty-nine.'

The train stopped. A railway policeman appeared at the carriage door. 'Sir.' He handed Sir Richard an envelope.

Sir Richard tore open the envelope, glanced at the note paper, and passed it to me. It said *The crisis has passed*.

Sir Richard's eyes told a different story.

Thirty-Eight

It was 10 p.m. when the Bentley drew up outside Bolton Hall, and not quite dark. Lazonby, who had sat beside the driver, jumped smartly from the car and opened my door. The chauffeur opened Sir Richard's door.

'Come.' Sir Richard took my arm and we walked towards the entrance of Bolton Hall.

There were just a few seconds when he and I were close to each other, with no one nearby to overhear.

'You suspect Indira.' I put the merest pressure on his arm.

His lips pursed tightly. He did not meet my eye. But he nodded, so slightly that afterwards, if necessary, he would be able to say I had misinterpreted him.

I did not feel ready to face her, not until I had taken in this new and unwelcome idea. I paused at the door.

'Will you enquire whether she wishes to speak with me tonight, or tomorrow? If it is tonight, I should like a few moments alone before I see her.'

'Very well. Lazonby will be here with an answer, when you are ready.'

I walked across the grounds, to the abbey ruins, and to the

graveyard. Where was the burial place that the white doe had haunted, I wondered. It was too dark to read inscriptions.

Who would take the blame for the attempted poisoning of Prince Jaya? Not Indira. That would be too much of a scandal. I could imagine it. Some Indian cook, new to the Yorkshire countryside, would be discovered to have made a foolish error in selecting a poisonous plant while picking herbs.

On the hill across the road, the Indian village of tents and marquees formed strange shapes against the background of Westy Bank Wood. Lanterns flickered as figures moved. It was a hypnotic sight. I left the graveyard and crossed, through the arch, onto the road.

As I drew closer, I picked out the figures of men, sitting cross-legged outside tents, and the red glow of cigarettes. I skirted the edge of the encampment. A faint and unpleasant smell permeated the air, a reminder of the sickness that had spread from the village. A pot steamed on a fire, giving off a spicy smell. An owl hooted. Nearby, some poor fellow retched.

I turned back, and began to retrace my steps. As I descended the incline, two figures emerged from a tent, one cuffing the other about the head, speaking rapidly in words I did not understand.

One of the men was Ijahar. He became suddenly obsequious, bowed to me and said, 'He does not finish polishing my master's shoes. I tell him to be sick is no excuse.'

They disappeared in the direction of Bolton Hall.

Lazonby waited for me at the entrance.

'The Maharani Indira will see you, Mrs Shackleton. I am to take you to her, if I can find my way through the maze.'

He led me once more to the room where I had previously met Indira.

As soon as he knocked, the door was opened by Mr Chana, who gave me the barest of acknowledgements as he left.

The gas lights in the room and the soft light from a lantern cast an eerie glow. My shadow loomed on the wall. I seemed to remember some superstition or prohibition about casting a shadow on an important person. Be careful where your shadow falls.

The astrologer's papers and parchments had been carelessly laid on a low table. Beyond the table, Indira sat on a cushion, her back to the wall.

It shocked me to see her. Black crescents under her eyes betrayed lack of sleep. Though such a short time had elapsed since I saw her last, I could swear her collarbones protruded more sharply. Her wrists looked thin enough to snap, yet she appeared composed, and had about her a steely determination.

'Sit down, Mrs Shackleton. Thank you for coming at such an hour. You will have heard of our new troubles.'

'Yes, but I am glad to hear of your brother-in-law Prince Jaya's recovery, your highness.'

I watched Indira's expression. She betrayed no emotion but the relief in her voice sounded genuine. 'It would have been a great blow to me if Jaya had not recovered. He is the one person on whom I can rely. We are both educated too well, both share the same outlook on the world.'

It was then that I noticed someone else in the corner. A young woman, her head covered, sat beside a small mound of scarlet cloth.

Indira followed my gaze. 'My son, Rajendra, and his ayah. I will not let him out of my sight.'

These were not the words of a poisoner, unless a very cunning poisoner. And if she were cunning, Jaya would be dead.

'What happened?'

'Sickness spread through our staff, shortly after we arrived. My father-in-law's doctor, Dr Habib, said that it may have been something to do with the change of water. The doctor became ill himself. Dr Simonson told us of sickness in the village, and that some children had been taken poorly. Though most of the village children have recovered, they came to stare at the strangers. My own little Rajendra is weakened from vomiting and diarrhoea. It lasted two days. Food did not remain with him for half an hour, even arrowroot and sago would not stay in his stomach. Our cook was badly affected and we had to draw on the services of another. So when Jaya became ill, water was boiled, arrowroot given. But this was something quite different, more severe. An emetic was administered, thanks to your Dr Simonson.'

I tried to bring to mind some details of poisons and treatments from the *Materia Medica* that I had at home but my brain felt sluggish. 'Does the doctor know what caused Prince Jaya's sickness?'

'Unfortunately, no. They are saying severe food poisoning, but I do not believe it.' She picked up one of the parchments from the low table. 'Our astrologer assured me that Jaya would survive, but I doubted. I feared the worst, even though it is foretold that Jaya is destined for great things.'

'What kind of great things?'

'He is very clever. Politics does not interest him. He has

335

all sorts of ideas about agriculture. But I did not ask you here to talk about Jaya. He is recovered and I hope we will soon be rid of the enemies in our midst.'

From the corner came a gentle murmur as the little boy moved in his sleep. The ayah made a soothing sound.

'Then how can I help?'

'Mrs Shackleton, I fear for my son. I have become his own taster of food, me, a princess, unable to trust those around me.'

'Surely you can trust your servants.'

'We have treachery beyond belief in our own household, all around us. My son must leave this house tonight. I have had the astrologer make calculations. Tonight is propitious for you to take Rajendra into hiding.'

'Me?'

Indira sat suddenly more erect. She threw back her shoulders and jutted her chin. 'That is why I asked you here. I want you to find a place of safety for him.'

'Tonight?'

'Now. We will leave by the door at the side.'

Grief had sent her half mad. She was not thinking straight. She turned to the ayah and spoke in her language.

The ayah answered.

'She says the servants will have retired. We will use their door. You have your car?'

'No.'

I tried to reason with her, and persuade her that some trusted person would watch over the boy. When this did not satisfy her, I suggested a room at the hotel.

She dismissed this suggestion with a wave of her hand. 'No! Too obvious. You must take us somewhere no one will think to look, and you must stay with him until I know what to do.'

'But Sir Richard Hartington is here, from the India Office, and you have the protection of the duke and duchess.'

'So did Jaya have all these protections. If it were not for Dr Simonson, he would be dead.'

'As long as you keep your son by you, he will surely be safe here.'

'It is time to take matters into my own hands. Do you have children?'

'No.'

'But you will understand. In all of nature, a mother will fight for her offspring.'

Having watched my cat's litter of kittens diminish from six to five overnight, I doubted that, but not Indira's determination.

'You have your trusted aides-de-camp. Won't they ensure the child's safety?'

'Jaya has his aides-de-camp, and the maharajah's doctor, and valet and servants and secretaries; much good they did him. Half of them sick, the other half useless. I want Rajendra out of this house. I want him somewhere where he will not be found, placed with a person who will guard him with his life.'

His life? Yet she was asking me.

'What about Mr Chana?'

'How can I know for certain? I believe he colluded in giving my husband a propitious day for a so-called marriage to the whore.'

'What will the maharajah and maharani say if I disappear with their grandson?'

'They are too distraught to think about this. Maharajah Shivram is with Jaya now, persuading him to take some tea and rice. They need not know. I will tell them tomorrow.'

'But I thought . . .'

'That I am a good Indian widow, who defers to everyone and has no mind of her own?'

'No.'

'My boy is now crown prince. I want him out of this house, away from this place of sickness.'

'I don't know this area. There is no one I can trust except . . .'

'Except whom?'

Reluctantly, I told her what no one else knew – that my former policeman assistant was lodged at the hotel. By now, I hoped that my housekeeper would also be there.

'Your highness, there is only one place I can think of at this time of night that will be vacant and you would not want your child to go there.'

'What is this place?'

'It is the cottage, rented by the man who accompanied your husband on his ride, Isaac Withers. He is in the hospital now and his son has moved there to be close to him so the cottage stands empty.'

'Then that will do.'

'It is a hovel.'

'As long as it is a safe hovel, I do not care.'

'It is about two miles away,' I said.

'Then let us go.' Indira stood, and spoke to the ayah.

Moments later, we left the house quietly by the servants' entrance, carrying an unlit lantern. I led the way. Indira followed. Behind her came the ayah carrying the child. Wishing

338

to avoid the road where we would be seen from the servants' tents on the other side, I followed the path across the fields, towards the woods near the river.

Only when we entered the woods did I light the lantern.

I glanced at the ayah. She was too slight to carry such a big boy, but he seemed exhausted. Perhaps taking him to a remote spot was not a good idea, but it was too late now.

I turned and looked back, having a feeling of being followed, but could see no one.

Once in the woods, there was little chance of our being observed, except by owls and foxes. Only when Indira gave a small cry did I remember the dainty sandals she wore, and realised that even through my stockings the nettles stung. The ayah did not let out a sound.

'Here.' I handed her the lantern. 'Take this. Let me carry the child now.'

She hesitated, but then, on a nod from the maharani, handed over her charge. The sleeping boy was a dead weight. I had seen a fireman carry a survivor from a burning house.

'Help me balance him over my shoulder.'

Indira took the lantern, and translated.

Gently, the ayah helped me transfer the child to my shoulder. Too late I realised that the fireman in question had much broader shoulders than I. Hoping desperately not to drop the crown prince on his crown and thereby deliver another blow to the dynasty, I struggled on.

A low roar from our right indicated how near we were to the Strid. Little moonlight filtered through the trees and we now relied on the light that the ayah carried. She had been reluctant to take the lead, to walk ahead of her mistress, but now she did, swinging the lantern a little. This had a dizzying effect and once more I turned to glance back, but could see no movement, and heard nothing but the hoot of an owl.

Everything looked different in the darkness. I feared I would miss the cottage. If so, we would walk into the morning at this rate.

It was the ayah, her eyes glued to the ground, who saw that the footpath veered to the left. From the outside, the stone dwelling with its thatched roof looked inviting.

The door was unlocked. I turned the knob. The door creaked open onto a single small room, the stone floor covered in dirty straw. As the ayah walked about with the lantern, light fell on a broken-back chair and a buffet by the empty fire grate. A few boards had been tacked together to make a table. On this sat a saucepan, thick with grease. The bed, once I realised that was its purpose, held only a striped mattress, with flocks peeping out of holes. There was no blanket.

'I'm so sorry. You can't stay here.'

'Tonight they will stay here,' Indira said firmly. 'You will stay with them. Tomorrow you will make a different arrangement.'

'Very well, if you insist. For tonight it will have to do. But I must go to the hotel, fetch some blankets and food and bring my assistant here to act as bodyguard.' She was about to interrupt, but I did not let her. 'Don't worry. I won't be seen. I will be back as quickly as I can, with Mr Sykes. He is utterly reliable.'

She protested. 'I cannot leave my son with only his ayah.'

'You stay here, your highness. When I return, I will take you back to Bolton Hall and Rajendra and the ayah will have a trusty bodyguard.'

The confidence in my voice belied fears that I might not wake Sykes from his slumber, or that the maharani would already have been missed. My reputation would hit the India Office dust if it became known that I had whisked the princess and her son away at dead of night and brought her to this hovel.

Smiling reassurances I did not feel, I left them with the lantern and walked back along the road to the hotel, glad of the moonlight now that the clouds had parted.

I walked, quickening my pace. The enormity of this folly hit me like a falling tree. Indira was crazed with grief and fear. I should have calmed her, called for Sir Richard.

No. I did not trust Sir Richard as far as Indira was concerned. But could I trust her, or myself?

What an idiot, to take important guests from the protection of the Duke and Duchess of Devonshire, leave them and a young servant alone and unprotected.

A sound startled me. I dared not stop to listen. Moments later, another sound, a whistle. I paused. Should I turn back? Too late.

If Indira and Rajendra were slaughtered before I could return, there would be only one person to blame. Kate Shackleton.

Thirty-Nine

It was almost midnight when I tiptoed to Sykes's room and tapped on the door. Fortunately, he had stayed awake, alert and fully dressed. Feeling a huge sense of relief at the sight of him, I half collapsed into the bucket chair, feeling suddenly exhausted.

Briefly, I explained the predicament.

He perched on the bed. 'Mrs Sugden is in the hotel. She is in a ground-floor room, opposite yours.'

'I hate to disturb her at this time.'

'I notice you don't hate to disturb me.'

He listened to my account of taking the princess, her child and his ayah to the Withers's cottage.

'How much of a hovel is it?'

'A tramp would think it heaven. Once the little boy wakes, he will either be delighted at the adventure, or horrified at the discomfort. We need to take bedding, and food.'

'Right.' Sykes untucked the sheets of his bed, placed the pillows on top and began to make a roll of the eiderdown, blankets and sheets.

'I'll do the same in my room. We'll need food.'

'I'll raid the kitchen.'

'Meet you by my motor.'

A few moments later, I tapped on Mrs Sugden's door. Unlike Sykes, she had decided that sleep was her preferred choice of passing the night. Fortunately she is a light sleeper. I explained the task, leaving out the state of the cottage. With a bit of luck and a dim lamp, she would not be too appalled until morning light.

In the time it took me to follow Sykes's example and roll my bedding, ready to be taken to the motor, Mrs Sugden was dressed and waiting.

Like three conspirators, we met by my motor and stared at it, considering the logistics. The motor was too small for the three of us to sit comfortably.

Sykes came up with the solution. The bedding and food would go in the dickey seat; Mrs Sugden in the passenger seat. He would ride on the running board.

It was a great relief to find my charges still alive.

Within half an hour, I had deposited Sykes and Mrs Sugden in the cottage with the ayah and Rajendra, who had woken and now looked surprisingly chipper at the prospect of spending a night in a dank cottage near a dark wood. In English, he told Mrs Sugden he was hungry, and spoke to the ayah about making his bed. Or at least, I assume that is what he said because she took most of the bedding and arranged it comfortably for him on the planks that served as the Withers's sleeping quarters.

Part one of my mission accomplished, I drove Indira back to Bolton Hall. One small snag was to find the side door closed.

Indira walked to the front and rang the door bell. I

waited, out of sight, until the butler eventually came to let her in.

Of course, there is always something one forgets. Back in my now familiar hotel room, I donned pyjamas, and looked at the stripped bed. A feeling of chill came over me. There was a simple solution: take the bedding from Mrs Sugden's room.

I crossed the hall. Unfortunately, Mrs Sugden, being a woman of foresight, had locked the door and taken her key with her.

But there would be a linen cupboard somewhere along the corridor. This entailed going back into my room for the flashlight, to ensure that I did not open doors with a room number and startle some unwary sleeper.

Cautiously, I walked the corridor, shining my torch left and right. There was no linen room, only a cupboard containing brushes and mops.

Then I remembered that on the floor above, there must be at least two linen cupboards because Ijahar had commandeered one as a laundry and storage room.

I tiptoed up the creaking stairs to the next floor.

To my surprise, Ijahar had not emptied his little room of his master's shirts, undergarments and his array of irons. I looked along the shelves anyway, in hopes of spotting some heavy drapery I might purloin. There were more undergarments, socks, shirts, soap, laundry materials including starch in a jar and two blue paper bags of powder, presumably washing powder. The poor man did not have a rich taste in snacks, only a few charcoal biscuits and a piece of root ginger. One of my older colleagues in the VAD, Marion

Calder, had sworn by charcoal biscuits, saying they did wonders for her indigestion. A bunch of nettles lay on the slatted shelf. Perhaps Ijahar drank nettle tea. I could conjure up a solemn conversation between him and Marion Calder regarding an efficacious diet for the healthy digestive tract.

I sniffed at the ginger. It protected against colds. On the rare occasions when we VAD nurses could procure a piece of ginger, we used it as an anti-emetic, the one sure way of keeping a patient from vomiting.

Ijahar had wanted flowers for his master's body and I found it touching that he had also placed flowers and leaves by a stack of starched shirts.

I left the little room, and walked along the corridor. To my disappointment the next cupboard contained the same array of brushes and mops as the cupboard on my own floor.

Facing a chilly night, I returned to my room, donned coat and socks and lay down to catch whatever sleep might come my way.

After a long while, I fell into a shallow sleep. It was one of those nights not just of disturbed dreams, but of voices. This happened to me sometimes. I would be spoken to in my sleep very clearly and yet entirely nonsensically.

This time the voice that woke me said, 'He is too young.'

These messages from nowhere are always somewhat terse.

I half woke, thinking that yes, Rajendra was too young to be dragged from his bed in the middle of the night. I fell back to sleep and saw Rajendra lying on the rough bed in the cottage. As is the way with dreams, I was also in the cottage, unseen. When a sudden noise startled Sykes and he ran to the cottage door, there was nothing I could do. He called Mrs Sugden's name.

I woke shivering, and not just from the cold. A sense of foreboding swept over me, as if the dream might be a warning. I was tempted to give up on sleep altogether and go out to my car. Had I given all the motoring blankets to Sykes and Mrs Sugden? I couldn't remember.

Wandering about in the middle of the night would be no good for me or anyone else. Putting on an extra cardigan, I forced myself to lie down again. Eventually, I slept, until light filtered into the room through the gap in the curtains. I woke thinking of that terse little phrase, 'He is too young.'

There were several interpretations for this piece of useless information, the most obvious being that Maharajah Narayan was too young to die.

I opened my eyes, and looked at the clock.

As I did so, something reared up from beside the bed, a writhing, twisting snake as tall as a tree, with hooded head, tiny eyes, open jaws, and a forked tongue pointing at me.

I froze. So did the snake, poised, elegant, offended, and then it swayed.

Stay still, I willed it, keeping my eyes on the dots of hatred that it wore for eyeballs.

I have not made a will. My library book is overdue.

Forty

Once in the corridor, I leaned against the wall, shaking with fear. Only the alarm clock had come between me and the snake, as I grabbed the clock, flung it, leapt from the bed and raced from the room, shutting the door behind me.

I looked at the bottom of the door, at the smallest of gaps. Did reptiles have the ability to flatten themselves and slither free? It might wend its way from room to room, first taking its revenge on me, then carefully poisoning guest after guest.

I do not know how long I stood there, barefoot, wearing only pyjamas, trembling. But they were moments of stunning clarity.

It is a cobra.

It is the dancing cobra belonging to the snake charmer.

Someone knows I sleep with the window open and has sent a dancing cobra to kill me. Someone has watched me, followed me; knows where I took the child. But there is only one snake. The child will be safe with Sykes and Sugden.

Never have I been so glad to see someone as when Rachel appeared at the end of the corridor, holding a tray.

She walked as far as Mrs Sugden's door, opposite mine. Good old Mrs Sugden, early riser.

Rachel stared at me.

'What's the matter, madam?'

'There's a snake in my room. It came in through the window.'

'We don't have snakes.'

'It's a cobra.'

'Was it a dream?'

I shook my head. 'Lock this door. Put something thick and heavy against the bottom, in case it tries to wriggle under.'

She put down the tray. 'I'll just . . . ' She tapped on Mrs Sugden's door.

I did not tell her that Mrs Sugden would not be there to receive her early morning tea.

Next, Rachel tried to insert her key into my lock. I could tell she was humouring me.

'It won't go in. Your own key is on the other side. Shall I . . . '

I stopped her from opening the door. 'Go find Mr Sergeant. Tell him to close my window from the outside, and then to come here straight away.'

She tapped on Mrs Sugden's door again.

'Never mind that. She's not there! Just go! Do as I say.'

As she turned and hurried along the corridor, I slid down, and sat with my back to the wall.

Be rational. Snakes cannot open doors. A cobra could not crawl through such a small gap. Think of something else.

I felt so very cold, so cold that my bones moaned a fore-telling of old age. Think of something else. Try and recall the dream I had before waking. A voice had spoken so clearly.

But that was not a real person. It was a dream voice, saying, 'He is too young.'

Poor Osbert Hannon was too young to drown; his baby son too young to lose his father.

'He is too young.'

Ijahar was too young to have worked as Maharajah Narayan's valet since Narayan was a child, which was what he told me when I first spoke to him. It can be difficult to tell a person's age if something else about them attracts your attention. With Ijahar, it had been the livid scar where his eyebrow should have been, and his over-anxious manner. Had he lied to me, or been confused by my questions?

Narayan must have been at least a dozen years older than Ijahar and would have had a valet before Ijahar was born. Perhaps I had misunderstood.

I recalled my first meeting with Ijahar, when he bowed, propped open the door of his little room and cut a pathetic figure, racked with anxiety about his master. Yet last night, he had strutted arrogantly, berating some poor young devil about not polishing his master's shoes.

Ijahar no longer had a master, or had he?

In and out like a jack-in-the-box, Sergeant had said of him. In and out of the hotel so often that no one would pay heed if he wandered hither, thither and yon, disappeared for long enough to kill, and to hide a body. The prince had been shot at close range. Ijahar could come within close range of his master. That was part of his job. Yet the idea was preposterous. Sir Richard was right. The man's servitude was too deeply ingrained for him to break a taboo and murder a prince. The notion went against all conventions, all sense, against the natural order. It simply could not be.

Yet why, when Prince Narayan's belongings had been cleared from the room, had so many bits and pieces been left behind in the linen closet? Not simply left, but adorned with flowers.

Mr Sergeant quick-marched along the corridor towards me. Rachel trotted after him. Without a word, he opened the door to my room, took the key from the lock, shut it again and locked the door.

'You believe me then?'

'I closed your window. The cobra has curled up in the wash basin. It must have been thirsty.'

'I suppose frightening someone half to death is thirsty work.'

'I've sent for the snake charmer. He should keep his creature under tighter control. Are you all right?'

'Mr Sergeant, Rachel, I need clothes and shoes, and I need them now.'

Twenty minutes passed before Rachel returned.

'Sorry, Mrs Shackleton. It's the best I could do.' Had there been time for dismay, the outfit Rachel produced would have brought it on by the bucket load. The tweed skirt would need two safety pins to stay up. The neat white blouse was, at least, beautifully ironed. A beige cardigan sported decorative bobbles which must have set the knitter something of a challenge. At least the bloomers were so well washed as to be threadbare.

'We could wait until the snake has gone,' she said helpfully, handing me a pair of lisle stockings.

We were in a vacant room, two doors from mine. 'No time.' As I dressed, I said, 'Tell me something about Prince Narayan's manservant.'

'Oh him. Nice as pie.'

Which translated from the Yorkshire means you would not trust him to carry a glass of water across the room.

'I notice he has left some stuff in the linen cupboard.'

'He has. He'd no inhibitions about taking over the place. It's supposed to be our Empire, but if you ask me, they're the ones who rule the roost. Look at the way they've taken over Bolton Hall, with all them tents outside. If I was to pitch a tent there, I'd be shifted along quick as you could say tug that forelock.'

The lisle stockings were on the baggy side.

'Rachel, there are irons in that little linen room, and starch, but it's a bit cramped for him to have done his laundry work there.'

'Oh he didn't do his laundry in there. We had bets on that he'd go to the river and wash the royal shirts on the rocks, like you see them doing in picture books. He came down to the cellar and took over the biggest sink, using his own scrubbing brush. He's not a laundry man, he says. If he was in India, he wouldn't do any laundry. He'd be too good for it.'

'And what about starching and ironing?'

'He helped himself to our starch didn't he? And the same with the irons, if he got to them first. He took up space on the table as if he owned the place.'

'You didn't like him,' I said, in my best mistress of understatement manner.

'He's shifty, that's what I think.'

My heart was starting to thump. Not because of Rachel's mistrust of Ijahar, but at the thought of the flowers, ginger, charcoal biscuits and bunches of nettles. Whatever Ijahar got

351

up to in that little room, valeting must have been far down on his list.

'Are you any good at identifying flowers?'

'I'm not bad. And I know the meanings, the language of flowers.'

'Come with me to the laundry room.'

As we left the room, I caught sight of myself in the glass and wished I hadn't.

Rachel turned her key in the lock. She led the way along the corridor. 'You're a detective aren't you?'

'Yes.'

'Mrs Metcalfe told me. You went to London.'

'I did.'

'Did you see Lydia? Her mam would like to know if she's all right.'

I felt a stab of guilt. 'Yes, she's very well.'

She must have been very well to climb out of a second-floor window and make a run for Paris. I would call and tell Mrs Metcalfe that Lydia had gone because it struck me that Lydia's first thought would not be to send her mother a postcard. "Climbed the Eiffel Tower today from the outside. Wish you were here."

We walked into the linen cupboard. Picking up one of Narayan's shirts, I shook it out and spread it on the shelf. Lifting the charcoal biscuits, ginger, nettles, blossoms and leaves, I placed them on the shirt.

'What a funny feller. Takes all sorts doesn't it, madam?'

'It does. Do you recognise those flowers?'

She did.

I tied the shirt into the kind of bundle a picture book tramp would carry over his shoulder on a stick.

'Rachel, the first minute you have, please bundle up the prince's linen. Lock it away somewhere, and if you are asked say . . . '

'By Ijahar?'

'Or anyone, say you haven't time just now but will find it later.'

That way, Ijahar would not suspect me of emptying his lair.

I hurried from the hotel and carried the items taken from the laundry room to my car.

Before I had time to start the engine, a voice practically shrieked at me.

'Mrs Shackleton!'

I turned to see Mr Sergeant, grim and shocked. 'What is it? Has the snake escaped?'

'The snake is still in your wash basin. Its owner is on his way, full of protestations that he believed it to be safely in its basket.'

'Then what is the matter?'

'All hell has broken out at the Hall. Maharajah Shivram Halkwaer is dead. He was found in his room by his servant this morning. Poisoned.'

Forty-One

At Bolton Hall, I parked my motor on the road, behind a line of Rolls-Royces and Bentleys.

I walked round to the front of the building. If I asked Indira a question about Ijahar, that might damn his prospects for life. To broach the matter with Sir Richard would be to risk being asked questions to which I had no answers, as yet.

It was then I saw Mr Chana, seated on the garden bench. Once more he wore the black turban and dark grey suit. He sat back, hands clasped in his lap. At first I thought he was looking at me, in my scarecrow-like garb, which I had forgotten until with every step my heels lifted from the ill-fitting shoes. But he was watching a finch that pecked at the grass. As I came closer, he offered a half-hearted greeting.

'My condolences, Mr Chana.'

'Ah, you have heard of Maharajah Shivram's death?'

'Yes.'

'I came out for air, not being needed at present.'

For him, this was a long speech. He had wasted so few words on me previously.

'I know this is the worst of times.' I took a chance. 'May I speak with you?'

'Of course.'

'I have a question.'

He inclined his head, as if all the better to listen.

'I understood that Ijahar had been in service to Maharajah Narayan, as his valet, since he and the prince were little boys.'

'That is not correct. He is too young.'

There should have been nothing eerie about his words echoing those of my dream, for there was only one other way for him to have said that: 'He is not old enough.' But he had said, 'He is too young.'

'My mistake then.'

'Perhaps not. Ijahar was valet to Prince Jaya since they were both six years old, so he has been valet to a prince since he was a little boy.'

'Then why was he with Maharajah Narayan?'

'Maharajah Shivram decreed that when at his school in Scotland, Prince Jaya must be like a British boy and pull on his own socks. No valet.'

His answer made me shiver. Ijahar did have another master: Jaya.

'But didn't Narayan have a valet of his own?'

'He died.'

I was tempted to ask how Narayan's valet had died, but perhaps that was another story.

A tiny detail came to mind. When I first talked to Lydia, Rachel had come to the door to ask if she needed help in packing. Ijahar had sent her. He would not have dared do that if he knew the maharajah would be returning.

Chana had refused to hear my question when I asked him about the exchange of telegrams and who else knew about the propitious date for the maharajah's marriage to Lydia Metcalfe. I could not be sure where his true loyalties lay, but I had to try.

'I heard that the astrologer was calculating a propitious day for the family to return to India, and that he had not yet found a day suitable for Jaya.'

I expected a sharp question about how I knew. Chana simply released his hands and upturned his palms. 'An auspicious day for one member of the royal family may not be an auspicious day for another.'

He gazed at a cloud that hovered just above the spot where smoke had risen from the funeral pyre. 'You have a question, Mrs Shackleton. What is your question?'

'Jaya had a horoscope that foretold greatness, a prediction that the qualities of his ancestors would shine in him.'

'I believe that to be the case.'

'Who are his ancestors?'

'Rajput on both sides. His mother came from the noblest of families.'

'Isn't it odd that a woman of such noble birth would be a second wife?'

'She was betrothed at a young age to the son of a fine dynasty, ruling a twenty-gun salute state. That young man died six months before the wedding. The princess came to the Maharajah Shivram Halkwaer of Gattiawan as his second wife, a match that brought honour to both families.'

'This horoscope of Jaya's, could it be interpreted as suggesting that he may succeed to the throne of Gattiawan?'

Chana turned and looked directly at me. He touched his

moustache, not in a gesture of vanity, but as if it may help him to think. 'Sometimes, when an astrologer, even the best astrologer, is asked to write a horoscope for a charming and high-born lady who asks about the future of her son, he may add a little flourish or a word of praise that will ripple through the lives of that mother and son.'

'Do you believe that is what happened in this case?'

'I have no way of knowing.'

'Where is Jaya now?'

'He found the women's distress unbearable. He went for a walk.'

'But he was so ill.'

'He has recovered.'

I stood up quickly. Jaya must know that Rajendra was no longer clinging to his mother's sari.

'Thank you, Mr Chana.'

I ran, ran back to my car, jumped in, started the engine, bumped a Rolls-Royce in my haste to be gone and drove up the winding lane, breaking all speed records.

Chana called after me, but the sound of the motor drowned his words.

Forty-Two

Leaving the car by the side of the road, I ran along the path towards the Withers's cottage, following the smell of burning, and the smoke that rose above the trees.

My fear of the snake was nothing compared with terror at the thought that I had sent the child, his ayah, Sykes and Mrs Sugden to their death in an inferno. Sparks shot into the air. I ran so fast, I thought my heart would burst.

At first I could make out no one through the smoke, cracking sounds and steady thudding noise of a toppling roof beam. Then I saw Mrs Sugden, beating at flames with a thick blanket. The ayah threw a bucket of water on burning thatch that had fallen.

'Where's the child?'

Mrs Sugden was choking, coughing. 'He's at the well, brave little chap, bringing water.' She waved an arm towards the rear of the cottage. 'Mr Sykes reckons we've to make a fire break, or the whole wood will catch light.'

Then I saw Sykes, beyond the ruin of the burning cottage, chopping down a tree that was in danger of catching light. Someone must see the smoke soon. Someone must come. This could not be left to a man, two women and a child.

Sykes called to me. 'Fetch help!'

Mrs Sugden began to cough. Now that I was closer, I could see that she and the ayah had done a good job of stopping the fire spreading. The burning thatch was contained within the bricks of the house, but for how long?

The ayah came back with another bucket of water and threw it on tongues of flame that licked the air.

'Good lass,' Mrs Sugden said.

I took the bucket from her, to give her a rest, and hurried towards the well. A second bucket had been left, half filled, waiting to be unhooked.

'Where is Rajendra?' I called. I had expected to see the child at the well.

When she heard her charge's name and the panic in my voice, the ayah came running. She coughed as she ran, holding her sari to her mouth. We looked about, and could not see him.

Then the ayah, whether by instinct or good hearing, ran towards the river.

Had the child gone to the river to cool himself from the heat of the fire, or to see whether he could more quickly draw water there?

The ayah reached the river's edge before me. She was calling out, panic in her voice.

The cry came from beyond the bend in the stream. A clump of trees blocked my view. And then I saw Jaya, thigh-deep in the water. He was standing over a floating pleat of linen.

'Rajendra!' I stepped into the stream, without stopping to

kick off my borrowed shoes, hurrying towards Jaya and the floating linen. Jaya stooped down and raised a spluttering, choking child from the water.

'He fell in, didn't you, old chap? Lucky thing for you I'm here to fish you out.'

The boy could not answer. He coughed and spluttered as Jaya patted him on the back.

The three of us stood in the middle of the stream. My legs felt suddenly numb with cold. Words would not come. Another moment and the choking child would have drowned. I reached out for him as he spewed river water.

Jaya drew him away from me. 'My nephew is in no danger. No thanks to you, for placing him in a house of straw. He slipped, that is all.'

When he could speak, when he had stopped spluttering, Rajendra echoed Jaya's words. 'I slipped.' He held his uncle's hand. They walked ahead of me, to the river bank. 'Uncle, come and put out the fire with me.'

'We do not dirty our hands. Your mother sent me to bring you to her.'

'What are you doing here, Jaya? How did you know Rajendra was here?'

'Your highness. Don't you mean, your highness?' He stared at me with a brazen look, one of his nostrils twitching with disdain. 'Out of my way.'

'How did you know he was here?'

He moved ahead of me still grasping his nephew's hand. 'This stupid person thought you were drowning. She can't help her ignorance. Perhaps she is a girl guide and needs to do a good deed. Let her find a blind person to take across a busy road. Let her put out the fire.'

'I fell in didn't I, Uncle Jaya?'

'You were trying to walk on water.'

The boy laughed and then became suddenly serious. 'We shouldn't play when father is dead.'

'We weren't playing. We were cooling ourselves after these stupid people tried to burn you alive.'

The depth of his arrogance almost unnerved me. Fury rose in my throat. 'No, you were not playing. You are in earnest, Jaya, but you won't get away with this.'

'Hold your tongue, woman. I have come here to break some news to my nephew, but not yet.'

Rajendra looked up at him. 'What news, Uncle?'

They reached the bank before me. I clung to the drenched skirt to keep it from falling from me. My shoes squelched as I stepped onto the grass.

At that moment, Mrs Sugden came panting on the scene. She snatched Rajendra and pulled him to her bosom.

'It's all right, Auntie.' He tried to free himself.

'That woman is not your auntie! Let him go, woman. You pollute him.'

I have never seen Mrs Sugden explode. She exploded now. 'I'll bloody pollute you. It was you set the house alight. I can smell the brimstone on you. I see it in your eyes. This boy's in my charge.'

It was a little late, but impressive.

Jaya moved towards her, to free his nephew from her grasp. She hit out at him, pushing him away.

His mask of charm slipped. 'Don't dare touch me, you unclean piece of filth. You are lower than an untouchable, beneath contempt.' He turned to include me in his tirade. 'Your days are numbered.' He pulled at Rajendra's arm. 'Raj and I will grind the British into the dust. When he is maharajah, we will throw out the British. India for the Indians.'

It was a scene that called for King Solomon. Neither Mrs Sugden nor Jaya would let go of the child. Then the ayah began to wail. Her cries distracted both Jaya and Mrs Sugden. Rajendra broke free and ran back towards the house.

Jim Sykes stood on the path. If he had not, I believe poor little Rajendra would have gone on running until he was out of the county. Sykes picked up the child and swung him high onto his shoulders.

'Come on, little feller. We still need help with the fire. It's down to a smoulder but it could spark up again with the wind.'

Mrs Sugden glared at Jaya, and turned her back on him.

He spat on the ground.

We reached the well.

Sykes, carrying Rajendra, walked towards the road.

Jaya came swaggering up from the river, a mocking smile on his lips.

I said, 'How did you know where to find him? Did you follow us last night, or was that your minion, Ijahar?'

'How dare you question me? If I hadn't come along, my nephew may have been burned alive.'

'If you hadn't come along there would have been no fire.'

'And you will be able to prove that, will you? Just like you proved that my brother was murdered? Oh, sorry, excuse me, that was a tragic accident.'

He began to walk back through the wood, along the path.

'My God.' Mrs Sugden put a hand to her heart. 'Never have I seen such evil, and I have seen evil.'

I shared her feeling. I wanted to see him taken to Skipton police station, charged with attempted murder and held until proof could be gathered of the shooting of his half brother and the poisoning of his father. But that would not happen. Not yet.

Jaya was walking back to Bolton Hall. Driving, we could be there before him. But Sykes, Mrs Sugden and the ayah were smoke blackened and still coughing. Rajendra and I were soaked to the skin. We were in no state to marshal an accusation, much less make it stick.

Sykes threw a bucket of water on flames that were beginning to rise. 'What will you do?'

'I'll take the child somewhere safe, again. This time, I'll be sure not to be followed.'

'I better stay here until this is properly out.'

'I'll raise the alarm.'

The four of us clambered into the car, Mrs Sugden beside me, fussing over my wet clothing, the ayah and wide-eyed Rajendra behind us.

I had to pull in on the narrow road to let the cart pass, pulled by two great horses, driven by Mr Upton, and packed with men and buckets.

'It's the Withers's cottage,' I called to him as he sped by.

Would Indira believe me, when I told her that the person she needed to fear was her young brother-in-law, the member of her husband's family whom she trusted above all others?

Chana had been wrong to say that no one knew of the exchange of telegrams regarding the maharajah's planned marriage. Jaya found out and told Indira, wanting to remain the faithful friend, the trusted brother-in-law. Or, Indira

363

found out and told Jaya, the only man in the family she could trust.

There had been an Indian on Bark Lane. His name was Jaya, and he believed himself destined for greatness.

Forty-Three

Dr Simonson was on his front doorstep, just about to leave the house. Key in hand, he stared in disbelief at us, the motley crew.

'Dr Simonson, I need you to allow Mrs Sugden, the little prince and his ayah to stay in your house for a few hours.'

'What has happened to you all?' He unlocked the door.

Not knowing where to begin, I said nothing. We stepped inside and into his kitchen where a fire glowed.

'I smell burning, and you're soaked.' He picked up the tongs and added a couple of large cobs to the fire. 'There are towels in the cupboard on the landing.'

Mrs Sugden wasted no time. She settled the ayah and the child by the fire and hurried up the stairs.

Clutching the shirt bundle, I drew the doctor into the dining room, and briefly told him what had happened.

'And it looks as if you have something to show me.'

Putting the bundle on the table, I undid the knots in the shirt.

'Good shirt.'

'It was Prince Narayan's. But it's not the shirt I want you to look at but what's in it. Could you tell me what it is?'

'Mrs Shackleton, only you could devise a party game at a moment like this. Shouldn't I be blindfolded and do it by touch and smell?' He picked up the ginger and sniffed. 'Root ginger.'

'An anti-emetic. If someone accidentally or on purposely dosed himself with poison, this would prevent him vomiting, would it not?'

'What are you suggesting?' He picked up a charcoal biscuit.

'And the biscuit would absorb poison.'

'Look, you need to change. I gave all my late wife's clothes to charity but there may be something up there and . . .'

'The charcoal, how else might it protect someone from poison?'

'Taken over weeks or months it would have a cumulative effect and . . . what's this all about?'

'And the nettles. That rash Jaya had. It was self-inflicted.'

'Prince Jaya?'

'Looking at all this together, doesn't it tell you something?'

'That I have in front of me a beautifully made monogrammed shirt, ginger, biscuits and flowers, etcetera.'

'Is it just the rhododendron flower that is poisonous, or the leaves also?'

'Both.' He picked up a rhododendron flower. Its petals began to fall.

'Jaya made himself ill, so as to avoid suspicion. Then he poisoned his father. How long would poison from the rhododendron take to act?'

'I suppose about six or eight hours.'

366

'Exactly. Overnight. That is why Maharajah Shivram was found dead this morning.'

'My God, woman, why didn't you tell me straight away?' He dropped the flower.

'Jaya poisoned his father last night, when the poor man was urging his son to take a little sustenance.'

The doctor let out a whistle. 'These are wild accusations.'

'Not in the least wild. If you want wild, imagine a cobra in my room this morning, imagine a cottage where Rajendra was taken for safety set on fire, imagine . . .'

'I take your point.' He opened a drawer in the sideboard and took out a gun. 'Here's my service revolver. I'll fetch the ammunition. Do you know how to use it?'

'I do.' The voice came from behind. It was Mrs Sugden.

When the doctor had gone upstairs for ammunition, Mrs Sugden picked up the revolver and snapped it open. 'Don't you worry, Mrs Shackleton. That great evil stoit won't pull his stunt again while I'm here. Dry yourself by the fire, madam, before you catch your death.'

But I wanted to lose no more time. Waiting only until Dr Simonson returned with ammunition, I watched Mrs Sugden load the revolver.

The dining room at Bolton Hall smelled of kippers, coffee and kedgeree. In my ill-fitting clothes, still wet from my wade in the Wharfe, I smelled of river water, burning timber and thatch, and sodden tweed. My feet squelched.

Smiling inanely at several guests, including the Duke and Duchess of Devonshire and Mr Chana, I plopped across to Sir Richard, muttering a general 'Excuse me' to the assembled eaters.

'I must speak with you.'

Unfazed, Sir Richard abandoned his kipper. I took this as less of a signal that he wanted, equally urgently, to speak with me and more of a snap decision that I must be expelled from the dining room.

He waited until we were out of earshot. 'What has happened to you?'

'I'll come to that. Jaya tried to murder Rajendra. You must have Ijahar taken where Jaya cannot interfere with him. Otherwise, you will never elicit a straight story about the murders.'

'You had better start at the beginning, but not here.'

The discreet Lazonby appeared from the woodwork. To his credit, Sir Richard did not hesitate for long. If I had asked him to put Jaya under arrest he would have demurred, but Ijahar was an easier matter.

'Lazonby, ask Chana to find Ijahar and take him somewhere private.'

'Lock him up, Mr Lazonby.'

'Mrs Shackleton and I will be in the library.'

Still not having fathomed the labyrinthine corridors, I let Sir Richard lead the way.

He listened in silence while I told him what had happened, starting with my interview with Indira, the flight to the cottage, my being entertained by a cobra in the early hours, the fire, the attempted drowning of Rajendra, and ending with my having, once more, taken the crown prince to safety.

'Princess Indira did what?' Sir Richard stared at me, showing the rare emotion of shocked incomprehensibility.

'She asked me to look after the little prince.'

'From the security of Bolton Hall to some hovel? You

should have told me. The poor lady is obviously under a huge strain.'

'The poor lady knows exactly what she is doing. Pin your ears back, Sir Richard. These murders . . . ' He opened his mouth to find some softer word. I persisted. 'These murders arise from Jaya's political ambitions, and his determination to claim what he sees as his rightful place as a descendant of the Rajputs. He knows this area, having been on shooting parties here in the past. He was the man seen on Bark Lane, count on it.'

Sir Richard shook his head. 'When his college term ended, he stayed with a university chum in Northumberland.'

'Have you confirmed that? See who will vouch for where he was last Friday. Question Ijahar about where his true loyalties lie.'

Lazonby appeared. 'I spoke to Chana, sir. He'll have the valet locked in an attic.'

Sir Richard nodded to his assistant. 'Get on the blower to the Wootten-Ferrers. Ask how long Prince Jaya stayed with them, and when he caught the train. I'm sure we can clear this up in no time.' As Lazonby left the room, Sir Richard frowned. 'Are you going to claim that Jaya poisoned himself and his own father?'

'Jaya recovered didn't he?'

'Because he is young and healthy.'

'Because he protected himself from the poison and induced vomiting, if indeed he took the poison. Did Maharajah Shivram vomit last night?'

'I don't know.'

'If not, test for ginger in his stomach. It is a known anti-emetic.'

'But Indians use ginger in their cuisine. It would not prove anything.'

'I am guessing that Jaya took advantage of the outbreak of sickness to make himself ill. He then poisoned his father. Given that the maharajah's doctor had been taken poorly, it was an ideal opportunity.'

'Mrs Shackleton, this is all very well and most interesting – an insight into how the detective mind works – but it gives us nothing definite. You come up with a plausible motive, but why would Maharajah Narayan's own valet conspire against him?'

'Perhaps Narayan mistreated him. What about the scar on his eyebrow?'

'I had the pleasure of meeting Prince Narayan on several occasions. He is not a man who would have mistreated an inferior.'

'Who last saw Maharajah Shivram alive?'

He paused. 'It was Jaya. Shivram encouraged his son to take nourishment.'

'As I thought, and Jaya urged him to partake in a last supper. I think you will find that the poison was from the rhododendron plant, carefully gathered by Ijahar for his master, Jaya, the man he has been devoted to since they were six years old.'

Still, Sir Richard hesitated. 'I suspected that the Maharajah of Kalathal . . . '

'And you suspected Indira. Please, Sir Richard, at least bear with me until you are able to check some facts. Jaya will be back here by now. If I am right, where will he stop? Do we wait for Indira to be murdered, for him to have a second, and this time successful attempt on the child's life?'

Sir Richard pulled the bell cord.

It seemed an age until the footman appeared. 'You rang, sir?'

'Find out the whereabouts of Prince Jaya. Come back and tell me.'

'I can tell you now, sir. Moments ago the prince was in his room, calling for his valet.'

'You do not know where the valet is. Is that clear?'

'It is clear and true, sir.'

Only when the footman had gone, did Sir Richard acknowledge the state of me, wild-haired, wet, and dressed in a tweed skirt adorned with safety pins.

I had left a wet stain on the plush seat.

It was my turn to hesitate.

'I have this in hand, Mrs Shackleton. No doubt you will wish to change before we go further.'

'Yes, but listen to me first. This is what I believe happened. On Friday, about noon, Prince Narayan received a telegram from Mr Chana, advising him of a propitious day for his wedding to Lydia. He knew he would leave Bolton Abbey soon, so decided he would fit in a little shooting. After he shot the doe, he set off riding to Halton East to see Presthope, his go-between, and ask whether he had yet spoken to Lydia's father. The prince never arrived at Halton East because on the way he met his step-brother, Jaya.'

Around the table in the centre of the library, we formed something like a small court of enquiry: Sir Richard, his assistant Lazonby, Dr Simonson, Dr Habib, and me.

Each person supplied his own small piece of the jigsaw puzzle.

Dr Simonson reported post mortem findings on Maharajah Shivram Halkwaer: poisoning due to his having taken a suffusion of rhododendron leaves in a small portion of curry or herb tea. Simonson had brought with him the silk shirt bundle of rhododendron flowers and leaves, ginger, charcoal biscuits and the bunch of nettles.

Lazonby referred to his notes, as if looking down would soften the words he had to say. 'The Wootton-Ferrers drove Prince Jaya to Newcastle for the London train last Thursday. He said he was joining his family at the Ritz. He did not.'

Dr Habib was the gentleman for whom the phrase a fine figure of a man had been coined. On a good day he would be an excellent advertisement for his profession. Now, he appeared ill and drawn. 'I was ill myself but I brought Prince Jaya's temperature down. It is true that the rash could have been self-inflicted by nettles. The prince was always interested in chemistry and botany.'

Dr Simonson gave Dr Habib a sympathetic glance. 'We were used to men feigning sickness in the armed forces, but it is not something one would expect of a royal prince.'

It annoyed me that Jaya was still free to wander about and had not been challenged. 'There is enough information to have Jaya and Ijahar taken to the police station for questioning.' Ijahar was still being questioned by Mr Chana, and reported to have said enough to incriminate himself.

Dr Habib's face had turned to stone.

'Much of this is circumstantial.' Sir Richard rose. 'Lazonby.'

'Yes, sir?'

'You have paper and pens with you?'

'I do.'

'I would like everyone at this table to write a statement of what they have said today, without collusion.' He left the room.

We remained at the table, like pupils kept back to write lines. Pens scratched. We did not so much as look at each other for the longest time.

Habib put down his pen. 'Ijahar – I never trusted that creature. He has good reason, though, to hate the British. His great grandfather was one of the sepoys in the rebellion of 1857.'

I was still writing. I wrote every detail since coming to Bolton Abbey last Saturday, as if my words would make the difference between finding a path to justice and truth and letting Jaya off to live a life in which, to quote the astrologer, 'the greatness of his ancestors would shine in him'.

We had all finished writing. The clock struck the hour. Sir Richard did not return. I began to feel concerned about Mrs Sugden, Rajendra and the ayah. If Jaya was as cold and calculating as I believed he was, they would be safe, for now. If the man was mad as a hatter, also a possibility, he might somehow find them and mow them down.

I wondered what the stars really had revealed about Jaya and his future.

Lazonby gathered in our statements.

Stop worrying, I told myself. Mrs Sugden is warned and armed.

The clock ticked on.

We grew restless.

Eventually, Sir Richard returned. 'I have spoken with his lordship.'

None of the men made comment.

'What about the police?'

'His lordship will deal with the matter.'

'How?'

'Appropriately, once all the facts are clear.'

Lazonby slid our statements into a manila folder and handed it to Sir Richard.

He was right, of course. I was being too hasty in expecting Jaya to be handcuffed and led away on the instant.

'Mr Lazonby will now give each of you a copy of the Official Secrets Act, which I require you to sign.'

Lazonby placed papers in front of me and the two doctors.

It reminded me of a school examination. I half expected Lazonby to warn us against turning over our papers before hearing the word Begin.

Dr Simonson pushed the paper away. 'Not necessary, sir. Patient confidentiality and all that, and as a matter of fact, I have already signed.'

Dr Habib followed his lead. 'My discretion is assured.'

At that moment, I wished I had spent some time acquiring a medical degree. It was clear that the Official Secrets Act had been brought into the room for one person alone: me.

Dr Simonson pushed back his chair. 'Mrs Shackleton, I'm setting off for home. Don't worry about Mrs Sugden and the prince and his ayah. They'll be safe now.'

'Thank you.'

The two doctors left.

The piece of paper lay in front of me. I did not pick up the pen.

Sir Richard gazed at a bookcase on the far wall. 'You will

perhaps wish to work for your country again, Mrs Shackleton.'

'Perhaps, but on a basis of trust. I don't believe my grandfather, Lord Rodpen, signed any such document when he served his country.'

Now was not the time to reveal that I had no notion what either my real or adopted grandfather had done. I only knew that I was entirely uneasy about what was happening, or more precisely what was not happening: arrests.

'How do I know something will be done? No one paid me any attention when I said that Prince Narayan was murdered.'

'Give me a short while, Mrs Shackleton.' Sir Richard tapped the manila folder containing our statements. 'I may be able to answer any questions you have, once we have perused these documents. Then I believe you will appreciate the importance of your signature.'

Mr Lazonby and I were left alone.

'Shall I ring for refreshments, Mrs Shackleton?'

'No, thank you. But you might explain something to me.'

'Of course, if I can.' He walked to the bell pull. 'But if you'll pardon my insistence, I'm ravenous myself and I'm betting that you'll join me.'

'You missed breakfast?'

'I did. And you too?'

I nodded.

He sat down opposite me. 'What did you want to me to explain?'

'Dr Habib said that Ijahar's grandfather took part in the Sepoy Rebellion. What did he mean?'

I wanted to know what prompted Ijahar to act in the way he had. Was it fear or love of Jaya, nationalism, a hatred of the British, or all of those motives?

'The chip has been passed shoulder to shoulder through generations. It was ridiculous. It should never have happened. Of course, it's the Indians who call it the rebellion, or the revolt. We call it the Indian Mutiny.'

Like every schoolchild, I had heard of the Indian Mutiny, the siege of Lucknow, and had seen pictures of British women and children dying of hunger, thirst and disease in some terrible tower.

'The Indian soldiers went mad, burned, slashed, slaughtered, men, women and children. It was a time of terror.' He made a steeple with his hands, long fingers that looked meant for playing the piano.

'Why?' And as I asked, I remembered vaguely, something to do with a breaking of taboos.

'Grievances, coming to a boil. You could say it was triggered by ammunition. The sepoys of Meerut refused to use the cartridges issued for Enfield rifles. The cartridges had to be greased and their paper ends bitten off. Rumour had it that the grease was a mixture of beef and pork fat, unclean to Moslems and a profound insult to Hindus.'

'And was it true, that it was beef and pork?'

'What matters is what those soldiers believed. Eighty-five sepoys refused Brevet-Colonel George Smyth's order to fire the Enfields. They were court-martialled for mutiny, stripped of their uniforms, and clapped in irons. The madness, the mutilations, the slaughter of everyone with a white face began the next day. Smyth didn't act quickly enough. The rebels went on to Delhi, to ferment

revolution. They ransacked the city. When British retri-
bution finally came, it was as terrible as anything the
Indians had perpetrated.'

For a long time, we waited for Sir Richard to return.
Refreshments came and went. The sun came out; the sun
disappeared behind a cloud. The clock chimed the half hour,
the hour, the half hour.

The door opened. As Sir Richard entered, Lazonby
left.

'Well Mrs Shackleton, we have had preliminary discussions. Naturally there is more to learn. Prince Jaya is now –
I suppose we might say – under house arrest. Ijahar has
proved helpful in supplying Mr Chana with a considerable
amount of information.'

'And what is to be done?'

'Jaya will be punished, depend upon it. But this cannot
come to trial. Imprisoned, he would be a hero to nationalist India. Execute him and we make a martyr. A democratic
India would not appeal to him at all but the masses would
not know that.'

'So what will happen?'

'He will be exiled and appear to have turned his back on
his country. People who matter will know what he has
done.'

'Is that all?'

'To a man like him, it is everything.'

'But he is a killer.'

'And remains a prince. He will do no more harm.'

'Is that all you can say?'

'It is too soon to say more. He will be allowed to attend
his father's funeral.'

'The murderer at his victim's funeral, that is not justice.'

'It is politics.' He sighed. 'I like it no more than you do, but needs must.'

Forty-Four

Almost two weeks had passed since Maharajah Shivram's cremation. I had heard that Jaya was gone from Bolton Abbey, banished from the scenes of his crimes.

Having received a request from Indira to see me before she left Yorkshire for London, I drove to Bolton Abbey. I wondered whether she would ask me about Lydia Metcalfe. If she did, how much should I tell her of what I had learned? My information came from James. He had written to me from France.

12 August, 1924
The Ritz, Paris

Dear Kate
Here I am in Paris. What would I have done without your valuable introductions? The Embassy staff are too slow to field at a fourth form cricket match and have their own snail-like ways of making themselves less than useless.

They are, however, making discreet enquiries of jewellers to ascertain whether a certain gem is thought to be on offer in any of the capitals of Europe.

Poor James. He seemed to think some naïve diamond merchant would hold up a hand and say, 'Ah yes, that is the dubte suraj ki chamak diamond. I am about to cut and slice Gattiawan's prized jewel.'

Your friends on the other hand, Miss Windham and Mr King, have been hospitable and charming to the nth degree. (Mr King is the only American I have met who understands the rules of cricket.) They know everyone in Paris and have made the acquaintance of Miss Metcalfe with a view to keeping me informed of her doings.

Miss Metcalfe's activities centre on parties, the theatre and suppers with her friends from the Folies Bergère. She frequently becomes tearful when asked about her maharajah, and excites a great deal of sympathy.

16 August
I had to break off this letter in haste when news came to me that Miss Metcalfe, who disappeared from view for several days, was on her way to Marseilles. This does not bode well. Here I am in Marseilles, knowing only an impoverished count and countess (if they truly be who they claim) who are acquainted with Mr King and Miss Windham. This supposed count and countess do their best, but their information is not of the highest quality. Fortunately, a young and bright chap from the consulate has come to my aid and informs me that Miss Metcalfe is booked on a berth to India. I have wired Sir Richard and await instructions. No doubt, she will be prevented from leaving.

19 August

This may be my last missive for some time. I have to hurry to board ship, having received a telegram from Sir Richard. I am to keep an eye on Miss Metcalfe and follow her to India. Please tell Mother not to worry.

Sir Richard assures me that my tailor has been informed and will send suitable clothing to await my arrival at the next port, wherever that may be. I should have liked more notice of this eventuality, as you can imagine.

Sorry, must break off now, and pass this to dear Mr King who has very kindly come to see me off and will give my letter to a chap who returns to London today and will post.

Your affectionate cousin, sending kind regards to all,
James

I decided against mentioning Lydia Metcalfe, unless Princess Indira brought up her name.

The tents and marquees were gone from the hill behind Bolton Hall. I parked at the rear of the house and walked round to the front. The bench where Mr Chana had sat stood vacant, yet welcoming. Who else would sit there in years to come, I wondered. They would look across the lawn, to the abbey, and beyond to the trees that rose on the far bank of the river, and have no notion of the high drama of these August days.

The young footman opened the door.

He led me to a bright room, perhaps the brightest the house had to offer. It was a music room, with chintz-covered chairs and sofas. I waited there until Indira arrived moments later.

She glided into the room, looking quite beautiful in a milky sari with barely a hint of silver. I thought of the last time I saw her, when she had been beside herself with worry and grief.

'Please sit down, Mrs Shackleton.'

'Your highness.'

'It will be just the two of us for lunch. The duchess is with my mother-in-law. I wanted the opportunity to thank you for everything you did.'

'I am glad to see you looking a little better.'

'You must have thought me quite mad when I asked you to take Rajendra to safety.'

'Not at all. Your instincts were right.'

She touched her perfect hair. No doubt some hairdresser had just been at work. How must it feel, I wondered, to be waited on, hand, foot and hair. I remembered Lydia Metcalfe, insisting that she preferred to 'do' for herself, without the attendance of servants she saw as enemies.

'You were the only person I could speak to at the time, and I will remember that, and that you saved the life of my child.'

'I am glad to have been of service. What will you do now?'

'We travel to London. No one with any sense would sail for India in August, but in September we will return.'

It occurred to me that Lydia Metcalfe had deliberately set off early, to be in Gattiawan first.

'When the time is propitious.'

She smiled. 'I think you do not believe in astrology.'

'I would not dismiss it. Jaya's mother must have had high hopes after his birth when she had his horoscope cast.'

'Yes. It will be a blow to her that she will never see her son again.'

'Do you have news of him?'

'Your government is still deciding where to send him. I believe he is now on Lindisfarne.'

'Holy Island.' Someone in government had a sense of humour.

'The high tide creates a natural curfew. I do not know where he will live out his days.'

'Any other man would face the death penalty for what he did.'

'And for what he tried to do. His attempt on my child's life was treason. Mr Chana tells me there is talk of sending him to the Isle of Man, or Tasmania. Jaya hates the sea.'

'I don't understand how you can be so calm about this.'

'Having failed, Jaya would gladly have died a martyr to his cause. The worst punishment will be exile from India, from Gattiawan, constantly watched, forever cursing his failure. I understand that he has begun drinking rather heavily. I suppose his minders encourage that. It will be a living death for him, and I am glad. Yet strange as it seems, I miss him. Or, rather, I miss the person I thought he was.'

Before I had time to reply, the footman tapped on the door and announced that luncheon would be served.

We stayed where we were for another moment.

'And the woman? Is there news of her?'

'She is under surveillance, and on a ship to India.'

'Going to collect her booty no doubt. It puzzles me that Jaya can be dealt with and prevented from travelling, yet a woman like that is free to maraud where she pleases.'

When would she speak of the diamond, I wondered?

383

I did not have long to wait. She smoothed her sari as we rose to go to the dining room. 'I had hoped you would retrieve the diamond. Do you think she has hidden it?'

'I don't know. I did wonder whether Jaya may have acquired it, through Ijahar.'

'I believe Ijahar would have been persuaded to confess, if that were the case.' Her voice was icy. 'She has it, Mrs Shackleton. I want it back, for my state, for my son, for India. Please do not give up.'

'I am not sure what else I can do.'

'Keep the diamond in your thoughts. Eventually, she will give herself away.'

We lunched on venison. Not knowing how long a deer must be hung, and how long after that it stays 'good', I wondered whether I might be biting into the white doe. This idea did nothing for my appetite, but I kept the thought to myself, and tried not to picture the doe so ingloriously trussed in Stanks's barn.

To provide light conversation, I told Indira that today civic officials from Bradford Corporation would be driven three miles through a tunnel, four hundred feet below ground, to place the last brick in a sewage system extension and declare it open.

'How extraordinary! I have never heard of anyone driving underground.'

A little voice came from under the table. 'I want to go!'

'Rajendra?' We looked under the table. There he sat, his eyes full of mischief. He would be a trickster and a practical joker, like his father.

'Come out of there. How rude!'

But we smiled.

'May I? I should like to drive through a tunnel.'

Indira and I exchanged a look.

Seeing his mother's hesitation, he seized the moment. 'I have never seen a car go in a tunnel. Please let me go.'

'What time does this ceremony take place?'

'This afternoon at three o'clock.'

'Will it be safe?'

'It will be safe to watch. We would not be allowed in the tunnel. That will be for the lord mayor and dignitaries.'

For the first time, Indira's eyes lit with amusement at the thought that Bradford aldermen would take precedence over Indian royalty.

'I could not possibly go. We would be seen. It would not do.' She took her boy's hand.

The little boy's eyes shone. I felt sorry for him, cooped up here, with no one of his own age to play with.

'You could ride with me, and view the event from a distance. There'll be so many spectators that we would not be spotted.'

'Very well, you shall go, and take my little crown prince.'

Rajendra tugged at his mother's arm. 'You come too.'

She hesitated. 'All right, but it is just between us, and we shall be incognito.'

The likelihood of Indira and Rajendra arriving incognito at Esholt Sewage Works would be as likely an event as my finding the Gattiawan diamond.

Half an hour later, we left by the side door, Indira in a Paris costume and hat with veil, Rajendra looking the perfect English boy in blazer, shorts and cap.

I was right about our failure to remain incognito. Indira had confided in the duchess.

When we arrived, we were met by a city official, an engineer, and Benjamin Jowett. We watched with some trepidation as the engineer led Rajendra by the hand to inspect the tunnels and take him for a ride to Esholt and back.

Mr Jowett reassured us. 'He will love it. I've done the trial run. An unforgettable experience. The exhausts make the most extraordinary noise, and the only illumination is from the head lamps. He will come out the other side singing that he wants to be an engineer.'

Indira bit her lip. 'What have I done, bringing him here?'

'He will enjoy it, your highness, and remember it forever.' Jowett produced a form from his inside pocket. 'Mrs Shackleton, I don't believe we have the pleasure of your membership in the Jowett club.'

It was December when I heard from James again. His letter lay on the hall stand. I dropped my bags of Christmas shopping and tore into it. We were hungry for news and wondered when, if ever, he planned to come home.

Dear Kate

Excuse my tardiness in writing to you. During the voyage, I was fit for nothing, keeping to my bunk as the vessel rolled. As we rounded the Cape, waves threatened to smash my porthole and engulf the cabin. The ship creaked, groaned and was ready to surrender. Indeed, seawater flooded my cabin to several inches, but I was so sick I cared not. I could keep nothing down, and now my clothes hang on me in a way that would shame a scarecrow. I scarcely have memories of the voyage, only the little pieces of information imparted to me by my steward who valiantly supplied sago, broth, arrowroot and tales of flying fish.

Now, after the most extraordinary journey by train and elephant, here I am in Gattiawan, having agreed to stay until the family return. I am lodged in the most splendid of palaces. If you thought Bolton Hall a difficult place to find one's way about, then this astonishing edifice would entirely flummox you. It is constructed of marble and gold, furnished with ivory and gilt furniture, and decorated with sumptuous velvets, silks and satins. You would love the garden. One part is planted entirely with chrysanthemums and dotted with fish ponds. The sounds at night are astounding — frogs and something like crickets, and jackals that howl. To say it is a land of contrasts is an understatement. I was not prepared for the squalor that exists beyond the walls of privilege and luxury.

But I must not spend pages telling you of my impressions and experiences, when I can hear you asking, 'But what of Lydia Metcalfe?'

She also travelled to Gattiawan, to the palace built for her by Narayan. How they do this in so short a time defeats me. I did not enter this palace of hers while she was in residence, although I was building up to making a call on her and enquiring after her intentions.

Before I was able to do so, one of the servants woke me early in the morning to tell me that she had set off towards the railway, riding on an elephant, with a herd of elephants following behind, one of them bearing a grand piano.

I immediately despatched messages to Delhi. Having done so, I finally visited her palace. It is a most splendid affair, with many bedrooms and bathrooms, and its own wells. I walked about, guided by one of the Halkwaer servants. She had stripped the place bare. Not a cushion or a teaspoon remained.

Thanks to my timely message, her entourage was stopped and searched. Unsurprisingly, the Gattiawan diamond was not discovered.

She is now setting sail for who knows where with everything that the late maharajah had bestowed upon her sailing with her.

Kate, India is the most extraordinary place. I never understood those old India hands who spoke of it with such longing, often without knowing they betrayed their fascination and nostalgia. Until you have seen an Indian sunset, you have missed a marvel of the world.

With kind regards to all from your affectionate cousin,
James

Forty-Five

To be invited by the Duke and Duchess of Devonshire to luncheon on Christmas Eve came as an unexpected surprise. Having been paid by the India Office for my investigations, and rewarded by Princess Indira, this seemed like an added bonus, a special thank you for the miniscule part I had played in ensuring the smooth continuation of our rule in India.

The sky was full of snow. I felt some misgivings as I set off, taking the precaution of including an extra blanket and a change of clothing, as well as my trusty boots. One never knows at this time of year what the weather will bring and whether even a motor as trusty as mine will need to be abandoned by the roadside.

There were twenty for luncheon, including Dr Simonson, who reminded me that I had not yet taken up his offer of a ride in the Bugatti. We exchanged addresses and telephone numbers over a glass of sherry. He seemed inordinately pleased to be sitting beside me at lunch. I was not too displeased myself.

Given the state of the weather, staying too long was not

a good idea. Dr Simonson and I were leaving at the same time, when the butler made a discreet beeline for me.

Dr Simonson hovered by the door.

The butler glanced about him before whispering, 'Her ladyship thought you might care to know that Miss Metcalfe is visiting her family.'

'Oh? How long has she been here?'

He hesitated. My guess was that the arrival of Miss Metcalfe and the despatch of my invitation to lunch would be suspiciously close to each other. So that was why I was here. Once more, I was expected to interrogate 'that woman'. Did someone really expect that I might burst in at the farmhouse and discover her at the kitchen table, eating mutton stew and polishing the Gattiawan diamond?

Dr Simonson took my hand as we reached our motors, mine parked neat as a spirit level, his cock-eyed. 'I know this is short notice, but I had not intended to go to Skipton Hospital New Year's Eve dance, Mrs Shackleton. If you were free to come with me, I should change my mind and accept the invitation with alacrity.'

I smiled. 'It seems a pity that you should miss the dance.'

'Then you'll say yes?'

'I should be glad to.'

'You may not say that when I dance with you.'

We parted with a smile, and on first name terms. And I should have driven straight home, before the blizzard, but I could not resist. After all, Lydia Metcalfe may not stay here for long. Who knew what country might next call her to ravish its ruler or dip her hand into its treasure trove?

As I drove from Bolton Abbey, the snow came in swirls, making it difficult to see, transforming the once familiar route into a mysterious journey. The rattle of the cattle grid alerted me to watch for the turning to the Metcalfe farm. Greyish white sheep stood disconsolately near the drystone wall, doing their best to find shelter. Perhaps someone would bring them in soon.

By the turn off I left the car and put on my boots, not wanting to risk driving up the lane. The snow fell faster now and if the weather turned I may not be able to drive back along the narrow track.

Halfway up the path, I caught sight of a figure on the edge of a copse. Something in the way she moved told me it was Lydia. I had not expected to see her out in the snow. There were footprints, where she had crossed a stile.

I crossed also and followed her steps into the copse. She was holding a basket.

'Lydia!'

She turned, and blinked in surprise. 'I didn't hear you.' She wore a man's army greatcoat, sleeves rolled up, a navy check scarf, and boots. 'It's the snow. Everything becomes so muffled.' She placed a branch of holly in the basket, next to a sprig of mistletoe.

'I'm surprised to see you back, Lydia. I thought you hated walking, and the countryside.'

'Who told you that?'

'I can't remember. Perhaps it was you.'

'Then I was lying.' She cut another branch of holly. 'Do you want some?'

'Yes please.'

'You know it doesn't belong to me to give you.'

'Doesn't it?'

She cut the mistletoe. 'It's his lordship's. All of this is

owned by one man.' She waved her arm, to indicate as far as the eye could see, which with snow falling fast was not very far, but I took her meaning.

'And do you mind that? You don't like the place after all. You couldn't wait to get away.'

'Who said that? My mother?'

'I don't remember.' I did not want to tell on Mrs Metcalfe.

'Well, it's not true. I love it here. I love it in May when the bluebells appear. I love when the orchids come out and you have to look so carefully to find them. Over there, there's a wild rose bush. I cut my finger on one of its thorns when I was little and I painted a white rose with my blood. This place is mine, Mrs Shackleton. Mine as it was my mother's and her mother's. But all of it is claimed – the land, the oak, the ash, the rabbit, the deer, the very birds of the air are his to shoot down. Can that be right? Do you ever think of that when you do their bidding? Do the hordes who come and pay them sixpence to walk across this little bit of England think, Why? How? Who gave it to them?'

The sky was now so white that it was like looking at a solid wall.

'I didn't know you felt so strongly, Lydia.'

'Well now you do know.'

Her sense of entitlement was bred in her bones. It came through her attachment, and she had left the place rather than live here knowing someone else claimed what she saw as her heritage. Before she had language, she felt injustice in her soul.

'Is that why you took the diamond?'

392

She pressed more holly and ivy into my arms. 'Go on, take it. Be my fellow conspirator.'

'If I'm you're fellow conspirator, will you at least tell me about the sunset diamond?'

'Do you know that Narayan planned to give the dubte suraj ki chamak to King George, in exchange for greater privileges and an expansion of territory?'

'No.'

'They're not entitled to it. They have enough, our rulers. It's someone else's turn.'

'But it's not yours. The diamond belongs to India. It belongs to Gattiawan.'

'It's like everything else. It belongs to whoever gets their paws on it.'

'When James Rodpen followed you to Paris, he lost track of you for a few days. Just for my own interest, where did you go?'

She laughed. 'You should have followed me. You would have liked Switzerland. And their bankers are so wonderfully helpful and discreet.'

'The diamond is in Switzerland?'

'In a safe bank, and a deep vault, under a lovely made up name and with only one person in the world who knows the alias, the combination and the whereabouts of the key.'

'That's theft.'

'I suppose some people would call it that. And I don't claim to be a Robin Hood, taking from the rich to give to the poor. Why should I? No one else does.' From the road came the sound of a motor horn. 'I think that's for you.'

We walked together back to the stile. Lydia took my holly and ivy and stood back as I clambered over. She handed me her basket, and then climbed across with such grace that it made me think of how she must have shimmied down from her second floor room at the Dorchester.

'Won't you change your mind about the diamond?'

'No. I only told you because I need to boast to someone about how clever I am. Since you are almost as clever as me, it may as well be you. But if you tell anyone, I'll deny it.'

She walked me back to the lane where Dr Simonson's Bugatti stood at the side of the road, parked straight for once, right behind my Jowett.

'Merry Christmas, Kate.'

'Merry Christmas, Lydia.'

I watched her walk back towards the farmhouse.

As I came closer, Dr Simonson climbed from his car and stood smiling, his feet planted firmly in snow. 'Your only chance of getting home tonight will be by train from Skipton.'

'If the trains are running.'

'If not, I do have a spare room.'

It was very late on Boxing Day when I reached home. The telephone was ringing as I walked through the door.

Mrs Sugden picked up the receiver. 'Mrs Shackleton's residence.' She covered the mouthpiece. 'It's your aunt. Shall I say you will telephone back to her?'

I shook my head and took the receiver. 'Hello, Aunt Berta.'

'At last! I thought you must be lost on the moors.'

'The snow was deep, crisp and even on Christmas Day in the Dales. I was perfectly snug.'

She did not want to hear about my white Christmas.

'I have had a wire from James. Have you heard?'

'Not since his letter.'

'He has had an offer . . . wait a minute, I shall read you the exact words . . . an offer of an administrative post from Her Highness Maharani Indira Halkwaer. He intends to accept.'

'Oh.'

'Is that all you can say, oh?'

'He could do worse. I liked her, and she was most generous to me.'

'Yes I know. But what will you do with a Rolls-Royce and a case of jewels? Ginny told me it has put you to the expense of garaging a motor you don't drive and buying a safe for clover emeralds that you refuse to wear.'

'Do you know anything more about this post that James has accepted?'

'Only what Richard tells me. Apparently the maharani and her mother-in-law intend to operate Gattiawan as some sort of matriarchal state, until the little prince is of age. They have all sorts of plans for social improvement. Oh, and the little prince will grow up to be an engineer who builds sewers. Well I don't see James fitting in with that sort of situation.'

'He may.'

'Do you think so?'

'If he has accepted.'

'But is he cut out for it?'

'Time will tell.'

'I disagree with leaving matters to the accident of time and place. That is a very male attitude to life. We must go see for ourselves. You know how persuadable James can be where ladies are concerned.'

I did not know, but preferred not to contradict.

'Are you still there, Kate?'

'Yes, Aunt. So will you and Uncle go to India?'

'Good heavens no. You and I must go.'

'Me?'

'Well, naturally, you involved him in this.'

'He involved me.'

'No matter, what's done is done, but it can be undone if necessary.'

'How?'

'We'll work that out on the voyage. How soon can you sail for India?'

After I hung up the receiver, I walked into my drawing room, very glad to be home. I poured myself a sherry. There were things I noticed in quite a different way. The curtains, which were here when we bought the house, are Madras embroideries, exquisite designs on a dark blue background. Three cushions are covered in hand-printed Delhi squares. The occasional table is a Bombay blackwood teapoy. On the landing, we have a fern in a Benares jardinière. India had come to me, without my ever really being aware of it, until my visit to Bolton Abbey. And there, India had almost overwhelmed me.

I have a lot to learn from my mother and aunt. They are very good at organising other people. Time for me to pick up a trick or two. Later, I would telephone my mother. She and Aunt Berta would enjoy a passage to India, but not I. Not any time soon.

Mrs Sugden popped her head around the door. 'I expect you've forgotten we're both invited over by the professor and his sister for drinks, spice cake, mince pies. And Christmas Day leftovers I don't doubt.'

'I had forgotten.'

'Plenty of time. We don't want to be first to arrive, last to go.'

'Shall we give ourselves a head start?'

'Go on then.'

I poured another glass of sherry. As we raised our glasses in belated Christmas greetings, I looked at Mrs Sugden as if for the first time, thinking back to that moment at Dr Simonson's when we were so worried about Rajendra's safety. She had taken Lucian Simonson's service revolver, snapped it open and popped in ammunition. Where did she learn that?

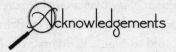

Acknowledgements

When researching her family tree, my friend Sylvia Gill discovered that most of her ancestors did not stray from Yorkshire. She was pleased to discover that a third cousin twice removed became a Folies Bergère dancer and married the Maharajah of Kapurthala. Stella Mudge (1904–1984) merited a chapter in Coralie Younger's fascinating book, *Wicked Women of the Raj: European women who broke society's rules and married Indian Princes*. A 1997 television programme explored Stella's life story and attempted to uncover a fortune thought to be held in the vaults of a Swiss bank. Unfortunately for Stella's next of kin, she had not divulged details of aliases and combinations. The treasure remains unclaimed.

Stella Mudge was the granddaughter of Yorkshire farmers. Lydia Metcalfe, in this story, is the daughter of Yorkshire farmers sent at an early age to live with her aunt and uncle in London. I have transformed Stella's parents, Joseph and Emily Mudge, into Lydia's aunt and uncle. Joseph Mudge was landlord of the Earl of Ellesmere, Bethnal Green.

The Indian princely states of Gattiawan, Kalathal and Gundel are figments of my imagination. Several books proved helpful for background research. These included *A Princess Remembers, the Memoirs of the Maharani of Jaipur*, Gayatri Devi; *Maharani, The Story of an Indian Princess* by Brinda, Maharani of Kapurthala as told to Elaine Williams; *The Princes of India in the Endgame of Empire, 1917–1947*, Ian Copland; *Lives of the Indian Princes*, Charles Allen and Sharada Dwivedi; *The Legacy of India*, ed GT Garratt; *The Memsahibs, The Women of Victorian India*, Pat Barr.

My agent, Judith Murdoch, told me about her visit to a lake near Lahore and the minaret built there by Emperor Jahangir as a monument to his pet deer. Dr Krishna Aggarwal, retired consultant anaesthetist, drew my attention to the story of the exiled Dalip (or Duleep) Singh, last Maharajah of the Sikh Empire, whose family's considerable property included the Koh-i-Noor diamond.

I explored various parts of the Yorkshire Dales, to find a suitable setting for the story. While walking through Westy Bank Wood on the Duke of Devonshire's estate at Bolton Abbey, I realised this was it. Bolton Hall is not open to the public and I did not seek permission to go inside, preferring to imagine it and the surrounding area as it was, or might have been. I enjoyed reading *Bolton Abbey, The Yorkshire Estate of the Dukes of Devonshire*, by John M Sheard, resident land agent.

Lydia Metcalfe and the other characters in this story are fictional. In 1924, when the story is set, the Duke of Devonshire was Colonial Secretary. He and the duchess appear as background characters.

Various questions arose during the writing. I am always grateful when friends patiently explain some detail that is beyond me. For their generous assistance, thanks to retired police officer Ralph Lindley; Eden Parish; Bill Spence (aka Jessica Blair); Noel Stokoe, editor of the *Jowetteer;* Barry Strickland-Hodge, Director, Academic Unit of Pharmacy, Radiography and Healthcare Science, Leeds University, and Viv Walsh, retired nurse.

Thanks to my sister Patricia McNeil for her continuing help and encouragement.

Special thanks to Caroline Kirkpatrick and all in editorial, design, production and publicity at Piatkus, and to Helen Chapman for her superb illustrations.

Kate Shackleton owes her appearance on the other side of the pond to agent Rebecca Winfield and the good offices of Pete Wolverton and Anne Brewer at Thomas Dunne Books/Minotaur.

A WOMAN UNKNOWN

THE WOMAN UNKNOWN: Deirdre Fitzpatrick is married to a man who wants to know where she really goes when supposedly taking care of her sick mother and calls on the expertise of Kate Shackleton, amateur sleuth extraordinaire to investigate.

THE GENTLEMAN: Everett Runcie is a banker facing ruin and disgrace. His American heiress wife will no longer pay for his mistakes, or tolerate his infidelity, and is seeking a divorce.

THE MURDER: When a chambermaid enters Runcie's hotel room, she expects to be a witness to adultery. Instead, she finds herself staring at a dead body. Suddenly Kate is thrown into the depths of an altogether more sinister investigation. Can she uncover the truth of her most complex, and personal, case to date?

MURDER IN THE AFTERNOON

Dead one minute
Young Harriet and her brother Austin have always been scared of
the quarry where their stone mason father works. So when they
find him dead on the cold ground, they scarper quick smart
and look for some help.

Alive the next?
When help arrives, however, the quarry is deserted and there is
no sign of the body. Were the children mistaken? Is their father
not dead? Did he simply get up and run away?

A sinister disappearing act . . .
It seems like another unusual case requiring the expertise of
Kate Shackleton. But for Kate this is one case where surprising
family ties makes it her most dangerous – and delicate – yet . . .